Warriors
of the
Blessed Realms

Chris McMahon is a novelist and short story writer based in Brisbane, writing everything from heroic fantasy and urban fantasy to hard SF. He is also an engineer, and blogs regularly about space science and exploration, and the growing catalogue of fascinating new exoplanet discoveries. He has a fourth-dan black belt in Moon Lee Tae Kwon Do and also enjoys movies and exploring narrow alleyways. Chris is very passionate about music, and loves singing and playing classical guitar. Website: www.chrismcmahon.net.

Also by Chris McMahon

The Jakirian Cycle

The Calvanni
Scytheman
Sorcerer

Science Fiction

The Tau Ceti Diversion

Warriors
of the
Blessed Realms

Chris McMahon

Warriors of the Blessed Realms

Chris McMahon

Published 2020 by Lanedd Press, an imprint of Pop & Top Publishers.
www.popandtop.com.au
Please direct all enquiries to the publisher at:
publisher@popandtop.com.au

ISBN: 9780980387056

Chris McMahon's website: www.chrismcmahon.net

To all the fantasy authors who have inspired me, enlivened my hungry imagination, and given me the heart to carry on, particularly David Gemmell, whose works imparted a life-long love of heroic fantasy.

Sydney Morning Mail
12th December 1999

Unexplained Homeless Deaths Continue.
Danny Critchfield

Another homeless man was found dead in Sydney's western suburbs yesterday, the seventh in less than a month. Police continue to be baffled by the deaths, so far ruling out initial theories of homicide or a new killer drug. The body of Johnny "Longjohn" Walker was discovered at 7:34 am yesterday by resident Majorie Thomas. "I thought it was a prank at first. You know, a dummy dressed up in old clothes. His face was so . . . blank. Empty. But when I got closer . . . oh! The smell! It was like he had been dead a week, not a few hours," said Mrs Thomas.

Anger is building in the local community, already frustrated by the homeless problem. "We are sick and tired of this. I'm trying to raise children in this street," said another resident yesterday, who did not want to be identified. "This is the second overdose in this area in a week."

Investigating officer Detective Sergeant Peter Holmes said yesterday. "As yet we have been unable to establish any cause of death, but we have ruled out overdose." State Health authorities continue to play down fears of a new, undetectable virus, but this has not stopped the rumours amongst Sydney's homeless community of the "Black Breath". Locals have begun wearing face masks.

The deaths have fuelled the local urban legend of Black Jack. "He's always looking," said one homeless man, only identified as "Pete" who was at the scene yesterday. "It's the End Times. End of the millennium. Jack's wanting the one that can open the door to the hot place [Hell] to let all the devils out. Midnight on December 31st. That's when it'll be. He's the one what's killin' them others."

Detective Sergeant Holmes denies any link to a killer. "We have no evidence of homicide, or of any other individual linking these deaths," he said.

Police investigations continue

Chapter 1

Brisbane, Australia — Earth
20th December 1999

Liam finished the cut, swinging his lean six-foot frame smoothly into a guard stance. He lifted his front foot, as though escaping a low strike, and stood balancing on one leg. Heat wrapped him in a humid envelope. Perspiration soaked into his thin T-shirt, gathering in the soft fabric rather than evaporate into the heavy, still, Brisbane air. Beneath his loose shirt, rivulets of sweat traced a slow line down his ridged abdominal muscles. His thigh flexed as it took the weight, and his breathing slowed.

The summer sun was hot. The brilliant blue of the sky broken only by the occasional threatening grey of storm clouds.

Someone hammered in the distance. Suburban repair work. In his mind, the sound swelled to a heavy booming, like the thud of a medieval ram being smashed into a iron-bound gate by the vanguard of an attacking army. The image of a ruined tower filled his vision. *Concentrate!* He looked up to check the position of his short-sword, raised above his head in a guarding position, then down to his left forearm, lowered to block a low thrust to his groin, but in his mind the tower drew closer. As though momentarily disembodied, he swept through the ruined doorway of the tower and on into a large hall. A high arched opening was set into the hall's far wall, filled with a flat grey light. Beyond the arched doorway, something tried to break through.

Liam blinked.

Normal sight returned in a rush. He felt a moment of disorientation. The visions were growing stronger despite his attempts to use a martial arts focus to keep them under control. Maybe he should just get out of Brisbane. Drive west to his uncle's property on the Darling Downs for a change of scenery. Following the death of his parents, it was the only home he had known. He smiled, remembering the long summer afternoons spent with his uncle on the property, both of them immersed in the ancient art of the sword. He could hear Aidan's voice as though he stood beside him. *It may seem awkward, many of the positions and techniques will, but it is about training your body. If you do the routines properly, you will react quickly to danger, and stay on balance under pressure.*

His head turned at the sound of a revving engine. His face lit in a smile as he recognised Shane's modified Celica, the gold coupe hugging the ground on low-profile tyres as it swept around the corner. The throaty engine roared, then subsided into a deep growl as it slowed. *Aftermarket extraction system.* His prospects had just gone from spending a quiet night in his flat to action and excitement.

Liam had always imagined post-graduation as a continuous party, but the celebrations had ended abruptly. The vague destination known as After Uni was here. He knew he had to start looking for jobs soon, but had been putting it off. There had been some good ones on offer, yet none of them just seemed right. Most of his friends had either gone travelling or found jobs elsewhere in the country . . . while Shane had simply dropped off the radar. The absence of friends made the void left by his now ex-girlfriend Deserie even more acute.

He stepped down into a low stance, the sword cutting laterally from behind his head to beyond his left shoulder with a low whistle. He spun again on his right heel, following the first cut with a second, then came to a finish. The powerful muscles of his chest and back ached from hefting the broad, double-edged short sword.

Liam ran a hand through his short black hair, now slicked with sweat. On the street below, Shane levered himself out of the Celica. It would be a few minutes before he made it up the steps to the back garden of the sloped block. Liam sheathed his weapon and took a deep breath. The afternoon heat seemed stifling, until a soft breeze moved through the garden, tossing the mango trees and cooling his skin.

He leant forward to stretch his right hamstring, enjoying the sun on his back, and the languid feeling that followed hard training. As he swapped to the other leg, he felt a gaze on his back. He could hear feet moving through the grass in long unhurried strides. Then he smelled the acrid scent of cigarette smoke.

Liam eased out of the stretch and looked up to see the

scowling face of his friend Shane, watching him with disdain as he drew on his cigarette. Liam had known Shane for five years, and had never once seen him raise a sweat — except in a nightclub.

"Shane! How are you, man?" asked Liam, deftly raising himself off the ground. "I haven't seen you for weeks. I've left messages—"

"Yeah, I've been around," said Shane. "Say, you're not going to stab me with that thing are you?" he asked, smiling wickedly as he pointed his cigarette at the sword.

Liam smiled. Shane could never resist a dig at him, particularly his obsession with martial arts and ancient weapons.

Liam and Shane had started Science together at the University of Queensland, and had become fast friends in the first few years. As Liam went on to honours in Chemistry, Shane had made a career out of partying. Liam had hardly seen him since graduation, but any annoyance vanished at the sight of him. It was typical of Shane to drop in without warning.

Shane had been a high school athlete. He was six-two, but his body had a rakish appearance, his skin taking on an unhealthy pallor from too much of the good life. He drew on his cigarette, exhaling with practised ease in a sort of motionless swagger. His eyes narrowed as a sudden breeze tossed his short blond hair.

"What brings you over here?" asked Liam.

"I was just passing through," said Shane, doing his best to sound aggrieved. "Thought I might drop in, but I'll leave if I need an appointment."

Liam laughed and took off his sword belt, walking over to the water tap for a welcome cool-down.

"So. What's happening?" asked Liam, splashing his face and neck with water.

Shane stood outside the radius of the tap's splashing flow, exhaling a cloud of rank smoke as he put on a winning smile. Shane favoured a particularly noxious brand of unfiltered imported cigarettes that left the tang of cloves hanging in the air.

"I was just on my way back to Benson Street. Thought you might want to come along?" That was Shane's share-house. Liam had spent more than a few wasted nights there.

"I'd rather go into the city," said Liam.

Shane groaned, as though he was talking to an idiot. "We're going to get high, man! We've just scored. Party while you can, man. Y2K! Only eleven days left. *The end is coming.*" He gave a high pitched, almost mocking laugh.

Liam ignored the tired old Y2K joke. That thing had been way too hyped. "You know I don't touch it anymore," said Liam, his heart lurching with sudden excitement despite himself. "Can't we just skip it and go into the city? Have a few beers?"

Shane took another drag on his cigarette. "Come on. You know you want to. I've got new shockies on the Celica. We can take a burn around Mount Coot-Tha first. It'll be fun. *Come on.*"

"OK. Just let me have a quick shower." As if he was going to say no.

Shane nodded at Liam's acceptance, his look of triumph fading to boredom. "Got any beer?"

"In the fridge."

Shane stamped his cigarette butt out with his heel on the damp concrete of the path and walked up the stairs. Liam raced past him, taking the stairs two at time, and headed for the kitchen. He reached into the fridge to retrieve two cold bottles of beer, handing one to Shane.

Shane twisted off the cap and took a long draught, his smile of pleasure genuine. "Ahh!"

Liam was always happy to see Shane. For a moment it was almost like two first-years stood in the kitchen, ready to explore the new freedom of University life. Then Shane's smile faded and Liam tensed as the silence stretched.

"Here. You should hear this CD!" Liam put on his latest find and dialled up the music, raising his beer to Shane.

Shane smiled and nodded his head in time to the fast-paced bluesy rock. "Not bad, mate."

"Let me run through the shower," said Liam, downing his beer.

Shane had already finished his. As Liam headed for the bathroom, Shane was already opening the fridge, grunting with effort as he helped himself.

"I'll be waiting on the back step!" called Shane, giving Liam an enthusiastic smile and thumbs up sign.

There was something odd about that, but in that split second, Liam could not place it. It was almost like . . . like Shane was trying too hard.

Chapter 2
Stonelake Gateway — Fourth Realm

Finn Evenstone landed lightly on top of a granite column. Less than a pace wide, the column extended scarcely an arm's-length above the wind-rippled surface of the lake. There was a regular series of them stretching between the stone stairs at the shoreline and the abandoned Gateway platform in the lake's centre. Finn had the familiar sensation of the cool air stinging his face and hands while inside his armour he was baking. He loosened a strap on his breastplate as he turned to watch the progress of his men. A good fit on the parade ground could be downright uncomfortable on exercise, or in combat. Yet, he reminded himself, nothing was as uncomfortable as a night in an outworld trench dodging Vault laser bursts and fragmentation grenades.

The Gateway platform and stairs had once been housed inside a single building, its wooden floor supported by stone columns driven deep into the lake sediments. The ancient structure had rotted away centuries ago. The naked columns now formed a regular grid, four wide across the width of the steps and twelve long between the steps and the old Gateway. He was halfway across. The Gateway platform itself was a monolithic structure of cut granite blocks that extended all the way to the lake bottom. It was now an island of pale stone, accessible only by boat, or across the columns. Finn grinned. Some of the wide, flat-topped columns had tilted, making them perilous to land on, particularly for warriors in full armour.

"Come on. It is only water!" called Finn.

He knew most of his warriors had expected an easy morning on the day of the Festival, but by now they should have known better. These men, this garrison, was his weapon. Like his gnarled fists, calloused after years of training in lethal open-handed techniques, and the Realm longsword at his hip, which could project a dampening field that neutralised Vault technology. If he was ever to take revenge, to make the Vault pay for the deaths of his father, his mother, and his brothers — and for the trail of destruction driven through his life — he needed all his weapons sharp.

He waved his warriors across. The muscles between his shoulder-blades bunched with tension as he saw their hesitation. If they feared water, what of Vault warriors like the siithe? Creatures as vicious and cunning as mad dogs, who tortured and feasted on their prisoners?

The first of his warriors to follow looked across at Finn from the stairs, his face pale.

"Take your time," said Finn. "Measure the distance. Never rush." He knew from bitter experience how reckless actions cost lives.

Threads of morning mist trailed across the water, swirling around the Gateway platform in the centre of the lake. A shaft of sunshine struck the lake surface, making it gleam in the new day. The Gateway itself was an arched doorway set on the far side of the platform, leading out into the lake waters, each doorpost a tall stone obelisk.

The warrior hurled himself forward. His booted feet skittered on the flat top of the first column before he stopped his slide. His face flushed with relief.

Finn let out a breath of relief, then turned, jumping across to the next column. His left boot slipped on the slick stone, and he halted his slide with a quick shift of position to correct his balance.

"Stupid exercise . . ." The grumbled complaint whispered across the water. "Damn Gateway's as dead as dead."

Finn leapt five more times, finally reaching the solid stone of the Gateway platform. He walked to the Gateway's arched opening, where visitors from Kgari, the world beyond the Gateway, had once emerged. The two obelisks were decorated with intricate carvings of native bees and forest trees. A peaceful scene. *A lie.* He reached out and touched the gap where the Axe of Evenstone had driven a wedge of stone from the leftmost obelisk. Finn's secret — which he had carried here from his own distant Third Realm — was that this Gateway was far from dead.

He shivered. It was from here that the Vault attack would come.

Finn turned back to his men. Dozens had followed onto the

blunt columns, and they were now strung out in a ragged line above the lake waters, while more waited at the shoreline. He pitched his voice to carry across the water. "You cannot always pick your own ground for battle. There might come a time when a little extra balance means the difference between life and death."

He eyed the men carefully, alert for any druidic devices. Although Realm biotechnology was commonly used in battle, he had banned its use on this exercise. Last month, he had caught one of the men in his garrison with an electronic viewing scope bought on the black market. It was illegal, non-Realm tech, and dangerous to rely on. Something like that might give a warrior an edge in training exercises, but come the time for real battle, the Realm dampening field would neutralise anything resembling Vault tech. *Steel and magic.* The only things you could trust. The Realm warrior's maxim.

A warrior sprang across the gap. He made it, then missed his balance. He threw himself flat, but could not halt his slide. His gauntleted fingers scrabbled desperately for purchase on the granite as he slid to the edge, then dropped into the water.

The men burst into laughter. Finn clenched his jaw, watching the water. The lake was shallow here, which was why Finn allowed the exercise. Armoured as they were, the men sank like anchors. The warrior's head broke the surface. He spat out water while more drained from his helmet. His angry, sodden face, and drenched hair, inspired a new wave of laughter.

"Captain Evenstone!" one of his young warriors called from the lakeshore.

"Yes, Keris!" said Finn.

Finn was fond of Keris, who had scarcely passed a year in his service to the High King. He was born in Stonelake. The only local boy to pass the gruelling entrance tests required for the High King's garrison for well over twenty years. It was not so long ago he would have been out here with his friends jumping from one column to the next. It was a popular game with the town youths. It was watching them, one idle afternoon, which had given Finn the idea.

"Captain Evenstone, the messenger from the High King has

arrived," said Keris. *The rider is early.*

"Right, lads. Back to the Tower!" ordered Finn.

The men still on the steps — who had yet to make the perilous journey out onto the columns — grinned at each other, while the others groaned and made their way back to the stairs.

Finn eyed Keris' battle gear as he reached the bank. He had an automatic reflex for that sort of thing. "Your scabbard is slung too low, guardsman. Hitch it up a handspan." The low-slung look was a tempting style for a new warrior, but the scabbard was liable to trip the wearer, especially when the sword was drawn and the sheath no longer weighed down by the weapon. As it was, the damn thing was likely to break his neck. Keris reached down to his belt, fingers scrambling. "Not now," said Finn. "Forward at the run!"

The arrival of the courier was always a cause for some excitement. Stonelake was isolated, and news of the Realms reached it slowly.

The men pulled instantly into disciplined ranks. The unlucky warrior who had fallen into the lake waded out of the reeds and joined them. He clanked and squelched along just behind Finn.

Finn looked across to Keris, who kept pace with him at the front, unsure whether to fall into ranks or not. The boy was nervous, clutching onto a scabbard that now flipped around wildly. Finn had forgotten how intimidating a Captain could be to a new warrior.

When Finn reached the courtyard inside the town gates, the horseman was at the walls. The courier galloped through the gates without waiting for the formal hail. The omission drew a hot look from Finn's lieutenant Endar, standing up on the battlement. The rider halted in the courtyard before Finn, amid a scattering of livestock and straw. His stallion snorted and tossed its head, chest heaving, its chestnut coat lathered with sweat.

At first Finn noticed only the horse. The stallion was exhausted, pushed far beyond his limits. Angry at the treatment of the animal, and concerned that the message must be urgent, Finn looked up to study the rider and recognised the man instantly. Zanthis, a companion and follower of prince Sentas.

His lip curling with disdain, Zanthis spurred the stallion

forward a pace, then reined him in hard, forcing him to rear. Finn dodged out of the way as iron-shod hooves flashed past his face.

"My apologies *Captain* Evenstone," said Zanthis with a mocking smile. "It is a difficult mount to control."

Two of Finn's men appeared at his side, ready to drag the courier off his horse.

Finn regarded Zanthis silently, slowly unclenching his fists. He let the cool clarity of his mind descend over his outrage and smiled. *Ah, yes.* The High King's courier is protected by the law, and cannot be accosted. *Damn, Sentas!* His foster-brother was still playing his games.

"Young, Zanthis," said Finn, in his best voice, which he knew would carry to the farthest corner of the courtyard. "Stonelake bids welcome to the courier of the High King! On behalf of the town, I offer you hospitality."

Zanthis met his gaze levelly, then spat into the straw at the horse's feet. A wave of shock swept through the crowd. On the very day of their great annual Festival, the courier of the High King had refused an offer of hospitality!

"I would no sooner stay in this pathetic backwater than marry a goat. Although perhaps that may be your pastime here."

At his side, Finn saw Keris' hand flash for his sword. His own hand shot out, seizing the young warrior's wrist before he drew. He cast a warning glance at the rest of his men.

Zanthis lifted the message-satchel from his saddle and tossed it to Finn, who snatched it from the air, his right fist closing on its rough fabric. The tension in Finn's clenched jaw was the only sign anything was amiss.

The courier dismounted. Finn motioned for a stable hand to take the horse.

"Now," said Zanthis, smoothing his fine silken breeches, which had been stained by horse sweat. "If you will provide me with a mount, I will be on my way back to the High Court," he said pleasantly. "You have no idea how much the place has changed, but then it has been years, has it not?"

Finn took his time looking through the messages in the bag, conscious of the absolute silence that had descended on the courtyard. Even the animals, sensing something, had grown quiet, and huddled against the lee of the wall away from the press of armoured men and onlookers.

Finn smiled as he saw a message from his sister Tallandra. Then his heart skipped a beat as he saw an official letter from the High King.

"Well!" demanded Zanthis.

Finn looked Zanthis in the eye, making a play of looking forgetful. "Ah, yes. A horse." Finn looked perplexed, then shrugged. "But my good courier, you already have a horse."

A look of shock came over Zanthis' face, and Finn knew what he was thinking. He had ruined his horse. If he must wait for it to recover before he left, he could be in Stonelake for weeks. Perhaps months, if it grew lame.

"I am the High King's courier!" stormed Zanthis, his face growing red. "I demand to have my needs met."

Finn nodded, carefully tying the bag. "And what urgent business draws you back to the High Court?"

Zanthis' jaw went slack. The couriers from the First Realm were regular visitors here. The High King's officials were bound to supply a courier of the High Court with any materials or succour they desired, provided they were on urgent business, and could prove this with a letter bearing the High King's seal. It was a safeguard that prevented the couriers from living the high life on the backs of the people.

Finn smiled, satisfied. He had cornered him, and Zanthis knew it. Once more he raised his voice. "Since I have offered the hospitality of Stonelake, and the High King's Tower, and you have so graciously refused, my obligations are fulfilled. But I am sure any number of townsfolk would be glad to offer you accommodations."

Finn gestured toward the assembled crowd. They remained silent for a long pause, then came a shout.

"There's plenty of room in my pigsty!"

The tension broke, amid laughter and derision, as the offers of accommodation came pouring in from the townsfolk — cesspits, old wells, water troughs — even a goat's pen.

Finn began to laugh as the townsfolk had their piece of flesh. His warriors relaxed.

Enraged, Zanthis closed on Finn. His voice lowered into a savage tone. "Very clever, Evenstone. Well choke on this. Sentas sends his regards. He says your sister has flowered into the very picture of womanhood in your absence. Just right for the *plucking*." Zanthis turned on his heel and strode through the crowd, to be lost amid the curving alleyways.

"Keris, take these," said Finn, retrieving Tallandra's letter, and the official dispatch with its High King's seal, before the grinning youth sprinted away.

"You men can return to your normal duties," said Finn. Then he noticed the guardsman who had fallen into the lake, still wet and miserable. "You had better get dry and warm first."

"Thank you, sir."

Chapter 3

Sydney, Australia — Earth
20th December 1999

Yolinda pulled the faded denim jacket closer around her shoulders, wincing as the chill wind sliced through the skyscraper shadows. A potato-chip packet skittered along the gutter, passing mounds of less mobile garbage as it went, the aluminium liner dull in the overcast grey of mid-morning.

She paused on the kerb, and waited for a break in the traffic, absently touching the grip of the 0.38 revolver holstered under her arm. *Damn this wind.* A sudden gust kicked up a cloud of dust from the dirty bitumen. Yolinda shivered with cold . . . and fear.

Around her the inner-city Sydney skyline rose in drab towers of featureless grey, each an aging monument to the death of the suburbs. The street was deserted. No boutique shops or shopping malls here. The district was purely commercial. No mirrored glass panels or fancy modern angles. Parallel lines of windows rose with depressing regularity, and Yolinda wondered what scene they would paint for a bored office-worker looking out onto the streets below. Would they see her as a lonely derelict? Another victim of heroin drifting around in numbness, dreaming of the next score? Her greasy, unwashed hair and pale face like a class banner, the dark circles under her eyes advertising her sickness.

The traffic thinned, and Yolinda shuffled across the street, thinking desperately. It had been over a week since Jay had contacted her, and even then he had been guarded. More than that, he had been *scared*. Jay was experienced. He had faced down shotguns, and defended himself with lethal force. What could rattle him like this? What he said made it plain there was something big going down, but what?

Yolinda had been undercover for just over a year. Despite being almost twenty-nine, in the right clothes she could pass for seventeen. She was a five foot nothing natural blonde with a small, finely boned face. She used to curse her height every time the nightclub bouncers checked her ID, but the Drug Squad had seen her potential immediately. She had only been in the Federal Drugs Taskforce for a few months before they sent her into the field as a liaison officer for deep cover operatives. When she had first gone undercover in Sydney, Jay — Federal Agent John Albert Troy — had been on the streets for three years. He had busted four major operations, and was close to the centre of the fifth. She had been amazed at his ability to think under pressure, and change his appearance in a moment: a different stance or expression, new mannerisms or gestures, all played to a fault. It seemed he had the ability to bluff his way out of anything. Yolinda had idolised him, but one week ago that had changed. The sound of fear in his voice had sent her universe into a spin.

This was to be no cosy meeting in a back street, getting reports to take back to headquarters. Jay was in danger, and this time she would be risking her life as well. There was no choice. She was his only contact outside the syndicate. "Meet me in one week," he had said, "at the usual place". Yolinda could still hear the disengaged tone as she held the phone to her ear after he cut the call. That was it. No explanation, nothing. Just the sound of his fear. The Agent in charge had issued approval for the meeting without hesitation.

Yolinda steadily drew closer to the rendezvous, the gun a cold lump of metal beneath her arm. She passed a group of young Vietnamese men on a street corner and looked down at her feet as she approached. They were small time dealers — nothing more than street kids with bad attitudes, deadly weapons, and no future. She casually watched them from the corner of her tired and aching eyes. They seemed jumpy, and were ready to run at the slightest sign of trouble. Usually they were cocky and confident.

Something was different on the streets today. Yolinda had been into all the usual low-life haunts. The places were deserted, regulars missing from the daytime bars, back-street dealing houses locked and empty. Was there a new player on the streets? First the Romanians, then the Vietnamese, the Japanese, now. . . who? Drug Squad intelligence had not been able to tell her anything. There had been some mysterious jailbreaks. Five inmates with heavy-duty records — assault, murder, rape, armed robbery — simply vanishing from maximum security. Serious criminals were loose, but how could that be connected to what was happening here, on the outside?

Yolinda had almost reached the contact point, an alleyway in the middle of sin-city, dark and sordid. She pulled the jacket tighter around her shoulders and turned into the mouth of the dirty lane, her ancient boots silent on the old cobbles. As she rounded the corner she saw Jay at the far end of the alley. He bled from multiple shallow cuts to his face. Two men had him bailed up against the wall. They had their backs to her. They were huge black men, built like weightlifters, with smooth shaven heads, dressed in matching leather jackets and blue denim jeans, all brand new. It was then that Yolinda noticed the wicked knives they held, the tips of the long double-edged serrated blades dripping blood.

Jay saw Yolinda. He surreptitiously waved her back. The men had not seen her yet. She still had the option of turning around and walking away, as if she had taken a wrong turn. A junkie too high to know the difference. She would be safe, and after all, Jay could take care of himself . . . *No.* That would mean deserting an officer in trouble, and missing an opportunity to find out what was happening. Yolinda continued into the alleyway. Her heart thudded faster as she slipped her right hand under her jacket to grip the handle of the 0.38. She could hear Jay's voice, high-pitched and pleading, rise over the low rumble of the black men's voices. There was a growl from one of the hulking men that froze her in her tracks. *It scarcely sounded human.*

Then everything happened at once.

Jay sidestepped, away from the men. He circled away from the wall, and drew his Glock 17. Light flashed as both knives rose. A gunshot boomed in the alley. One of the big men flew back, but the second closed the gap with startling speed. The man gripped Jay's hand — gun and all — and twisted it away. The gun fired again, the bullet striking a cloud of brick dust off the alley wall. Taking a short step forward, the man sunk his serrated long-knife into Jay's heart, all the way to the hilt. The man, still holding Jay's hand, and the gun, then ripped the knife out with a savage downward twist. Yolinda watched, still frozen, as Jay fell. He tumbled to the ground, as boneless as a bag of laundry. The undercover agent's mouth was open, his eyes wide in shock. There was a flood of blood. It steamed in the cool air. Jay shuddered then went still. The knifeman released Jay's hand. The Glock clattered on the cobbles. Yolinda watched the blood spread out across the grimy alley surface. The crimson flood split as it reached the fallen gun, moved around it, then the two streams rejoined. The pool broadened and spread until it reached the base of the graffiti-strewn wall. *There was so much. So much blood.*

Yolinda's eyes were drawn back to Jay's lifeless face.

Her hand trembled on the grip of the revolver.

Chapter 4

City of Minoras — Shadow World beyond the Third Realm
Fifteen years earlier . . .

Vespar retreated into the shadows.

He could feel the rough texture of the cold stone wall through the back of his gown, and shivered as he pressed into it. An armoured troop carrier rumbled through the night, the low throb of its engine and the sound of its rubberized tread softened by distance, counterpoint to the edge of quiet despair that seeped through Minoras' seedy backstreets. The soot-filled air stung his throat, leaving the nauseating taste of acid.

Tanya's townhouse was just across the narrow street, yet he hesitated. Its crumbling facade appeared still and silent to normal vision, but through his thurjun's sight it was alive with Shades — spirit creatures that preyed on the living. They drew together and cavorted like vultures above a dying man, waiting to feed. His mind groped and stuttered, trying to make sense of it. A Shade swarm like this one should not appear in an outpost city like Minoras, not this close to a Gateway into the Blessed Realms. Never in his long career as a thurjun, not even within the Vaults of Sheol where the krell ruled, had he seen such a concentration of darkness. It meant that a powerful servant of a krell lord was close. With them would be blood priests, siithe warriors, Dark Thurjuns . . . and worse.

Vespar had dedicated his life to fighting the Vaults of Sheol, empires that thrived on destruction and pillage, drawing the lifeblood of a thousand races into their dark hearts. Enemies of the Blessed Realms. *His* enemies.

His heart burned in shame. How had it come to this? Visiting the Shadow Worlds in secret? Without an escort? Without the consent of his lord? He was no warrior, sneaking to the tavern or the brothels, he was a senior thurjun of Lord Evenstone's court, in control of the Minoras Gateway.

His hand went instinctively to his chest, but he had left his mionanail pendant — his only weapon — back in the citadel, too fearful the Realm device would fall into the wrong hands. As skilled as he was in the thurjun's craft, without his mionanail to power his magic he could summon only phantoms and illusions. Against any normal enemy perhaps that would be enough. But against the Shades and the living servants of the krell?

He had risked all of this for her.

Tanya.

Why did she obsess him so? And why had her demands for secrecy bound him so tightly? He had not even discussed her with Morin, his lifetime friend and fellow thurjun.

It was forbidden for any of the subjects of the Blessed Realms to journey alone into the Shadow Worlds — dark dominions between the Vaults of Sheol and the Blessed Realms. The dangers were great, the fragile bulwarks too thinly defended. Yet he, in his arrogance, had allowed himself to believe he was stronger than normal men. Above them in power, and beyond them in discipline. Protected by his thurjun's sight, he believed he would see the dangers, and easily avoid them.

His duty was clear. As thurjun to Lord Evenstone, he should report the Shade swarm immediately. It would mean explaining it all. His affair. His lies.

He gasped as an intense nausea gripped him. His legs quivered in sudden weakness. He leant back against the wall, waiting for it to pass. He tried to breathe evenly. Erotic memories flooded his mind. A wave of heat rose from his groin and his heart raced.

He cursed the day he first saw Tanya's beautiful, empty face. Even then he had sensed something beneath her approach, yet the sweet flattery, her seeming emotional insecurity and need for him, had drawn him back. He looked across the street to her narrow tenement, and the nausea inexplicably vanished.

Vespar had met Tanya Ger'Van at a reception in the Exarch's palace, while attending in his official function as Realm ambassador to Minoras. A widowed royal — a Seatess no less — distantly related to the Exarch himself, Tanya had been delightful and charming. Very correct. Very formal. He had accepted her invitation to visit with pleasure, arriving at her townhouse escorted by a full squad of warriors, as required by Realm law. It had been harmless enough, a simple first meeting, yet she had broken down in his arms, pleading that he return in secret, fearing that the Exarch's court would paint her as a Realm consort. He sternly refused. But strangely, he had returned alone within days. The first of many secret sojourns. She had played the innocent well, shyly removing the heavy court clothes with shaking hands. Yet slowly, she had led him ever deeper into debauchery, increasingly using drugs, introducing her slaves into their lovemaking, until he scarcely recognized himself. Where was the strict thurjun who had scorned the weaknesses of lesser men? The unerring follower of a strict moral code that had limited the assignations of a lifetime to less than he could count on one hand? There had always been something lurking under the surface of her mind, but it was elusive, and he had let himself think she was truly that fearful of pubic embarrassment.

His temples pounded. His breathing grew rapid, and the nausea rose once more. He flinched as the door opened. Tanya appeared on the steps. She was wrapped in a heavy robe. Her sensual lips curled into a smile as she saw him in the shadows. She let the robe fall open to reveal a translucent negligee. Her nipples were taut beneath the silky fabric. The dark triangle of her mons vivid against her pale flesh. She filled his vision. He trembled with the memory of pleasure, and groaned as the nausea receded. *Scandalous.* Was this the woman who tearfully begged him to come alone to protect her reputation? The seemingly chaste and proper Seatess who invited him to visit?

Vespar stumbled forward into the street.

He heard a scream. An abyss opened under his feet. A man struggled at the lip of the chasm, howling in fear as darkness yawned beneath him. The grip of the hapless victim slowly weakened and the man looked up at Vespar in terror — and he saw his own face. His mind recoiled. Sharpened.

The vision fell away. The spell that had drawn him forward shattered under his new focus. He found himself in the middle of the street, halfway to the townhouse.

Sorcery!

The Shades — vague shadows of pain in the darkness — stopped their swooping motions and flitted toward him.

Vespar ran for his life.

As he fled, the night blurred. Confusion took hold, and his mind filled with the memories of those nights of flesh and abandon. For a while it had been so sweet, so deliciously sweet, despite the agony of breaking his own moral codes and the laws of the Realms . . . especially to a man who had only moderate success with women in his youth, and was now so far past his prime.

Vespar took the four steps at a run and looked up with astonishment to find himself at the townhouse door. Despite his attempt to flee, the Shades had turned him around. They now pressed on his shoulders, urging him on. The door opened. Reality grew soft as he drifted into the red-lit interior. The door closed.

She was there.

At the sight of her, his mind filled with a rushing sound, a confusion of images centred on her face. Tanya melted into his side, caressing him, passing him a gilded cup filled to the brim with dark red wine, smelling strongly of narcotic. He had craved it. Craved her. Longed to touch her. Before him, the large room was crowded. A retinue of siithe warriors and fiends surrounded the massive grey bulk of a krell lord. His armoured form dwarfed the chair of twisted iron he used as a throne. His siithe bodyguards were armed with pulse lasers, sonic mines, and huge thick-bladed falcatas. He should have known none other than a krell lord would be attended by such a host of Shades. Fear and alarm rose beneath the thickened surface of his mind. They were distant things now, hardly sensed beneath the furnace roar of his desire.

The krell's eyes expanded to fill Vespar's world. His mind tore through Vespar's defences, flensing the hide of his soul, stripping him away. The pain was unlike anything Vespar had ever felt. He screamed, fighting back with every skill he knew. The krell drew him on, step by step. Vespar shuffled closer. With each step, another measure of his will drained away.

The force of the krell's presence flattened him, reducing him to an insignificant, two-dimensional creature. He felt no fear. The krell's wet and glistening eyes held him. A fierce exhilaration and arousal rose in him as Tanya and her bed-mates pulled him to the furs and cushions at the foot of the krell's throne. His thurjun's robe was cast aside. He was vaguely aware of the taste of the drugged wine. The empty goblet tumbled from numb fingers. Those nights of pleasure in his memory were nothing to the sensations he experienced now. A white-hot fury of savage lust engulfed him, its borders defined by the bloodshot irises of the krell's eyes. His last defences were ripped away. Beneath his heady, impossible elation, the bright fabric of his soul shrank as the krell took his repast, casting in place the heavy chains of spirit that would make Vespar his thrall.

When the fury of the sexual union had flared and died, and Vespar lay sated and buoyed by the piquancy of the drugs, the krell turned away from him.

Vespar's disciplined mind snapped back into shape.

He sat naked in a pit of vileness. The furs were rank and rotten, stained with blood and entrails. The krell lord was revealed as a dark grey behemoth of vaguely human proportions, his hide wet and glistening with sticky fluid, the thick, armoured plates of the wedge-shaped head crowned with yellowed and chipped horns in rows like shark's teeth. At the krell's side was a skeletally thin human, his stark blue eyes contemptuous and cruel beneath his close-cropped hair and aristocratic visage. To his far right, standing apart from the dagger-toothed siithe warriors, was a sight that startled Vespar. A seraphin, a creature of the High God, had joined with the Vaults of Sheol. Its raiment of bright light had gone, and in its place it wore a cloak of red fire. The dark limbs within the nimbus were immobile, the face, as always, unreadable. Its six wings beat a slow time.

Tanya had risen. Her female attendants covered her nakedness with a dark leather robe. She sipped from a golden cup and stared at Vespar. Eyes empty. Appraising. Her hair had been drawn back into a net of gold lace. He scarcely recognized her.

"Seatess?" he croaked.

"Welcome, thurjun."

"Tanya. What have you done to me?" asked Vespar.

"Tanya? I am Uzar, you weak-minded fool. A priestess of VoYannan."

VoYannan! Lord of the Vault of Seven Horns!

Trembling, Vespar rose and donned his stained robe. The soft women were gone, and no attendants came to him. The siithe warriors crowded closer, penning him in. Their small, dark eyes followed every movement, and their tongues flicked across their pointed teeth, as though in anticipation. Their thick fingers played over their falcata hilts, as though eager to put the heavy blades to work on his flesh. Vespar's stomach clenched at the rank scent of their dark, thickset bodies.

Vespar understood everything. The seduction. His entrapment. The slow building of the dark compulsion that had led him here. The Seatess Tanya Ger'Van had never existed. His very first step into Minoras to see this trickster creature had led him inexorably to this moment. His own pride had been his downfall. He had been too arrogant to believe that the Vault could conquer his mind. Too protective of his reputation to admit the liaison.

His one consolation was that not even Uzar could make him break the strict prohibition against risking Realm technology in the Shadow Worlds, despite her continual requests that he bring it "for his own safety". His precious mionanail was safe. In the Vault's hands it would have been too terrible a weapon. He tried to gather his thoughts. To plan some escape.

Then the krell spoke.

Chapter 5
City of Minoras — Shadow World beyond the Third Realm

"Uzar," said the krell. His deep voice shook Vespar's chest like a drum. "You said you would have a compulsion on the thurjun within a month. Yet you have kept me waiting a year."

Uzar paled. "It took me longer than I expected, Mighty One. I had to build the spell slowly, lest he read my intent." She bowed her head, gaze fixed to the floor.

The krell growled, and turned to a knot of priests in red robes that lurked in the shadow-draped verges of the room.

"Show me the omens!" The krell's words struck Vespar's mind like a bloodied hammer. He fell to his knees in shock.

Two priests rushed forward to the base of the throne, drawing a dull-eyed, naked slave between them. The slave was in his prime, the skin around his heavy shackles broken and bleeding: a testament to earlier struggles. One of the priests nodded, and a heavily muscled, lower-caste priest came forward slowly, a small reptile gripped tightly at arm's length. Even through the slave's drugged state, terror cast its grip. The man began to struggle feebly. Tremendously weakened by the drug, the two emaciated priests held him easily. As the squirming beast drew close to the terrified slave, a fourth priest came forward with a long ceremonial dagger and sliced open the man's stomach with a single, deft cut. The slave gave a strangled yelp of pain and surprise, then his eyes glazed. With practiced efficiency, the handler forced the ferocious, starving lizard into the bleeding cavity. With precisely choreographed movements, the four priests stepped back three paces.

For an instant, the slave made no move. The lizard squirmed beneath his skin and sheets of blood ran from the cut and down his legs to pool at his feet. His mouth opened soundlessly. Then he screamed. He collapsed to the floor and writhed in agony.

Vespar pushed himself upright, then turned away. The thurjun tried to block his ears, but was unable to shield himself from the sickening wet sounds that issued forth from the dying slave as the animal ripped its way free in a frenzy of teeth and claw.

They removed the slave's body, and the handler expertly retrieved the now sated lizard with a noose of wire on a pole, which he drew tight about its leathery neck before leading it away. Once the area was clear, the two leading priests returned to study the scattered pattern of blood and entrails that had been cast outward across the furs at the base of the throne — the place where, moments before, Vespar had rutted like an animal. He squeezed his eyes shut, fighting despair. He forced them open again.

The priests consulted at length, then approached the dais. "My Lord VoYannan!"

The krell sat forward. A low and menacing growl issued from his throat.

"The omens remain favourable. A krell spawn issuing from a union with the virgin priestess, Sephany, will be subject to your will for eternity. Your power will be increased beyond measure."

"And of all the Blessed Realms, she is the only one?"

The priest bowed quickly, clenching his fists into his robe. He was shaking. "Yes, Lord. Such a being of light comes only once an aeon to humankind."

The krell surged to his feet and instantly the entourage were gripped with the same savage desire, as though the court were a single entity. Even Vespar surged forward, ready to kill, before he checked himself.

"Proceed with the attack!" raged VoYannan.

For the first time, the thin aide at the krell's side spoke. "My Lord," said the man.

VoYannan faced the man. "Procarrus." VoYannan seemed to measure him for a moment, as though sizing up a meal. "Speak."

Vespar felt a dark hurricane of fear swirl inside his heart at the mention of the name. Procarrus. The Archfiend. *Sworn enemy of House Evenstone.*

"Have we gained the means to pass through the portal?" asked Procarrus.

The krell lord growled and turned. Once more, Vespar found himself the subject of that paralysing gaze. Yet, this time, there was no exhilaration. Instead, he felt a dull pain in his heart as the krell drained him to his core, stripping away his will.

"Will you open the gate, thurjun?"

A hand gripped his soul, with it came a cold emptiness that promised an instant and final death. Now came the price of his folly. He was being asked to open the portal to the Third Realm of the Blessed, to the very hearthstone of Lord Evenstone's tower. The sleeping place of his children. It meant nothing less than the death of hundreds of men Vespar had sworn to protect with his life, and possible ruin for the entire Third Realm. Millions of lives. It was a betrayal of the gravest kind. How could he do other than refuse, even though it meant his life?

His tongue froze, defiance dead before it was born. His determination drained away. Ashamed, he heard himself whimpering in fear, yet he was unable to move or turn away. In those few moments of lustful fury, he had committed the ultimate stupidity. He had let the krell invade him to the core of his being.

Just when it seemed he must die from emptiness, his body and mind were filled with pleasure. His whimpering turned to laughter as he reached arousal and climax in a rapid, endless cycle. He floated on a warm, carnal sea. The krell lord was no longer before him; instead, it was his liege, Lord Evenstone himself. "Vespar, my loyal thurjun," he said, "will you open the gate for my warriors tonight?"

"Yes, Lord. Yes. I would do anything for you."

In an instant, the vision was gone. Vespar was left trembling and retching on the bloody furs at the krell's feet. He scrambled back in disgust.

The cold, cold, blade of reality, slid into his brain.

There was only one escape.

Death.

He rushed forward, drew a dagger from one of his siithe captors, and using both hands, stabbed at his heart with all his strength.

The strike halted mid-thrust.

The dagger fell from fingers he could not feel. Astonished, Vespar was seized by two hulking siithe, one on each arm, and held immobile. He looked up to see the krell lord watching him through watering green eyes, edged with rheumy film. Beside his master, the cruel face of the Archfiend creased into a savage smile.

"Raise the cohorts of Seven Horns!" stormed Procarrus. Siithe warriors and slaves hurtled into motion.

"Tonight Evenstone Tower will burn in the fires of Sheol!"

Chapter 6
Brisbane, Australia — Earth
20th December 1999

Liam laughed with delight, revelling in the thrill. Shane took the corners at a flying pace, leaving tyre marks across the bitumen. They raced through the suburbs, music blaring as Shane pushed his worked Celica to the limit.

The sun was setting as they arrived at Shane's share-house, armed with more beer. Shane was completely broke, as usual, so Liam had bought a carton. What were a few cans between friends? Besides, Shane had agreed to go out on the town later, and had driven Liam to the ATM to get cash. "Better get out a few hundred," said Shane. "Who knows where we'll end up?" Liam had smiled as he pushed the buttons, but that smile had faltered as he noticed Shane eyeing the notes. There was some weird undertone there he could not decipher. Again, he put it out of his mind.

Outside the old Queenslander in Benson Street, two big Harleys lay parked on the curb, each at the same lazy slant.

Liam reached for the car door.

"Let's have a beer before we go in," said Shane.

Liam sensed Shane had something to say.

"OK," said Liam. He broke the side of the carton, still cold from the bottle-shop fridge, and pulled out two cans, handing one to Shane. "What's on your mind?"

The silence stretched. "Some of us are putting together a big score tonight. Bulk quantity. Good stuff too. We're just a bit short on cash."

Liam groaned. There was always something. He suppressed his anger as he realised the whole visit was set up for that one question. That explained the ATM. He must be desperate, thought Liam. After all these months, he must have finally run out of credit with his family and biker friends. He remained silent.

Shane lit a cigarette. "How about it?"

Liam felt his heart squeezed. "No. Sorry. The answer has to be no. I don't smoke anymore. I told you that."

"Yeah, yeah. Mister Fitness. Then lend me the cash. I'll pay you back."

"I can't afford that. Not until I get a job."

Shane laughed. "You're sitting on four hundred bills, man. You can afford it. I don't have a cent left in my account."

Their eyes met for an instant. Shane could be so damn insistent. Liam weighed his own determination against the potential dent in one of his few remaining friendships.

Shane took another long draw on his cigarette. The atmosphere in the car was stifling. The stink of cloves overpowering.

"The stuff's from the Coast. If we can put together a grand we can get an excellent deal, otherwise we'll be paying a premium. Mick and Warren are in as well, we only need another two-fifty. That leaves one-fifty for beers in town. Come on!" said Shane, giving Liam a smile and nodding his head. Liam was reminded of that last smiling look before he headed in for the shower. His stomach clenched at the realisation. *It was all a put on.* That was the worst. Shane was supposed to be his friend, yet he was working him like a mark.

Liam took another mouthful of the beer despite the sick feeling in his stomach and shook his head. "Look, just . . . No. Let's just go in."

Shane watched Liam with a predatory gleam in his eye, but merely nodded. He dropped his butt into his can, where it extinguished with a hiss in the beer dregs. He lit another cigarette, watching Liam without a trace of emotion, as though he were studying a wall of painted graffiti. His face was drawn. Liam could tell he was more than just irritated. "Can I have another beer?" asked Shane gruffly, the deal forgotten. For now.

Liam nodded. "Sure. Help yourself."

Shane pulled out another of his beers. He ripped it open, then reached over to turn up the stereo, quickly draining the can as the music pumped. It was dance music. Shane used to like rock.

"Just going to have a quick racehorse," said Shane, taking a skinny joint from his glove box and lighting it up. He took a drag and offered it to Liam, laughing to himself as Liam silently refused. Smoke curled through the air, the pungent, distinctive aroma of marijuana making Liam's heart beat fast in automatic desire. *Pavlov's dog.*

Liam started to roll down his window, trying to escape the cloud.

"Leave it up. Too much wind," said Shane.

Liam tapped the floor with his foot. "Can't you smoke that inside the house?"

Shane held up his hand and shook his head, his lungs full of smoke.

Damn it!

Liam looked across at a small park across the road. He forced his muscles to relax and let a calm flow through his mind. After years of meditation, it was like a reflex. There were two flowering bushes near the swings, both with huge blossoms, the long fronds that supported them bending down under their weight. One of the flowers was purest white, the other blood-red. His vision unfocussed. A woman appeared, dressed in white. She was soft and elegant. Her raven-black hair gleamed in the sun, yet her face was twisted in fear and pain. Her dress had been torn open in a ragged tear, its white cloth spattered with blood.

"Oh, my God! She's been attacked!" said Liam in alarm.

"Who?" asked Shane. He opened his window and flicked out the butt of the joint.

"That woman. Look!" Liam pointed across the road.

There was nothing there.

Just the big bushes, tossing in the wind, the flowers jostling each other. It was another vision.

"Shit, Liam!" said Shane, laughing. "Oh, I forgot. *'I don't need that stuff to get high'*," said Shane in a mocking falsetto. "Seeing things already?"

Liam gritted his teeth, regretting ever saying that to Shane. "Leave it out, mate."

"OK. OK. Don't get touchy. Let's go," said Shane, climbing out of the lowered sedan and coming around to Liam's side.

"Here, let me carry that for you," said Shane, hefting what was left of the carton onto his shoulder.

They made their way up the stairs to the front verandah.

Shane ignored the ornately panelled wooden door with its archaic centrally-mounted doorknob and headed for a set of French doors to his right. Shane flipped open one of the French doors and walked through into the front living room. Liam watched his own reflection in the glass of the other door as he walked across the landing. He wore a tight black tee under a loose collared shirt and stretch jeans, showing a spare frame without a trace of fat, the muscles lean and powerfully compact. His straight black hair was cropped at collar length, and shone almost blue in the hot sun, framing a soft, pleasant face with deep-set blue eyes.

Inside the house, it was dark and humid. It smelled of stale beer and marijuana. Around a dozen people sat languidly on mismatched couches in the living room. Two bearded bikies sat together, one of them holding a set of leather saddle-bags with long fringes. Heavy rock blared from the stereo.

The biker nursing the bags turned to watch Liam. Scruffy beard, beer-gut, armless leather vest and faded blue tats on stretched skin, the shape of the biceps hidden by body fat. His bulk hinted at real muscle though, beneath the fat. The flat stare was practised, and Liam guessed he was used to intimidating people. Liam met his gaze, sizing him up. He knew how slow someone like that would move if it ever came down to it, despite the posturing. The biker frowned and turned to Shane.

Shane's cattle-dog bitch, Thatcher, was on the back balcony staring hopefully into the living room. At the sight of the visitors she lifted up her head, waging her tale hopefully, then lowered it again, resting it on her paws. She looked bored.

Shane put on a winning smile and went straight to the bikie with the saddle-bag. "Phil! How's it going mate! Have a beer," he said, handing over one from Liam's carton. *No Y2K jokes here,* thought Liam.

Shane handed around the beers in a miraculous outpouring of goodwill. Liam clenched his jaw as he saw his carton dwindle.

Phil and Shane swapped a bit of chat while the other biker drank steadily and did his best to look tough.

"Let's get to it," said Phil.

The balcony doors into the living room were slammed closed

and the curtains drawn.

The silent biker spread out a newspaper on the floor, then Phil set out bags of marijuana from the saddle-bag in neat rows while Shane measured the weights with a set of portable scales, and checked the weed's freshness and quality.

Satisfied, Shane nodded to two other share-house guys. All three pulled out wads of cash. Shane fronted half — five-hundred dollars. He had been carrying it the whole time, including when they bought the beer. *Too broke to afford it, huh?*

A water pipe materialised, and at Phil's nod, the other biker packed the cone and passed it to Shane. He smiled as he lit the pipe, inhaling the thick white smoke with hungry enthusiasm. The pipe was passed around the group.

Liam waved the pipe away and took another beer, biding his time. The money changed hands and the bikers left. Then the whole crowd burst out onto the rear balcony trailing a cloud of smoke and laughter. The roar of motorbikes vibrated through the air from the street below as the Harleys fired up.

Within minutes they were growling into the distance.

Liam looked around at the crowd of stoners.

What the hell am I doing here?

Chapter 7

Sydney, Australia — Earth
20th December 1999

Yolinda's knees went weak.

A fog descended onto her thoughts. Distantly, she recognised the symptoms of shock. Her hand still gripped the handle of the revolver. Then her training kicked in. She deliberately slowed her breathing, and forced herself to take deep, even breaths. *Assess the situation.* The man Jay had shot got nimbly off the ground. He appeared unharmed. She blinked in surprise. The man bent down to Jay's body then carved a deep gash across his throat that nearly severed Jay's head from his shoulders. The knifeman grunted, as though in satisfaction, picked up Jay's Glock, and slipped it into the inside pocket of his big leather jacket. The automatic pistol looked like a toy in the knifeman's massive hand. Jay was dead. She expected the men to leave the scene of the murder, yet they did not. Instead they squatted down on either side of Jay's corpse and began to slice away his clothing. *What the fuck?*

Yolinda backed away.

Her heel hit a bottle, which rolled across the cobbles with the distinctive tinkle of glass on stone. Both men whipped around to face her. Their lips drew back in a snarl. Rows of jagged, pointed teeth gleamed like carved ivory.

Yolinda had seen Jay get off a clean shot, right at centre body mass. She could even see the hole in the jacket, through which the wound was slowly bleeding. It was right where the man's heart should be. Yet the 9mm Parabellum round had done nothing. Jay was still dead. Disembowelled. Decapitated. She had seen how fast they could move. Could she take out two of them before they closed on her? She might be able to get one clean shot to the head, then . . . *No.* Maybe with an assault rifle from 100 metres, but not three paces away with a 0.38 revolver.

Sirens began to sound in the distance.

It took all her willpower, but slowly Yolinda released her grip on the 0.38. Time for some distraction. *Misdirection.*

Yolinda pointed at the corpse.

"How am I going to get my stuff?" Yolinda demanded, play-acting fury. "You've killed my dealer, you queer bastards!"

The teeth vanished. Yolinda found herself studying the weirdest faces she had ever seen. God they were ugly! If there had only been one of them she might have assumed he was disfigured at birth, but they were as identical as twins split from the same egg. Their faces sloped forward, with a shrunken forehead and heavy jutting chin, their ears pointed and swept back. They were completely hairless, and watched her with dark, colourless eyes. The one Jay shot took the lead, stepping toward her. She stepped back, forcing herself to keep her hands away from the gun.

"You wan' smack?" he asked.

"Yeah, I want smack, you moron. How am I going to get it now?" she snapped.

The man turned to his dark-skinned companion and spoke rapidly in a foreign language. Yolinda struggled to listen, desperate to identify anything that might give the Task Force a clue, but she could not catch anything. The language was rough and guttural, and the conversation was over before she could make out a single word.

The leader turned back to her. "You follow. You get smack."

Yolinda's heart fluttered. "How much?"

The two men took up positions on either side of her, and marched her out of the alleyway, taking hold of her arms. She did not like how this was turning out and covered her anxiety with aggression. "I said how much, you ugly sons-of-bitches!" screeched Yolinda, twisting out of their grip.

Instantly she felt pain at her back as two lethally sharpened blades were pressed to her spine — right through her jacket and into her flesh. She gasped at the sudden pain. *Goddamn it, they were fast.*

"Maybe you get it for free. We go see boss-man."

Yolinda forced herself to relax. "OK."

The knives withdrew.

The policewoman took over, and she made herself think objectively. Here was a chance to meet someone a little higher up the food chain. If she played her cards right, she could make Jay's death mean something. Get on the inside now, then in a few weeks bust them all. It would only take one phone call. Then she would have plenty of time to slip away, after she had gained their confidence.

But what if they wanted more than just a drug sale? Up until now she had only been acting a part. Yolinda had never shot up, let alone been into anything as serious as heroine. A chill of fear gripped her. What if they wanted another sort of payment? Yolinda looked sideways at the two men in disgust, unable to suppress a shudder at the thought of being pressed up against one of them.

If Yolinda thought that any of the passers-by would come to her aid, she was mistaken. Not so much as a single eyelid fluttered in her direction. They took her to a large panel van with darkened windows, and roughly threw her into the back. The van screeched off into the traffic like it was exiting a warzone. Yolinda tumbled across the hard floor, trying to steady herself. The rear of the van was like a cell. The upholstery hung from the ceiling in tatters. The light that filtered through the darkened panes lit patches of old dried blood. As she braced herself, her palm came down on something slippery and hard. She lifted it up to the light. Then screamed. *It was a severed finger*. She flung it away. Then Yolinda saw an ear, and other things she did not want to name. Vomit climbed into her throat. Closing her eyes for a moment, she swallowed down bile. *Think!*

They had not searched her — yet. She took off her jacket, and the shoulder holster and gun. She stashed the holster in the cavity between the seat back and rear floor, covering it with rubbish. She pushed the gun down into the crotch of her dirty, baggy jeans, before donning her jacket once more. Then she waited. At least the short-barrelled revolver was compact.

Alone in the semi-darkness, Yolinda fought her fear. How had she gone from a plum job in Canberra profiling major drug syndicates to this? She knew the answer. *Because it hadn't been enough*. Coming from a housing commission home with a heroin-addicted mother, she had wanted to take the fight to the streets. To work undercover. Well, here she was. Back in Sydney, the battleground of her childhood. The fact that undercover operatives were all but forbidden to keep any long-term relationships was something Yolinda preferred not to reflect on too deeply.

The van came to a halt. Yolinda struggled to calm herself, but thousands of years of human evolution had begun to betray her. These animals were psychotic murderers! Was she insane? What lead was worth a horrible death at the hands of these freaks? Against this chorus of fear, Yolinda sought to assert her training. It, and all the long, lonely years of her youth, all told her the same thing. Only a clear head would save her. Jay had chosen his moment, but he had lost, paying with his life. His error had been to assume a bullet would stop these bastards when a bullet would not. They were not . . . human?

The van doors slammed open. They were parked on the curb. A flood of light from the streetlamps revealed the grizzly rubbish and ugly stains inside the van in all their detail. Yolinda was seized by her arms and led into a run-down industrial building. The long grass on the curb, the discoloured concrete and rusted roller-doors all suggested long abandonment. Next to the building, a hastily erected chain-link fence surrounded a partially demolished house. Its roof had collapsed onto a massive pile of brick and cracked asbestos sheeting, as though the earth had tried to suck it into some subterranean dream.

Yolinda was hauled through a set of glass doors labelled "Teros Graphics" in faded letters. Inside, two dark-skinned men — again virtually identical to her captors — guarded the inside of the doorway. They were dressed in dark leathers, studded like old-fashioned leather armour, and each carried a falcata. An ancient weapon Yolinda recognised. A heavy, cleaver-like sword with a distinctive curve, which was double-edged from its midpoint to its tip. It took prodigious strength to wield, and had the cutting power of an axe. It could cut off arms at the shoulder, and sever heads with ease.

One of the guards hitched his weapon onto his belt and began an efficient search of Yolinda, carefully feeling her arms, torso, and legs, for any sign of a concealed weapon. He stank of rotten meat and excrement. Her heart was racing as the dark-skinned warrior ran his hands up her inner thighs. Carefully choosing her moment she slapped the warrior's hand away from her crotch in mock indignation and danced away from her two captors, screaming obscenities. The warrior growled. He hefted his falcata and advanced on her, his mouth pulled back to reveal his pointed teeth. Yolinda backed away as quickly as she could. Still screaming, she tripped on a raised section of tattered carpet, and fell onto her back.

The guard's falcata fell like a guillotine blade. In a blur, another hand shot out, taking a grip on the warrior's wrist and stopping the blade inches from her face. Yolinda let out a breath and looked across to see it was one of her captors, the one who Jay had shot. Muscles bunching, the dark-skinned man forced the other warrior back. After a brief argument in their guttural tongue, the warrior resumed his station, and the incident was forgotten.

Her two captors hoisted her off the floor and dragged her through a pair of disused offices — the rotted carpets smelling of mildew — and into the rear of the factory. Here the concrete slab had been broken open. A series of rough steps had been cut into the dark native rock beneath. A string of incandescent bulbs lit the stairs with pale yellow. Four more dark-skinned warriors stood guard, armed with falcatas. A fetid stench rose from the cavity into the deserted factory.

As Yolinda was led down the stairs, her head began to spin, as though the ties that bound reality were loosening. Darkness. Bodies. The savage teeth and empty eyes of the warriors. Beneath the factory floor, under the honest industry of a bygone era, the stairway gave access to a vast underground chamber. The ceiling was crowded with stalactites, except for one bulging section that was secured with rock bolts, as though to contain a recent collapse. *The trashed house*, she realised. The space was lit with torches and a few scattered light bulbs. In the rough centre of the cavern, a pool of mercurial flame turned rapidly on its own axis, spewing twisted beings into the gloom. The nightmare figures rose from the surface of the flame as thought born from a vast, tainted cauldron. She blinked, trying to clear her eyes, but the image remained. She looked desperately around the room, instinctively looking for an escape. Two men in dark robes — one with a bulky device hanging from his neck — stood in the flickering shadows near the pool of flame. There was also some sort of . . . man-beast. Sensing her gaze, it rose to its feet, the all-too-human eyes leering. It panted and grunted, dribbling green and clotted mucus from its slack, over-toothed jaws. She looked away, not wanting to believe what she saw. An indolent mass of bodies covered the floor, unmoving beneath a blanket of drug paraphernalia.

The men pushed her to her knees before a raised dais. On the throne sat an emaciated man in draping robes. He fixed her with a gaze that shot through her like a bolt from a rivet-gun. At the base of the raised throne, a woman dressed as a priestess was crying silently. With a shock, Yolinda recognised her. Vicki. A small-time dealer who also ran scams in the markets on Sundays, ripping off an endless series of weekend hopefuls with a regular line of palm-reading and tarot.

The light within the man's eyes grew, and began to push into her. The cavern faded, and she was a child again. Her stepfather Nick was calling her, for those games he liked to play. But she hid. There was always a place he could not find her. Against his anger, despite the indifference of her mother, she would cling to the life raft of her childhood like precious flotsam. Her will would not be broken. She, only a child, he a grown man in the full power of his twisted potency — yet she would defy him. Within her secret hiding place, clutching her rag-doll, she waited for him to lose patience and turn his anger and lust onto her mother instead.

It seemed a lifetime of waiting, but at last he was gone.

Yolinda's vision cleared. She was back in the cavern. In the horror of the moment, rather than the horror of her past.

What the hell had she stumbled into?

"I cannot read her," said the Archfiend, in the language of the Vault.

"Shall we kill her?" asked his siithe captain.

"No. She seems dull-witted. Perhaps the drugs have vanquished her mind," he lied. "Put her with the others. We will use her as entertainment. But make sure she takes the lotus first. Whatever mind she has must be clouded. I will tolerate no free will."

"Why not give her to the Shademaster?" suggested the siithe. The warrior ran his tongue across his pointed teeth.

Procarrus' gaze flicked to the dark-robed figure of his Shademaster, Oth'Seth, walking slowly through the dreamers at the base of the throne. His hood and long sleeves concealed face and skin. Procarrus instinctively strengthened his mental defences. It was Oth'Seth who had possessed the Gate-opener — from more than a world away. The Shademaster would have no difficulty with the new slave, but her mind might end up a shattered mess. Then she would be nothing but meat. The siithe had fed enough. Procarrus liked to keep them hungry.

"No. I will break her myself. Was the spy dealt with?" asked Procarrus, changing the subject.

"Yes, lord. It was as you said. He was a guardsman of the police." The siithe smiled. "They are weak."

Procarrus permitted himself a small smile and waved the siithe from his presence. He returned his mind to the dream-realm, from which he drew both power and knowledge. The captives that writhed beneath him were his map and key to this world. Using techniques perfected over centuries, he drained them mind, body, and soul. They fuelled Procarrus, while giving him direct knowledge of the language, customs, and geography he needed to direct his conquest. The campaign would soon begin — but first he must breach the Stonelake Gateway, capture the priestess, and deliver her to VoYannan.

He tightened his fist around the Fragment, a stone section severed in antiquity from one of the primary Realm Gateways, as he considered the new addition to his court. This *Yolinda*. He already knew her name. The rest would follow. He would draw everything that she was from her.

The woman watched him defiantly as a siithe pushed a needle into her veins. Her gaze drew dreamy as the wave of euphoria took her. Procarrus thrust into her mind. Again she hid, withdrawing to some quiet corner. He sensed her feeling of victory and smashed his clenched fist down onto the arm of his throne. The wood splintered with a *crack*. She was adept, but he would still break her.

"Bring her closer," said the Archfiend.

Chapter 8

Evenstone Tower — Third Realm

Fifteen years earlier . . .

Finn woke in darkness. His heart beat wildly, yet he could hear nothing but the soft, regular breathing of his little sister Tallandra across the room, her wild hair a dark mass across her pillow. Then, for a moment, he thought he heard one of his father's war hounds, yelping in pain.

"It could not be," said Finn. Those hounds were fearless.

He looked around, noting the familiar shapes of his books, and the wriggling form of his latest experiment in its glass-walled enclosure.

A high unnatural wailing cut through the night.

Finn slipped out of bed. He turned the spigot on the glowglobe and light poured from the now saturated glowbeast within.

Tallandra woke with a start. "What! What is it?"

"I . . . I am not sure," said Finn. *What could make a sound like that?*

A tremor ran through the floor, as though the whole tower were being struck by a huge hammer. Dust fell from the ancient rafters. There was a second blow, even more powerful than the first. More followed, becoming stronger.

He pushed his desk back from the wall and reached behind it for his new longsword, given to him by his father for his thirteenth birthday. He rushed to the door, but it opened before he could reach it. A slender warrior stood in the doorway with a shield and longsword, long hair unbound.

"Mother?" said Finn. It was. His beautiful mother, Erel Evenstone, her delicate face now drawn with fear. "Why are you . . .?"

"Finn, go back to bed."

"But . . ."

Finn looked past his mother into the room beyond, and saw his older brothers Kas and Levin at the head of the stairs, both armed and armoured, and ready to move down. Evenstone

Tower was under attack!

Tallandra rushed to the door, still clutching her pillow.

"Mother, what's happening?" Tally looked paler than her white sleeping shift.

"Look," said Finn, pointing.

Staggering up the stairs was one of their father's thurjuns, the front his robe soaked with blood. Finn knew him. It was Morin, Lord-thurjun of the Evenstone Gateway. He heard Levin shout a question, his voice taut with shock, but it did not register in his mind. Finn's vision was filled with the blood. The shredded mess of Morin's stomach.

His mother rushed to Morin's side.

"The enemy is here. Inside the tower," gasped Morin. "I have set a Shield on the stairs, reinforced with my mionanail. But it will not last long against a seraphin."

His mother blanched at the mention of the seraphin. It did not make sense, thought Finn. A seraphin was an angel of the High God, sheathed in white. Why would one attack them?

"Morin, we must get you to a healer!" said Erel

Morin waved her away. "Lord Evenstone is dead. Venn . . . dead. The Archfiend is upon us." He struggled for breath, his shattered ribs a mass of pain. "I have to get you and the children to safety."

"How did this happen, Morin?" Silent tears tracked down parchment-white cheeks. Her sword trembled in her grasp, as though it had grown in weight.

"Vespar. He . . . betrayed us."

"It is blood. Blood on his robe!" said Tallandra, eyes wide. He could hear the edge of panic in her voice. His own mind was numb. *Father was dead? His brother Venn, dead?* No. It was impossible. It was a mistake.

"It is not as bad as it looks, Tally," said Finn, his voice hardly as confident or reassuring as he wanted it to be.

"What do you think you are doing with that?" said Kaz, pointing at Finn's longsword with his own weapon.

"Same thing you are," said Finn defiantly, staring back at Kaz. But Kaz just looked away. He seemed funny. Sick maybe. *He does not think I can fight, but I will show him. I will show them all.*

Finn tightened his grip on his sword. He had been doing extra practice in secret, long hours when he should have been studying the theory of druidic devices.

"You will have to go with mother, Tally. I am staying here with Kaz and Levin," said Finn.

"I am scared, Finn," said Tally, her voice shaking.

"It is alright, Tally. We will not let any of them through," he said, looking enviously at Kaz's and Levin's armour. If he had been allowed to train as a warrior, he too would have been gifted a set of custom made armour. Instead he was forced to train in a borrowed armoury outfit. *They think I am fit only for the druids. I will show them.*

Mother looked at him and Tally and her eyes grew sharp. Then she was in motion. "Up the stairs. Quickly. Both of you! To the roof. Morin!" The last was to the thurjun, who staggered after Lady Evenstone with stolid determination.

"I have to stay. To fight with Kaz and Levin," said Finn.

Erel looked down at Finn's sword, as though noticing it for the first time.

"No. No, Finn. Quickly," she said, taking his arm.

Finn shook off her hand. "I can fight!" Everyone knew that Evenstones were invincible in battle. Right now his father was probably wreaking havoc with the attackers. Kaz and Levin were probably dying to get downstairs and into it. A real battle! He could hardly believe his luck.

"No!" snapped Erel. "You are just a boy. An apprentice druid, for the love of Lugh! Leave it to your brothers."

Finn let his sword droop, the tip dragging on the stone as he was herded along by his mother.

At the base of the stairs, he looked back angrily at his brothers, but he noticed something odd. Levin also had that sick look. Kaz looked back at him. Just before the curve of the circular stairs cut off the view, he had one last look at Kaz's face. And he realised. Kaz was scared. *Terrified.* Finn's heart pounded, the fear shooting across that one contact like contagion. He looked at his mother, then Morin. They were *all* terrified. *It . . . could not be true? Could it? Father . . .*

A massive concussion shook the tower. The masonry around

them groaned as the huge stone blocks ground against each other. Tally clutched at his arm, sniffling as tears streaked down her face. Then the east wall crumbled with a roar of falling stone and snapping timber. The whole tower tilted dangerously, and wide gaps opened in the stairs. There was a piercing ululation that tore at Finn's eardrums. Tally screamed, her voice lost within the power of the unearthly cry. Finn's breath caught in his throat. Hair stood up on the back of his neck. It was the same as he had heard before, except closer.

Half-way up the stairs, he heard Kaz and Levin yell a challenge . . . then they screamed. The cries ended abruptly. He had a sick feeling in his stomach. Finn shivered in the chill air coming down from the roof.

Where were his father and the other Evenstone warriors?

Morin and Erel exchanged quick, desperate words, and his mother ran back down the stairs while they continued up. She was going to face it. She was going to fight while he was sent with the children. But if it could so easily deal with Kaz and Levin . . . his heart thudded. His head swam.

He did not want her to die! He did not want anyone to die.

They were barely on the roof when Morin stopped.

"Morin?" asked Finn.

He heard his mother yell the Evenstone war cry. Then there was nothing. No sound of battle. Nothing. He looked back, waiting for his mother to emerge from the top of the tower stairs. Hoping . . . despairing. *It was true, by the High God, it was all true.*

Beside him Tally was shaking, taking short, gasping breaths. He squeezed her hand and tried to smile, but any words of comfort died in his throat.

Morin fell to his knees. The thurjun's leggings glistened wetly in the night. Blood. Morin was dying.

"Quickly, children. Help me stand. We must reach the side of the tower. I must be within sight of the ardanaith to draw on its power."

Finn looked back for his mother, but there was nothing but the dark emptiness of the stairs and . . . something else. Coming closer.

Finn and Tallandra helped Morin to his feet.

Then it appeared.

A beast of red flames, its dark limbs a blur within its sheath of power.

Tally's eyes widened, her mouth open in a silent scream. This thing had killed his mother. His father. His brothers. Finn began to shake once more, but it had nothing to do with the cold. The sword dropped from his weakened fingers. It struck the stone roof with a dull clang. Finn backed away, nausea writhing inside him. He pulled at Tally, but she would not come.

Then the flames expanded, filling the roof with lurid red.

And the Dark Seraphin came for them.

Chapter 9
Brisbane, Australia — Earth
20th December 1999

Liam walked to the balcony railing, taking a cool sip of his beer and inhaling the fresh twilight air with relief.

Shane wandered over, a grin plastered on his face. "Hey, it's not too late. You can still buy in," he said, his eyes gleaming.

Liam stared at Shane and shook his head. *The guy will not take no for an answer.* "Say, when are we heading into town?"

Shane shrugged. "Don't feel like it now. I'm just going to hang out here." Liam felt an undercurrent in Shane's manner. He knew he was pissed off Liam had not cut in on the deal. He had forgotten how petty Shane could be — and how he changed when he smoked. Became more sarcastic. More vindictive.

Thatcher ran up to Shane with a hessian bag in her teeth. Shane took hold of the bag, trying to take it out of Thatcher's mouth, and the game of tug-of-war began. It was one of Thatcher's favourites. She growled menacingly as Shane pulled it suddenly to the side.

"Hey, Shane. Want another one?" One of the guys held up the water pipe.

"Yeah!"

Thatcher took advantage of the distraction to rip the hessian bag out of Shane's hands and ran over to the corner of the balcony. She lay the bag down then sat on her prize, watching them. Her eyes shone with victory, daring them to try to take it back.

"What are you doing for Christmas?" asked Shane.

"No plans so far," said Liam. His uncle Aidan was tied up with business. He often travelled.

"A group of us are going up to Fraser Island for a few weeks. We'll probably stay up around Central Station. Maybe check out the resort nightclubs. It should be good."

Liam took another swig of the beer, starting to relax again.

"You should come over. Give me a ring and I'll let you know what barge we're going on," said Shane.

The evening glow filtered onto the balcony through an unkempt tangle of greenery and runaway vines, which shot up around the house, hiding the neighbours from view. Liam looked out into the twilight sky, imagining himself out on the bay amid the freshness of the sea and the vitality of the rainforests.

"The islands," mused Liam. "Aren't you worried about the fall of civilisation while we're away?"

"Well. If Y2K does hit, what better place to be? We can survive on nuts and berries," said Shane.

"I haven't been over there for years. That would be magic. Let's do it."

"Excellent. Oh — you still have your four-wheel-drive?"

"The Suburu? Yeah, I still have it," said Liam.

"Great. You can give us a lift."

The night drew on, the remains of his beer carton long gone, and Liam found himself seeking something else to spur on his sense of excitement. Then the water pipe started going around. What harm could one do? *No.* He had told himself a thousand times. A person with his hyperactive mind, and his dark moods, should not take the stuff.

Shane walked over toward him. His face smiling and friendly. "Here, Liam."

He paused.

"Oh, come on!" groaned Shane. The whole group was looking at him — the only one not smoking. Refusing it seemed like refusing friendship.

"OK."

Once he had one, it was hard to stop. It was always the same. He had lost count by the time he noticed Shane watching him. Liam could not understand the gleam of victory in his eyes.

His mind flew around the night. Images grew. Swirls of colour, like bright sails raised above a thousand ships of joy. Each expanded then burst apart. He heard himself laughing. Then saw the perplexed looks on the faces of the small crowd as he got lost in the high.

Power surged through him.

He saw starships above a wasted plain. A thousand slaves

chained to the will of one dark master. He searched for his face, but it remained out of reach, just a void within the deeper shadows.

He turned and saw another world. One of green fields and majestic towers that floated as high as the clouds.

Then all too abruptly, he sank into a dark well.

The bright lights were gone. Savage thoughts tore at him, like sharks in a frenzy. Driven by his loneliness. His lack of direction. The empty void in his heart where the love of his family should have been — where instead there was an orphan's pain. He could not marshal his thoughts, or focus his energy. People were talking to him, but he could not remember what they said from one moment to the next.

For one brief moment, he became aware they were laughing at him. In that instant, his senses focussed, as though he was tuning into the sights and sounds from some faraway place.

"Liam!" It was Shane. "You still with us there, buddy?" Shane gave a short laugh and pointed at him with his cigarette. "Liam could never take grass. Look at him! He's totally wasted."

Liam felt the contempt as though it were acid.

He stood and wandered away from the group, toward the corner of the balcony. It had been raining, and the moisture glistened on the leaves. The air was cool and refreshing. The plants around the balcony glowed with life. Liam held onto them, reaching out with the arms of his spirit to feel their vital pulse. Their energy flowed into him, tingling across his arms, legs, and chest. He gave no thought to what he did. His mind floated in a quiescent haze. It was as natural as breathing.

He felt something at his leg and looked down to see Thatcher offering him the hessian bag in a hopeful gesture. Liam reached down and stroked the short hair on her head.

"Sorry, Thatch. Not in the mood."

The dog whined, looking back at the group at the table, and then back at Liam, before curling up at his feet.

A quick glance showed that Shane was settled in for the night. The bastard had never intended going to the city. There was nothing for him here, he realised, and he knew Shane would never drive him home — at least not tonight. He decided to walk back to his flat, even if he had to cross half of Brisbane.

Liam vaulted over the balcony in a single movement, falling one storey to land lightly on his feet. Thatcher barked and raced down the outside stairs. It felt good to be in motion, and he was astonished that he could have felt so low only minutes before. Without looking back, he set out across the street, toward the river. He heard Shane calling out.

"Liam! Where are you going?" Laughter, and muffled conversation. "Liam!" More laughter, then he was too far away to hear them.

A sense of tremendous relief washed through him.

He heard someone shouting back at the house. Then Thatcher appeared at his side. He realised Shane had been calling her back.

"It's a bit of a walk, Thatch. You sure you want to hang out with crazy Liam?"

Thatch gave a him a brief look, then trotted on ahead.

"I'll take that as a yes."

*

Liam fumbled for his keys in the dark.

Inside his flat, he looked at the clock. 4:00 am. He knew he should sleep, but he was too keyed up. Unlike most people, who were relaxed into torpor by the drug, marijuana gave him insomnia. The walk through the tree-filled streets of the suburbs had also filled him with a restless energy that circled his stomach like a trapped snake.

Liam went to the fridge to get himself a drink of water. Thatcher followed his every movement. He took an old pot from the cupboard and filled it with tap water, placing it on the floor. Thatcher lapped at it gratefully.

He took his glass and walked out onto the enclosed veranda, flicking on the lights. He paused for a moment, looking at his easel, and the mess of paints and colours that littered the desk there. They were covered with dust. It had been a while.

He took off the easel cover and looked critically at the work. He had been trying for months to copy a complex piece of Celtic knotwork from an old book his uncle had given him. But try as he might, he could never get it. The lines were there — it was an exact copy — yet it did not *feel* the same. He sighed with frustration and re-covered his easel, moving to the desk to push aside the scattered brushes and paints and retrieve a sketchpad from the bottom of the pile. Maybe he was starting with too much complexity. Perhaps if he could render it in simple, faint outlines, he could get the feeling right, then add the colour and swirling layers that confounded him.

He seated himself at the table, the drawing on his left, the sketchpad to his right, and a light pencil in his hand. He took a deep, shuddering breath, and began.

Hours later, he was still at it. The copies were exact, and yet not *right*. He tried to draw it with increasing simplicity, but failed. He discarded his latest effort and drained the last of his water, looking across at Thatcher with a sigh. She was fast asleep, curled up in a corner of the enclosed balcony on top of the bunched-up easel cover. *Bitch*, he thought, chuckling to himself at the pun.

Finally, in frustration, he closed his eyes and tried to draw the swirl in his mind. He had been staring at it for hours. It was waiting for him. Carefully he reconstructed every line, growing excited with every mental brush. It was working! Then something else began to happen. That restless energy, gathered from the living landscape of Brisbane, which had been tumbling around inside him, shot through him, lacing itself into the knotwork. It was perfect!

He opened his eyes, then lurched back in shock. His chair flew backwards, waking Thatcher, who jumped up with a yelp and began to race around the verandah, barking furiously.

The interlace lay before him, swirling and moving in living colours. Within its fabric, all the scattered debris from the desk rotated in mid-air. Discarded sketches, tubes of paint, the sketchbook, scraps of paper — all moved inside the glowing pattern.

He was startled by a muted bashing on the wall.

"Shut that almighty racket up!" It was his neighbour.

As though a twig had snapped underfoot, something gave way. The paints, papers, and brushes, fell to the floor. The swirling interlace shot toward him like an iron filing to a magnet.

Liam saw a flash of colour, then was lost in darkness.

*

He woke with a jolt of sudden alarm.

The morning sun streamed through the windows. The phone was ringing. Thatcher was gone, and the back door was swinging ajar. He raced to the living room, and snatched the brown plastic handset from its cradle. The spiral chord stretched out between the end of the handset and the heavy plastic base with its old rotary dialler.

"Yeah!" The effort of talking set his head throbbing.

"Mr Durrow?" The voice was grave and official.

Liam's heart raced. "Yes. I'm Liam Durrow."

The man cleared his throat. "Ah, Mr Durrow. I have been trying to reach you for almost twenty-four hours. My name is John Peters, one of the directors of the Durrow Trust."

"Durrow Trust?"

"Your uncle never discussed the Trust with you?" Peters' dry voice grew tense.

"No." A cold feeling grew in Liam's stomach. "What is it?"

"I'm afraid I have some dreadful news. Your uncle has been killed in an accident."

Liam dropped the phone and sank to the floor, burying his head in his hands. Dimly, he could hear Peters' voice, mouse-like, from the handset as it swung back and forth like a pendulum on its spiral chord. "Mr Durrow! Mr Durrow? Are you there? As beneficiary of the Trust, and heir of the late Aidan Durrow, there are urgent matters to be finalised. Mr Durrow?" Peters grew more agitated.

Reluctantly, Liam picked up the handset.

"I'm here."

Chapter 10
Stonelake Gateway — Fourth Realm

Finn headed for the battlements. He found himself a comfortable corner of the guard tower in which to lean, out of the wind, yet still within the broad sunshine of late morning. He tucked the official dispatch into his belt, then with care, opened Tallandra's letter, sighing with affection at her neat lettering. A faint scent of perfume rose from the parchment. A small pressed flower fell out as he opened the last fold. His hand moved fast to catch it, the stem clasped gently between thumb and forefinger. It was a pretty thing. Its violet colour still vibrant.

The letter followed a typical pattern. On the surface it was a rambling tale of court gossip. There had been another state marriage. A Gateway in the Second Realm had changed hands, moving from one aristocratic house in decline to another on the ascendant. A new general had been promoted from the ranks of Realm captains, the woman only a little older than Finn himself. She had been a star graduate when he had begun his time at the Academy, he remembered. He scanned it all quickly, then paused to concentrate. The real message lay hidden. He and Tallandra had long ago established their own cipher. Finn was now so adept at its translation he no longer needed pen and paper. *Ah.* Pressure was growing on his sister to marry. The blood link to Evenstone was highly sought after — as was the power and wealth that flowed from control of a major Realm Gateway. Tallandra was a talented woman. As a ward of the High King, that talent was alloyed with first class connections. She could have excelled in any field, from religious orders and the druidic sciences to warcraft. Yet she had chosen to navigate the treacherous waters of politics. In the guise of a flighty high-born prize, she had worked tirelessly to cement their claim on Evenstone Tower. Her machinations had defeated at least three attempts to take possession of it. His decision to virtually kill his career in a backwater like Stonelake, with its apparently dead Gateway, had made her work exceedingly difficult.

The same night of terror that had ignited Finn's thirst for

revenge had created something else in Tallandra. An intense desire to rebuild their home. To return. She wanted him to reclaim their birthright. He wanted that too. But first . . . he had to stop Procarrus.

Finn carefully folded the flower into the letter and slid the parchment into a trouser pocket. Tallandra knew why he had requested Stonelake for his first command, yet had disagreed violently with the decision. It had evolved into a major argument that had threatened to create a permanent rift between them. They had reconciled, forced to admit they needed each other, but it had been hard. Court observers had considered Stonelake an extremely odd choice for an honours graduate of the Academy who had earned swift promotion in the Shadow Worlds. Yet for Finn, ambition and position counted for nothing against the chance to strike back at the same fiends that killed their family.

Impatient now, he broke the seal on the official dispatch and swiftly unfolded the heavy parchment.

Finn Evenstone, his Most High Majesty's Captain Charged with the Defence of the Stonelake Gateway, Fourth Realm.

Captain Evenstone, it is with regret that the office of the High King must decline yet another request for additional troop placements for the Stonelake garrison. Despite your latest lengthy and exhaustive missive, the strategists of the High King see no legitimate threat at Stonelake Gateway, which has remained inactive for more than a millennium.

Reports of your work at Stonelake are exemplary, however. News that the country bandits have been subdued is a credit to your command, since they have been a persistent threat to trade in the Fourth Realm. As a consequence of this reduced threat in the area, the station at Stonelake is being downgraded to secondary command status.

I am hereby commanded to inform you that your commission at Stonelake is being terminated. The office of the High King has need of officers of your standing and ability in active stations. On behalf of the High King, I am hereby requesting and requiring that you surrender your command and pass all responsibilities to your second-in-command, Lieutenant Endar, then, without

Finn walked to a heatglobe set against the inner wall of the parapet. He crushed the parchment into a ball, his knuckles growing white around it. For a long moment he stared down, through the shimmering heat haze, at the heatbeast swimming in its broth of nutrient solution. He threw the crushed ball of parchment into the metal mesh basket that housed the heatglobe. At first the wax seal melted, running like a small red river, then a tiny tendril of smoke curled upwards. A moment later the whole ball popped into flame. Such a gesture was only possible when Stonelake's ardanaith slumbered. The Realm defensive device usually prevented simple combustion inside the town.

"Captain Evenstone."

Finn drew a slow breath as Keris climbed the battlement stairs. The young warrior's scabbard was hitched up to a proper height now. Finn could not help smiling. He was eager, this one.

"Yes, guardsman."

"The festivities are about to begin."

Finn looked up. The sun was high in the sky. He nodded. "Tell the councillors I will be there directly."

"Yes, sir," said Keris, turning back down the stairs.

The Festival commemorated a battle that saved the town. Long millennia ago, the Vault had threatened to break through the Gateway into the Fourth Realm and overrun it. Finn's ancestor, Thurn Evenstone, had driven the Vault legions back through the portal, striking down the Archfiend Procarrus with a blow so powerful it cleaved a wedge of stone from the Gate. The Fragment had been kept by his family as a keepsake. Nothing more than a curio that sat atop the great hall's mantelpiece in Evenstone Tower, beside the ancient Axe. Procarrus, having survived his defeat and grown to power once more, had seized both the Axe and the Fragment on the night Finn's family were killed. The Fragment, imbued with the energies of the Gateway, could be used by a Dark Thurjun of the Vault to strike through at Stonelake. Finn had waited here for years, never knowing when the Gateway would open to disgorge Vault forces onto an unsuspecting world. He regretted nothing. They had been good years here, devoted to training his troops and honing his own skills. He had pleaded with the High King for the threat to be taken seriously, but had been dismissed. Worse. He had been forbidden from speaking of it publicly. The High King's counsellors had feared an "unnecessary" panic. So Finn had pursued his quest alone.

Yet now time had run out.

His desire for revenge, to strike a blow at the Vault, warred with his loyalty to the High King. What should he do? No one had seen the dispatch, yet how long could he ignore a direct order? He could leave the High King's service. That would make him nothing but a mercenary. His dream of leading an army against the Vault — against Procarrus and the Archfiend's krell master VoYannan — would be destroyed. He also knew that any outright defiance of the High King would risk his titles. Tallandra would never forgive such a move.

There was a strange irony in the fact that the line of Evenstone began here in remote Stonelake, with the deeds of his famous ancestor. He hoped it would not end here as well.

Chapter 11
Stonelake Gateway — Fourth Realm

Finn greeted the townsfolk warmly as made his way through the maze of streets and alleys to the town square. After five years there were few faces he did not recognise. He nodded to the town butcher, and waved to the elderly Priestess of Brigit, who was shepherding her latest recruits to the festival in single file, as though the young women in their pure-white vestments were nothing more than unruly schoolchildren. The thought of leaving these people defenceless tore at him. The siithe had no mercy.

A small crowd grew behind him as he walked. Every year since he had arrived he had suggested that someone else lead the ceremony, and every year the Council insisted that, as an Evenstone, only he deserved the special place of honour. As he emerged into the square, he was buffeted by the sea of excited voices. The place was packed. The main procession, which traditionally began at midday, was already assembled. The costumed figures drew the eye, a vivid tableau of bright colour in the warm spring sunshine. A great bonfire was burning at the square's far end, blocking the path of the procession. Morin waited beside it. The thurjun was a large man, well past middle years, with solemn blue eyes, wavy grey hair, and a neatly trimmed beard. Although portly, his stout frame gave the impression of strength. Beads of sweat dotted his forehead, driven off the thurjun's skin by the bonfire's heat. He saw Finn and smiled a greeting as the warrior approached the fire. The roaring flames were now outside the radius of power of the High King's Tower, within which no fire would burn. Usually the reach of the Tower's ardanaith extended beyond the boundaries of the valley, but for the ceremony, Morin had adjusted its mechanism to retract its field of effect.

Finn took his place at the head of the procession. Behind him, men and women decked out in bright faux armour of painted wood and coloured cloth brandished outlandish spears, shields, and swords, in mock defiance of the Vaults of Sheol — a loose confederation of individual krell empires that had threatened the

Realms since time immemorial.

Finn took a ceremonial axe from the town chancellor, symbolic of the Axe of Evenstone.

Morin stepped forward and raised his arms, his left hand open and his right holding his staff. His blue robe and golden belt gleamed in the sun.

"We go forth to still the Fires of Sheol!" called Morin.

A look of fierce determination overtook Morin's face as he prepared his spell. Finn's arm twitched with tension as a memory stole into his mind. It was two years before his captain's commission. An active posting on one of the Vault Shadow Worlds. The face of a young warrior bled across his mind, his face and upper torso ravaged by radiation burns. The man had not been much older than Keris. *We cannot hold them,* the young warrior had pleaded. *We need the dampening field. Now!* Morin had been beside Finn, ready to activate a powerful Realm field at his command. Finn had waited. Waited until the siithe warriors were close enough to smell. The explosions and multi-coloured flashes of Vault weaponry jarred his mind, then gradually faded into sunshine as the memory ghosted away.

Smiling faces surrounded him.

Finn watched Morin with his thurjun's sight as the interlace took shape. No warrior of the Blessed Realms reached commission rank without some talent in that direction. It spun as it expanded, translucent and ghost-like in the noonday sun. The reds, greens and blues grew more defined, dazzling his eyes with restless movement. Then Morin touched his hand to the mionanail pendant about his neck. The interlace swelled with power channelled outward from the mionanail. The interlace bloated like an enormous jellyfish, then flashed away, encapsulating the bonfire in a Realm dampening field.

The great leaping flames vanished. The piled coals and timbers creaked and groaned as they collapsed into a blackened, cooling heap.

Finn took his cue and stepped forward, raising the axe.

"We will not fear the fires of Sheol!" shouted Finn.

"WE WILL NOT FEAR THE FIRES OF SHEOL!" The voices of the crowd crashed into the walls and buildings around them.

Finn charged. The people behind him roared. The procession surged forward behind him. Two flanks of screaming children swept out from the column, both left and right, and ran at the inert bonfire. They struck the cooling timbers like a stampeding herd, sending a cloud of ash into the air with shouts of excitement. They rampaged on through the pile, scattering it, and raising a cloud of fine soot. Finn grinned as he saw Keris in the group, hidden within a ridiculous suit of bright yellow wooden armour and waving an oversized sword and shield with telltale precision.

Finn increased his pace. Coals crunched beneath his boots. The crowd raced with him through the blackened debris and down to the western gate. The procession surged out of the citadel. They ran across the wide grassy fields beyond the wall and down the hill to Stonelake itself, where the stark ruins of the Gateway kept their lonely vigil.

When they reached the lakeshore, waiting musicians struck up a tune. The furious race ended in laughter, and the column dissolved into loose groups, which meandered through the food stalls. Impromptu teams began to form for the Festival games.

Finn handed the axe back to the smiling chancellor, and drifted through the crowd. He paused briefly to watch Morin draw another interlace, admiring his skill. The magic form soared toward the citadel, sinking through the rock walls of the High King's Tower to the ardanaith's core. A shimmer rose in the air, like a ripple on a lake's surface, spreading out from the Tower in all directions. A group of children playing with fireworks gave a disappointed cry as their toys abruptly ceased to explode. Morin shrugged at them with a friendly smile and the kids packed away their fireworks for another year.

Finn looked through the crowd, noting that the rudeness of the High King's messenger had not done too much harm to his status. Zanthis, surrounded by an adoring audience of young women and boys, swaggered arrogantly as he recounted tales of the High Court and the First Realm. A large crowd of townsfolk stood nearby, trying to look nonchalant, but doing their best to listen in.

Feeling the sudden need for solitude, and more relaxed now

that Stonelake's defences had been restored, Finn set out around the lake to take in some of the spring air. The sunshine was soft and warm, and glistened on the lake. The high ranges behind Stonelake, green and majestic, and the blue sky above them, were reflected perfectly in the water. He saw himself there, a young man of middle height with a compact, lean frame, and close-cropped blonde hair. A dragonfly swept past, touching down briefly on the water and sending ripples through the image.

"Enjoying the spring weather?"

Finn turned to see Morin striding across the grassy verge.

He had not been aware of the point when he made the decision, but as Morin approached he knew he would defy the High King's orders. Nothing could take him from Stonelake. Not before the Vault struck. He had waited too long, sacrificed too much, to baulk now. Tallandra . . . would see it as a betrayal, his action perhaps forcing her into a political marriage to a Realm general of sufficient status to take control of the Evenstone lands.

"Er . . . Yes. Very pleasant," said Finn.

Morin gave Finn a sharp look, intuiting some sort of dissembling on his part. Finn quickly moved to fill the gap.

"A wonderful Festival, Morin. Once again your manipulation of the ardanaith was masterful." He flashed Morin a grin.

"Well . . . thank you." Morin's eyes narrowed. "Is there something on your mind?"

Finn did not answer straight away. He stepped forward and laid his hand on Morin's shoulder. This man, more than anyone else, had been his real father. He had been there for him whenever he needed him. Had followed him to the frontiers when Finn had been nothing more than a young officer fresh from the Academy, and then into the self-imposed exile of Stonelake.

"You have been a good friend, Morin. And I thank you. For all that has gone before and what is to come."

Morin's eyes widened. "So there is something."

"Nothing that need concern you, old friend. Enjoy the rest of the Festival."

Finn turned and headed back toward the gates of the Stonelake citadel.

"Finn, wait!" called Morin. "*Finn.*"

Chapter 12
Stonelake Gateway – Fourth Realm

Sephany shivered in the cold.

The mirrored surface of the Chamber of Silence drew the heat from the room like a hungry winter night. She had been meditating for less than an hour, but her legs were numb from lack of circulation. With delicate care, she shifted on the hard surface. She winced as the rustling sounds from her gown were amplified by the wall's magic to the din of marching feet in an autumn forest. Slowly drawing breath, she let the sound subside and forced herself to concentrate. To block out the pain and the cold.

She centred her mind, and once more sought to find the centre of her harmony: the colour that could not be painted, the sound that was beyond hearing. The ocean of her breathing, and the cold, receded.

Images rose into the stillness of her mind.

The face of her first love, Damast. His eyes shadowed with disappointment as he turned away from her for the last time. The orchards of her distant home, boughs swaying in a gentle breeze. The smell of the long grass in spring. The worn wood of the kitchen table, smoothed by the jostling elbows of three generations. Her mother beside the hearth, apron stained with flour and grease. Her mother's smile as Sephany took a bite from a fresh-baked berry pie, the silence filled with just the two of them as the sticky filling trickled down her fingers and chin.

As she had been taught, Sephany gently turned her mind toward the eternal, allowing the other thoughts to flow past. As though falling beyond herself, her mind filled with profound emptiness. A sound felt. An absence understood. The scent of nothing. She was connected to the fertile bed of existence. She let her awareness expand. Energy swelled in her mind's eye. She had stepped to the point beyond time.

She heard screams in the Temple corridors, and her mind sped toward them. There was blood on the walls, guardians and priestesses scattered obscenely in death, bloody rag-dolls, ripped and broken. Siithe warriors, bearing war-axes, and their cleaver-like falcata, strode the halls. Their coarse shouts and laughter a chilling punctuation to their death-strokes as they waded deep into slaughter.

Sephany sought to relax, to detach herself from the vision, to allow it to pass from her along the stream of consciousness as her earlier thoughts had done. But the energy pouring into her third eye swelled. The images grew sharper, the fear in the victim's screams more palpable. She could smell the rankness of the siithe, the foulness of blood and faeces as the dead emptied their bowels, the scents mixed obscenely with the familiar Temple incense.

Still, Sephany let the images fill her mind, not allowing herself to react, knowing that the walls of the Chamber would amplify the slightest sound or movement. As she watched, the death toll grew. New friends and teachers lay together, cold and empty in death. The siithe, inflamed with lust and hunger, feasted on flesh, both living and dead. Sephany began to shake. The rustling of her vestments rose to the sound of crashing masonry.

The vision grew steadily more real. The siithe closer. *I can accept my death*, she thought. They were looking at her now. One raised his weapon for the kill. The bloody blade fell, but Gerla, her chapter-mother, threw herself before it. Her life was severed in an instant as she accepted death in Sephany's place. Sephany collapsed onto the marble floor, shielding her eyes with her hands. She was still there, in the Chamber, but her mind was in the future. She screamed as the images kept coming. The sound was amplified instantly. It hit her like a crashing wave.

The siithe in her vision stepped forward, over Gerla's corpse, ready to kill. Then there was a shouted command, from a thin, almost skeletal man, and the siithe paused. The man's dark, empty eyes assessed her with a coldness that stabbed into her mind with icy fingers. She knew him. *The Archfiend.* "She is the one. Take her."

The siithe seized her.

The scene shifted. Now she was at the top of a steep precipice, carved by ancient winds from blood-red stone. The siithe threw her from the cliff. She screamed as she fell. Sephany twisted to see what was below her. It was a huge gaping maw, opening wide to swallow her whole.

In the darkness above the cavernous mouth, the eyes opened.

Chapter 13
Court of the krell lord VoYannan — Vault of Seven Horns

VoYannan sat motionless on his dark throne.

The slow rise and fall of his stomach was the only sign of life. Through the eyes of his thralls he surveyed his domain. Fifty-eight worlds, sixteen firmly within the Vault of Seven Horns, and forty-two Shadow Worlds he was yet to fully subjugate. Across this vast dominion, millions were chained to his will. Each had knelt before him over the eons, and each fed his mind now through the bonds of spirit. Some — the more powerful ones — had dwelt within his court while he perfected his control over them. His mind swelled with the power. With practised ease, he banished the minute effects of aging from his body and restored his fierce vitality.

The krell drew his mind back to his court, flowing his consciousness into one of his new favourites: Rith'an, former High Councillor of the planet Oleth. VoYannan sighed with pleasure, buoyed by thoughts of his recent conquests. *Ah, he is a prize, this one.* Rith'an's soul was fat and largely untapped. VoYannan eagerly sucked off its layers. He could hear Rith'an's wails of despair as his core was drawn out, and this only added spice to the snack. The Oleth had resisted him for three millennia, but at last they had fallen. Procarrus had brought him Rith'an as a prize.

VoYannan was in the mood for some erotic stimulation. He filled Rith'an's body with lust, then rode the man's consciousness as he rutted with his semi-conscious companion. *Soon, I will have my bride*, thought VoYannan, groaning deep in his throat as the man climaxed. The krell withdrew his consciousness. The pleasure had been brief, and left him unsatisfied. Always, he limited himself to this shadow-lust, fearing the birth of another krell spawn to challenge his power. That would change once he had Sephany.

Thoughts of his bride made VoYannan impatient. He opened his eyes and surveyed his court. Narcotic smoke swirled through the air, pooling in the darkened corners. Below his dais, the chamber was packed with a mass of intertwined bodies. They were an odd assemblage of species, perhaps a hundred sentients in all, their races of origin difficult to discern beneath a camouflage of deformity. VoYannan's power had twisted their bodies into shocking parodies of their former selves. Many were completely insane. VoYannan manipulated each of their minds expertly. This was the genius of the krell — the ability to maintain an endless number of simultaneous mental landscapes and thought patterns. All other creatures, sentients and non-sentients alike, could be subsumed, to become extensions of a krell's will. Each new thrall fuelled their talent and swelled their minds. The only sounds in the court were animal grunts of pleasure, those of copulation, and the occasional gasp of pain or fear as one of the court sought to challenge his will, and was brought to heel. Most had been here for years, lost inside the whirlpool of the krell's mind. He had been lax, he realised. He should have cast most of them out to make room for fresh stock.

His gaze fell on Vespar, who had emerged as leader of a small group of captured Realm thurjuns. He suppressed his irritation. These few struggled to halt their slide into oblivion, keeping their corner of the room clean and vigorously defending it against the thralls who had succumbed to him. VoYannan tolerated the little group because they sometimes operated the Gateways for his legions. Their natural gifts also gave them an abundance of spiritual energy and allowed them to weather the feasts better than most.

VoYannan ended the dreamscapes.

Cries of fear and disgust filled the room as his thralls simultaneously awakened. The siithe warriors advanced, their thick-bladed weapons raised to strike, and the naked crowd cowered back and fell silent.

The krell waved one of his siithe bodyguard toward him. "Bring me Procarrus."

"Yes, Lord!" The siithe warrior bowed, then shuffled away.

"Two dreamers have perished, my Lord," said one of the siithe.

VoYannan waved his assent for the dead to be taken to the siithe food pits. He did not permit them to feed in his presence.

Vespar wept bitterly, as he always did when the dreams faded.

He cast a look of pure hatred at VoYannan — but not for too long. The beast was obscene, and dangerous to cross, sensitive even to errant thoughts. The krell's wet hide glistened. The thick armoured plates of his wedge-shaped head were surmounted with rows of horns that grew constantly, sharp and white in the crown's centre where they appeared almost as teeth, yellowed and chipped around the outside of the head, where they stood up as long as a man's forearm. As always, sight of the krell took Vespar straight back to the first night he saw the loathsome creature. When he had betrayed Evenstone. He thought bitterly of the seemingly innocent Tanya — the krell priestess Uzar — who had manipulated him so easily. *Weak-minded fool*, she had called him. His arrogance had been utterly shattered that night. Only hours later, lost in an erotic dreamscape of the krell's creation, he had opened the Gateway from Minoras to the Third Realm and condemned the Evenstone family, and hundreds of others, to death. When the attack was over, and the krell had released him, Vespar had seen everything with terrible clarity. He had not thought such despair possible. How little he had known. He had learned new depths of it since.

Servants entered the court with trays of food, bringing Vespar back to the present. The dreamers shuffled forward, most more animal than sentient. He felt a gentle touch on his shoulder. Vespar turned to smile at the female Thorin who had been his firm companion throughout this nightmare. She stood upright on huge legs designed for leaping, balanced by a thick tail. Her head was feline, her body covered in short black fur, with a marsupial pouch.

Vespar's body had changed since his seduction. His legs had grown thin and crippled, his arms skeletal and emaciated, whereas his belly and genitals had grown distended out of all proportion. He was shamed by his appearance, and desperately wished that he could cover himself, but the krell forbade any coverings, preferring to strip any vestige of dignity from his minions. Like most of them, Vespar longed for the erotic pleasure and escape of the dream, but also feared it, knowing how the krell used mental distraction to weaken his thralls' defences and drain them of power and will.

The Archfiend entered the court.

Vespar's laboured breathing grew harsher as the man's arrogant gaze swept across his group. Vespar saw the disdain, and looked down. From the gossip of the court, he knew the Archfiend was from a distant and primitive world called the Roman Empire. Procarrus had been cast by the thurjuns of that place into the Vault of Seven Horns, where he was enslaved. But the Archfiend had excelled beneath VoYannan. He had learnt a measure of his master's skill and had kept himself virtually immortal for thousands of years. He had also managed to shield himself from the powers of the krell and contain the forces that would have otherwise warped his body out of all recognition.

Procarrus raised his right hand toward VoYannan's throne in salute. He wore a simple white robe, with a slim silver circlet set around his tightly cropped hair. His spare features were unblemished, his face clean-shaven. His skin glistened with perfumed oils, and at his side he wore a slim longsword, the ancient bronze scabbard set with red enamel and intricate designs of silver and gold. This was a mark of special favour, since few were permitted a weapon in the krell's presence.

"You sent for me, sire?"

The focus in the krell's eyes sharpened. Vespar sensed the fragments of the krell's vast mind drawing back into his hideous shell. The sheer *presence* of beast blazed from the green depths. There was a susurrus of whimpers from the thralls. Even Procarrus took an involuntary step backwards. *Unusual*, thought Vespar. *Perhaps Procarrus is out of favour.*

"What news do you have?" asked VoYannan.

Procarrus straightened his back and returned the krell lord's gaze. "Our thurjuns and Shademasters have found a Gateway into the realm we seek. My Shademaster Oth'Seth now seeks a mind receptive to our will. One with the talent to open the way."

"Why must I wait? You know of this planet. You were spawned there, and have led our forces there before." The unspoken threat in the krell's voice sent chills down Vespar's spine.

"My Lord," replied Procarrus evenly, seemingly unperturbed by his krell lord's ill-humour. "The Gateways used for the last conquest were closed or blocked by the Realms, long ago. We must open a new Gateway. The arts of the thurjun have been mostly lost within this realm, to find one with the skills we seek, then to entrap them —"

VoYannan roared.

Siithe guards ran to the dais. They surrounded Procarrus in a circle of edged steel. VoYannan bared yellowed teeth. His feral eyes glistened with hunger. "How long must I wait till I have my bride?" For a heartbeat Vespar, along with the whole court, struggled for breath, his heart clenched in the vice of VoYannan's will.

Inside the circle of siithe guards, Procarrus sank to his knees. "Please, my Lord!" gasped Procarrus. "We are constantly seeking. We. . . *I* will not fail you!"

The krell released Procarrus, who fell forward onto the cold stone. Slowly, the Archfiend rose to his feet. He faced VoYannan in silence. Tension gathered in the air.

"You best not fail me, Procarrus. I want this Realm priestess."

"We shall seize her, sire, and cast her at your feet."

Thick mucus oozed from pores in the krell's hide. It gleamed sickening yellow in the torchlight. It signalled relaxation, Vespar knew. Sounds of motion and whispered conversations grew in the room. VoYannan waved the Archfiend from his presence. Procarrus saluted and left the court. The siithe warriors reluctantly parted to let him pass.

VoYannan swept his gaze across the room and hissed. "Fetch me my champion, Balos. I am in the mood for some sport."

The thralls backed away, wailing in fear, but the siithe herded them back. They knew what was coming.

Vespar trembled. And shut his eyes.

Chapter 14
Stonelake Gateway — Fourth Realm

A scream cut through the air.

It was a young woman's voice, filled with terror. It seemed so at odds with the Festival atmosphere that Finn did not react at first. Then the screaming started again, and this time it did not stop. It rose in pitch to become a continuous, hysterical wailing. *So loud!* He darted around his desk and snatched up his sword belt. He buckled it on as he slipped through the door. Finn ran down the Tower stairs to the great hall. Three of his junior lieutenants had lingered here to share a post-Festival cup of ale. The men were already on their feet. "Join me," he ordered. "You," he said, pointing to one of them. "Alert the wall guards."

A warrior ran into the hall, passing the lieutenant Finn had sent to the wall. He saw Finn and pulled up short. "It is coming from the Temple, Captain."

His stomach flipped. Was it the Vault? He swiftly got his thoughts under control. Whatever it was, he would face it with a cool head.

When Finn reached the Temple of the High God, he found a crowd of weary Festival-goers gathered at the broad steps, rapidly sobering under the continual assault of the eerie screaming. "Make way!" Finn had to shout to make himself heard. Dazed, the crowd parted.

"Draw your swords!" ordered Finn.

Blades bared, Finn and his men ran into the Temple's main public chamber. The vaulted ceiling above them was lost in shadow. They circled, alert for any movement. The painted decorations on the nave columns danced in the light of the High God's Flame, which flickered on its mionanail base by the main altar. *Nothing.* The place was empty. Finn led his men past the altar and into an access corridor. Like most of the Temple, the corridor was lit by a series of lamps set into wall-niches. The corridor continued in both directions, and three doorways were visible, each sealed with a thick curtain. Visibility was poor. The burning oil released the subtle scent of sandalwood. The screaming continued, loud and inexplicable. They were closer to it. The sound was jarring in this sacred place of whispers, song, and chant.

Finn caught sight of movement in his peripheral vision and spun to his left. The shape resolved into a stocky robed figure, running toward them. He saw a familiar face.

"Morin!" Finn lowered his sword.

The thurjun was breathing heavily. *He must have entered through a side gate.*

"What is it, Finn?" asked Morin, leaning on his staff.

"I do not know, but we will soon find out." Finn pushed aside one of the heavy curtains and entered the sacrosanct inner chambers. A middle-aged priestess rushed toward them, her gold and orange vestments draped over a simple white robe. She was clearly relieved to see Morin, though she gave Finn and his warriors a disapproving glare.

"Lord Morin. Thank the High God. It is our young Priestess, Sephany. None of our Prayers seem to calm her."

"Sephany? What has happened to her?" asked Finn.

The priestess looked at Finn coldly. "Put up your sword, warrior. And remove your men from the Temple."

Finn sheathed his weapon. "My men remain. At least until we know the danger." He held her gaze.

"Follow me." The older woman led them through a confusing maze of corridors and chambers. The screaming grew closer. Louder. They entered a small room, crowded with robed figures. The noise was deafening. Beyond it was another, smaller chamber. Inside this second chamber, five priestesses struggled to calm a young woman, barely more than a girl, who screamed hysterically. Her face was pale. Her long black hair in disarray.

"Sephany!" said Finn, taking a step toward her. Morin grabbed his arm to stop him. Frustration tore at Finn.

Sephany had pushed herself up against the wall of the tiny chamber, which was so cramped it was impossible for the others to surround her. Although slight, she fended off their advances with manic strength. Her screams reverberated around the walls. It was like being inside the dome of a ringing bell!

Finn covered his ears. "What is causing such a damned noise!"

"Do not defile the holiest of holies with your tongue!" snapped the priestess.

The High Priest, Korbeth, came over to Finn. He was large man, his face blunt and coarse, as though carved from granite, his broad shoulders giving the impression of strength. His tonsure, shaved in a crescent across the front of his head, only served to emphasise the bluffness of his face.

Korbeth laid a hand on the shoulder of the priestess, his voice melodious and calm, yet impressive in volume as he made himself heard over the din. "Teris, the Captain meant no harm. Could you help Morin calm the girl? I need to speak to Captain Evenstone."

Teris glared at Finn, but at a second look from the High Priest, she left them.

"This is the Chamber of Silence," said Korbeth. "One of the holiest parts of the Temple. Within it, a breath sounds as though it is a mighty wind, a stray thought becomes a careless whisper. It is here that we give some of our mightiest Prayers to the High God above. The room forces our initiates to still their bodies, slow their breathing, and calm their mind." Korbeth sighed and smiled at Finn. "Most of them are quieter than this!"

Finn looked into the room. He now noticed that the small chamber funnelled upward as though it were a tall chimney, yet one designed to convey sound, not hot air. He could find no place for a concealed mechanism, and assumed that the stone itself must possess some quality of amplification.

Morin stepped into the Chamber. A coloured pattern formed in the air before him, and they watched spellbound as he gathered his power and sent the swirling form darting toward Sephany. The colours wrapped themselves around her, then grew brighter as they stretched across her skin, pulsing with a gradually slowing rhythm. Sephany's eyes grew less manic, and at last she stopped screaming.

They all sighed with relief. Finn's ears rang in the silence.

At the sight of Finn, Sephany broke away from the priestesses and fled to him, gripping onto his armour. He put his arm around her protectively. Her dark brown eyes, when they found his, were still dreamy and unfocussed, looking past him — and through him. A chill ran up his spine.

"It was the Archfiend!" she whispered. "He was here in the Temple, surrounded by a band of dark-clad siithe warriors. Slaying, killing . . ."

Finn gripped the pommel of his sword in automatic reflex. He had dreaded this day, yet he had longed for it too. For justice. *The Archfiend.* The chief commander of the Vault of Seven Horns below VoYannan. He had the blood of thousands on his hands, including Finn's own family.

Sephany paused to take a breath. She turned sharply to stare at the High Priest. "Korbeth was slain."

One look at her distraught face, and Finn wanted nothing more than to take her back to the Tower, but that was not possible. He looked around at the assembled clergy, noting their disapproving eyes. Such physical contact was inappropriate, he realised. He took her wrists and gently moved her to arm's length. It seemed to Finn that her soft, beautiful face glowed with an inner light.

"You had a vision?"

Sephany nodded. "A powerful one. They are coming for me." Her voice was low and calm, so at odds with the terror-filled screaming. It held a strength and conviction that impressed him. She had left her fear behind, despite her certainty that danger threatened.

Teris stepped forward. She took Sephany firmly by the arm and drew her away.

Sephany cried out and reached for him. "Let me go with Finn, please!"

Sephany had lived under his protection in the Tower for the last year as she undertook the initial Temple rites. High King Torren had issued him sealed orders to care for and protect her until her formal initiation as priestess of the High God. The orders had soon proved superfluous. Finn had grown to love her like his own sister. Earlier today, Sephany had taken the vows of an initiate, attending a series of secret ceremonies attended only by Temple clergy. This removed her from his care and put her under the protection of the Temple. He had no right to interfere.

"Calm yourself child! You are not the first to have strange visions in the Chamber. The others had the sense to hold their tongues!" snapped Teris.

Sephany's eyes were sad as she was led away. It took every measure of self-control Finn had to let her go.

Only hours before, he had been torn at losing his chance at revenge, wondering how long he could defy the High King's orders. Now he was filled with remorse. How could he have forgotten that the Vault attack would mean the loss of innocent lives? How much was his revenge worth? He and Morin had never understood why the Vault were so intent on Stonelake. Now he had the answer. *Sephany.* They were coming for her. Why? Her last look, and the unwanted knowledge in her eyes, haunted him. He silently vowed to do anything in his power to protect her.

The High King's orders meant nothing now.
The Archfiend was coming.

*

Finn woke with a start.

He rolled out of bed and drew his sword, falling instinctively into a fighting stance. His heart hammered. He blinked, looking into the darkness. *Nothing.* Just the dream gain.

He leaned his forehead against the cold stone of the wall.

The memories were as sharp as ever.

Morin had driven the Archfiend Procarrus and the seraphin back, using the power of the ardanaith. Then he had sealed the Gateway.

The night had become a blur of running men and shouted orders. The injured Morin was carried away, leaving the thirteen year old Finn and eight year old Tallandra to wander like ghosts through the confusion. The mutilated corpses of his brothers, mother, and father, had been set out in the great hall. All in a row. Priests and healers came, but they could do little more than close the eyes of the fallen, clean away the blood from their faces, and cover their bodies with blankets. Tallandra would not let him go. She kept whimpering, on and on. Finn was silent, as though his

78

heart had solidified into some twisted gemstone. A Priestess tried to take them to the Temple, but Finn had ordered her away.

A tall warrior came to them as they sat by the bodies in the great hall.

"Finn."

He looked up.

"I am Captain Fell, of the High King's guard. You will have to come with me."

"No. I cannot . . . this is my home."

Fell grimaced. "Not any more, son. The Evenstone Gateway is now under the direct control of the High King. You and your sister are to travel to Tir, in the First Realm."

"But . . ." he said, reaching out to touch the cold hand of his mother. For the first time, tears touched his cheeks.

"You can do nothing for them now."

He *had* done nothing. Nothing to save them.

"Who did this?" asked Finn, tears streaking his face.

"One of the krell. VoYannan, most likely. He holds sway in Minoras, beyond the Evenstone Gateway."

"Then one day, I am going to make him pay."

Fell shook his head slightly. He started to reply, then stopped. Finn met his gaze calmly. The warrior looked over at Finn's slain family then back to him and Tallandra. Fell took a deep breath and let it out slowly. "It would take a mighty army to vanquish VoYannan. He is Lord of the Vault of Seven Horns — many, many, dark worlds."

"Then one day I will lead that army, right into the Vaults of Sheol," said Finn.

"I pray that comes to pass. In the mean time, let me take you away from here."

Finn returned to the present.

He lifted his blade. It was an ancient thing. Once carried by his father. He sheathed it.

After all this time, he would have his chance to fight.

Chapter 15

Toowoomba, Queensland, Australia — Earth
23rd December 1999

Rain descended from a clouded sky. It soaked through Liam's new, ill-fitting black suit, and made puddles in the rich red basaltic soil that waited to fill Aidan's grave. It was a heavy storm. Strangely cold for December, even for Toowoomba's high elevation. The true chill was deeper, though. Inside him.

The priest's voice was the only sound above the rain. The words filtered past him, finding no lodgement, and certainly offering no consolation. A crowd of around forty had gathered at the gravesite, dressed for mourning in black suits and sombre dresses. Liam was bewildered by these strangers in their expensive clothes and designer jewellery, who cast knowing glances in his direction. They had passed words of sympathy to him before the service, discharging their duty, yet their condolences left him flat. Liam had not expected so many, and had been too stunned by grief, and the whirlwind of events, to organise any wake.

Liam became aware that the priest had stopped speaking. *The service is over*, he realised. The priest said goodbye to Liam, exchanged some last, solemn words, then hurried through the increasing rain to his waiting car. The crowd dispersed slowly, almost reluctantly. Some gathered in groups, talking in low tones as they looked in his direction, but they too, eventually, left. Liam remained at the gravesite, his gaze fixed on the casket. When he looked up from the coffin, he found a small man at his side, sheltering under a large black umbrella, another tucked under his arm.

The man's pale blue eyes were full of sympathy, and he smoothed his sparse greying locks methodically across his balding pate with a black comb as he considered Liam. "Mr Durrow, I am John Peters."

Liam recognised his voice, and nodded imperceptibly. The man paused out of respect. For a long moment they both stared into the grave, where the dirt the mourners had thrown atop the coffin was being washed off the deep red mahogany lid.

Liam's mind began to function again, emerging from the numbness that had seized him since he had heard the news three days ago. There was no one left. His parents had died when he was a child, and Aidan had been the only family he had known. He had underestimated how much his uncle had meant to him. His plans for the future counted for nothing in the face of his grief.

"And now the mantle of Keeper falls to you," said Peters.

It took Liam a moment to focus on Peters' words.

"Keeper? What do you mean?" asked Liam.

Peters looked shocked for a moment. Then his face flushed red. "This . . . makes it all very difficult. I had hoped your uncle would have explained *some* of this to you, at least. We had agreed that a large part of it would be withheld, but . . ." Peters sighed. "No doubt Aidan had his reasons."

Anger gripped Liam. This stranger — the man who had told him Aidan was dead — was blathering some bloody nonsense at his uncle's funeral. He found he was not coherent enough to form a reply, even to this . . . outrage.

"Please, Mr Durrow, let me take you out of this rain. Come to my offices in Toowoomba, and I will tell you everything I know."

Peters offered Liam the spare black umbrella. The man was genuine in his concern, and it was this, and not the rain, which impelled him to accept. Liam clicked it open and spread it against the deluge. As though it were a signal to himself, he turned away from the grave, whispering, "Goodbye, Uncle Aidan."

Liam followed Peters to an old Rolls Royce, parked neatly at the curb. The rain ran down its highly polished black paintwork in flowing rivulets, beading briefly before being urged on by the continuing downfall. It spoke to Liam of money. Old money. Peters opened the door for him, and Liam hesitated to sit on the immaculate beige leather in his soaked clothes. Peters saw his dilemma and retrieved a thick towel from the boot. He handed the towel to Liam, then urged him inside. Liam dried himself as well as he could, suddenly conscious of the fact that he had been standing in the rain for the last hour, spread the towel on the passenger seat, and slipped inside the car.

The car started with a low roar, and they drove to the city

centre. It was strange seeing Toowoomba again, so much a part of his childhood. It seemed smaller. The last time he stayed in Toowoomba was two years ago. He and Aidan had come for the Festival of Flowers. It seemed another lifetime. Queens Park was empty now, and he let his gaze wander across the grand trees as they drove by.

"My family have served yours for many years, Liam. Centuries in fact. Not that it makes this any easier for you."

The numbness in Liam's mind vanished. He looked at Peters again. *Really* looked at him. He had thought of Peters as nothing more than a lawyer, yet the man had a quiet intensity that made a nonsense of that.

"Served?"

"Yes. Served the Keepers."

Something squirmed in Liam's stomach. He had a sense of his life swinging on the moment. The rational part of his brain rebelled, yet all the things he should have said, he knew would ring false. Some, deep, deep part of him had been waiting for this. The rain, the cluttered houses of Toowoomba, and their green cloak of vegetation, all flared brighter, as though his mind had come to life.

"Tell me everything."

"Please have a seat, Mr Durrow."

Dressed in dry clothes — courtesy of Peters — Liam seated himself in front of Peters' antique wooden desk. The huge old thing dominated the room, which was lined with modern filing cabinets and floor to ceiling shelves filled with law books and other references. The tall glass windows that faced the street admitted a soft afternoon light. Through them, Liam saw cars move slowly down the main street three storeys below, cautious in the driving summer rain. A solitary pedestrian struggled past, trying to keep dry under his umbrella.

Peters seated himself at his desk, surveying the wooden tabletop like the lord of his domain. "Would you like some tea, Mr Durrow?" Peters looked at his watch. "My goodness, look at the time! Perhaps some sandwiches as well?"

He nodded, still overcome with a sense of unreality. "Call me

Liam, please."

Peters smiled warmly and pressed the intercom button on his telephone. "Ellen, could you bring us some tea and sandwiches please?"

A young, light-hearted voice called back through the intercom, "Oh! Uncle John. You're back. Sure. I'll get something sorted for you."

"Now." Peters walked across his office to the bookshelves. He pressed a hidden release, and a section of shelving swung open, revealing a small concealed safe. He manipulated the tumblers with quick, deft movements, and opened the thick metal door. Peters removed a large envelope and an elaborately decorated box, then closed the safe and replaced the shelving. It closed without a sound. Peters reverently placed the box on the desk and sat across from Liam. It was a beautiful thing, decorated with a twisting pattern of gold and silver, and set with gemstones. About the size of a shoebox, but flatter. Peters weighed the envelope in his hand. After a thoughtful pause, he tore through the thick brown paper and removed a large pendant, some papers, and another sealed envelope with Liam's name written across the front.

"I've known your uncle for a good many years. Most of my working life in fact. I also knew your parents . . ." Peters looked slowly through the papers. "So many memories," he whispered to himself.

Liam could remember little of his parents. He was only six when they were killed in a plane crash. He had a vague memory of them explaining that he had to visit with his uncle while they went on a trip. He had waited, but they never returned. He used to dream of that crash, playing it over and over in his mind, imagining it a thousand ways. Usually it was a scene from Hell — flames and screaming — his mother reaching out to him, his father calling out as they fell endlessly from a turning sky.

"This is yours now."

The sound of Peters voice brought Liam back to the present. He took the teardrop-shaped pendant from Peters' outstretched hand. Once, long ago, he had seen his father wearing this. He turned it over reverently, marvelling at the detail on its surface.

The size of a man's palm, it was dark green in colour, with a dull gem set in the centre. At first glance, it seemed to be made of fired clay, yet it felt cool and smooth like metal. Liam lifted it to the light and found that there were highlights within it that glittered like flecks of gold. A Celtic knotwork — a design of marvellous complexity — was worked into its surface. It seemed to defy the eyes with its subtle twists and turns, yet Liam could feel the pattern, as he had felt a very different pattern three nights before. The one that had suspended his art equipment above his desk in a rotating pinwheel.

"The Will is quite clear," said Peters, taking one last glance before putting the document aside. "You are the sole heir of Aidan Durrow."

Liam looked up from his examination of the pendant. He gripped it in his left fist. Its edge dug into his palm, but the pain was a welcome anchor.

"The Trust," asked Liam, straightening in his chair. "Was it something my uncle set up?"

"Oh, no. The Trust has been in existence for hundreds of years. It is just a convenient way of administering the Durrow fortune."

"Fortune?" Liam's stomach dropped through the floor.

A smartly dressed young woman entered the room carrying a silver tray bearing sandwiches and tea. She was short, but unlike her uncle, slim and graceful, with a pleasant face softened by light grey-blue eyes, and wavy dark blonde hair. Ellen looked around twenty. She carefully placed the tray on the table and smiled nervously at Liam. "Hello, Mr Durrow." The silence grew awkward. She lowered her voice into a conciliatory tone. "Sorry to hear the news about Aidan."

"Er . . . thanks," replied Liam.

She began to lay the lunch out on the polished wooden tabletop. As she placed the teacup and saucer in front of Liam, he noticed her hands shook. She stood back with the tray. "We have all heard so much about you, Mr Durrow."

To Liam's amazement, he realised that Ellen held him in a kind of awe. She seemed on the verge of asking him something.

"Thank you, Ellen," said Peters.

She left. Disappointed, but resigned.

Peters sighed, reaching for a sandwich. "Yes, well. Back to business." He took one bite then scanned the paperwork in front of him.

"The Durrow fortune is kept diversified. Your family has built up tremendous assets over the centuries, mostly in shares and properties, although we do have some businesses. Let me see . . ." Peters reached behind him into a filing cabinet and retrieved a thick file, looking carefully through the pages and nodding to himself. "Yes. At last appraisal, it would be worth, conservatively, just under seven hundred million US dollars."

Liam froze, the sandwich suspended halfway to his mouth. "And this is mine?"

Peters smiled. "Well yes, technically. At least part of it. The Trust has been set up to prevent any one generation of your family from having too much control over the assets, however you will be entitled to a significant income. But let me assure you, Mr Durrow — Liam — that considerable resources are available to you at any given time, including the use of any of the properties. I have a list here . . ."

Liam understood Ellen's awe of him. He was rich!

Peters continued. "But you must understand, Mr Durrow, that considerable responsibility comes with your family's heritage. Especially now that only two of you remain. I hope for all our sakes that at least one of you has many children."

"Two? You mean I have a living relative?"

"Yes, Liam. You have a distant cousin, who is also in the direct line of descent." He paused as he retrieved another file from the cabinet. "Teag Durrow. Thirty-one years of age. Native of Canada, although God only knows where he might be now. He only contacts us for money."

"How can I contact him?"

"I can leave messages for him, Liam. But before you pursue Teag around the globe, there are other things that must be done. You will not help yourself by latching onto Teag. He is totally irresponsible. Before you do anything, you must become comfortable with your role."

"Why didn't Aidan tell me about Teag?"

"It was a decision made by both your uncle and myself. Teag

was to have the pendant. When your parents and his died in the plane crash, it was Teag, being the eldest, who we hoped would take up the mantle of Keeper. But he had been brought up with full exposure to the realities of his position, the wealth and the privilege, with none of the guidance. Teag refused to accept his responsibilities. He even refused to believe in the truth. Instead he chose to abuse the wealth his ancestors had accumulated to aid the Durrows in their sacred trust," Peters had grown serious, and placed a hand on the jewelled box. "As a consequence, Aidan and I felt it was better you were insulated from that danger. Liam, you have to understand, you are our last hope."

What did Peters mean by *Keeper*? He kept using that word.

Peters continued. "It was traditional for the adult members of the Durrow clan to gather together to decide on matters related to the administration of the Trust, and to vote on the leadership of the family. It had always been done this way. The leader of the clan would be elected from those considered the most able. The last meeting was held in Canada. At a small estate in the country. Your family — parents, uncles, cousins, and both your grandparents — had all decided to fly to Montreal for the weekend in a small hired jet. No one really knows what went wrong."

Peters sighed. "Your uncle had agreed to mind you. He was quite upset he was to miss the gathering, but it was fortunate for us. You and your cousin Teag were the only family members under voting age, and are now the only surviving Durrows."

Liam waited, his inner tension growing, needing to ask the question, yet fearing the answer.

"How did my uncle die, Mr Peters?"

Chapter 16
Fourth Realm

Finn's grey stallion swept over the mountain steppes.

The morning sun was bright, and Stonelake was far behind him. Crisp mountain air rushed past in a torrent, numbing his face and hands. He drank in the cool freshness of the day and revelled in it. This was the Blessed Realms, where law and land were one. Each city, town, and hamlet, was bordered by wide tracts of unfettered nature. He was south of Stonelake, racing across a series of hills that rose to a forested plateau, now lost in cloud. Had he travelled to the north, he would have still found wilderness: rolling hills that stretched out to the horizon, open and free, with crests of wild, fertile woodland. Although his own Third Realm was far away, this was also his home, and as a warrior of the Blessed Realms, he was sworn to defend it.

Finn had seen the Shadow Worlds. He knew what the Vault did to the planets they conquered. They raped them. Poisoned them. Enslaved the population. Took what they could use and reduced the rest to ash.

And the Vault was coming.

The stallion powered up the slope. He turned him south-east, reluctantly slowing as he neared the forest's edge. He found the track to Genna's lodge and let the stallion find his own pace as he pushed through the fern understorey. The light was dim in the towering rainforest. The air cool. As Finn's eyes adjusted, his heart soared. Scores of delicate flowers grew against the living canvass of the forest in vibrant colours of red, orange, purple, white, and yellow. Coloured birds shot through the air, from the leaf-strewn floor to the high boughs of the strangler vines and their rich, stolen bounty. Finn stilled his mind and strained to hear the song behind the silence, to be at one with the forest, but that sense of peace was elusive. Instead, images of his dead family rose to the surface of his mind. His doubts were close behind. He remembered the awesome power of the Dark Seraphin, and the ruthlessness of the near-immortal Archfiend. Could he defeat them when they came?

Fear knotted his stomach. It was swamped immediately by rage. He urged the grey up the steep track, pushing him to a gallop. The stallion answered eagerly. He was still fresh and brimming with energy. Such speed was dangerous on the forest track, but the thrill of risk cleared his mind and lifted his mood.

Finn broke into the clearing where Genna's people had built their lodges. Each was a low-set A-frame, crafted with care and skill. The huge entrance beams swarmed with mythical beasts and forest animals, all meticulously carved into the mountain cedar. The shelters were irregular in size, each built from fallen forest timbers of different dimensions. It was the way of Genna's people to leave no mark upon the land. As he had expected, most of the lodges were empty. This was only one of the camps of Genna's people. They had a score of them in the great forests of the Realm, and they seldom stayed long in any one place. When they moved on they left a Guardian, like Genna, to maintain the camp.

Finn reined in outside Genna's lodge. "Up, Genna!"

Finn grinned as he heard Genna's curt reply. He did not know many words in his friend's language . . . but he knew these.

Finn had met the dark-skinned native years ago, when he first took his commission at Stonelake. Genna had been chosen by his people to greet the new garrison Captain. Since then they had become close friends. Genna's tribe were an ancient people, rumoured to have come originally from Kgari, the world beyond the Stonelake Gateway. They, and their cousins on that lost, distant world, were the original custodians of the Gateway, dating back to the times when the portals were held open for all to pass freely. The ancient of war in which Thurn Evenstone had driven back the Vault's incursion had cost Genna's people dearly. When the Gateway closed, they had been cut off from Kgari.

Genna emerged from his lodge, a finely cut cloak of animal skins fastened around his ebony shoulders with a silver chain. His dark, handsome face was lit with a sardonic smile, and his black eyes glowed with mischief. Decorations of carved bone were worked into his wiry black hair. It would be a mistake to think Genna unsophisticated, despite the way he styled himself. Like many of his tribe's men, he had been sent to train as a warrior of the Blessed Realms. He was more conversant with Vault tech than most Stonelake townsfolk.

"You are up early for a court-bred boy. Has the day got you by the ear, eh?" asked Genna.

"It has indeed, and filled my head with the notion of some hunting."

Genna wore loose cloth trousers, his feet bare. His face was finely featured, tapering from a strong, wide brow to a narrow chin, with the wide nose of his people. Behind Genna, in the doorway of his lodge, Finn briefly glimpsed Genna's youngest wife, Tarragini, through the gap in the hide curtain. Their eyes met for an instant, then she was gone, darting back out of sight. Finn had met her only once before. She was beautiful and stately, but shy.

Genna looked up through the sparse canopy and watched the sky, reading the clouds. "Hunting," he mused. "Mmm."

Finn waited for the idea to sink in.

Genna's people never did anything in a hurry.

It was almost noon, and all was silent. Finn drew that stillness into himself. He squatted down, trying to catch his breath. There were beads of moisture on the leaves from the night rain, which dripped slowly to the forest floor. Each caught the light as it fell, a liquid lens vanishing into the thick humus.

"Here," whispered Genna. He pointed at a splayed footprint in the mud.

They had set out on foot, and had been hunting for hours, climbing up gullies and scrambling down treacherously damp slopes, navigating around, under, and over, moss-covered rocks, creeper-laden trees and fallen giants dotted with multi-coloured fungi. Finn was armed with a hunting bow, Genna with some finely crafted spears, a spear thrower, and two boomerangs, which were tucked into his woven belt.

Finn bent closer. The print was made by a cassowary, a large, aggressive forest bird with a solid ridge on its head — and very sharp talons.

"He goes to drink. Come." Genna set off in pursuit.

Finn took a moment to string his compact recurve bow before

following, trying to emulate Genna's swift, silent progress.

He recognised the trail. They were heading for High Lake. A deep pool perched high up on the range. It was a favourite place for Genna's people to fish, and a good place to hunt. With his tribe gone, the forest animals would be even more relaxed about approaching the water.

When they reached the thick growth around the lake, Genna raised his hand. Finn settled back onto his haunches. Genna gently drew back a branch to give them a view of the lake. The cassowary was at the lakeshore, watching the forest warily between quick gulps of mountain water.

Genna pointed at Finn, then the bird, as if to say, *be my guest.* Finn nodded his thanks, then turned to focus on the bird. He slipped an arrow from his quiver. He rose from his crouch to a standing position and sighted along the ash shaft. The bird raised its head once, but remained still. The shot was perfectly lined up. Then red flame rose in his mind. He heard again the seraphin's scream of fury. Knew its awesome power as it came for him. His hand trembled. The arrow released, sailing high. The bird flinched, then ran for the trees.

Finn swore. He clenched his fist to still the tremor.

Genna looked at Finn in surprise, then darted out from the concealing cover. He reached back to his belt and launched a small boomerang in one smooth movement. Finn knew the smaller boomerangs were not used for killing. Genna was attempting to get the bird to shy from the canopy, to give him another chance at a shot.

Finn fitted another arrow to the bow.

The boomerang arced across the lake's surface, cutting low across the bird's escape. The cassowary shied back in a flurry of feathers, the wings opening in an instinctive defence. For that brief moment it was unsure which way to go. Finn was ready. He loosed. The arrow shot fifty paces to its mark. But in that fraction of a second, the bird turned. The arrow struck the raised right wing, passing harmlessly through the feathers and into the forest beyond. Then the bird was gone.

Genna stepped forward and caught the boomerang on its return arc, snatching it neatly from the air.

They ran across the shore. Finn saw his second arrow quivering in the trunk of a tall pine. The was no sign of the first. He pulled the arrow free and turned it over in his hands. "That bird is long gone now."

"Unlike you to miss an easy shot," said Genna, watching him closely.

Finn nodded, not trusting himself to speak.

Genna smiled and put a hand on his shoulder, looking deep into his eyes. "We are hunting the bird. But something is hunting you."

Finn tried to smile, but failed. "The Vault is coming, Genna. To Stonelake."

"And you fear its strength?"

Finn nodded, unwilling to speak his fears aloud.

Genna smiled. "Whatever comes, we will face it together. You are not alone, Finn. You have friends, and many warriors who would die for you."

"That is what I am afraid of. My mistakes will mean their deaths — or worse — failure for us all."

"The only decision you need to make is whether to fight or not. The rest?" Genna shrugged. "Let it take care of itself."

Genna walked over to the lake and squatted at the water's edge. He drank from a cupped hand, then splashed the icy water across his face and neck. "Still plenty of day left. Why not follow the bird?"

Finn looked up at the sky. Rain seemed unlikely, and it had been weeks since he had simply lost himself like this. "Why not."

Finn also slaked his thirst with the cool mountain water. Refreshed, he unstrung his bow and slung it across his back.

They moved through the forest at a steady jog, Genna pausing only to check the sign. His gentle, dark hands would come within a hair's-breadth of the ground, as though he could feel the fading heat of the bird's feet in the forest litter. Its trail led them down the mountain, toward Stonelake. The flatter country around the lower, larger lake was popular with the birds for roosting. The forest was wetter at the base of the ridge, rich with forage and fruiting trees. As they descended further, moving away from the high rainforest, the travelling grew easier as the forest opened up.

It was twilight by the time they were in sight of Stonelake. A group of three cassowaries were foraging just back from the lakeshore, which was deserted at this time of the day. Genna laid down his bundle of spears and chose one, fitting it to his thrower while Finn strung his bow. The group were over seventy paces away, but the two companions were not going to move closer. If the birds scented them, they would disappear into the darkening forest in a flash of feathers, and that would be that.

"He is the one on the right," said Genna. He stepped forward and launched his spear. The black shaft curved high into the sky while Finn's arrow, loosed from the powerful bow, cut almost horizontally. The arrow flashed past the bird's head, just nicking the crest, causing it to rear, and alerting the other birds. Then the spear struck it squarely in the body, knocking it from its feet. They raced after it, finally subduing the dangerous bird while Genna dealt it a clean deathblow with his knife.

Finn stalked across the clearing to retrieve his arrow. "Missed again!"

Genna laughed. "You always have to show off. Only you would have gone for a head shot over that distance."

They quickly butchered the bird, Genna removing the feathers with a small, razor-sharp scraper. Then they built a fire by the lakeside, near the Gateway steps. Genna seasoned the bird with some forest herbs, and glazed it with some wild honey he had brought along. Finally, the two friends sat by the shore, chatting easily as the bird roasted on a makeshift spit, sizzling with fat. Then they feasted. The herbs and glaze worked well with the bird's strong-tasting meat, but it was still a little tough for Finn's taste. Still, he could not have been happier. He was a peace, one with the night, and feeling, at least in part, the simple joy of existence that Genna's people pursued with an artist's dedication.

As they sat in the moonlight, the stars outlined against a cloudless sky, Finn watched the play of the firelight on the ancient stonework of the Stonelake Gateway. He thought of the Fragment. Saw his father — a towering hero to the younger Finn — proudly lifting Evenstone's axe from the lintel above the fireplace to show him. The Fragment, nothing then but an ancient keepsake that once excited his fancies, had always lain beside it.

He missed his father, his mother, and his brothers. Every year on the anniversary of their deaths, memories swarmed around him.

"It is not wise to stir the past beside a Gateway my friend," said Genna.

"No," said Finn. His friend had the uncanny ability to guess his thoughts.

They sat in silence for a time. Then Genna rose smoothly and packed away the uneaten meat with the other parts of the bird he could use. Finn put out the fire.

"Do you want to stay in the Tower tonight?" asked Finn

Genna smiled and looked up at the ridge behind them. "It's a fine night. I'll make my way back up the track."

Finn shook his head in admiration. Who else would travel that distance through the forest at night? Genna hoisted his pack and started up the trail.

"What about my horse!" yelled Finn.

"I will bring him down tomorrow!"

Finn set off toward the citadel. Within minutes he was passing through the city gate. At peace, and renewed.

He was ready.

Chapter 17

Toowoomba, Queensland, Australia — Earth
23rd December 1999

The room was silent.

Liam waited for Peters' answer.

"Your uncle died in an accident," said Peters eventually. "One which none of us could have foreseen. He had agreed to use his skills as Keeper to help two lost travellers locate their home world. This he did — but at a price. Not knowing who he was, the defenders of the Orin home planet killed your uncle moments after he found it. The two travellers assured me they had no idea such defences were in place, and I believe them. They are peaceful scientists, and leave the defence of their planet to their more warlike brethren. It was a tragedy."

This sounded insane. Maybe he *should* talk to Teag. Liam's frustration boiled over. "Alien worlds? *What the hell?* And what's this about being 'Keeper'?"

Peters held up his hand. "Please, Liam." Peters pushed the jewelled box toward him.

"This is the Book of Elements. Its ancient name is the Book of Duile. It is the last of the many copies made during the great flowering of Celtic culture in the seventh century. The monks who transcribed this book did so under the direction of your ancestors. Within is a record of their knowledge, written in an ancient, symbolic script. I cannot help you decipher it. Aidan was the last who knew the language. I only hope he managed to pass something of it on to you."

Liam reached forward and lifted the jewelled lid. Inside was an ancient leather-bound book. The cover, the *cumtach*, was of sheet silver, set with intricate designs that matched the lid of the box. More precious jewels were set into the pattern with care and artistry. Liam was awed by the cumtach's beauty, and soon found himself lost in the intricate turns and spirals.

"Liam, please! *Cover the book!*"

Liam looked up to see that Peters was kneeling on the floor with his head bowed. He replaced the cover. For the first time he understood the gravity and respect with which Peters treated his heritage. He also had his first real sense of the others who had worked silently through the centuries to maintain the Durrow fortunes and help the Keepers perform their mysterious duties.

Peters took his seat again. He smoothed back his hair, clearly embarrassed by his own reaction. "This is not the place to examine the book. You must return to your uncle's property before you explore it any further."

Peters handed the sealed letter to Liam.

"This is from your uncle. He left it in case he was taken unexpectedly. Before he had a chance to explain things.

"Now. I should take care of some minor formalities. Then I think I should leave you in peace for a while to take all this in. We can meet again tomorrow, or if you need to talk, this is my number." Peters handed him a business card.

Peters had Liam sign a quick succession of papers then led him back to the Rolls. Within half an hour, they were on the open highway, heading south-west from Toowoomba toward his uncle's property on the Darling Downs. The storm had passed, leaving clear, unblemished sky

Liam opened the letter.

His heart skipped a beat as he recognised Aidan's neat handwriting. Outside, the familiar scenery slipped by.

Dear Liam,

If you are reading this, I have been taken from you.

I have tried to be a father to you. To teach you the values that have always mattered to our family. You will need them now that you are alone. You must be strong, Liam. You will lead the house of Durrow through a new century. Lead it well, and with the strength of grace.

By now Peters will have told you of Teag, and our decision to keep you in ignorance of the family's past. For this I apologise, but we believed it was necessary. You now have the mionanail pendant, and the Book of Elements. These are the tools of the Keeper. Do not underestimate, or endanger, either, for they are priceless. In time you will use these to grow in power, and then, and only then, will you truly understand. I pray that a call from the Blessed Realms will not come in your lifetime, but you must work hard — to be worthy — if that call should come. Pray for guidance.

Our family is an ancient one. Originally Irish, in the seventeenth century our ancestors fled the English advance, first to the Scottish Highlands, then on to Brittany. In the nineteenth century, amidst the Great Depression of the 1870s, and sensing the coming storms of the next century, the Durrow leaders decided it was time to flee Europe. Some of the family moved to Canada, others to Australia, others remained behind. The Durrows have learned to keep a low profile, and what enemies you may have will never consider seeking you on the Downs.

In ancient times, our ancestors were clan chieftains in the remote west of Ireland, and even in those times, the knowledge our family guarded was old. Our blood is of the Tuatha de Danann, Ireland's elder race.

The key to understanding your powers is in your blood. Any progeny you sire will also share your power — but our family do not conceive easily, or with just anyone. At some time in your life, if you are fortunate, you will feel drawn to another like you, with the blood of an elder race. It is only through her that our family will live once more. I have had a long life, yet I have never found that rare connection.

Once, in the first flowering dawn of mankind's history, some peoples of the Earth walked the paths between worlds. Our ancestors were among them. The Earth was free and wild, untainted by chaos. In these times, the Blessed Realms were open to us.

Then the legions of the Vaults of Sheol visited Earth, seeking to use the Gateways that existed here to attack the Blessed Realms. Most of the elder race defied them, and paid for that defiance with their lives. We were of the few that survived, aided by warriors of the Blessed Realms. After a bitter battle between these dark forces and the armies of the Realms, it was agreed that the Gateways be closed. Frustrated, the Vault left the Earth to seek other ways to strike at the Realms.

Before they left, the elders of the Blessed Realms gave knowledge and power to those who could open and control these Gateways. Your task Liam, and the task of our family, is to maintain this knowledge, in case it is ever needed again.

Liam turned the letter over, searching for more, but found a blank page.

Could all this really be true? Surely not — and yet — all his life he had felt something within him, some dimension he could not comprehend, which held him apart from others.

"The Durrow family have built up an extensive network of observers worldwide, who seek out all sorts of unexplained phenomena," said Peters.

Liam put down the letter, staring through the roadside trees and out across the open grazing country to the distant blue sky. Watching the scenery calmed him. It seemed so mundane. So ordinary. It helped him to centre himself as Peters continued.

"The Orin scientists landed in the pacific, barely alive inside their little spacecraft. They were testing the first experimental Orin star-drive. They were lost, and doomed to be either killed or taken as specimens for examination by the major powers. Your uncle, thankfully, intervened. They were transported secretly to Australia, with their craft. For this, and the sacrifice your uncle made for them, they are deeply grateful."

"When did all this happen?"

"Within the last few months," said Peters.

"My uncle died helping aliens . . ." *Sure. Why not.* What was next? Bigfoot? He still did not have the faintest idea what a Keeper was. Liam certainly did not feel qualified to further a tradition he was in total ignorance of.

"Should you ever need the Orin, they will help you in any way they can."

Liam's temples pounded in response to an internal pressure that had been building since Peters' first mention of "Keeper" at the gravesite. As much as he wanted answers, he needed distance first. This was all too much.

The Rolls approached a familiar bend in the road, which signalled the entrance to his uncle's property. *His property.* The Rolls turned in, then glided along a well graded dirt road that led into a hollow in the side of a ridge, where his uncle had built his house. *Our home.* A low-roofed portico extended out from the entrance to the top of the driveway. In the middle of the front yard, like an island inside the horseshoe shaped driveway, was a rainforest garden set around a gurgling pond. The plants were well established, and gave the house a sleepy, lived-in aspect. It was all so familiar, and yet so foreign without Aidan there to greet him.

"Liam. I hate to have to leave you like this, but I have pressing business back in town. I've arranged for Lilly to be here to meet you." Lilly was Aidan's housekeeper.

Liam stepped out of the car, clutching the letter like a lifeline. The Book of Elements an awkward weight in hands. Looking at its jewelled cover made him feel like he had robbed a jewellery store . . . or a museum.

"I'll be going now, Liam!"

He waved as Peters turned his Rolls back toward Toowoomba and his strange and secretive life. A life spent serving his family. Serving him.

Liam walked toward the house, shoes crunching on gravel. The enormity of everything he had learned weighed on him. He was richer than he could have ever dreamed, yet bound by a duty he could scarcely understand. He felt as though somehow he had betrayed Aidan, as though he had traded his newfound wealth for Aidan's life. Now he was also asked to believe in worlds that existed beyond mysterious Gateways, evil beings that once descended to Earth from the skies, and lost alien scientists. It should have been funny, but it was not.

Lilly, a short rotund woman wearing a floral-print dress and flat shoes, came out of the house to meet him, an expression of sympathy on her careworn face. "Welcome home, Liam. I'm so sorry to hear about Aidan." She patted him on the shoulder. That simple gesture and few words meant so much more than all the words he had received from strangers. Lilly was at least someone who had shared their lives. She had been with Aidan for as long as he could remember, and had been a de facto mother to him.

Liam hugged her, reassured by her warmth and solidity. "Thanks, Lil."

She ushered Liam into the lounge room and motioned for him to sit down while she poured him a glass of orange juice from a carton. Liam had not drunk store-bought OJ since he moved out of home to college accommodation at the University of Queensland in Brisbane three years ago — he found it insipid — but the gesture was too heart-warming to refuse.

"Do you want anything else, sweetie? A sandwich? Cuppa?"

Liam shook his head.

Lilly hesitated for a moment. "I'll only be here for another half-hour. Do you want me to sit with you?"

"No, that's OK. I think I just need to be alone." He could not very well discuss his new status as Keeper with Lilly. *Whatever a Keeper was.*

"Alright, then. I'll just finish up and go. I'm only a phone call away, OK?"

"Thanks, Lilly."

She gave him a warm smile and bustled away. That's how she was, always in motion, always doing something. He felt a sense of relief to be alone at last. For a long time he sat, just looking out through the tall glass windows into the eastern sky. His mind was blank, washed clean by the sheer intensity of everything he had experienced.

He heard the jangle of keys and the quick clatter of Lilly's flat shoes on the tiles.

"I'm off, Liam," she said, trotting through the room. "Sure you'll be OK?"

"Yep. Don't worry," said Liam.

He heard her car start, then shoot off up the gravel drive. Another familiar sound.

Liam was left with the empty house, with memories . . . and questions.

Chapter 18
Toowoomba, Queensland, Australia — Earth

The rain was gone.

The clouds in the eastern sky glowed with shades of gold, yellow and pink as the last rays of the setting sun reached across from the west. Outside, the light was fading rapidly, and Liam roused himself, flicking switches and filling the living area of the house with light. Tomorrow he would return to Toowoomba and pick up his car, but for tonight, he would rest. He had his room here — at least that much was familiar — and a wardrobe full of clothes. At some point, he would have to go through his uncle's personal effects, but that could wait.

Liam gathered the jewelled box under his arm, and for want of a better place for it, looped the pendant around his neck and made for his room. He stripped off his borrowed clothes and damp underwear, and gratefully immersed himself in the luxury of a hot shower. Strangely reluctant to remove the pendant, he left it around his neck. A few minutes later he emerged from the steaming bathroom, feeling more himself again. He had hardly slept since the news of Aidan's death reached him — and he longed to plunge himself into the sleep of exhaustion.

Dressed once more, Liam lifted the jewelled lid from the box. The precious metals and jewels in the cover alone would be worth a fortune. To think it had been preserved by his family for almost thirteen centuries! He was scared to touch it, but even so . . . could not resist taking the precious book from its sheet-silver reliquary so that he could hold it in his hands. As he lifted it out, something caught Liam's eye. Concealed by the book, in a niche at the bottom of the box, lay an antique bronze key, shaped like the letter F, but with a complex set of smaller branching arms on the main limbs. On the shaft of the key, a miniature interlace was set into metal, worked cunningly in silver and gold. As though it were as natural as breathing, Liam concentrated on the interlace, his fatigued mind slowly but surely building the pattern. As he did so, he felt a gentle swelling of energy from the pendant and gasped in surprise. At his sharp intake of breath, the subtle energies raced through him and into the pattern. A brief light flashed before his eyes, and Liam had a clear vision of Aidan's trophy cupboard. Of course! The only place in the whole house that was always secured. *The key had shown him the lock.*

The hairs on Liam's arms stood on end. In a moment of clarity he understood that his visions were somehow part of his heritage — a gift of the Keeper — and *not* his only gift. He could manipulate energies he barely understood. This was not fantasy. It was real.

He gathered the Book of Elements and the key and walked through the darkened house toward Aidan's bedroom and its small adjoining living area. Liam paused on the threshold and turned on the lights, regarding the trophy cupboard with awe. It was a tall display cabinet, set into the wall, and fronted with glass. It was filled with intriguing artefacts that Aidan had collected over the years. His uncle had an outrageous story to tell about each one, stories that Liam had listened to with fascination as a child, and which he had later set aside with the Easter Bunny and Father Christmas. So much of his childhood was symbolised by these few treasures, and so many of his fondest memories were of this cosy room — the thick carpets by the fire, the old-fashioned lounge setting, and the endless bookshelves filled with mysterious books. He would gaze for hours at those thick-bound volumes, and at the impossibly mysterious treasures in the trophy cupboard, dreaming of the day he would hold them in his hands. He could not count the times he fantasised about breaking the glass and fleeing with his prizes before Aidan discovered him.

He looked at each of these artefacts now, both as an adult, and as a child. There was an old Zippo lighter from World War Two, lovingly polished and set on a little raised platform of creamy parachute silk; a set of antique binoculars from the Great War; a long and lethal looking bayonet, highly polished and set beside its black metal sheath; a silver fob-watch, its hands set forever at seven minutes past eleven; a swag of polished war medals, and a German Luger pistol. Out of place amid the modern memorabilia was a polished hunting horn set with silver chasings and a thick leather strap. Once, Aidan had Liam convinced he had fought in the Boer War, the Great War, and World War Two — collecting each of the items himself — which would have made him at least one hundred and twenty years old. He had also claimed that the hunting horn was none other than that of the Forest Lord Cernunnos, and would bring luck to those who sounded it in good faith within the forest.

Liam slipped the key into the long slit of the keyhole. The odd shape fitted perfectly. He turned it. There was a loud *click*. His heart hammered.

He stepped back and opened the door to the display case. It swung smoothly away from the wall, and as it opened, the neat shelving behind it swung backwards, revealing a steeply sloping stone stairwell lit by a row of florescent lights, which were now blinking to life. Clutching the heavy jewelled box to his chest, Liam descended into the cool depths below the house. Behind him, the display swung closed, sealing him in. *Sensors.* The stairwell was carved from the dark basalt of the ridge, and descended more than three storeys into a natural cavern. The cave was small, and roughly elliptical, but open at the far end, where the cave continued, but narrowed rapidly. The cavern was furnished as a chapel. The walls carefully dressed to smooth dark stone. An old wooden crucifix was set high on one of the walls. It was intricately carved, and shaped in the Celtic fashion, with a sun-wheel centred on the cross. Wooden seats and an altar were placed in a regular arrangement, with low tables around the walls set with fat beeswax candles.

Liam placed the heavy jewelled box on one of the tables against the wall and lit a single candle before kneeling at one of the pews. The pendant swung out from around his neck and clattered against the wood. He prayed out of respect for the chapel, and in memory of Aidan. His mind filled with questions. Why would Aidan have hidden this place from him? Liam had been brought up Catholic, and had attended mass with Aidan many times. His uncle would have no cause to feel shame about his faith.

He was too tired to think.

As he prayed, his mind subtly shifted. He had the strange illusion that he knelt in a fast flowing river. He could hear it rushing around him, cool and potent. He put the image down to exhaustion, and struggled to clear his mind, but his body betrayed him. Before he knew it, he was lying on the thick carpet that covered the chapel floor. Unknown energy swept around him, ebbing, flowing, swirling. A circling storm of life. Liam reached out, through the eye of that whirling maelstrom, and found himself suspended between worlds. He could see a doorway, sealed with a heavy bar. There was a knocking at that door. Insistent. Growing louder.

Open the door, Liam. He jerked at the sound of Aidan's voice in his mind.

At one with the swirling energies, Liam reached forward with the arms of his spirit and cast aside the locking bar. Then he flung those ancient doors wide open.

And his mind plunged headlong into an alien world.

Liam was in a dense forest.

A quarter moon showed through a high canopy of palm fronds, its light hardly penetrating the thick growth. The darkness was alive with alien sounds. Screeches and rattles in the treetops. Sibilant calls from the undergrowth. The bushes rustled to his left. A dark blur of fur and legs sped across his path. Below his feet, Liam could see the slimy texture of rotting vegetation, but he could feel nothing. His feet passed above the ground on a cushion of air.

"Where am I?"

Further into the undergrowth, a regular croaking started. A bird? A frog? He could not tell. Liam walked deeper into the forest. He had done plenty of bushwalking in the native sub-tropical forests and drier lowland scrub of Queensland and was amazed at his trouble-free progress. He never once snagged his clothing, tripped or slid on the wet clay, despite the darkness. Liam reached out to touch the ragged trunk of a tree fern. He missed, his hand disappearing into the dark mass of fern fronds adjacent. His head swam. He stumbled.

Liam tried again. This time he watched carefully. *My hand is passing right through the trunk.* He could feel a slight resistance, but that was it. His stomach clenched with panic. Then Liam noticed other things. Despite the darkness, he could still see. The trees and undergrowth were outlined by a faint tracery of flowing energy. A soft blue luminescence. Every little corner of the forest stood out, even the fungi, fixed to the trunks like miniature fans. Animals appeared as bright bundles, lit in subtle neon as they scampered and darted through the forest.

On impulse, Liam called out. "Cooooee!"

The night noises grew louder. That scared him most of all. If he had sounded off like that in any *normal* night forest the animals would quieten down, assessing a potential threat. *That means they can't hear me!* Am I dreaming? *Think, goddamn it!*

Liam could vaguely remember returning to his uncle's property. There had been a book, an old book, and a key . . . *Damn!* His memories slipped away like greasy fish.

"How did I come to be here?"

Behind him, Liam could see the opening in the forest where he had first appeared. Standing like a sentinel inside the clearing was an ancient chapel, built from unmortared stone. The plain granite walls shone a ghostly white in the moonlight. Liam remembered emerging from the chapel, confused, and yet drawn by a sense of something . . . He had come a long way. Yes. He had made a journey. He had been called here.

A bright light in the distance caught his eye.

"How the hell am I supposed to see anything stuck in this?" said Liam, sweeping his arm around him at the forest. "I need to get up above the canopy."

Liam looked up and imagined floating high above the forest, suspended like a kite. He immediately shot through the thick canopy. He raced up into the open sky without disturbing so much as a single frond.

"Stop!"

Liam stopped dead.

If he had been scared before, now he was terrified.

He floated above the forest, poised like a skydiver, but utterly motionless. Alien stars spread across the sky in a vast panorama. Sharp and clear.

At the crest of a hill, some distance away, stood a tall circle of rough-hewn stone megaliths, with a huge bonfire inside it. An ocean stretched out from the base of the hill toward the horizon.

Thought became motion. He flashed through the sky.

Within a heartbeat, Liam was above the stone circle. Below him, a ring of dancers circled around a central altar stone, each decked out with feathered masks of stone and wood. They were dressed in loincloths, both men and women bare-chested, their skin painted with swirls of gold, red, blue, and white. Beads of amber shone like jewels in their flaxen hair. The flames of the bonfire erupted into the night, engulfing Liam in an orange-red haze. He emerged startled, but unharmed. When the flames cleared, Liam descended toward the circle to stand beside a blackened altar stone. It was littered with sacrifices of wild grain, roots, and fish. Far below the hilltop, was a bright crescent of white beach. Heavy surf pounded the shore, and glittered with tropical luminescence. A score of streamlined canoes and outrigger craft were drawn up on the sand. A stiff on-shore breeze surged across the hilltop, and Liam could smell the salt in the air, yet not a single strand of his hair tossed in the wind.

Around Liam, the dancers fell to the ground and lay prostrate, their faces pushed into the wet earth. Only one figure remained standing, a well-muscled native who held a feathered rod of wood in his right hand. His mask depicted a wild boar with yellowed, bloody tusks set into the red wood. The shaman stared directly at Liam and spoke something in a language that seemed like a cross between Gaelic and German. Liam did not bother to respond. The whole event had taken on the texture of a dreamscape. Then the man gathered himself and reached out toward him. The presence of the shaman washed across Liam. His dreamy complacency vanished. He could feel the shaman's awe and fear, and instinctively knew that the shaman could feel his own growing alarm. Across the empathic link, the shaman sent his thoughts. "Do you come from the stone-place?" asked the shaman, mind-to-mind.

Liam was shocked to hear the man's voice in his head, and his thoughts tumbled out like a bag of marbles. *Yes, I have come from the small chapel. Is this place real? Where am I?*

The shaman seemed confused. "Do you come from the stone-place in the clearing?" The shaman pointed down the hill and into the darkened valley, unmistakably indicating the stone oratory.

Liam began to gain some control over his thoughts. He looked past the fearsome mask at the grey eyes of the shaman and replied with his mind. "Yes."

The shaman relaxed. "Good. That is good." The shaman bowed to him, then continued in the mind-speech. "Greetings Guardian. I too am of the ancient blood. My name is Iffa, thurjun of the Veniti."

The word thurjun was unfamiliar to Liam, but from the context of the man's thoughts he gathered it was some sort of shaman or magician. Liam focussed his thoughts, and responded. "I am Liam Durrow."

Iffa smiled, revealing a row of perfect white teeth. He bowed again and walked toward the centre of the stone circle. He motioned for Liam to follow. "Come. Another has been waiting to greet you. He has reached back from the Distant and Unknown Dream seeking you. We must guide his path back to this time."

Back to this time?

Liam followed the shaman, walking around the prostrate figures as though he were solid, rather than a ghost-figure. Set slightly off-centre within the larger ring of megaliths was a second circle, constructed of smaller, darker stones. The smaller megaliths were hunched over, like once soaring trees weathered to stumps across an unknowable age.

Iffa raised his arms.

The mass of brightly coloured feathers fell back from the tip of his wooden sceptre, and for the first time Liam noticed the dark green stone set into the top of the decorated staff. It was shaped like a teardrop, and fixed onto the carved wood with dark resin. Across the surface of the stone swept an intricate tracery. *It was the twin of his own pendant!* Energy emanated from the stone, growing into a small white cloud. Iffa drew the energy into himself then wove it into a complex matrix that quivered with power. The woven form shuddered and sought to fly free. It was held there by the force of Iffa's will. With a hiss, Iffa pointed his sceptre toward the centre of the smaller circle. The matrix shot forward and expanded to fill the space within the circle. It rotated rapidly. The whirling maelstrom cycled through the spectrum, sending slivers of coloured light shooting off like streamers. It hummed like a powerful engine. The earth beneath his feet trembled and stirred. The fearful cries of the Veniti filled the night as the power of the spell grew. As the tempo increased, the swirling shape faded, replaced by a pillar of white light. A tongue of fire the height of a man emerged from the pillar and came toward Liam. As it detached itself from the blinding whiteness, he could make out a face within it, the head shaved in an archaic tonsure, a crescent across the front the head. A bluff face with a kindly smile, and yet with eyes that burned with knowledge like twin fires. Liam was suddenly afraid. He looked around for Iffa, but the shaman had fallen to his knees.

The being of light drew closer. Inside the flame, fainter faces and dimly seen figures flitted around the first man's face. Visions, glimpsed only for a moment.

"I walked the halls of time for an age to seek you here," spoke the shining figure. "Are you from the realm beyond Stonelake? Kgari?"

Liam paused, unsure where or what Stonelake, or Kgari, were.

"I came here through the oratory. A small stone chapel," replied Liam.

The man reached out and touched Liam. Where the hand wrapped around his arm, a flood of warmth entered him. It felt like joy. His fears dissolved.

"Show me."

Liam thought of the small oratory. Instantly, they were inside it. The light from the nimbus that surrounded the man lit the interior with gold and orange. Liam heard the energies of the place roaring like a distant wind.

"Show me the realm beyond," said the man.

Liam grew cautious. "Who are you?"

The man smiled. "I was once — long ago — a High Priest called Korbeth."

Chapter 19
Veniti World

Liam searched the bright face of the flaming spirit. The being that called himself Korbeth.

"Now I am one with the spirit of my Temple. In your time I am still flesh and blood, and ignorant of my own fate," said Korbeth.

"How did you find me?" asked Liam.

"I found your uncle Aidan in the Island of Peace. Through him I sought you. To urge you to open a Gateway into this realm."

Then Liam remembered Aidan's voice in his mind, urging him to open the door, and he knew it was true.

Liam reached out with his mind. He and the once-Priest Korbeth appeared in the stone cavern below Aidan's house — hovering above Liam's prone body.

"Yes, I can feel it! This is Kgari!" said Korbeth. "Come, Liam. I have things to show you, and time is short."

Liam yelped in surprise as they sped up through the solid rock of the Downs and into Earth's night sky. The stars fled past in a blur, then resolved as the motion ceased.

Korbeth closed his eyes and reached out with his mind.

"I can feel them," he thought to Liam. "Yes. I know how they came." Then they were racing again. This time when they slowed they were hovering over a suburban landscape dotted with run-down industrial buildings and tattered residences.

"This is the place where the Vaults of Sheol found the path to your world," said Korbeth. "This is your past."

They descended. As they neared the ground, Liam heard the sounds of a party. They passed through an old iron roof and into a darkened living room. As they drew closer, Liam could see it was mostly a crowd of young women, dressed in black, and loaded with rings, arcane bracelets and pendants.

"Look for the centre."

Liam did as Korbeth suggested. Parts of the vision were ghostly, while others were more solid. Then he found it. *The focus.* Three women, like dark suns, orbited by the others. As the night flashed by, the crowd dwindled, leaving a handful of young women lounging in the smoke-filled room. The three women began to chant, instinctively drawing upon the energies of the earth, the Ouija board at their feet now ignored. At first they were buoyed by a feeling of exhilaration as they were filled with power — unaware of the ancient, spiritual nature of the place upon which the house had been built — but the energy they had summoned was quickly captured by another: an unseen mind watching from another world. Abruptly they fell back onto the floor in a swoon. They began to writhe, their hands playing over their bodies in desperation as they were filled with arousal.

Distracted, their minds were open.

The onlookers were transfixed by the lewd display. Some grew aroused, others merely fascinated. They had not yet tasted fear. As the convulsions grew more frantic, the watchers roused themselves from their drug-induced lethargy and tried to bring the women out of their shared trance. The three women were soon writhing not in ecstasy . . . but in agony. When the white foam from their mouths began to tinge with blood, the onlookers panicked. The thick smoke of the living room was now heavy with fear. A white, sickly-pale energy.

The three women twisted in pain.

Two of them exploded outward in a showering of blood, like burst containers.

As if in a dream, the remaining woman opened her eyes and rose to her feet. Liam watched, horrified, as she drew the life-energies of the dead women into herself. A dark voice now whispered to her, giving her the knowledge to create the interlace that would open a Gateway. The energies were bloody red, and were woven true.

"The woman has the blood of the ancients," sent Korbeth sadly.

The ground under the house shuddered, then collapsed. The screams of the women were lost in the thunder of cascading earth as a vast natural cavern opened beneath them. Within that cavern, the ruddy glow of the death-energies was the only light. Those energies wove around the space. They spun faster and faster around the standing form of the woman, then transformed to a quivering, liquid mirror of quicksilver. She cast her mind into the Vault. She was answered.

And the Gateway was opened.

An acrid stench issued from the circle of light. Stale, fetid air, laden with grit and soot, filled the cavern. A skeletally thin man, dressed in Roman costume, stepped from the Gateway. He was flanked by enormously muscled warriors with dark, leather-like skin, bald heads, and pointed teeth. At a wave from the man, the warriors ran past the Gate-opener and fell upon the dazed women that had survived the collapse with their falcatas, hacking them down.

"Siithe," said Korbeth, in disgust. "Led by the Archfiend himself. Procarrus."

Liam could not tear his eyes away. "We have to stop them!"

Korbeth took Liam's arm, holding him in place. "It has already happened. You must open the Gateway to Stonelake. That is your task."

Liam began to protest, but Korbeth motioned him to silence.

"Come, Liam. I will show you what you can do to help us defeat them."

Liam turned from the carnage and they rose up into the night sky once more, leaving the memories of nightmare behind them.

Korbeth grew still. Focused.

Then the once-Priest laughed with pleasure. His fire-bright eyes fixed on Liam. "I have found it. *Come!*"

They sped north, across land and sea, and time — the sun and moon racing each other through the sky — until at last they hovered above a darkened lake, surrounded by thick stands of eucalyptus trees and wallum heath, native flowering shrubland. Cresting the hills above the lake was a full moon. Korbeth pointed this out to Liam. "The full moon will mark the time. It is here, Liam. Here you will open the Gateway for Finn."

"But where is this?"

Korbeth released Liam's arm.

The flame that surrounded Korbeth flared brighter, then vanished.

Korbeth was gone.

How am I to open the Gateway?

A wind began to gather. It grew in strength, forcing him back
to his body. He heard Korbeth's voice, at the very limit of his
hearing. *"There is an ancient ally here to aid you. My task is done. Now
I can rest, and the Spirit of the Temple can return . . . goodbye, Liam."*

Liam woke, gasping for breath.

The single candle he had lit in the chapel had burnt low. He
had a pounding headache. An unnatural drowsiness washed
over him, threatening to drag him back into sleep. He struggled
to his feet and looked for something to fix him to reality. He
shivered as he remembered the vision of the dark-skinned
warriors and their red-stained blades. The fallen bodies of the
women. A knot of fear tightened in his belly. He would have liked
to believe it was all a dream. That he could push it aside and go
on with his life. He knew it was not.

The call had come.

Chapter 20

At sea, off the east coast of Queensland – Earth
26th December 1999

Yolinda was aware of nothing but the drone of the cruiser's engines. The vibration sawed through the cold floor and into her skull. The sound was all her slippery consciousness could grip, and she returned to it again and again through the long darkness, groping for it each time she emerged from the sticky depths of her mind.

Silence.

She lay for a long while, hovering on the borders of a dream. Then, when she finally moved, a pain ripped through her right temple. Rank, slaughterhouse images, flooded her mind. Memories of her capture and the strange court beneath the factory floor. Snatches of conversation surfaced like scum; talk of Procarrus, Sephany... VoYannan. There had been screams, sharp and terrifying, cut off abruptly by the blades of the siithe. A stinging pain as her captors had forced another needle into her arm, filling her with numbing poison. More darkness. Then they were herded into the back of a van, penned in like cattle. She could remember one woman sobbing in the darkness. A hopeless, forlorn sound.

There had also been dreams. An endless dreamscape of terror as the Archfiend pursued her in the guise of her stepfather, Nick. Yolinda had run, her eight-year-old dream-legs pumping in fear. Once he almost had her, but she had kicked out and fled, leaving him with the rag-doll. His fury had been monumental. Once, she had roused from a dream to hear her captors talking in the rough tongue of the Vault. Still linked to the Archfiend's mind, she had somehow understood the words.

"Shall we throw her to the feast, Lord?" asked Ossis, the siithe captain.

"No. Keep her apart, and leave her within the span of the dark lotus. She is not what she seems." Procarrus had sighed with frustration. "I know she is close to breaking – then her mind and soul will be mine."

Time had passed after that, leaving only a vapour trail of darkened images as the remnants of Procarrus' court were ushered out of the vans and into the pitch-black bowels of a huge ocean cruiser. She caught a fleeting glimpse of grubby dockland before its dark hull swallowed them. Then days in the packed company of slaves. The stench of the siithe and the constant sound of the engines.

Yolinda slowed her breathing and cracked her eyes open. She lay on her side, knees drawn up. A shaft of light stabbed through a porthole and into the dank atmosphere with all the blinding strength of summer. A wave of nausea hit her as she scanned the hull around her body. It was littered with filth and gore, and alive with maggots. Flies buzzed through the stench. How many days had she lain like this? Inside the crotch of her baggy jeans, inside her panties, the cold metal of the 0.38 stung her skin. *So, no rape then.* Not yet, anyway.

She felt the Archfiend's absence as though a blade had been withdrawn from her skull. The relief was indescribable. Without knowing *how* she knew, she was certain he was no longer on the boat. Methodically she began to scan the room. Two siithe guards stood by a narrow circular stairway, while a third squatted close by, rummaging in the human debris.

Five women lay on the floor like Yolinda, lost in drug-induced stupor. One was sitting against a bulkhead with a cigarette butt in her hand, her clothes in shreds. Her eyes were vacant, and the cigarette in her hand had burnt away unnoticed. She could see no trace of Vicki.

The siithe closest to Yolinda gave up on his search and moved over to her, drawing a large, thick-bladed skinning knife from his belt.

One of the siithe by the door spoke in the language of the Vault. "Leave that one. The Archfiend wants her for himself." The meaning of the words echoed strangely in her mind.

The siithe turned back to the others at the doorway. "He wants her soul, not her body. She will be good for pleasure."

"If you damage her, Ossis will skin you, fool."

The siithe ignored them. He turned Yolinda onto her back and sliced open her shirt. Panic threatened to engulf her. Slowly, deliberately, Yolinda opened her eyes wider.

The siithe immediately moved his blade to her throat.

Forcing a smile, Yolinda reached down and began to undo her jeans, button by button. The siithe grunted. Sheathing his knife he reached down to open the crotch of his leather armour. His penis flipped out — huge and twisted — covered with rough skin and tufts of coarse hair. Bile rose in Yolinda's throat, leaving the taste of acid. In anticipation, the siithe lowered himself to his knees, his rank, hot breath gushing over her face. Yolinda kicked off her runners and began to slip off her jeans. She reached inside and gripped the pistol. The siithe's mouth hung open like a gaping cavern. The sharpened teeth stained black and yellow.

Yolinda had seen how fast these siithe were. Surprise was the key. Inch by agonising inch, she brought up the gun, keeping her hand below his line of sight. The siithe's body blocked the view of the two warriors at the stairwell. Yolinda kicked off her jeans. As he moved to position himself between her legs, she pushed the gun into his mouth and pulled the trigger. One motion. A moment of rage darkened his face before the back of his head exploded outward in a spray of blood, shattered bone and brain. Her hand hummed with the recoil.

The other two siithe surged into motion.

Yolinda rolled onto her knees. Fear squeezed her heart in a vice. Jay had shot one of these bastards point-blank in the chest, and it had no effect. But as she had just discovered, they could be killed, provided they were hit in the right place. She had no idea where they were vulnerable in the body, so it would have to be the head. It seemed their skulls were thick, like a natural helmet. She had been able to kill her rapist by shooting up through his mouth, below the brow ridge. Yolinda sighted the closest warrior along her barrel and shot him in the left eye. The siithe catapulted backwards. The second was already on her, raising his weapon. Yolinda threw herself to the left. His huge cleaver-like weapon thudded into the deck where she had been seconds before. She rolled to her feet and ran at the siithe, trying to knock him off balance. It was like hitting a brick wall. The collision stopped her dead. He stumbled. That gave her enough time to jam the revolver's stubby barrel into his ear and pull the trigger. *Point-*

blank. Her bullet ripped into his skull, but did not exit. The warrior staggered sideways, turned to face her, then dropped to his knees. He stared at her, eyes blank, then fell forward to the deck. Dead.

Shouts sounded from the deck above. Her ears rang from the shots. She had done it. She had killed all three of them. Now she had to escape.

Surrounding the bodies, the human slaves of the Archfiend were motionless. Yolinda ran to the porthole, opening the small round window. Squinting against the glare, she saw an island shoreline tangled with mangroves, with yachts and other cruisers at anchor in a sheltered bay. There was no way she could squeeze through that porthole — even a child would find it hard. Desperately she looked around for somewhere to hide. She could hear booted feet on the metal rungs of the curving stairs and knew she had only moments. There was a cupboard built into the void behind the stairwell. Beside the window was a low stool with a collection of whisky bottles and an ashtray filled with cigarette butts. Blood was everywhere.

Yolinda started to shake. Gritting her teeth, she pushed aside a tide of panic and forced herself to think. She swept everything off the stool and tossed it all through the porthole, just as the booted feet of the siithe guards became visible on the spiral staircase. The bottles and ashtray hit the water with a loud splash. She heard one of the guards growl with anger and increase his pace. Yolinda grabbed the stool and positioned it below the porthole, as though it had been used as a step. If she could not escape through the narrow opening, she would have to make them *think* she had. Yolinda fled into the shadows behind the stairs and slipped inside the small cupboard there, squeezing in beside musty life vests and folded tarps of oily canvas. She pulled the access door shut, but left a tiny crack open. Through that tiny sliver of vision, she watched as guards swarmed into the room. *One . . . two. Shit. Five.* Yolinda's heart sank. So far she had been lucky. But against five siithe? Only three bullets remained in the revolver. Yolinda started shaking again. A fever of withdrawal and shock swept through her. This time she could not make it stop. She watched in terror as the siithe examined the corpses and the porthole, methodically searching the room. The drug mist receded, and the impact of everything registered fully in her mind.

Yolinda listened, but the speech of the guards had become a mix of known and unknown words. All foreign. *Strange.* When she woke, hadn't she been able to understand them? She knew her memories were no dream. Nausea rose as images of slaughter came flooding back. She tried to swallow it down, but could not. She dry-retched into the life jackets and tarpaulins, shaking and crying. The gun slipped from her fingers and clattered against the hull. Yolinda looked up through the crack and whimpered in fear. For a moment she was so weak she could not move. One of the siithe had heard the noise and was making for the cupboard. She could see every scar and ugly line on that cruel, blunt face. Desperately, she groped in the dark, searching for the gun.

When the siithe was only paces from the cupboard, the other four Vault warriors began a violent argument, shouting in their harsh, guttural tongue. The warrior swiftly turned and strode back into the room, growling and raising his falcata. Opening the door a fraction wider, Yolinda fought another wave of nausea as she saw what they were doing. They were arguing over the bodies of the siithe, efficiently stripping them of their armour and butchering them, squabbling over choice cuts, and eagerly cramming the raw flesh into their mouths. Yolinda was shocked to see that one of the siithe she killed had been a female. From their looks, they were impossible to tell apart.

Yolinda squeezed her eyes shut. Don't think about what you just saw. *Don't think about it!* She finally found the gun. She clutched it to her chest. Then she settled down to wait, ignoring the horrid grunts of animal satisfaction and loud-mouthed chewing from the siithe. *What the hell were they?*

Hours later, the siithe finally left the cabin. Yolinda crept out of the cupboard, fighting cramping muscles at every movement. She checked the prone women for signs of life. The five sprawled on the floor were alive, but comatose. She could not rouse them. The woman who had sat herself up against the bulkhead had no pulse. Yolinda closed the dead woman's eyes, plucked the cold cigarette from her fingers, and arranged her torn clothing to cover her better. It was a shitty way to die. Someone was going to pay for this. *First escape. Then get backup.*

She hunted among the grisly remains of the butchered siithe for her bloodstained jeans and shoes. Shuddering with revulsion, she slipped them on. The blood had partially dried, making the denim as stiff as cardboard. Once more, she pushed the stubby 0.38 down into the crotch. She saw a glint of steel. Pushing aside the piled-up debris, she found the siithe's sheathed knife. She carefully slid the sheath between her belt and the waistband of her jeans, at her back. A quick search of the cabin revealed a pile of discarded clothing in the corner, from which she selected a snug dark purple T-shirt to replace her ruined blouse. Yolinda tried not to think of the previous owner, who had probably died to feed the siithe's appetites.

Yolinda wanted to get out of the cabin before they returned. Wanted to run. She almost did, then her training kicked in, forcing her to stop and assess. To strategize. As brutal and inhuman as the siithe were, they were no more than muscle. Procarrus was the kingpin. This was still a Task Force operation aimed at taking down his drug import network. She had gone well past reasonable suspicion — she had been witness to murder — but her superiors would need tangible evidence to justify mobilising a major operation in the field. Their objective was always to catch the perps in the act of drug importation, that was the prize, but there was other evidence she could gather. Right here in plain sight. She snatched up a packet of heroin and a bag of marijuana and pushed them deep into the pockets of her jeans. Each was sealed in an airtight snap-lock bag and wrapped tightly in plastic. The chemical signature of the heroin would tell the Federal techs a lot about its source.

Time to get out of here.

Chapter 21
Off the east coast of Queensland — Earth

Yolinda crept up the circular stairs, each foot placed with care on the fan-shaped metal treads. She paused just before the main cabin and listened. She heard only a faint snoring. Teeth grinding together, stomach roiling, she took the next step, bringing her eyes above floor level.

The main cabin was well above the water line, with doors opening to the gangway on either side of the boat. She saw the five siithe guards. *Asleep*. That explained the snoring. Procarrus — the crazy nutter who called himself *the Archfiend* — was not there. Most of the siithe muscle-men were also missing. Hardly daring to breathe, she continued up the narrow curving stairs to the steering deck. It was deserted. She had a panoramic view of a sandy beach and a forested mainland. There were a series of low-set buildings to her left, set back into the scrub. Perhaps upmarket resort accommodation. Further down the beach she saw a shop and cafe, surrounded with people. There was a short jetty, beyond which the shoreline was thick with mangroves right down to the waterline. That was what she had seen before, through the porthole. The boat was anchored maybe three hundred metres offshore. Eight other boats were moored nearby. Six sailing boats and two powered craft. None of them was a large as the Archfiend's black multi-deck cruiser.

She searched through the draws and cupboards on the steering deck, seeking more evidence, but found only maps. Most were standard marine navigational charts of Australia's east coast, although there was one of Fiji, and another of Noumea. Then something caught her eye. Wedged into a gap behind the wheel, was another map, stained and roughly folded, as though casually pushed there by someone who had been piloting the boat. She grabbed it and spread it out on the console. It was a detailed map of Fraser Island, a large sand island off Australia's east coast. A route had been marked across the island's interior in waxy red lines. She carefully folded the map and slipped it into her back pocket.

Yolinda studied the shoreline. Her first plan had been to get off the ship as soon as possible. She could do that, and lose herself in the crowd, but how fast could she find a phone? She still had no idea where she was. She had no money. No ID. Then she saw the ship's radio set. Yolinda switched the radio to an emergency channel and tried to transmit a distress signal, whispering into the handset.

No response.

The needles on the radio deck display, which showed the incoming signal strength, were moving, but there was no sound. Was the speaker turned off? She searched the deck. The damn thing *was* turned off. She flipped the switch. Voices blared out. There were scores of people on the air, all Aussies by the sound of them. *Christ!* She scrambled to turn down the sound. Too late.

"So? What do we have here, eh?" said someone behind her.

Yolinda spun around. He was big and ugly, and she recognised him instantly. Indian Joe — that's what they'd nicknamed him in prison. His chest was bare, showing a web of tattoos. He was one of the recent escapees.

"The black guys said one of you tarts had got away, but not quite, hey?"

There was no way she could reach the gun in time. She slipped her hand behind her back. Curled it around the hilt of the knife.

Indian Joe looked at her through bleary, bloodshot eyes. His lust and cruelty were transparent.

Anger flared in Yolinda. She was sick of being pushed around. If she could face the siithe, she could face anything. Noticing the narrow stairwell, a plan formed.

Yolinda pulled out the knife.

He laughed. "What do you think you are going to do with that? What do you think you *could* do, sweetheart?"

She came at him. Feinted with a stab. As she expected, he tried to grab her knife-arm, but she was quicker. She whipped her hand away from his grasp and slashed out with the razored edge, opening a savage cut on his forearm.

"AHHH! You *bitch!*"

Yolinda pressed him. She flashed the blade in front of his face. He backed up, toward the stairway. He growled and bunched himself to charge. She feinted forward again. This time he backed away immediately. His right foot slipped on the top of the hatch, and with a yelp of surprise, he tumbled straight down.

Voices.

Siithe and men.

Yolinda ran to the steering deck's port-side door. She yanked at the handle. It did not budge. "God no!" She sprinted to the starboard door. *Locked.* She looked between the tiny porthole in the starboard door and the wide glass panels of the steering deck. Yolinda dropped the knife and scrambled up on the console. She tugged out the revolver and slammed the butt into the glass. It splintered. She struck again. Then again. The whole pane shattered into pebbles of safety glass.

The head of a siithe warrior appeared on the stairs.

Yolinda ducked out through the shattered window and stood up on the narrow sill. The main deck of the cruiser was three storeys down, and below that, the glimmering surface of the ocean. There was an animal growl behind her. The sound fuelled her muscles on a primeval level.

She jumped.

Pain flared in her left thigh. Glass flew up from the broken sill as a siithe falcata thudded into the console. One fraction of a second later and it would have taken her leg off.

Yolinda hit the water with a stunning impact. It squeezed the air from her lungs. Water was all around her. The pain in her thigh was intense, but she struggled away from the boat, keeping under water for as long as she could. The heavy fabric of her jeans weighed her down. She pushed on. She was *not* returning to that hell. Her lungs burned, but images of the carnage she had left behind fuelled her determination. Swimming with the revolver clutched in her right hand was awkward, but there was no way in hell she was letting it go. Eventually she saw a sandy bottom. She found her footing and thrust her head up above the surface, gasping for air. Yolinda splashed through the shallows to the beach, her legs like rubber, her skin chaffed from the wet denim.

Yolinda looked behind her. A man had followed her into the water from the Archfiend's cruiser, and was striking out for the shore in pursuit. She ran for it. She sprinted along the hard sand toward the shops and the milling crowd until she was close enough to read the sign.

KOOKABURRA BAY RESORT. FRASER ISLAND.

A painful cramp in her right calf forced her to shift into an awkward shuffling limp. She glanced behind her. The man had cleared the water and was closing fast. *Roberts.* Another escapee and model citizen. Big and mean.
Give me a break!
Yolinda was less than twenty metres from the crowded café. Christmas decorations glittered in the window. She looked between Roberts and the shops ahead. She would reached them before Roberts closed on her. The 0.38 was still gripped in her right fist. She was certain it would fire without a problem — any water would be long gone from the short barrel — but there were innocent bystanders close by. Roberts did not look armed. She shoved the gun into her rear waistband and dropped the T-shirt over it. Then she was there. In the crowd.

Yolinda stopped, gasping for breath. Her jeans were soaking wet. She took the drug packets out of her pockets and checked for water damage. They had both survived the swim. Her T-shirt was drying rapidly, so she stuffed them under it and tucked it in at front to keep them in position. She did not want to risk any further damage to the evidence.

Fraser Island must be the location of the drug drop. Why else would Procarrus bother to drag his crazy bunch of killers all the way up here from Sydney? Maybe the drugs were coming in on another boat. That would make sense. She knew Fraser Island had no permanent police presence. Right now she was on her own. Desperately, Yolinda cast around for anyone who could help her. Two young men were climbing out of an old Subaru four-wheel drive. The driver was tall and athletic and was looking down at the door as he locked the car. His friend was lanky to the point of skinny, and watched her with a friendly smile as he lit up a cigarette. He was leaning against the car, dressed in a Hawaiian shirt, cream coloured slacks, and sandshoes.

Yolinda approached the cigarette smoker. He looked pale in the sunshine.

She could tell them she was a Federal Agent, but that might work against her. Most people were inclined to back off when they found out. Besides, how could she prove it without ID? She took a deep breath. They may not help Federal Agent Yolinda Paris, but maybe they would help Yolinda the junkie. It seemed she would have to keep her cover, for now.

"Hi," ventured Yolinda.

"Hi," returned the man, with a bright smile. "I'm, Shane."

"Yolinda."

Shane grabbed a pack of cigarettes from his pocket, flipped open the lip and tapped the bottom of the box with his finger. A single cigarette popped half way out of the box. He had done it all in one motion, with an easy charm. Despite herself, she smiled. His enthusiasm was infectious.

Yolinda shook her head. "No thanks." Her heart was hammering. Time was running out.

"You have to help me," said Yolinda. She looked behind her to check on Roberts.

Shane drew on his cigarette and watched Yolinda carefully for a few seconds, saying nothing. His eyes dropped to her arm. Yolinda self-consciously covered the needle marks with her other hand. She looked up to see his attention had moved on to her wet jeans and T-shirt as he assessed her figure.

Yolinda tensed.

"What's happening?" asked Shane.

Yolinda turned and pointed. "That guy has been following me. He . . . tried to attack me before." There was no way she could tell them the truth. Besides, even now she wasn't sure what had been real, and what had been drug-induced hallucination.

Shane took a slow drag on his cigarette. "Really? Why?"

Yolinda shook her head.

Roberts was closing on her. She needed help. *Now.*

Shane watched the guy for a few seconds, then turned to Liam. "Hey, Liam. This guy coming up the road attacked her," said Shane, nodding toward Yolinda. As he watched Liam, Shane's eyes took on a predatory gleam, although he continued to smile.

"Her name is Yolinda."

Liam moved around from the other side of the car. "Yolinda?" he asked her.

She nodded, struck by Liam's deep blue eyes. She immediately sensed a depth to him, a gravity that was odd in someone his age. Even so, beside Shane, he seemed very young.

Liam put his keys in his pocket and pointed at Roberts, who was rapidly approaching. "This guy?"

Yolinda nodded. She was sorry she had involved them. Roberts was tough and experienced thug. She remembered from his dossier that he had beaten men to death with his bare hands. He was a serious threat. Roberts slowed as he approached Shane and Liam.

Whatever happened, she was *not* going back to that boat. Yolinda's hand moved to the small of her back, where the stubby revolver was tucked into her waistband. She stopped. She had to stay undercover, at least until she could make contact with the Federal Police. Drawing the gun would raise way too many questions. If she lost Procarrus now, Jay's death would mean nothing. She had to nail that sonofabitch.

Her moment of indecision cost her.

Roberts darted forward. Before she could even flinch, he grabbed her right arm. *Damn it.* His grip was like a steel vice. The bones of her wrist ground together painfully.

"Come on luv'," said Roberts, dragging her with him easily.

She panicked, instinctively arching her back to resist. The movement tugged the end of her T-shirt from her front waistband. Two packets flopped onto the bitumen. One white. One green.

She heard Shane's surprised voice behind her. "Hey, Liam. That's dope!"

Calming herself, she stepped forward and stiffened her arm, sweeping it in a tight circle to dislodge Roberts' grip. She kicked him in the shin and danced away.

Roberts let out a yelp. "*You cunt!*"

Shane blew out a cloud of cigarette smoke. "Do you actually know this guy?"

Yolinda shook her head. "No. I don't!"

Roberts smiled, and tried to laugh, but the sound came out like a sick croak. "Sure she does. It's just a game. Newlyweds, you know." He lunged forward to grab her again, but she sidestepped, sending a quick jab at his left eye with the stiffened fingers of her right hand. He dodged the strike. His eyes glittered with malice.

Shane motioned to Liam with his chin and they both stepped in front of Yolinda, blocking Roberts.

"Hey! Back off!" yelled Shane.

Roberts bridled. He had run to fat in prison, but was still muscled like an A-grade footballer. "She's coming with me, mate," he said, meeting Shane's gaze. "You reckon' you could stop me?"

Shane smiled and lifted his hands in the air. "We don't want any trouble. What's the big deal?" Shane's voice was suddenly conciliatory. He backed away slowly toward Yolinda, leaving Liam in front.

Liam looked across at Shane in disbelief. "What are you doing?"

Shane was leaving Liam to fight alone. Yolinda stepped forward to help, but Shane stopped her with a touch on her arm.

"Liam's a martial arts expert," he said, a gleam of mischief in his eyes. "I'm sure he can handle it."

Liam went pale, but he gritted his teeth and stepped toward Roberts.

Chapter 22
Fraser Island, Queensland, Australia — Earth

Yolinda's eyes flicked anxiously between Roberts and Liam as the two men closed on each other. Roberts looked like he was *twice* Liam's weight. The escaped prisoner was also vicious, and street-smart.

"That's far enough," said Liam, his voice low and menacing. He radiated strength and determination. Yolinda looked at Liam in surprise, reevaluating him.

Shane's eyes flicked between the two packets of drugs and Liam, smiling as though it was all a game. What was going on here?

Roberts shuffled closer. He shrugged, forcing a laugh. "Come on mate," said Roberts, as though to a friend.

Yolinda saw it coming, but it caught Liam off guard. Roberts' fake smile twisted into a grimace as he turned the shrug into a quick series of punches that thundered at Liam's face.

Instantly, Liam brought his guard up, deflecting all but the first punch, which left his lip bleeding. Roberts stepped in, but Liam kicked him in the stomach, sending the bulky thug flying back off his feet. The big man landed on his back. He hit bitumen with a heavy thud and cracked his head on the pavement. He lay stunned.

Liam hesitated, unsure whether to attack the fallen man. *No streetfighter then*, thought Yolinda.

Roberts recovered. He growled in rage, scrambled off the ground, and threw himself at the younger man. Liam met the charge with a fast combination of punches. The big man was forced to stop as he ducked the blows. Then Roberts delivered a savage kick to Liam's groin. Liam's hand swept down, blocking the kick with a forearm. Liam winced in pain. Then Liam sidestepped, sending a straight right into Roberts' face, breaking the bridge of his nose. *The kid can punch.* Blood flared on Roberts' face and he staggered back, eyes watering. Liam followed in, his left leg snapping out. Yolinda did not even see the kick connect. Roberts' head snapped back. He tottered back, then thudded onto his arse. The big man sat on the bitumen. There was no quick recovery this time.

By this time the fight had drawn a crowd from the outdoor resort bar nearby, including the two bouncers. Roberts pushed himself to his feet. He took in the two bouncers, then glared at Yolinda and Liam. Swearing, he ran back down the beach toward the cruiser. He would be back soon . . . with reinforcements.

Yolinda came up beside Liam and laid a hand on his shoulder.

"Thank you, Liam. You saved my life."

Liam nodded. He lifted his right arm and made a fist, massaging his forearm. "Man, that guy can kick hard."

Shane walked up to Liam and lit another cigarette.

"Hey, Liam. You alright, buddy?"

Liam gave him a withering stare. "Yeah. Apart from a split lip and damn-near-broken arm. Fine."

Shane scooped up the bags of heroin and marijuana. "Hey! What have we here?"

Yolinda snatched them out of Shane's hands and pushed them into her pants pockets.

"Sorry," said Shane with perfect innocence. "Are you alright, Yolinda?"

Yolinda was angry that Shane had not stuck with Liam, but when he smiled she softened. His concern seemed genuine, and he had tried to help after all. Maybe it had just taken him by surprise.

"Hey, let's all go for a drive and have a joint!" said Shane, his eyes on the bulge in Yolinda's pocket where she had hidden the weed.

Liam shook his head. "I don't believe you, Shane."

Yolinda looked back over her shoulder at the beach. *They would be here soon.*

Out of danger, now was the time to make contact with the Federal Police. She had the two bags of evidence, and she could testify to the bizarre, sickening, things she had witnessed. Yet . . . those events seemed increasingly improbable in the cold light of day. It was not enough. She had to follow Procarrus. Catch him and his people in the act. To do that, she needed transport, and a local guide. Yolinda eyed the two young men speculatively.

Perhaps there was a way . . . She looked into the back of their car and her eyes lit on a camera. Perfect.

"Give me a lift out of here, right now . . . no questions asked . . . and you can have as many joints as you want," said Yolinda, forcing a smile. She winced as she realised that she was offering evidence in return for favours, but she had done worse undercover. The bag of heroin would stay untouched. She would make sure of that.

"Where do you want to go?" asked Liam.

Yolinda took the map from her back pocket and carefully spread it on the bonnet of the car. She had half expected it to be ruined, but the chart had a waterproof coating. It showed only slight water damage along the edges, and in the creases where it had been folded.

"We are here," said Liam, pointing at the island's north-west coast.

There it was. *Kookaburra Bay.* It was a small developed area etched in yellow. Most of the map was the dark green of national parkland. The red lines, drawn in grease pencil, were still there. They showed route a north from Kookaburra Bay. She followed it with her finger to a small lake, set back inside the national park. *Maybe the drugs were not arriving on a boat, but on a plane? Perhaps a hidden airstrip?* Procarrus must be there already with most of his men, waiting for the drop. If she could photograph them actually importing drugs she would really have them. She stabbed at the lake with her finger.

"There. I have to get to that lake."

Liam frowned. "Lake?" He met Yolinda's eyes and studied her with an uncomfortable intensity. She sensed a conflict inside him. Some internal mechanics she could not grasp. Finally, he nodded. "OK. I can take you."

"Of course we can help." Shane's eyes gleamed.

"Thankyou. First I need a change of clothes, and a phone," said Yolinda.

"You can use my mobile," said Liam, taking a cell phone from his pocket and handing it to her.

"Thanks." Yolinda took a deep shuddering breath. A wave of relief swept through her, making her giddy.

"When do we . . . ," said Shane, making a parody of smoking a joint then spreading his arms to fly like an aeroplane. His face split in an idiot grin.

Yolinda started laughing, and could not stop. Escaping those murdering bastards seemed like a miracle. Soon her sides ached, and Shane joined her.

Then images of the last few terrible days came to her, starting with Jay's bleeding corpse and ending with the young woman propped up against the bulkhead, her glazed eyes staring into death. She sobered rapidly. Her training kicked in. *Dehydration. Shock. Lack of food. Probable withdrawal.* Hysteria.

Shane sensed the change. He dropped his cigarette to the pavement and ground it out with his heel. His eyes never left her.

Yolinda felt guilty putting Liam and Shane in danger, but she had no choice. There *was* no one else. After everything she had been through, she was not about lose the trail. She wanted to get those bastards. For Jay.

She turned her back on Shane and flipped open the mobile phone, walking away to give herself some privacy. She keyed in a collect number and waited for the answer. "ID?" prompted the operator. Yolinda gave it. She was put through to her Sydney squad and arranged for them to notify the local police on the mainland and send men over to the resort. There would be a little reception waiting for Procarrus and his men when they returned to Kookaburra Bay.

*

Liam winced as the Suburu hit another bump.

Shane was driving, throwing the car around every twist and turn in the road, trying to impress Yolinda with his rally driving skills. Liam's arm had rapidly stiffened up, and he had asked Shane to drive. A decision he was beginning to regret. He was in the back, Yolinda in the front passenger seat.

Clear golden shafts of afternoon sun slanted into the cabin from the west, lighting their faces. The track went north, and followed the island's western shore. Every now and then he glimpsed blue sea through the scrub. Liam looked across at

Yolinda. The first thing that struck him was that she was older than she looked. He was not sure how he knew — maybe it was her eyes. From the expression on her face he did not have to be a genius to figure out what she thought of Shane's driving. Her skin was pale against her new cream-coloured long-sleeved blouse. Yolinda looked better with her hair tied back in a ponytail, but it did make the dark circles under her bloodshot eyes more prominent. She had binned everything she had been wearing when they met. Yolinda had bought a whole new outfit, right down to new running shoes, giving the store her credit card details from memory. She had lost her purse somewhere — apparently.

"Do you think you could slow down," said Yolinda, clasping her stomach.

Shane gave a high-pitched laugh and flicked the steering wheel, narrowly missing a fallen branch on the road. The car sped faster and Shane laughed again, delighting in his control of the vehicle, and its passengers.

Yolinda's hand flew to her mouth. "*Stop! Stop the car!*"

"Oh, Christ! You're not going to spew are you?" asked Shane.

Shane slammed on the brakes. The car slipped on the soft sand and slewed to a stop. Yolinda fumbled with the door catch and scrambled out of the cabin, racing over the verge and down to the seashore.

Shane grunted in disgust. "Wonder what's got into her?"

Yolinda had left the two packets of drugs on the top of the dashboard to dry. Shane snatched up the marijuana. He ripped open the clear-wrap, broke the seal on the waterproof bag, and inhaled the moist scent with satisfaction.

Shane looked back at Liam with a sly smile.

"You always have to push it," snapped Liam. "Put it back."

Shane shrugged, took some cigarette papers out of his pocket and started making himself a joint. "She said we could have it," he laughed. "We gave her a lift."

Disgusted, Liam flicked open the door and followed Yolinda. He was worried about her. She had looked positively green when she left the car.

"What's the matter, buddy!" called Shane. Marijuana smoke

followed on the breeze as Shane lit up. Then a wave of sound hit him as Shane cranked up the stereo. Liam struggled down the steep path to the sea.

He found Yolinda on her knees at the shoreline. The calm waters of Hervey Bay stretched out from the shore without a ripple. She was past vomiting now. She was dry retching, her stomach knotted in pain. Instinctively, Liam moved up beside her and laid his hand on her back. As often happened when he saw somebody in pain, or sick, he became aware of an energy flow moving from his torso into his hands, tingling like the faintest touch of electricity. He directed the flow into her back and instantly connected with her pain, and the waves of sickness that engulfed her body. She trembled. Sweat broke out on her forehead.

If the touch bothered her, Yolinda was in no state to complain.

The sun was setting over the bay. As the hush of dusk descended, the light changed from gold to soft crimson, lighting up the wallum heath and scribbly gums behind them in elegant shades of red. It was a moment of stillness. The breeze had dropped to nothing, and the bay's surface was as clear as glass, glittering with the last rays of the sun. Then the light was gone. Liam could feel the open forest at his back, and the deep well of the earth's calm beneath him. He regulated his breathing and began to draw on the energies of twilight, becoming part of the shore. One with the trees and the sand. It was as though he completed a circuit, and he and Yolinda were components within it. Energy flowed into Liam, and along its rhythmic pulse travelled Yolinda's pain and nausea. The energy pooled inside the pendant. Liam was startled by a memory. A story Aidan used to tell him. The Druid in the Trees. He recalled a picture from Aidan's storybook. An ancient, grey-bearded man, crouched on the ground beneath an oak tree, listening to the earth with an ear pressed to the ground. He could not recall the story, but what he did remember was how the boughs of the oak twisted and intertwined around themselves. *My God! It's an interlace!*

Liam concentrated, forming the pattern in his mind. The accumulated energy rushed from his pendant and into the form. Transformed, it swept through him and Yolinda.

Liam gasped and opened his eyes. The pain in his arm was gone! He laughed in astonishment. The twilight world around him glowed with life.

Yolinda rose to her feet. She stood in the twilight, watching him carefully. She had more colour in her face now.

"Better?" asked Liam.

"Throwing up must have helped. That and the sea air. Even my leg feels better." Her eyes narrowed. "You seem . . . strange."

He looked at the darkened sky. In the west, no crescent moon appeared above the horizon. Not tonight. This was the last night of the full moon, and it would rise behind him, hidden by the bulk of the island.

The full moon!

The lake.

For weeks he had been driving himself crazy trying to understand his vision. To find some clue that would lead him to the right place. Weeks in which his own doubts had grown. "This is the place!" What had Korbeth told him in the dream? *The full moon will mark the time. It is here, Liam. Here you will open the Gateway for Finn.* "But who is Finn?" wondered Liam aloud as he absently scanned the shore. Shane was calling out from the ridge, but the words were indistinct.

"Are you OK, Liam?" asked Yolinda.

Liam realised how vague he must seem. "Yeah I'm fine. We better go see what all the racket is about," he said, referring to Shane.

Yolinda grabbed his arm. When he saw the hardness in her eyes it stopped him cold. "We need to find that lake."

Goosebumps rose on his skin. Yolinda's features were hard to read in the deepening twilight. He longed to confide in her, to tell her of the visions of the strange, thin man, dressed in Roman costume, and the huge dark-skinned warriors, but he hesitated.

"Who are you, Yolinda?"

Yolinda sighed. "I'm a Federal Agent. Drugs Taskforce."

"And why do you want to get to this lake so badly?"

Yolinda's eyes searched his face. "My partner and I were tracking a drug ring. I think this is where they are bringing in the merchandise. Maybe a hidden airstrip. But I have to catch them in the act. I need to gather evidence. I need your camera."

Disappointment seized Liam, and he was more confused than ever. He had expected strange, otherworldly revelations, not something so tied to his own world.

"OK. I'll help you get to this lake." Liam looked up at the sky. "It will be fully dark well before we get there."

"That's OK. Just get me there. I'll do the rest. Say nothing to Shane." Yolinda pulled a stainless steel revolver from the pocket of her new baggy blue jeans. She flipped it open and checked the load, then slipped it back out of sight. "Let's go."

They clambered up the sandy slope to the car. Shane was lounging on the front seat, door open, well into his third joint. The Doors were blaring from the stereo. When he saw them coming, he groaned and sat up. "About time! Get in."

Shane pushed himself back up into the driver's seat and started to shut the door.

Liam grabbed the door before it closed. "Where do you think you're going?"

"Back to the resort," said Shane.

Liam was in no mood for Shane. He needed to get to this lake, and it was not for a drug bust, whatever Agent Yolinda thought. He pulled the door out of Shane's hands. "Out."

Shane grunted, and slouched around the car into the backseat, still clutching the bag of marijuana. Too stoned to argue.

Now in the driver's seat, Liam turned down the stereo. He switched on the cabin light and studied Yolinda's map while she settled into the front passenger's seat.

"OK." Liam turned the ignition, and the engine flared to life. "The turnoff to the lake is about eight kays north, right off this road."

"What do you mean, lake?" asked Shane. "It's almost night for chrissake. What the hell are we going to do at a lake in the middle of the night? Skinny dip?" Shane's eyes flicked to Yolinda, his eyes lingering on her body.

Yolinda snatched the bag of weed out of Shane's hand. "Just sit back and stay quiet."

"Why?" Shane was suddenly fierce. All pretence at charm was gone. His glittering eyes dissected her in unconcealed analysis.

Yolinda opened her mouth as though to explain, then closed it again. She clenched her jaw. "Just drive, Liam."

Liam accelerated onto the track and off into the night.

"Fuck!" Shane reached for a cigarette. "OK. Let's go to the lake. Should we do some wildlife spotting? How about a frigging nature tour?"

Liam watched Shane in the rear-vision mirror and could tell he was fuming. They travelled on through the dark in silence.

"Turn up the music," barked Shane, exhaling a cloud of cigarette smoke that filled the cabin with the scent of cloves.

Yolinda reached forward and turned it off.

"Christ! The least you can do is leave the music on," whined Shane.

Yolinda turned and gave him a cold look. He groaned and sunk his head into his hands. "Great. This is going to be a barrel of laughs. Nature boy and party girl."

Chapter 23
Fraser Island, Queensland, Australia — Earth

The fresh sea air surged through the car's open windows, carrying the aromatic scent of the forest with it. Liam and Yolinda strained to see the road ahead as the thin headlight beams stabbed forward into the darkness. Later, the moon would light the track, but now it was pitch black. The road wound on, climbing up into the island's interior.

Shane had fallen asleep and was snoring loudly. Liam turned to get a quick glimpse of him. He was sprawled across the back seat, held up only by the seatbelt, his body flopping around with the car's motion. "I can't believe he's sleeping through this."

Yolinda followed Liam's gaze. "The dope was probably laced with narcotics," she said. "Don't worry. He'll be OK. *There!*" Yolinda pointed.

On their right, a road veered off from the main track and ran down into a darkened valley. Large signposts stood on either side of the road.

AREA CLOSED FOR REVEGETATION.

Yolinda flicked on the cabin light and checked the map. "This has to be it." She turned off the light.

The track had been closed off with a tall chain-link fence that stretched to the forest on either side. In the centre was a wide vehicle gate. The galvanised metal gleamed new in the headlights. The gate stood ajar. A heavy padlock lay intact on the sand, still locked into the discarded chain.

"The chain's been cut," said Liam.

They looked at each other.

"Someone has been this way. Recently," said Liam.

"Well what are you waiting for!" she snapped.

"OK. OK." Liam swung the car onto the track and eased through the gate.

"Sorry. The few last days are just beginning to tell," said Yolinda.

Liam looked across at Yolinda. The map shook in her hands. She was at the limit of her endurance. He wanted to ask her what had happened to her, but knew it was not the time.

"How is your leg?" he asked instead.

"Throbbing. And I haven't eaten in days. But I don't care about that. I just want to get these bastards. I . . . want it over."

The track grew rough, and Liam had to slow as they drove around low-lying boughs and fallen logs. From the damage on the track, it was obvious that some heavy vehicles had been this way recently. The small trees that had grown up in the middle of the closed track had been snapped and forced back on themselves, while fallen logs had been pushed out of the way.

After around twenty minutes, punctuated only by a cacophony of night noises, and Shane's snoring, they broke through a thickly overgrown section of the track into a clearing. The road continued on, but outlined clearly in the Subaru's headlights were three big, black, Toyota Landcruisers, all empty.

Liam came to a halt.

"Take the car a bit further in and pull off into the scrub. We need to hide it," said Yolinda. She reached behind the seat and picked up Liam's digital camera from the rear passenger footwell, slipping it into her pocket. Then she drew the revolver.

Liam drove slowly past the clearing, then pulled off the road. The Subaru rocked violently as Liam manoeuvred the four-wheel-drive over a pile of fallen debris. He parked it under a stand of eucalypts.

Shane sat up. "What's happening? Are we back at the resort yet? Christ! Is that real?" Shane had spotted the revolver.

"Shut up!" Yolinda drew a shuddering breath. "Look, just stay quiet, OK?"

As soon as Liam cut the ignition she reached across and took the keys, then she slid out of the car. Liam and Shane piled out behind her. The three of them walked to the middle of the clearing, which had been a parking area for visitors to the lake before the area was closed. Yolinda turned in a circle, trying to get her bearings.

"Damn! Where's the lake?" said Yolinda.

Liam studied the forest. It was thickly overgrown on either

side of the road. If there had been any walking tracks down to the water they would be hard to spot in the dark.

Yolinda grew impatient. "Look. You two stay here. And stay out of sight!"

She disappeared into the forest on the north side of the clearing. Liam looked around, suddenly recognising the landscape from his vision. He walked to the southern verge and could just make out an old track. There was faint light to his left, and he saw the rising moon through the trees.

This was it.

"Liam," said Shane, his voice tense.

Liam looked south. The lake *was* down there. Yolinda had gone the wrong way!

"Liam?" Shane walked over to where Liam was standing. "Liam. What the fuck are we doing out here?"

From the tone of Shane's voice, Liam realised he had come down from the dope.

"Liam! Talk to me buddy? You're not veging out on me are you?"

Anger flared through Liam, but he did not dignify Shane's taunt with a reply. "She's a cop," he said.

"Yolinda?"

Liam nodded.

"Bullshit."

"She is. You saw the gun. This is some drug-bust or something. She said to stay in the car. Just stay in the car."

Shane grunted. "Give me the keys."

"She's got them."

"Shit!"

Liam looked at the full moon, now huge and bright above the eastern hills. Everything was the same as his vision. The night. The moon. The stands of eucalypts and thick wallum heath. It matched perfectly. That meant . . . that the vision was real! Korbeth. The Veniti. The spirit of Aidan, whispering for him to open the door. All real. He felt his own power rise. Something was going to happen tonight that would make the Keeper magic he had experienced so far look like nothing. All he had to do was find the lake. He set off into the bush.

"Liam? Where are you going?"

Liam could just see the path. He followed the walking track through the thick scrub, moving carefully. Soon the track began to slope downward. Behind him he heard Shane call out. "Liam. Come back, you fucking fruitcake!"

"Stay with the car!" Liam yelled back.

Branches broke and twigs snapped behind him as Shane followed.

Liam crested a small rise. Through a gap in the trees, had his first view of the lake. There was a group of people on the shore, clearly visible in the moonlight, including two heavily built, black-clad warriors. Liam froze, his heart beating fast. They were identical to the brutal creatures that had emerged from the cavern Gateway under the collapsed house, which he had seen in the first part of his vision. *Siithe*, Korbeth had called them. The priest had not said anything about *them* being here. A small, dark-haired woman sat on the shore with them, dressed in a ragged black dress. The woman held a wedge of stone in her hands, and stared into it, transfixed. Two figures lay prostrate at the lake's edge. One struggled, bound hand and foot, while the other lay strangely twisted on the sand. As his eyes adjusted, Liam could see the second figure was partly dismembered, and surrounded by a dark stain of spreading blood. *Butchered!* His stomach heaved.

The woman abruptly jerked to her feet. The two siithe beside her grew alert. For a while she stared vacantly at nothing, then she pointed at the trussed captive struggling at her feet. Liam heard a muffled cry of terror. The prisoner was woman.

The dark-haired woman turned slightly, and her features were outlined by the glow of the fire. *The Gate-opener from the vision.* Her face, although beautiful, was devoid of feeling — as perfect and empty as a shop-store mannequin. She directed the two warriors to place the bound woman before her.

"Kill her," she said. The words were spoken quietly, but Liam could hear them clearly across the surface of the lake. The bush around him, alive with noises only moments before, grew quiet.

With brutal efficiency, one of the siithe slashed a knife across the captive's throat. Blood gushed from the wound. As her struggles grew weaker, the siithe laid her onto the sand at the water's edge. Liam was appalled, yet transfixed. He shivered as a the temperature plummeted.

A pall of mist formed above the lake.

As he had seen once before, in Korbeth's vision, the woman raised her hands before the corpse, the stone Fragment in her right hand, like a talisman. A ringing started in Liam's ears, which grew swiftly to a deafening roar. His head rocked as though hit by a sudden wave, then his vision expanded. The forest around him was outlined in shades of tranquil green, the water a deep, dark blue. A dirty crimson vapour welled up from the corpse, flowing from the sliced throat, the womb, and groin. The dark-haired woman inhaled the energy. It built inside her, pooling in her head and stomach. The stone in her right hand glowed a brilliant white.

Leaving the corpse, the Gate-opener waded into the lake.

Skilfully, the woman wove a complex interlace above the lake waters. It hovered there. Insubstantial. Liam knew instinctively that the pattern's ghost-like energies were only visible to enhanced vision. Liam followed every loop and turn, committing it to memory. The overall shape of the pattern was echoed in the one inscribed on his own pendant. The hairs stood up on his arms.

With a cry, the woman channelled her gathered energies into the interlace. It spun rapidly, sinking toward the lake surface where it floated just above the water. It grew in brilliance until it shone with an intense white light that illuminated the lakeshore. The woman waded out into the lake centre and stood inside the swirling pattern. She held up the Fragment.

The Earth's energies surged beneath him.

The Gateway opened.

"Liam! Where are you?" Liam's heart leapt into his throat.

Shane!

Alerted by Shane's voice, one of the siithe spun around, hefting his falcata. With a low growl, he scanned the shore. The siithe spotted Liam instantly, outlined in the Gateway's brilliant glow. He called to the other siithe warrior and began to smash his way through the bush toward him.

Chapter 24
Stonelake Gateway — Fourth Realm

The scream of the Clarion ripped through the air.

Finn ran for the Temple, issuing orders as he went. *Stonelake is under attack.* He had feared this so long, he was surprised to feel so calm. Runners had been dispatched to all the duty stations. The garrison roused. Men were heading for the walls, where they would gather under the command of Endar, his most experienced officer. Stonelake would be sealed tight. Finn's place was with them, yet his instinct, and Sephany's prophecy, urged him to the Temple of the High God. Finn had ordered a squad to meet him there, but they would be minutes — precious minutes — away. He spotted Lieutenant Uris in the street, running to his station on the wall. "Follow me," he ordered instead. The warrior turned on his heel and raced after him. Finn gripped his sword with grim determination and prayed he would not be too late.

He and Uris reached the Temple to see lightly armoured temple guards in savage close-quarter fighting with armoured siithe. Although he had been expecting it, nothing could have prepared him for the shock of seeing Vault troops in Stonelake. One of the temple guards fell beneath a falcata, the heavy blade shearing through the haft of his ceremonial spear to cut deep into his shoulder. The guard screamed in mortal agony. Finn forced himself to focus. These siithe would be only part of the main group, left to finish off the last resistance here while others penetrated the Temple. He could not pause to engage them. He had to find Sephany.

"Come on!" called Finn. He sprinted past the fighting warriors and up the steps, Uris at his heels.

A huge siithe struck out from the shadows.

Finn swayed aside in automatic reflex. He turned on the balls of his feet and swept his blade through its neck in a backhanded blow. The heavy falcata dropped from the warrior's slackened grasp as the headless body toppled.

Inside the main Temple hall, two guards fought back-to-back on the dais, protecting the altar and the ghostly Flame of the High

God from five siithe. Korbeth knelt before the altar, deep in prayer, seemingly oblivious to the battle. The siithe rushed the guardians. One of the dark-skinned warriors was impaled on a spear, but the temple guard, his spear trapped, was cut down by a second siithe. The remaining guardian screamed as the siithe converged on him from all sides, their falcatas battering him to the steps in a cloud of bloody spray.

"Korbeth!"

Korbeth opened his eyes and looked at Finn. His face was serene. His eyes sad and resigned. A tendril of spirit touched Finn, and he heard the High Priest's voice in his mind. *Save the girl.*

Horrified, Finn watched as the siithe closed in.

Korbeth stood. He closed his eyes and raised his arms, as though inviting an embrace.

"*No!*" yelled Finn.

The falcatas cut down, driving Korbeth to the ground. The priest's blood splattered over the white altar-cloth and hissed into the sacred Flame. As his body struck the stone, the High God's Flame extinguished. The hall plunged into darkness.

A woman's scream cut through the air.

Sephany!

A whirlwind burst through Finn. With Uris at his side, they drove into the siithe, unleashing a righteous, deadly fury. The darkness was filled with darting blades and the grunts and howls of siithe. Finn touched the mionanail inside the sword's pommel lightly with his mind, filling himself with its power. He sent a spinning interlace out from his mind's eye. There was an explosion of light. A hovering ball, like a miniature white sun, floated above him.

The two remaining siithe warriors gave bestial screams, pained by the light. Finn leapt forward, bringing his longsword down in a cutting stroke that cleaved straight through the thick skull of the leading siithe. The remaining Vault warrior fell quickly, with both their blades buried deep in its abdomen, each spearing one of its two hearts. The siithe fell heavily, its body pumping dark ichor. The light from his sword-spell illuminated the bloody, dismembered corpse of Korbeth in awful clarity.

Finn's breath caught in his throat. There was no time for grief. *Not now.*

"Sephany!" yelled Finn.

They sped into the Temple's inner sanctum, past the bloody bodies of temple guardians, clergy, and the shattered remnants of relics and icons.

A flurry of movement to Finn's right caused him to spin, his sword held at the ready.

"Captain Evenstone. Thank the High God!"

"Teris!"

Finn sheathed his sword, and with Uris' aid, lifted the elderly priestess to her feet. The ball of light hovered to his left, above the longsword's scabbard.

"They have taken her. My poor Sephany. How could we have known? A true vision? How could we have known?" Her hands shook uncontrollably.

"Where have they taken her?" asked Finn.

"The Gate of Sunsets," said the priestess. Her eyes cleared. "This way." She led them through the Temple to a small exit concealed cleverly in the stonework, which now swung open. Thanking the priestess, Finn and Uris slipped through the stone doorway into a small space behind an external altar, outside the Temple's western wall. Finn now recognised the place. The glowing ball cast its light on a small garden where passers-by could stop and pray. The trampled hedges and ornamental plants showed that a large body of siithe had passed this way. From here they would make for the Gateway.

They broke into a run. Finn extinguished the glowing ball with a mental command. He wove through the streets he knew so well, heading for Stonelake's western gate. Fearing an attack from the Gateway, Finn had positioned most of his troops on the western wall. He ran up the steps and saw Endar, dressed in full battle gear, waiting for him.

"What is the state of the battle, Endar?" asked Finn.

The older warrior had the sort of focussed intensity that inspired confidence in his men. It reassured Finn now. "The squad that followed you to the Temple has dispatched the siithe in the courtyard. There were casualties."

Images of the dead from the Temple flashed through Finn's mind, accompanied by a sickening dread. He had seen action before at the frontiers of the Blessed Realms as young officer, yet nothing like this. Somehow the horror of the Vault had been easier to deal with in the Shadow Worlds.

"The main party of siithe has abducted the young priestess, Sephany," said Finn. "Have you seen any sign of them?"

"We came up against a handful of siithe on the wall with ropes and grapples. That is probably how they entered Stonelake. We dispatched them. As for this larger group, we have not seen them yet," said Endar.

"They must be still inside the walls," said Finn. The ramparts were now lined with men, thanks to his planning, and Endar's efficiency. His heart flowered with hope. *Now he had them.*

"Lord Morin?"

"The thurjun has left for the Gateway," said Endar.

"Excellent," said Finn. All was going according to plan. Morin would secure the Gateway, cutting off their escape.

A loud concussion came from the north. Finn flinched. A section of wall collapsed with a roar of falling masonry. Men screamed.

Finn and Endar rushed along the top of the battlement. Below them, only a hundred paces distant, they could see a group of around twenty siithe led by a slim human warrior. They filed through the breach in the wall and pounded down to the darkened lakeshore. Sephany was with them, bound and gagged, her white dress splashed with red.

"They are heading for the Gateway. Endar. Hold the wall. Squad! With me!" shouted Finn. He sped down the steps and north to the ruined wall, a squad of twenty warriors following him. They were the only reserve he had. A full scale Vault attack could be imminent. He could not take men more without potentially sacrificing the walls.

Ignoring the screams of the injured men buried under the fallen masonry, Finn led his warriors through the breach and after the siithe. He knew Endar would soon be on hand to free the men, but that did not make ignoring their pleas any easier. Ahead of them, a brilliant flare of light lit the open field like a flash of summer lightning. Standing alone before the Stonelake Gateway, his portly figure outlined in shadow, was Morin. Even though it was what they had planned, Finn's stomach clenched at the thought of his old friend and mentor facing them alone.

A second flash exploded from the lakeshore, flaring angry red. In the crimson light, Finn saw Morin struggling to hold a Shield spell against a thin, emaciated man in ancient armour of black metal, who was countering the thurjun with dark magic. A man with cruel, aristocratic features, and closely cropped hair. *The Archfiend.* The killer of his family. The destroyer of his dreams.

Penned by Morin's barrier, the siithe initially milled about in confusion while Procarrus countered with bolt after bolt of explosive force. At a curt command from the Archfiend, some of the siithe set into the barrier with their weapons, seeking to weaken Morin. Others had begun to spread out, probing the invisible wall with their falcatas, seeking to stretch Morin's powers still further. Finn's heart squeezed in his chest. Morin would have to falter soon, then he would be at the mercy of the Archfiend and his siithe.

Red fury washed over Finn's vision. "Form a fighting wedge! Forward at the run!"

At the head of the wedge, Finn drew his longsword and ran at the siithe. He screamed a warcry, giving vent to his rage and fury. His men answered him. A wall of outrage thundered across the cold turf to the retreating backs of the siithe. At the sound of their warcries, some of the siithe turned to meet the onslaught. Stationary, they could do little but fall back as Finn led his warriors through their massed ranks directly toward the Archfiend, seeking to pin him against Morin's barrier. Individual combats broke out on all sides of the wedge. Three siithe fell in the first moments.

The wedge stalled, but Finn pushed on into the packed ranks. The siithe gave ground and circled back in to surround his warriors, striking the unprotected rear of the wedge. Warriors screamed as the heavy falcatas took a terrible toll. Instinctively, the twelve warriors at the rear of the wedge broke away to form a fighting circle, and the wedge collapsed. They were completely surrounded. These warriors watched helplessly as the top of the wedge — led by Finn — drew away.

Finn, with six warriors at his back, was now desperately outnumbered. Seizing their chance to kill Finn, the siithe pressed into the small, isolated group. Two warriors fell behind Finn, while he and his four remaining men fought to survive.

Screams and curses filled the air, outlined in flashes of crimson and white from the magical battle. Four more siithe fell, yet the remaining Vault warriors had managed to push the circle of warriors back toward Stonelake, leaving Finn and his men even more isolated.

Finn fought with precision and manic strength. The ground behind him was littered with fallen siithe. Disembowelled. Beheaded. All slain in moments. His victories had come at a cost. Only two warriors remained to guard his back. Procarrus was close now, paces away, defended by only four siithe, one of which held the unconscious Sephany.

"PROCARRUS!" yelled Finn.

The Archfiend snapped his head back toward Finn. Procarrus' eyes burned with a dark fire of hate. That instant of recognition existed outside time. A moment of stillness surrounded by the maelstrom of battle.

The Archfiend turned back to the barrier. He extended his hands toward the siithe warriors guarding him. The siithe bellowed in pain as Procarrus drew out their life energies. He was building to a single, massive, strike. Three siithe collapsed, leaving only the siithe carrying Sephany. Procarrus sent a wave of red at Morin's barrier. As it struck, it sank into the invisible wall like dye sinking into a casting of molten glass. Morin's barrier, visible now, quivered and began to vibrate like resonating crystal. Then it exploded in a burst of white light.

Finn and the two warriors at his back were briefly stunned, regaining their composure only to find themselves swamped by the remaining siithe as they fled to the Gateway. One of Finn's warriors fell to a passing cut from a falcata, while Finn and Uris, the remaining warrior at his side, were separated by the sheer weight of the stampede.

Finn retreated, defending himself against two of the savage brutes before a stunning blow struck him from behind, sending his silver helm spinning into the darkness and driving him to his knees. Blood spurted from the wound on his head, blinding him as he struggled to rise. An armoured boot cracked into his ribs, and sent him sprawling.

His sword flew from his hand.

Finn wiped the blood from his eyes. A siithe towered above him. It roared an obscene oath and raised a double-headed war axe, ready to strike.

Chapter 25
Fraser Island, Queensland, Australia — Earth

Liam ran.

Behind him, the siithe roared. The warrior's falcata crashed down through the wallum only paces away. Driven headlong by fear, Liam was soon lost in the heavy scrub. Branches tore at him like claws, ripping his skin, and his feet snagged on fallen wood buried in the undergrowth. Finally, he broke through into a small clearing. He ran, tripped, and sprawled face-first into a stand of tall ferns. Winded, he struggled to rise as a shadowed figure broke through the dark wall of forest. It came straight at him.

His cry of terror froze in his throat as he recognised Shane.

"What's going on, man?" asked Shane, reaching forward to help Liam up.

With a bellow of rage, the siithe warrior smashed his way into the clearing. The bulky warrior came straight at them.

"Shit!" said Shane. He dropped Liam and ran for his life in the other direction.

The warrior was terrifying. Never once did Liam consider facing him. He scrambled to his feet and ran into another thick stand of wallum. Inside the low-set, tangled shrubland, the warrior's bulk worked against him, and Liam managed to give himself a lead.

Liam broke through into another clearing. He looked around desperately for somewhere to hide. At the clearing's edge was a huge eucalypt with a hollow trunk. With no time to think, Liam ran to the tree, squeezing into the narrow fissure. Cobwebs draped across his face. He shuddered as something scuttled across his cheek. He stifled his cry of disgust and turned to face the fissure's entrance, trying not to breathe.

The siithe broke into the clearing. He swept the area with his dark, beady eyes. He looked directly at the tree but did not see Liam. With a guttural curse, the siithe gave up the pursuit and turned back to the lake.

Liam let out a breath.

Guardian?

Liam jumped at the voice in his head.

He backed out of the darkness of the tree-bole into the clearing. He blinked in wonder as a huge glowing snake, swirling with ochre, yellow, and white lights, emerged from the tree. It raised its head and slithered toward him. The snake circled the clearing, sweeping its luminescent bulk around him in a whirlpool of colour. It was huge — over twenty metres long — the body almost a metre thick, and tapering at the tail and narrow head. The snake stopped, and lifted its head toward him. Eyes of pulsing gold bored into Liam, probing deep. He experienced its ancient power, and had a sense of maleness. Then he remembered Korbeth's mention of an ally at the Fraser Gateway.

The Way has opened. I have tasted the Ancient-Evil-One, but you . . . you are the . . . Keeper.

"Yes. Liam Durrow."

I am Munnagurra. Much of what I was has faded, yet some strength remains. Perhaps enough. Follow. Quickly.

Munnagurra uncoiled himself in a sleek, graceful motion, and slipped back toward the lake, drawing Liam along. In the snake's bright wake, Liam saw an ancient, overgrown trail. The panicked flight from the lake had seemed eternal, yet the journey back took only a few minutes. They crested the rise before the shore, and Liam paused to survey the scene. The Gateway still flared open above the lake, the Gate-opener within it. Her raised hand grasped the Fragment. The Archfiend and his siithe warriors emerged from the brightness of the Gateway, falling into the shallow lake waters. Liam recognised Procarrus from Korbeth's vision. One of his warriors carried a young woman dressed in a simple white shift. She sagged in the siithe's arms, unconscious.

Munnagurra surged down the rise, making directly for the Gateway.

"They will see us," said Liam, running to keep up.

Stay within my light and you will be hidden, Keeper.

They reached the shore and continued into the lake. The water deepened. Liam pushed through the chest-high waters inside Munnagurra's ghostly brilliance. They soon neared the Gateway, concealed by the magic of the Guardian snake. Liam held his breath as the Archfiend strode to the shoreline. His was barely ten paces away.

Procarrus gave a curt command. The Gate-opener lowered her hands and sagged back in exhaustion. He was plunged into darkness. Liam *felt* the Gateway close.

"Bring the Fragment!" commanded Procarrus in English.

Munnagurra sped toward the Gate-opener. Fearful of leaving the serpent's concealing magic, Liam followed. Munnagurra spun around the woman then tripped her over with a flick of his tail. She screamed and fell into the lake, hands flailing for balance. The Fragment flew from her grasp. Her cry cut off abruptly as her head disappeared beneath the surface. With the speed of a striking cobra, Munnagurra snatched the Fragment in his mouth and swam away. Liam followed.

Procarrus stormed into the water, hauling the small woman to her feet. "You fool! Where is the Fragment!"

The woman cowered in fear. "It slipped when I fell."

"Imbecile!" Procarrus struck the woman savagely, spinning her into the water. He waved his warriors into the lake. "Find the Fragment!"

The siithe scoured the lake bottom for the Fragment. Finally, finding nothing, they returned to shore, one approaching the Archfiend to report. Procarrus screamed in rage, his longsword sweeping from his scabbard to stab into the siithe's side. It seemed a light wound to Liam, yet the siithe screamed and struggled, unable to pull away from Procarrus. Moments later, the warrior slumped to the ground, clearly dead. Procarrus walked to the shore, leaving the siithe's lifeless corpse on the sand. He spoke rapidly in a harsh language. The remaining siithe methodically stripped the dead warrior. Within minutes, they were all gone.

Munnagurra circled around Liam then grew still. The light inside the spirit snake grew in intensity until it saturated Liam. He felt the energy flowing into him, through him . . . and into the pendant. The flow ceased.

Munnagurra lifted his head, presenting Liam with the Fragment.

Take it and open the Gateway. I am spent.

Liam took the Fragment. The snake curled itself into a coil and sank through the lake waters, its colours fading.

Liam waded to the shore. His clothes were soaked by the chill lake water. He began to shiver in the slight breeze. The stone Fragment was heavy in his fist. Solid. Undeniably real.

Chapter 26
Stonelake Gateway — Fourth Realm

Time slowed as the siithe struck.

Finn started to roll, but was not fast enough. *The axe will cut right through my armour.* He braced himself for the death blow.

A heavy black shaft struck the siithe low in the abdomen. The siithe bellowed in pain. The impact was enough to turn the Vault warrior's body, and Finn gasped as the battle-axe thudded into the grass beside his head. The tapered metal head of the thick war-spear had cut through the siithe's leather armour and pierced both its hearts. The siithe staggered back and collapsed. Its body twitched, then lay still.

The battle swept past Finn and the remaining siithe fled to the Gateway. The Stonelake warriors who had formed the fighting circle rushed to Finn's side. He scrambled to his feet. Finn searched the darkness from which the spear had flown. Genna melted out from the forest verge. In his left hand he held a small shield of dark wood, reinforced with bands of black steel. In his right hand he gripped a long-hafted war axe. Genna ducked under a sweeping blow from a fleeing siithe warrior and swung the axe's small, hooked head into the back of the siithe's left knee. The siithe tumbled. Its scream cut short as Genna's follow-up blow cleaved its skull in two.

Finn snatched up his longsword. Only paces away, Morin stood unharmed. The old thurjun leant on his staff, exhausted. The remaining siithe were being led to the Gateway by the Archfiend. Sephany was still with them, a limp prize in the arms of a huge siithe. The Archfiend's skeletal form was outlined against the silver glow of the Gateway. The siithe began to move up the wide stone flagstones and into the ancient structure.

"Come on!" yelled Finn, leading his warriors directly to the Gate. Genna fell into step beside him.

Morin struggled after them.

Finn and Genna were still thirty paces from the Gateway when the last of the siithe disappeared through it, and the light faded. For a long moment they stood in silence. Overwhelmed with fatigue, Finn sat heavily on the Gateway stairs.

"Should we summon reinforcements from the wall, Captain?" asked Uris, the last of those who had stood with Finn at the top of the fighting wedge.

Finn considered their situation. It was unlikely that the Gateway would be opened, and even if by some miracle they could open it, he could not take Morin with him since the thurjun would be needed here to operate this end of the Gateway. He slammed a fist into his palm. This was what he had always feared. He had begged the office of the High King for a second thurjun at Stonelake so one could travel with him to Kgari and secure the Gateway there. He sighed. It was too late now. If the Gateway *did* open he would have to follow regardless. A full company would probably hinder their progress in the distant world of Kgari, presumably now fallen to the Vault. A small team of experienced warriors would be ideal.

"Take the dead and wounded back to Stonelake and help Endar to clear away the . . . debris at the wall." Finn could not bring himself to speak of the crushed bodies there. "Give orders for a squad of experienced men to be assembled. Send them here with field supplies and ask my aides to gather my equipment."

"What of the siithe bodies?"

"Leave them where they lie until the High Priest . . ." Finn faltered as vivid images of Korbeth's death flooded his mind. "Until someone from the Temple can perform the rituals.

"Make sure nothing is removed from the siithe bodies. Understood? No one is to go near them. Their Shades will be powerful."

"Yes, Captain."

Morin finally reached them. He greeted Finn and Genna gravely, before studying the Gateway intently. After a long pause he sighed. "I am sorry Finn, but the Gateway is fully closed." He shook his head. "This is what I feared. With that Fragment — imbued with the resonant energy of the Gateway — they need only one Dark Thurjun in Kgari to open a passage."

Finn's fist tightened on his sword hilt. He knew that only an integral section removed from a Gateway as ancient as Stonelake's could be used in this way. The Fragment had stood within the flux of the open Gateway for millennia; its very essence imbued with the same energies a thurjun of the Fourth Realm would use to open the Gateway.

Genna stirred, tilting his head as though listening. "I can hear the Dreaming of Munnagurra."

Finn stood. "Is the Gateway reopening?"

Morin's face creased in desperate concentration. "I am sorry. I can detect nothing."

"What is Munnagurra?" asked Finn.

"He is the serpent who guards the lake," replied Genna.

Finn was in no mood for riddles. "Can the Gateway be opened or not?"

Morin shook his head. "Only if — by some miracle — a thurjun of Kgari reaches through to touch my mind, and we can work together to raise the energies required."

Seeking calm, and trying to give himself time to think, Finn cleaned the siithe blood off his sword. For a time they waited in silence, then across the field they heard a crowd gasp in wonder. They looked back at the wall breach and saw the gap outlined by a golden glow. Finn blinked as a tall flame appeared there.

Finn sheathed his sword and rose swiftly. "What is it, Morin?"

"I am not sure."

The flame surged through the gap, followed by excited townsfolk. It flitted across the lawn to the battleground, where Uris and his men were solemnly attending to the dead and wounded. The flame reached the site of the battle and flickered between each of the fallen siithe, bathing the darkened corpses in ethereal light.

"Praise the High God!" exclaimed Morin. "It is the Temple Flame."

At the scene of the battle, Finn's troops fell to their knees. They watched, spellbound, as the Flame moved to each siithe corpse, cleansing it of dark Shades. From the last of the fallen siithe, the Flame shot toward Finn and his small company.

The towering Flame halted just a few paces away.

"Korbeth!" said Finn.

Within the Flame, surrounded by a flickering sea of faces, Korbeth lay outlined in glittering shades of white. The ghostly outlines of his vestments were a crystalline echo of those he had worn in real life, and reflected the Flame's brightness.

"Yes, Finn. But not only Korbeth. To have power in this world I have joined with the Flame. I am one with the Spirit of the Temple."

"The siithe have escaped us, Korbeth. Sephany is gone. We have failed you."

Korbeth smiled. "You always were too hard on yourself Finn. The battle has only started."

"But the Gateway is closed to us," said Morin.

"That is why I joined with the Flame." Korbeth smiled at them, and their hearts lifted. "When the siithe invaded the Temple, I foresaw your plight." Korbeth turned and spoke with one of the figures beside him, although they heard nothing. Korbeth turned back to them. "Time is short. I leave now to travel the Paths. Fear not. If thurjuns loyal to the Realms dwell in Kgari, I shall find them."

The Flame flashed up the stairs and through the silent pillars of the Gateway, disappearing as quietly as a ghost.

"A closed Gateway is no barrier to the spirit," said Morin softly.

A crowd swelled out from the breach in the walls, following the path of the Flame. Hundreds of them, most holding glowglobe torches. They surged across the green to the Gateway.

"The Flame cleansed the Temple!"

"Did you see the image of Korbeth in the Flame?"

"I saw High Priestess Kiri."

"But she died fifty years ago!"

Finn could hardly believe it. After the desecration of the Temple, and all the deaths, the men and women in the crowd were in a state of rapture.

He recognised the older priestess, Teris.

"Teris, what is going on?"

Teris made her way through the crowd to Finn. Her eyes were wide and shining. "It is a miracle! When the High God's Flame died, we felt all hope was lost. But then it reappeared in the main chambers, clothing the immortal form of Korbeth himself!

"The Flame cleansed the Temple. Casting out all the siithe

Shades, freeing us of the desecration!"

A temple guardian, a huge man with a savage cut to his forehead, came to stand beside Teris. "The Flame moved through the town, cleansing each of the fallen Vault warriors in turn," said the guardian. "Just as well. Only Korbeth and two other priestesses could performed the banishing rituals, and none of them survived the attack. Another priestess is travelling from Jasper, but she is hours away."

Siithe Shades faded quickly in the Shadow Worlds. Here, the very nature of the Realms increased their strength. Cases of possession were rare, but not unknown. It paid to be cautious.

"Finn!" called Morin.

Behind him, the Stonelake Gateway flared to life.

Chapter 27

Fraser Island, Queensland, Australia — Earth

Liam looked around the darkened shoreline. He tensed at the sound of movement, but relaxed as he saw Yolinda sprint across the sand to the corpses. She examined the two slain women, then the dead siithe. She took photographs, the flash bright against the sand, then looked around. When she saw Liam, she ran over to him.

"I saw the light. Am I too late? What did you see?"

"They were here," said Liam, "but they've gone. About ten minutes ago."

"The dead women?"

"They killed them in a ritual. The dead warrior was slain by the leader. A tall, thin man." The title of Archfiend, or the name Procarrus, would mean nothing to the Federal Agent, thought Liam.

"Did you see them handling any drugs? Did you hear a plane?"

"A plane . . . no. But they were carrying another woman. She looked unconscious."

"Damn! I've missed them. I'm going to follow them in the car, but you stay here, Liam. I don't want you involved in a potentially deadly situation, OK?"

Liam nodded, hardly listening. He was on the threshold of something his family had been preparing for since antiquity. His head was full of magic, and he was already planning how to recreate the form the Gate-opener had used.

"Give me your mobile," she ordered.

Liam fished it out of his damp pocket and handed it over. She pocketed it quickly. Yolinda checked her revolver's load, then she set off up the slope, dodging through the thick bush in the direction of the overgrown carpark.

Liam waded back out into the lake. To the Gateway. The water's surface was flat and dark. He could feel the Gateway's power, and through the Fragment, the resonating echo of the distant world beyond it. He calmed his mind. Then, with the skill of an artist, he began to draw the Gate-opening interlace.

Shane stumbled out of the undergrowth and walked to the lakeshore. He laughed when he saw Liam chest-high in the lake water. "You stupid fuckwit. You're tripping aren't you, Liam? Where'd ya' get the tabs?"

Then Shane saw the prone forms on the shore. "Christ! Are they bodies!" He touched one of the women's corpses. "Stone cold." He moved to the dead siithe. "Hey, will you look at this guy?" Shane rummaged through the leather pouch that hung from the siithe's belt. He came up empty. His companions had stripped the dead warrior of his Vault weapons and wealth, leaving only the armour. Shane rolled the siithe's corpse onto its front. He searched behind the siithe's backplate, his hand emerging with a black pistol. He whistled.

"Look at this, mate!" Shane waded out to where Liam was standing in the lake. He held up a semi-automatic pistol, examining it in the moonlight, rubbing away the blood with a broad smile. "I wonder how much it's worth?"

Liam ignored Shane. He refused to be distracted from his task. He could feel the energies of the recently opened Gateway stirring once more. He had completed the pattern. He raised the Fragment above him, into the centre of the form, which spun and glittered before his enhanced sight. At this point the Gate-opener had injected energy into the form. Of course! He touched the pendant with his mind and felt the power of Munnagurra within it.

"You're a fucking fruitloop, Liam," said Shane, when he got no reaction.

A tower of flame appeared above the waters. Within the flame Liam recognised Korbeth, his eyes focussed on a distant horizon. He did not see Liam. The flame swept past him and disappeared.

Liam carefully filled the interlace with the energy stored in the pendant. It transformed.

A spinning disc of brilliant white appeared above the waters.

"What the f—" muttered Shane, pushing the pistol into his belt.

Liam could feel the energies of Earth reach through space, where they met and joined with the energies of a distant world, drawn together by the Fragment, which resonated powerfully in his hand. Liam cast his thoughts through the Gateway and encountered Morin's outreaching mind. In a brief moment, Liam knew Morin, a thurjun of the High Court of the Blessed Realms, and Morin knew Liam, the Keeper of ancient knowledge.

Two warriors emerged from the Gateway, falling with surprised shouts into the shallow waters. They recovered quickly and circled. Seeing no threat, they lowered their weapons.

"Finn," said a blonde warrior pointing at himself. "Genna," he said indicating the other.

"Liam," he replied.

Shane shook his head. "Maybe *I'm* tripping."

The warriors nodded their thanks to Liam then pushed through the water to the lakeshore. As he stood on the sand there, Liam saw that Finn was dressed in archaic silver armour. The two travellers examined the bodies, then conversed rapidly in an unfamiliar language. Genna bent to examine the siithe tracks. The two men talked again, then both looked back expectantly at the opened Gateway.

For Liam, a new world — a new destiny — beckoned through that Gateway.

Shane grabbed Liam's arm. "This is crap. Let's hotwire the Subi and get the fuck out of here."

The Gateway energies were fading, and beyond Liam's power to sustain with the drained pendant. Through the brilliance, Liam saw Morin and a crowd gathered by a lakeshore. He could not let this chance at destiny pass him by. He took a step forward.

Still gripping Liam's arm, Shane followed.

No Liam, stay on Kgari to operate the Gateway! Morin's plea came too late.

Liam felt himself lifted up. Shane was drawn through with him. They appeared on a raised stone platform in the middle of another lake. A series of tilted columns led like elevated stepping-stones to a set of stairs at the lakeshore. Morin stared at them, shocked. The thurjun called across to Liam, but his language was indecipherable. Surrounding the lakeshore were hundreds of people, all watching in hushed expectation. A group of around twenty armoured warriors were sprinting up onto the Gateway steps at the lakeshore, equipped with heavy packs. *That's who Finn and Genna were waiting for.* They were too late. The Gateway was closed.

Beside Liam, Shane laughed. "Hey, can we do that again?"

*

Yolinda pushed past the last of the thick undergrowth and stumbled into the clearing, exhausted, bruised, and bleeding. She saw the dark bulk of the Suburu beneath the trees. "*Finally.*" Yolinda took a moment to catch her breath. Pushing through the wallum heath was like rubbing up against sandpaper. Her frustration at missing the drug-drop burned inside her. She had lost a chance to gather crucial intelligence on Procarrus' operation. Yolinda had been out of position, in the scrub north of the lake, when it all went down. It was only when the lights went on above the lake that she realised she had gone the wrong way. They had been off by the time she got back. By the amount of illumination, probably a bank of 1000 Watt halogen floodlights, run by a generator.

Yolinda slid into the Subaru. She put the camera on the seat and started the car. She engaged the four-wheel-drive, reversed onto the track, then sped after the Landcruisers. She took Liam's phone out of her pocket and flipped it open. She punched in the police number from memory. With any luck, the local cops would already be on the island.

As she drove, dodging fallen branches and low-slung boughs, Yolinda thought furiously. If it *had* been a drug drop, then a seaplane must have landed on the lake. That was what puzzled Yolinda. The lake was easily big enough, but out here in the bush she would have heard a plane landing from kilometres away, and Liam had seen no plane. And the generator for the lights — wouldn't she have heard that fire up?

Her hands tightened on the steering wheel.

Yolinda increased her speed, driving one-handed while she held the phone to her ear. There was no dial tone at all. Nothing. Out of range?

Her speed increased.

158

Yolinda turned a corner — too sharply. The back of the Subaru slid across the soft track. She tried to correct, then saw a tree across the road. Yolinda dropped the phone and screamed. She turned the wheel and hit the brakes, but there was no traction on the soft sand. The Subaru skidded across the sand and slammed sideways into the tree. She was catapulted into the passenger seat in a shower of broken glass.

She blacked out.

Yolinda blinked, unsure how much time had passed. The engine had stalled. The dashboard was lit up with warning lights. Liam's camera was a smashed ruin. Still giddy from the crash, she took out the memory stick and slid it into her pocket. Scrabbling about in the footwell, she found the phone. She turned on the cabin light and examined it. There were no lights on the phone display. The thing was dead. And wet. Come to think of it, Liam's clothes had been drenched. The idiot had left it in his pocket and gone swimming. "Goddamn it." She threw the phone onto the dashboard in disgust, then clambered out of the car. When she stood up, her knees gave way. She sagged against the car, and waited until her strength returned. *I seriously need to eat something.* Recovered, she checked the Suburu. There was no damage to the radiator or engine, which meant the car could still be driven, but the side that had hit the tree was crumpled into a mass of twisted metal.

"Sorry, Liam."

There was a broad drag mark in the sand where the fallen eucalypt had been towed out of the forest and positioned across the road. From the broad tyre prints in the sand, one of the big Landcruisers had been used. There was no way she could move the tree using the underpowered Suburu, even if she had a tow rope. Her only chance was to go around it. She scouted the verge of the track and decided there was enough room for the smaller four-wheel-drive to squeeze between the end of the log and the scrub beside the road. *Worth a try.*

Yolinda climbed back into the cabin and started the engine. The car moved easily at first, broken glass and bent panels creaking as she separated from the trunk, but then the car stopped dead. She gently increased the acceleration, then tried "rocking" the car — alternating between forward and reverse gears and turning the wheel slightly with each change of direction. It was no good. She was stuck. Yolinda climbed out. She had missed it before, but now that the car had pulled away from the trunk she could see that a thick branch had speared into the front left panel of the car, pinning it in place. She walked right around the car. The wheels were sunk to the axles in the soft sand. Even if she could somehow separate the car from the tree she was completely bogged.

Yolinda slammed her palm onto the roof of the car. "Damn it!"

She needed a miracle.

Chapter 28
Fraser Island, Queensland, Australia — Earth

Finn watched as Genna finished his chant.

His friend had begun the accompanying dance slowly, building the delicate magic with precise steps that grew more frenzied as the chant built in volume. Then Genna landed in a complete stop, both hands raised, and called out into the night. A single, powerful, word. Finn had seen this spell before, and he remained motionless as Genna's Call raced across the forest.

Two stocky island horses crashed through the undergrowth into the clearing, their chests heaving. They were a pair of stallions, deep chestnut, snorting as they scented humans. They were small, their protruding ribs showing they were underfed, making their heads and hooves seem large in comparison. Genna talked softly to them, walking close on silent feet until he was standing right in front of them. He touched each on the forehead. Each whinnied in turn, and came forward to nuzzle his face, relaxed and docile.

Genna smiled. "At least something works." He had tried to raise the local people with his bull-roarer — an oblong piece of shaped wood on a long piece of string that produced a loud droning sound when spun in a circle. Hearing that, any Guardians nearby would have come to investigate, but Genna got no answer. The fact that there were no camps close to the lake, a prime spot, clearly worried Genna.

Genna patted the two horses softly, making clicking and cooing noises. They responded with low whinnies. "These two have agreed to carry us."

Finn smiled. "You are a master of your art, young Genna."

Genna chuckled. "Young! I am a grandfather remember."

"Oh I forgot. You start early up in the forest," said Finn, grinning.

Finn sprang onto the back of his horse, lightly gripping the mane for support. He urged the horse into a gallop, following the unmistakable tyre-prints of the siithe vehicles along the track. He heard the soft, thudding hoof-falls of Genna's stallion behind him. Genna had read the sign, and was convinced one of the siithe had been carrying someone when they reached their transports. It had to be Sephany.

They heard a crash, followed by the sound of shattering glass. They halted their mounts and listened, but heard nothing more than the regular rasping of the local crickets. They continued on. Then, as they rounded a bend, they saw a tree across the track, the wreck of a vehicle beside it. With no time to slow, they spurred their mounts forward and jumped the tree. The rear hoof of Genna's mount clipped the tree trunk. They landed heavily and reined in their labouring mounts. Turning his horse, Finn saw a woman come toward them, hand raised in greeting. The woman was slight in build, and yet Finn was wary, recognising strength of purpose in her movements.

She called out to them, but the words were incomprehensible.

Finn shook his head. "Do you recognise it, Genna?"

"No," said Genna. "Use your mind."

Finn nodded. All warriors and thurjuns of the Blessed Realms were trained in special techniques that sped the acquisition of language; literally taking the words straight out of a person's head. Few mastered the skills, but a warrior of Finn's calibre was an expert. Concentrating, he summoned his thurjun's sight. He sent a tendril of spirit snaking across the gap toward the woman.

Contact.

He could feel her turmoil and frustration. She was also in pain, and in desperate need of aid. Her determination was overwhelming.

Finn strengthened the bond. Now, as she spoke, he could hear her thoughts as well. The words and the thoughts were taken directly into his brain, to the areas of language recognition. Now she had only to speak a word once and he would recognise it immediately thereafter. Learning to speak would be slower. Linked as they were, mind-to-mind, the woman would also understand him and receive some knowledge of the Realm language, although her level of retention depended on her innate talent. Finn felt the gentle touch of Genna's spirit on his own, and realised his friend had joined the mental bond.

"Can you give me a ride?" asked the woman.

"Where are you going?" asked Finn.

"I have to get back to Kookaburra Bay," she said. A mental image flashed through Finn's mind of a series of low-set buildings by the sea, surrounded by more of the steel vehicles.

"We are chasing siithe warriors," said Finn. "It may be too dangerous."

The woman looked shocked for an instant, but her face became set. "I am a *guardswoman/warrior*. I am also pursuing the criminals." One of the words had not had a direct equivalent in the Realm language, but he received the association as a direct concept. Finn felt her honesty and conviction. She was a warrior of Kgari, also in pursuit of the siithe. Finn sighed with relief. Perhaps the Vault had less hold over Kgari than he had feared.

"Quickly then," said Finn, lowering an arm.

She gripped his hand and he hauled her into the saddle behind him. He was puzzled at her lack of weapons or armour, but did not comment.

Still connected mind-to-mind, he continued to talk to her. "How far ahead of us is Procarrus?"

He could feel her surprise at the question, and her alarm as she took in the sword at his waist and the silver armour, which had been hidden, until now, by the night's gloom.

"Only a few minutes ahead, but they are *riding/on/in machine/vehicles*."

Finn paused to absorb the information. She must mean the transports. The word had sounded like "karr".

Finn and Genna urged their mounts forward. The track opened out into sparsely vegetated heathland, its white sand easily visible in the moonlight. They picked up speed. By the way the woman's weight fell behind him, Finn could tell she did not ride often. He leant forward to help her balance.

"What is your name?" asked Finn.

"The *Nation's Guard/warrior* Yolinda Paris," she replied.

"I am Finn, Captain of Stonelake Tower, Fourth Realm. This is Genna, one of the traditional Guardians of the Stonelake Gateway."

Yolinda was silent for a long moment, tense and ill at ease. Was his relief premature? He was burning with curiosity about

Kgari, but held his tongue. He had a feeling they had a few surprises ahead of them. He had other concerns. How could he face Procarrus' dark magic without the aid of a thurjun? He had been shocked when the Kgari thurjun had stepped back through the Gateway to Stonelake. The squad of warriors he ordered to follow must have been only moments behind him when the Gateway closed. If they did rescue Sephany and slay the siithe, what then? How would they return? He forced himself to relax. There *must* be another thurjun in Kgari.

Finn let the mind-bond fall away. The technique was powerful, but took intense concentration and considerable energy. Finn sensed Yolinda's distrust as the bond faded. This puzzled him. If their goal was the same, what was she concerned about?

They rode in silence for around two hours, making good time. The road began to descend and Finn could smell the sea. The stallion was tiring fast, unused to carrying heavy loads, let alone an armoured man and a woman. They glimpsed lights ahead of them and slowed.

"We should go on foot from here," said Finn.

"It is a palace," said Genna in amazement, looking at the beautifully lit structure ahead, with its tall glass windows and elegantly sloped roof. Other smaller structures of similar design clustered around it. Finn could see a darkened beach and calm bay below, the lights of the few boats there twinkling across the distance.

"Kookaburra Bay," said Yolinda.

They dismounted.

Genna thanked each of the horses in turn, then tapped them sharply on the forehead. Each shook his head and jumped back in fright. Turning together, the stallions bolted back along the track and were quickly out of sight.

Yolinda put a hand on Finn's arm. "You. . . not . . . speak. . ."

Finn could only understand fragments of what she was saying. He took a moment to reestablish the bond.

"I said, why won't you speak English?"

Finn smiled. From her question, Yolinda obviously had not realised their communication to date had only been possible with the mind-bond. In fact, she was even using some Realm words without knowing it.

"We will try," said Finn.

Yolinda grew serious. "I don't know where you two came from, but I owe you *one/debt* for helping me. However, I am a *soldier/guard*, and you now have to stand aside. I have *talked/called* to the local *soldier/guards,* and they will be waiting to *ambush/capture* the *siithe/criminals*."

Finn smiled. "We are also seeking the siithe. Why can we not work together? Help your guardsmen?"

Yolinda sighed, eyeing the pair critically. When they had first met on the track, she had been wary, conscious of her mission. Then when they had started talking she had been overwhelmed by Finn's strength of character and honesty in a way she had never experienced before. Despite Finn's strange accent, which had seemed to echo inside her fatigued mind, she had been more than willing to trust them both. The coincidence that they were both in pursuit of the same gang had not seemed strange.

Then, on the road south, it was as though she had suddenly come back to her senses. Yolinda blamed drug withdrawal, and the shock of the crash, for her dreamy compliance and started thinking critically. She could not resolve what she saw. Two men, dressed in medieval reenactment gear, riding horses — without saddles — through the night. When they reached Kookaburra Bay, she had decided they should be taken into custody for questioning. Their knowledge of Procarrus and the "siithe" gang was enough to raise questions. And she would stop at nothing to find the answers.

But now, her determination to arrest these two men was being challenged again, by an overwhelming sense of Finn's integrity. Finn's words seemed to resound clearly in her head, but she could hear strange words beneath them. His mouth moved strangely, like an actor in a dubbed movie.

Yolinda's anxiety, her exhaustion and frustration, boiled over. She pulled out the police revolver and levelled it at Finn and Genna.

"Back off!" she ordered. She moved slowly away from Finn

and Genna.

Finn's hand fell to the hilt of his sword. "We mean you no harm, guardsman Yolinda Paris."

A glow flickered at the hilt of Finn's sword. *Something* flowed out from him, making her stomach lurch. Yolinda reacted instantly. She aimed at Finn's sword-arm and pulled the trigger.

There was a click as the hammer fell. Then nothing.

Yolinda fired again.

Click.

With a sick feeling, she realised the seawater must have ruined the 0.38 loads. She backed away down the track. When she was twenty paces away, she broke into a run. Somewhere in Kookaburra Bay the local police would be waiting for her. She had to contact them and stop Procarrus' boat from leaving the bay.

Chapter 29

Fraser Island, Queensland, Australia — Earth

Finn and Genna watched Yolinda disappear down the track.

"I do not think the local warriors are going to be much help," said Genna.

Finn nodded. His unease was growing. The warrior Yolinda had impressed him with her determination and sense of purpose. He did not want her for an enemy. The siithe would be hard enough to handle.

Finn drew his sword. The power of the mionanail pulsed through his hand. They advanced on the palace. As they neared it, the lights began to wink out, first the streetlights, then the lights in the main buildings. Each taken by the advancing dampening wave projected by Finn's weapon. Soon every building — right down to the waterline — was in darkness. He could hear astonished cries as people found themselves in blackout.

"This world runs on Vault technology," said Finn.

"Technology once used by the Realms," said Genna.

"In ancient times."

"I have seen no other signs of the Vault here," insisted Genna.

They followed the wheel-tracks of the siithe vehicles down onto a wide sandy beach. They found the black, box-shaped "karrs" parked at the shoreline.

Genna knelt at the water's edge and inspected the marks left in the sand. "They went out from here in a small boat."

"Can you see them?"

Genna's people were famed for their extraordinary eyesight. He studied each of the boats anchored inside the bay, settling on a large black vessel, lit up with lights fore and aft. "There, Finn. The black ship! High up in the wheelhouse." The unmistakable form of a siithe.

"Got you!" *Procarrus was close.*

Finn heard the boat powering up its engines. The cruiser was just beyond the normal range of his sword, but he knew how to stop them. He raised his sword and concentrated. Using a simple form that Morin had taught him, he extended the weapon's range. The sword pulsed warmly in his hand and the dampening wave lengthened.

The ship's lights cut to dark. Its engine died a moment later.

"What now?" asked Genna.

"We board the ship and take back Sephany."

"What of the Archfiend?" asked Genna.

"He will be weakened by his battle with Morin."

"Hopefully."

"We may not get a better chance. We know nothing of this world, and cannot assume the local guards will help us." He thought of Yolinda. "Now we need a boat."

Finn and Genna scoured the shoreline. They soon found a small craft, constructed of inflated tubes around a flat metal hull, tied up to a tree above the waterline. It was equipped with a pair of oars. They untied the rope and ran it down to the water.

They were suddenly surrounded by men. They wore uniforms with bulky, shapeless breastplates, and were equipped with small projectile weapons similar to Yolinda's. Primitive technology, thankfully. That did not mean he and Genna were not in danger. One of them, clearly the leader, yelled a command in the local language. He looked prepared to kill.

Finn was anxious to complete the pursuit. He refused to come this far only to be stopped now. He shook his head at the local guard and motioned for Genna to continue. The men continued to shout warnings, which Finn ignored. He and Genna lowered the boat into the water and Genna leapt lightly into the craft.

The leader of the guards barked an order. Their weapons, rendered harmless by Finn's sword, sounded a series of metallic clicks as hammers fell on latent caps. There were more shouts, accompanied by bewildered looks, but the leader was thinking fast. He ordered the men sheath their guns and draw short wooden clubs. They closed on Finn, now alone at the shoreline. Genna stood up in the boat, ready to join him. "Stay there," ordered Finn.

The local guards surged at him. It quickly became obvious they had not been trained to attack together. Half of them got in the way of the others. Finn blocked the attacks easily. He was reluctant to kill or wound. He sent two onto their knees with the flat of his blade to the sides of their unprotected heads, and smashed the heavy pommel down on the leader's head. He fell, unconscious. The others soon retreated, bruised and cursing.

Finn raced for the boat. He had one foot inside it when he sensed someone behind him. He turned, his sword raised in readiness to strike, then recognised Yolinda. Here was a chance to set things straight, perhaps even enlist the aid of the local forces. He lowered his sword, preparing to use the mind-bridge. He took a step toward her.

Yolinda's arm whipped out at him. It came fast and high, from his left. He raised his sword to deflect the blow, instinctively angling the blade in a cut that would have severed Yolinda's arm. He slowed the strike, wasting precious moments as he turned the blade to use the flat. The heel of her gun slammed into his temple. There was an explosion of white light. He staggered against the boat, releasing his sword, which fell into the boat. The dampening field immediately collapsed. Then the others were on him. He tried to shake them off, but there were too many. Genna started toward him, intent on helping, but Finn kicked at the boat instead, sending it out into the water.

"Go!" ordered Finn.

Reluctantly, Genna pushed further out into the water. The guardsmen waded in after him, but were soon out of their depth in the channel. Genna took up the oars and rowed out into the bay. He disappeared from sight around the point.

Lights flared on throughout the bay. The guards shouted in surprise and pain as their pieces discharged in their hip holsters. Yolinda's revolver roared as both struck rounds went off simultaneously, flaring brightly. The recoil jarred her wrist and the gun flew onto the sand.

Across the water, the engines on the black cruiser flared to life, and with a roar, it powered out of the bay.

"Sephany . . . ," whispered Finn.

Then blackness took him.

Yolinda and two Queensland Police constables carried Finn back to their temporary headquarters, which had been set up in one of the Kookaburra Bay outbuildings. Sergeant Haynes, a thickset man with dark hair, who stood around six feet, was inside when they arrived, talking on a landline. He had a surgical pad pressed to the back of his head with his free hand. Although she technically only held the rank of constable, all the Queensland Police, including Sergeant Haynes, gave her a wary respect. The Australian Federal Police tended to be secretive, but received cooperation across all facets of law enforcement. Once her credentials as an AFP undercover operative had been confirmed, the locals had been eager to help. Being the one who took Finn down did not hurt her street cred either.

"Yes, sir." Haynes eyes narrowed in concentration as he listened to the person on the other side of the phone conversation. From his manner, Yolinda guessed it was a senior Queensland Police officer. "I understand, sir. I will."

"He's heavier than he looks," said one of the constables. They laid the unconscious Finn on a desk and took position on either side, guarding the prisoner. From their expressions they were just hoping Finn would wake up and try something. No policeman liked to be taken down by a perp. They wanted payback.

The mainland police had come to Fraser in force, but none of them had any special training. They were country cops. One had a gunshot wound to his calf, superficial thankfully, another had a bullet lodged in his right foot, a third had suffered powder burns to his right thigh, another had a broken right arm. All of them had bruises from Finn's sword. Except Yolinda. The four wounded officers were being treated in the resort's infirmary while they waited for a helicopter airlift.

The wound to Sergeant Haynes' head had bled profusely. He had refused treatment. The blood had formed a nondescript brown splash on the back of his light blue uniform shirt. Head wounds always bled a lot. "I will, sir." Haynes put down the receiver. He took away the surgical pad and checked it. It glistened with fresh blood, a startling red under the room's fluorescents. He grimaced and pushed the pad back against the wound.

"I don't understand what happened to our guns," said Sergeant Haynes. "They could not all misfire exactly the same way."

"Then fire all at once." Yolinda had been given an icepack by the resort staff. She held it on her right hand. It still throbbed from the jarring recoil when two bullets in her 0.38 fired at the same time — none of them actually in the chamber. She was lucky the exploding brass had missed her.

"The Hervey Bay Water Police are on the case. We'll find that boat." Haynes jerked a thumb at Finn. "I assume you want him transferred to Brisbane?"

Yolinda shook her head. "Sydney." She had just got off the phone herself. In her case, from a conversation with Superintendent Esco, who headed up the Federal Drugs Task Force. It had been a tough telephone call. It had been the first chance she had to tell him about Jay's death. "I heard about the coordination with the water police. My boss has pulled some strings as well. There's a navy patrol boat coming south from Mackay to help with the search."

Haynes narrowed his eyes. "You must really want these guys, Agent Paris."

"You have no idea." Yolinda held out her right hand. "Can I use your cuffs, Sergeant?"

Haynes gave her a tight grin. "Be my guest. That prick really nailed me. He was bloody fast." He slipped the cuffs out of his belt holder and passed them to Yolinda.

She opened the cuffs as she walked over to the unconscious Finn. She snapped them shut on his wrists, hands in front, since he was laying on his back. "Help me get this gear off him. We should also remove any personal effects."

Haynes tossed the bloody gauze into the trash and joined her.

Yolinda's gaze was drawn to Finn's face as she stripped him of his archaic armour. There was strength there. Purpose. Even in repose. She could not rid herself of the memory of their meeting on the track. He could have easily knocked her unconscious with that sword, even killed her. She had seen him deal with the police squad and could hardly believe one man could be that proficient with such an ancient weapon. But when he faced her he hesitated. The last thing she remembered was the light of concern in his eyes. He had been worried he might harm her — then she had used that moment's hesitation to lay him out. Feelings of guilt and betrayal settled in her stomach like molten lead. She rebelled against them. *What did she owe him?* She had a job to do. A duty to bring down the guilty.

Yolinda straightened up and took a breath of the night air. If Finn was innocent, he would go free. But not before he told her everything he knew.

With Finn stripped and secure, she remembered something else. "We need to send a unit up the west coast of the island. There are two young men up there that need a lift. Do you have a map?"

Haynes nodded.

"I'll show you where."

Chapter 30
Stonelake Gateway — Fourth Realm

The Gateway's light faded.

Hundreds of people crowded the lakeshore. They were outlined in the white glare of weird torches, which ended in large bulbs that glowed without flame. They were dressed in an odd assortment of rustic clothing and stood silently, watching the gate. It was as though they were waiting for something. A sign . . . or a blessing. Liam stared around him in amazement. He had appeared on an ancient platform built of the same light grey stone as the Fragment. Alien stars filled the sky, along with a full moon identical in size and position to one he had seen so recently in Earth's sky. The high walls and towers of a medieval fortress town rose nearby.

"What the fu—" Shane lost his footing on the wet stone and fell between the Gateway pillars, off the edge of the platform, and into the lake. He emerged a moment later in waist-high water. "*Fuck!*"

Shane's outburst broke the impasse.

A buzz of excited conversation swept the crowd. The thurjun, Morin, motioned for two Stonelake warriors to help Shane out of the lake. The squad of warriors that had run up onto the steps with such urgency, now filed back onto the lakeshore. Their leader looked across at Morin, who motioned for him to wait.

Liam skipped across the columns and landed lightly on the steps.

Morin greeted Liam formally in a foreign language.

"Sorry, I don't understand," said Liam.

Morin's presence swelled. The man's spirit surrounded Liam. There was a surge of magic and Liam felt a shock of connection. Then, a moment later, the mental link took hold.

"Welcome to Stonelake, Liam," said Morin in the Realm tongue. "I am Morin."

Liam heard both the words, and the thoughts behind them, giving him a strangely disjointed, but immediate, comprehension. He responded in English. "Thank you, Morin."

He instinctively knew that Morin would also understand *his* thoughts. The experience was a revelation.

"Is there another thurjun in Kgari who can reopen the Gateway?" asked Morin. Liam immediately sensed how important this was to Morin.

"No . . . I was alone. I could not hold it open any longer. Sorry." Without the power gifted to him by Munnagurra, he would not have been able to open it at all.

Morin nodded gravely. He turned to the squad leader, who had rushed to follow Finn through the Gateway, only to find it closed. "Take your men back to Stonelake. There is no way through — for now."

The lead warrior looked back at Liam, his jaw clenched, then led his men away.

Shane emerged from the lake, gasping with shock at the cold, but watching everything with a familiar look of calculation.

"Why are all these people gathered here?" asked Liam.

"They followed the Flame. They witnessed the opening of the Gateway and watched as Finn and Genna passed through on their quest to rescue the priestess Sephany."

A mental picture of the priestess Sephany flashed through Liam's mind. He gasped in recognition.

"The girl with the siithe!" said Liam.

"Yes," replied Morin. "The siithe came through the Gateway, using the Fragment, to capture Sephany." Morin pointed at the small wedge of grey stone in Liam's hand. It was still warm from the energies that had passed through it.

Liam nodded, and held the Fragment out to Morin.

Morin took the stone and studied it intently. "This was the tool the Archfiend used to strike through the Gateway. At one time the Stonelake Gateway was a primary Gateway. In the first age of the Realms it was kept open at all times. So that all could come and go from Kgari as they pleased."

"Kgari?"

Morin frowned. "Is that not the name of your world?"

Liam shook his head. "We know it as Earth."

"*Earth*," said Morin, repeating the word.

The thurjun sighed and turned back to the crowd, which was

beginning to break apart and drift back toward the distant town.

"Finn led a desperate battle here. The cost was high. All that remains now is the gruesome task of removing the dead and piling the siithe corpses onto a funeral pyre."

Liam remained silent, unsure what to say.

Morin weighed the Fragment in his palm. "Finn's family died for this. It is time to prevent it from being used again."

The mind-bond dissolved. Liam sensed power rise in Morin again. He was startled when Morin rose gently into the air, hovering there unsupported. Then he *floated* across to the Gateway platform. Once there, he reached up to the tall carved obelisk on the left side of the Gateway and fitted the Fragment into a wedge-shaped crevice.

Liam's vision swam. A multi-coloured shape appeared in front of the older man. A white haze issued from the pendant at Morin's neck and flowed through the lens of the form. Heat flowed from his hands into the stone, concentrating at the join. The Fragment glowed red hot, then cooled as he took his hands away. Liam gaped at this demonstration of power, realising that what he had experienced so far was merely a hint of what was to come.

Morin returned to the lakeshore with the same suspended mode of flight. He casually reestablished the mind-bond. "The Fragment has been rejoined to the Gateway. Now it can never be used against us again. We have only the betrayal of a Realm thurjun to consider."

"Realm?" queried Liam.

Morin looked at Liam quizzically, then nodded to himself. "You and your friend should come to the Tower with me. I can sense how strange all of this is to you."

Liam followed Morin across the wide field toward Stonelake. Shane followed, flanked by two warriors. His friend was silent, but his eyes were hard. He reached into his top pocket for a cigarette, but the water had ruined his packet. In disgust, he threw them to the ground — near a bloodstain left by a fallen warrior. One of the two escorts stooped to pick up the packet, giving Shane a stern look. The warrior inspected it, pushed it into his belt, then rested his hand on his sword hilt. It was a menacing gesture. Shane shrugged.

Part of the town's wall had collapsed, and the site was a swarm of activity. A stand of large glowing globes had been erected, and townsfolk and warriors had set up a human chain to remove the fallen masonry. Liam had at first taken the glass globes to be some sort of electric light, but up close he could see a living creature within, glowing brightly and floating in a clear solution. The strange torches used by the crowd were smaller versions of these glowglobes, set onto wooden handles. Some sort of biotechnology.

Morin led them through the town to the Tower. All the while he was locked in conversation with Liam, describing the Fourth Realm, Stonelake, and the Blessed Realms. They passed through the great hall to a room in the complex adjacent to the Tower. Morin left the two warriors who had escorted them from the lakeshore to guard the room. "I must hurry away. Dry clothes are coming for your friend. Ask these men if you need anything else."

"Are you alright, Shane?" asked Liam, when they were alone.

"What the fuck do you think?"

A few minutes later a servant arrived with dry clothes. As Shane changed, he stared at Liam with a murderous glare. Dry once more, he reached for his top pocket then cursed as he realised his cigarettes were gone. "What's going on, Liam?"

Liam opened the windows at the rear of the room, taking a breath of the fresh night air. He could see an alleyway below, lit with glowglobes. The street surface was cobbled, and sloped to the centre to make a shallow drain. A couple were walking slowly along the narrow way. It could be London in the seventeenth century, he thought, except with glowglobes instead of lamps. He smelled baking bread on the breeze. This is Stonelake. The Fourth Realm of the Blessed. An alien planet! A thrill of excitement shot through him. His inherited talent as Keeper had brought them here. The enormity of that step between worlds was still sinking in.

Shane walked over to Liam, blocking his view. He stared at Liam with a sarcastic gleam in his eye. "What's the matter? Cat got your tongue?"

Only hours ago, Liam had witnessed the cold-blooded murder

of a bound victim. Until tonight, the legacy of his family had been a distant thing. Now he realised, more than ever, what he had been entrusted with.

"Back off, Shane."

Shane grunted and leant casually on the sill. "Can you at least tell me where we are? I don't need to be a genius to figure out we are not on Fraser Island anymore."

"We are in the Fourth Realm of the Blessed. In a Gateway outpost called Stonelake."

"You're an idiot, Liam. Just because you believe anything doesn't mean I will. And where's this 'Fourth Realm?'"

"Another planet," said Liam.

"Bullshit!" said Shane, cutting the air with his palm. He was truly pissed.

The doors flew open. The two warriors, keyed to full alertness, watched them from the doorway.

"This is a set-up," said Shane. "Don't think I don't know about the big inheritance."

"*What?*"

Shane swaggered. "Yeah I know. I know people who know people. Just like I know you've put all this together. Somehow. Drugged me and taken me to one of those freak-show reenactments they have in Europe. You were always into that fantasy crap.

"What's the language anyway? Swedish? It's bullshit, Liam. Bullshit. Get me out of here. *Now*. Just get me a cigarette first."

"I can't."

"Bullshit." Shane turned and stalked out of the room, shouldering past the guards.

The two guards looked back at Liam, as though they expected him to order Shane back. In that pause, Shane smiled at him from the doorway and lifted his shirt to show him the dark butt of the automatic pistol tucked into his waistband.

"Wait," said Liam, but Shane just walked away.

The two warriors conferred quickly. One followed Shane. Liam stood in the doorway and watched them both disappear around the end of the corridor. This *was* all real. Shane would have to find out the hard way.

Liam smiled at the Stonelake warrior, who nodded in recognition.

"Not . . . good. . . ," said the warrior.

Liam was surprised that he could pick up some of the Realm words, even without a mental bond. His mind had absorbed the language with astounding rapidity.

Liam concentrated for a moment, then replied in the Realm tongue. "Yes. Not good."

Shane wandered down the stairwell, retracing his path through the hall and out into the night. He was pleased that no one interfered with his progress, not even the warrior who shadowed him. He was a big guy, but he did not seem too bright.

"Cigarette? Smoke?" Shane parodied a smoking motion.

The warrior shook his head. Whether he understand or not, Shane had no idea. Okay, if it was all a game, he would play.

Shane looked up. The stars looked really strange. *I must be way up in the northern latitudes.* No. Not cold enough. It was winter there at the moment. Maybe South America? Some weird enclave of non-Spanish speakers? Argentina?

He went to the wall to watch the backbreaking work of shifting the fallen stone. He walked through the crowd, trying to find someone who spoke English, but with no luck. They all looked at him like *he* was the crazy one. As the work proceeded, the mangled forms of the guards who had been on the wall were gradually uncovered and removed. The workers continued in solemn silence. Shane pushed through to get a better view, but was soon bored.

Flames flared to life on the field out beyond the town. Shane scrambled through the breached wall and set out across the field to get a closer look. They were burning what looked like bodies. More staged crap! The bodies on the lakeshore back on Fraser though . . . he was pretty sure they had been real. He frowned, trying to make sense of it all. The greasy smoke rising off the pyres was ghastly. He skirted the plume, approaching the solemn ring of warriors around the lit pyres from upwind. The guard shadowed him.

One of the warriors standing by the fire was smoking a pipe.

Like a starving man, Shane made straight for the smoker. The slightly overweight man initially refused Shane's requests, but when Shane offered to trade him his thick silver wrist-chain, the man nodded, giving him the pipe and a pouch of tobacco. Shane eagerly packed the pipe and lit the bowl from the pyre. The warriors glared at him, but said nothing. *It's all fake anyway.* He initially choked on the heavy blend, but was soon sighing with satisfaction. Time passed. His escort grew impatient, shifting from foot to foot. Shane considered hanging around longer just to aggravate the man, but was too bored.

Shane walked back to the town, puffing on the pipe as he walked. What had Liam called this place? Stonelake. He angled his walk to arrive back at the broken wall. He knew his way back from there.

Just shy of the wall, the smouldering flame in his pipe abruptly died. Shane cursed and pulled a lighter from his pocket, but it would not fire up.

"Damn."

Shane checked the gas, but there was plenty of fuel. Shaking his head, he put away the pipe and lighter, and settled back to watch the guards as they hauled away the masonry. The crowd cried out, scrambling back like someone had threatened to detonate a bomb. One of the warriors shouted an order, and a young guard ran into the town. Shane pushed into the space they had vacated. The workers had uncovered the crushed body of one of those ugly black thugs. This body looked real, just like the one at the lake. There was just too much blood and gore to fake. He looked around at the crowd. They seemed truly scared of it. Hard to know why, he thought, it was just dead meat.

Shane knelt beside the corpse.

His escort barked an order and drew his sword. Shane looked up. He knew the warrior would not come any closer. The thrill of defiance made him grin with pleasure. He rifled through the armour and pouches of the dead thug. With a curse, the warrior sheathed his sword and waited for him at the edge of the circle. *This is the best fun I've had all night!* Not one person in the crowd dared to come close enough to stop him. He was looking for ammunition, but he found nothing but stage props made up to look like withered body parts. He grunted in contempt. He stood up, disappointed. A wave of dizziness overtook him, and his heart clenched with sharp pain. He stepped back. The wind changed and he choked on a mouthful of smoke from the funeral pyre.

The crowd backed away from him.

Shane's head cleared. He was drained and weary, and staggered over to lean against a wall, trying to catch his breath. His gaze was drawn inexorably toward the thug's body. *Contact.* A hot lust flooded Shane. The world went red. A sudden erection took his breath away, then eased.

"Wow. What a hit!"

It's time to find some action!

He started walking, then with a burst of speed, he ducked through the tight backstreets, darting left and right at random. The big man in his heavy armour called out angry commands, but did not stand a chance of closing the distance. Shane soon lost him. Alone at last, he refilled the pipe and tried to light it. *Nothing.* No flame from the lighter. "*Fuck.*" He tucked the pipe and lighter away.

Shane walked slowly toward the more lit sections of the town. He knew what he wanted, and he knew he would get it. He flicked his tongue across his teeth. Strange, he thought, they seemed too flat.

Chapter 31
Stonelake Gateway — Fourth Realm

Morin watched the burning funeral pyres from his Tower window. Heavy black smoke shrouded the battlefield. The surviving warriors kept vigil, grim and silent.

He touched his stomach where the seraphin's blades had cut him, so long ago. The pain had been intense. The wound severe. He had stayed on his feet long enough to create a Shield in the tower stairway, then collapsed. He had sacrificed his mionanail, fixing it into the centre of the Shield to power the spell. He lay there on the steps, paralysed by pain, as the seraphin hit the glowing barrier like a whirlwind of fire, knowing it was only a matter of time before his mionanail was drained of power and the Shield failed. Sheer will had driven him to his feet and up the narrow stairway to the family apartments. Erel Evenstone, Finn's mother, and Finn's two brothers, Kas and Levin, had all died to give him time to reach the roof with Finn and Tallandra. There, he had been within sight of the High King's Tower . . . and within reach of the ardanaith that slumbered within. It had taken the ardanaith's full power to beat back the seraphin long enough for he and his other thurjuns to join forces. Together, they had pushed the Archfiend's army back to Minoras, and sealed the Gateway. The fate of the Third Realm had hovered on the edge the abyss that night.

Now, finally, the attack on Stonelake.

He had waited fifteen years for this night. A night born in Vespar's betrayal. Now warriors lay cold and still on the floor of the temple, being prepared for burial, while the siithe burned. A score of priests and priestesses had been slain, and despite everything, Sephany had been taken. By a miracle, Liam had been on hand to open the way for Finn. Now at least, Finn and Genna could take the fight to the Vault, and try to free Sephany. Morin knew the krell. VoYannan must plan to use Sephany to increase his power . . . and not in a trivial way. This was all part of a larger strategy that ended with the destruction of the Realms. They *must* find a way to thwart his plans.

Morin sat by the heatglobe, warming his hands.

According to Liam, knowledge of the Blessed Realms had vanished from the histories of Earth. Liam's thurjun's skills were a remnant, passed down in secret through his family line. He was talented, but unique. This meant that Earth was a prime target. If Earth was taken, the Vaults of Sheol would have one more staging post from which to launch assaults on the Blessed Realms. After a thousand years of isolation, Stonelake would become a front-line outpost. He also had another problem: no one remained on Earth to open the Stonelake Gateway. Even if Finn succeeded, how would he return? How would additional forces from the Realms reach him, or even hope to stop the Vault occupation of Earth?

Morin shook his head.

These were problems only the College of Thurjuns would be able to solve. That meant a journey across the Realms to the High Court — for both him and Liam. In any case, the High Court must be notified of the attack on Stonelake, the capture of Sephany, and the reactivation of the Gateway.

Closing his eyes, Morin steadied his mind.

He drew on his last mental reserves and reached across the planet to Dromar, the capital of the Fourth Realm, and the community of Seekers there. Long range mental communication was an extension of the same skill a thurjun used to reach through a closed Gateway to a receptive mind on the other side. Although to reach so far, to such a specific location, required a highly trained focus and an innate talent. An image of the Dromar night fled across his vision, and he sensed that his consciousness had stretched the distance, despite his fatigue. He called out a mental greeting.

Morin was answered by an elderly Seeker, keeping vigil in the night. He quickly relayed what had happened in Stonelake, and then sat back to rest. The message would now be passed through a network of Seekers across three worlds to the High Court. The speed at which the message reached the Court would depend on the Seekers who were on duty when the message was received, and their range. The reply would have to be returned through the same network. It would be hours, at least.

Morin disrobed and settled back on his narrow bed. Sleep did not come swiftly. He was haunted by images of Procarrus, the siithe, and the slain Stonelake warriors. The last tore at him. Men and women dead on the same ground where they had celebrated a Festival only days ago. Finally, he drifted into a restless sleep.

"Morin!"

Morin sat up in alarm. He turned up the spigot on his lamp, flooding the light-chamber with nutrient. The small, jelly-like animal within the device began to glow, emitting a clear white light. He could see the bar in place across the door. The room was empty.

"Morin, are you listening?" It was a young woman's voice.

Morin clambered out of bed. As his mind cleared, he realised that the voice was in his head. He settled himself into his chair and concentrated on receiving the signal. "Morin," came the voice once more. Mental voices were often no more than thoughts, lacking any sense of the sender, but her voice was powerful and clear, as though she was in the room with him.

"Yes, it is Morin. I can hear you well," replied Morin using his mind.

"I am Seeker Tirini."

Morin was puzzled. "I have met most of the Seekers at Dromar. I do not remember you. Are you new to the order?"

Morin heard laughter, and saw a bare stone room where a slender woman and a man sat together. Then the image was gone. The man at the table beside the young woman — sitting with his usual impatience — was Kevrin, Master Thurjun and head of the College of Thurjuns.

"I am new to the order, but I am not at Dromar. I am at the High Court."

Morin was astonished. There had not been a Seeker of such power in his lifetime. The gift to reach through space, across such massive distances, was nothing short of miraculous.

"Forgive my astonishment," said Morin. "For one so young, you have remarkable powers."

"Can we begin?" asked Kevrin. Tirini communicated his words through the bond.

The image of the room flooded back to Morin, and it was as

though he was sitting with Tirini in the flesh. He looked at Kevrin. "Kevrin, can you hear me?"

"Yes, Morin. And I am eager to be finished with this midnight foolery."

"Has the council considered the news?" asked Morin.

Kevrin nodded. "Yes. And we have met with the High King. There is clearly nothing we can do from here. We need you to bring the Earth thurjun to the First Realm. Then we can study his knowledge more thoroughly. Once we know how the Vault forces are entering Earth, we will know how to proceed. High King Torren has decided to send a small company of warriors through the Vault worlds to close their Gateway to Earth. We need you both here as soon as possible."

"And what of a replacement for me here?"

"One has already been sent," snapped Kevrin. "You have your instructions."

Kevrin stood up and left room. The image wavered.

Tirini apologised. "Sorry, Morin. I cannot hold the link steady."

Bemused at her humility, Morin shook his head. "Thank you for helping us."

"Goodbye, Morin." The image of her soft, oval shaped face, and startling green eyes, flashed before his mind's eye, her lips curved in a shy smile. She looked young. Perhaps only nineteen.

"Goodbye, great Seeker."

Morin could hear the sound of Tirini giggling, then the link was gone.

Chapter 32
Fraser Island, Queensland, Australia — Earth
26th December 1999

Procarrus used a simple trick of magic to enhance his eyesight. He watched, across the intervening strip of water, as the Realm Captain was captured by the local guardsmen. Deep within the belly of the cruiser, the engines rumbled back to life, sending vibrations up through his bootheels. The lights of his stern cabin flicked on. The Realm dampening field had faded. Lights came on across the bay.

He laughed in triumph. "Incompetent fools. This world will be easy to destroy, my friend. They do not know their friends from their foes."

At his feet, Barsus growled. His hound longed for combat. Procarrus absently bent down to pat the thick bristles that grew behind Barsus' massive head. "I know, Barsus. But I must keep you hidden. The siithe can pass as locals here. You would cause a little too much alarm. Soon, my friend, we will have a siithe legion in Sydney. Then you will be free to rend and tear as you will."

Barsus shut his mouth with a menacing clack and ground his teeth in frustration. Once Procarrus' centurion, Barsus had long ago lost his speech. He was truly a Hound of Chaos — twisted by the power of the Vault. He had a man's strengths and appetites, with the bear-sized body of a beast, huge jaws, and gleaming eyes set deep in an armoured skull.

Procarrus considered his own reflection in the glass of the cabin doors. He had neatly cropped hair and a youthful face, although his body appeared thin and wasted. This was deceptive. Beneath his robes, his twisted muscles and tendons were imbued with supernatural strength.

Procarrus was pleased with his victory in Stonelake, yet the personal cost had been high. Energies carefully garnered over centuries had been squandered in a few hours. The Fragment, a vital key to the Stonelake Gateway, had been lost, closing the Gateway to Vault forces . . . and somehow the Realm Captain had been able to follow them. His grip on the hilt of his longsword tightened. Procarrus forced his hand to relax, and lifted it into the steering deck's dim light to examine the skin. There were blemishes there. The signs of aging, no longer held back by magic, were taking hold. He would need to replenish his powers, and quickly.

"Come, Barsus."

The Archfiend descended to the large cabin serving as his court. Two huge siithe took up station on either side of him, while Barsus padded across the boards at his right. Despite all the forces that he had left to guard the boat, one of his slaves had escaped. The small blond woman. His failure to dominate her mind rankled him.

He took his seat on the dais and swept a predatory gaze across the room. Dim globes had been set along the roof, but most of the light issued from a large brazier in the room's centre, which had charred the nearby deck boards. Flames danced in the coals and cast menacing shadows across the metal bulkheads. The remaining slave-women cowered. He smiled. Nothing heightened his appetite like fear. The Gate-opener Vicki was chained to the base of his throne. She watched him through a fringe of long hair, a dark bruise — the mark of his hand — coloured her pale cheek. The slaves were deathly silent, hardly daring to breathe. They had long ago recovered from the drugs, and their eyes swept in terror from the armoured siithe, to the gruesome body parts that littered the floor, and back to him. The stench was offensive. Procarrus was displeased with his siithe. Just like any servants, the brutes always had to be kept in hand. He had no problem with their appetites, only the mess they left. It offended his Roman sensibilities.

Procarrus beckoned his siithe captain toward him. "Ossis. Bring the priestess."

Ossis gave the command. Two siithe warriors left the room at a run, their boots clattering on the metal treads of the stairwell as they climbed to the upper decks.

Procarrus studied the assembled slaves. "Now. Which one of you will grace their lord's table?" The ragged group looked back at him in incomprehension, failing to understand the common

Vault language he had used.

The siithe around the room snickered, though. At his side, Barsus grunted with lust. He liked to have his way with the victims — dead or alive.

Procarrus' eyes settled on each of the women in turn. One in particular had taken his interest — perhaps there was still a spark of defiance left in her? *Interesting*. He was about to summon her closer when he heard the gruff curses of the siithe and the sound of chains echoing down the narrow stairwell. The two siithe led Sephany into the room and forced her to her knees below the dais. She was dressed in the thin nightclothes in which she had been seized. Her white shift was stained with blood from the wound on her temple. Dried blood matted her dark hair.

Procarrus watched her in the flickering light. He remained silent, knowing it would unnerve her. She would look into him, and she would see nothing but the cold emptiness of her own death.

Despite the heat, Sephany shivered. He smiled as he saw the fear in her eyes. She looked up at him, searching his face. For a moment, her fear grew, then a quiet determination took hold. Gradually her shivering subsided. Her lips moved in a silent prayer.

His stomach twisted in anger. "Do you know who I am?" he asked in the Realm tongue.

Sephany met his gaze evenly. "Yes. You are one of the lieutenants of the Vault. A fiend."

Procarrus was enraged by her calm. Barsus growled and rose to his feet. The Hound's deep-set yellow eyes fixed on Sephany with an avaricious gleam, his teeth set to rend.

Procarrus placed a hand on Barsus' shoulder to restrain him.

"I am Procarrus. *Archfiend* of the Vault. I serve at the right hand of VoYannan — master of the Vault of Seven Horns."

Sephany remained silent.

Procarrus unleashed his power. He sent burning tendrils spearing into her mind.

She screamed.

"Can you feel it?" he said. "Can you feel my hot, tearing grasp?"

Sephany quietened. Calm once more, she began to pray, this time out loud. "I open myself to the light of the High God. I place myself under the High God's protection."

Procarrus laughed in contempt. He feasted on the innocence of her fresh, young mind. He sought out each hidden corner, testing for weaknesses. Whispers of prayer rose around him like a teasing wind, and he laughed again. Then his inner sight was blinded by a rushing wall of white light. It burned away his reaching mental tendrils with searing pain. Procarrus gasped and withdrew. He surged to his feet, advancing on her until he was close enough to spit in her face. To further enrage him, she refused to meet his gaze, denying him any sense of closure. Her mouth moved in prayer.

"You will not fare so well against VoYannan. He will take your mind, pitiful priestess, then plant a demon seed in your belly that will grow fat as it devours your soul. *A Seed that will rip its way from your wasted carcass.*"

Sephany's eyes opened in shock. Her prayer faltered. *Now I have your attention.*

Procarrus raised his arm to strike her down, then stepped back and reasserted his control. VoYannan wanted her unharmed.

"Take her out of my sight. And clean her wounds. After all . . . she is our master's bride." He laughed as she was taken away, yet he felt no triumph. His hunger was greater than ever. He could feel a weakness taking hold of his limbs. That, he would *not* tolerate.

"It is time to feed," declared Procarrus.

The siithe grinned, bloody strips of meat hanging between their teeth. They always enjoyed his leavings.

Barsus fixed his eyes on the Gate-opener, drooling with lust. Vicki trembled. Procarrus inclined his head, giving permission. "Do what you will with her, Barsus. But leave her alive."

"No!" screamed Vicki as Barsus leapt onto her, his weight knocking her flat.

"Be silent," snapped Procarrus. Vicki bit her lip until it bled. Her eyes were glazed with horror as Barsus tore at her clothing. Procarrus had no energy to waste on illusion. She would have to suffer each moment of her punishment with no escape, and so learn the consequences of the Fragment's loss.

Procarrus assessed the slaves, deciding who to drain. Then he had another idea. *Yes.* The one who allowed the prisoner to escape.

"Bring me the one named Indian Joe."

Chapter 33
High Road from Stonelake — Fourth Realm

Liam gripped the edge of the chariot to keep his balance.

The excitement of their forward rush as they hurtled along the High Road sent his heart racing. He and Morin were in the lead chariot, while Shane and the courier Zanthis travelled behind them in a second vehicle.

"At least the weather is with us," said Morin, his words distinct across the mind-bond.

Liam looked up at the dawn sky. The clouds blazed gold above the rising sun. "It's breathtaking." Stonelake and its wooded valley were long behind them.

Liam and Morin's charioteer, Bran, leant out over the team with the casual ease of an expert, carefully scanning the road ahead. Each of the chariots was drawn by a matched pair of horses, and was of superb lightweight construction, with metal leaf-springs insulating the riders from the roughness of the road. Provisions for the journey were secured to the side with rope bindings. Both the charioteers wore sleeveless leather vests with loose coloured trousers. Although short and wiry, their arms were impressively muscled, with forearms like a dockworker.

The light dimmed as they entered a narrow forested gorge. Birds darted through the thick canopy, sometimes keeping pace with them before darting back into the greenery. Then the High Road dipped and cut sharply to the right. The gorge opened out into a vast fertile plain that sloped down to their right. The scenery reminded Liam of Ireland. He saw dozens of tiny hamlets, clusters of stone-built houses amid long rows of crops that swayed gently in the breeze, and green paddocks divided by low-set stone walls, where livestock with strangely elongated heads grazed with steady determination on the new grass.

The glare soon had him wishing for a pair of sunglasses, and the ache in his back and feet for a padded car seat. As the hours passed, Liam's grasp of the Realm language grew rapidly. Around mid-morning Morin let the mind-bond drop. Liam was amazed to realise he could converse normally in Morin's language. Somehow he had absorbed more vocabulary and grammar than he had heard Morin use. Much more. There had been a subconscious transfer across the shared mind-bond.

"How long will it take to reach the First Realm?" asked Liam.

"If luck is with us, less than a week."

"And where do we stop tonight?" asked Liam.

"Tonight we will camp at the border forest."

"The border forest?"

"I still forget how foreign the Realms are to you, Liam. Let me explain," said Morin. "The six Realms of the Blessed are bound by the law of the High King. Since ancient times it has been decreed that 'each of the Realms be girt in green'. Each Realm province must be held within the grasp of a natural landscape, whether that be desert, icescape, or forest. In that way, the balance of nature is kept, and the natural creatures have tracts of land on which to travel."

"And what of the High Road?" asked Liam. "Does that pass through these border areas?"

Morin smiled. "Well, yes and no. The High Road travels to the border forest of Stonelake province, but once within the forest, we must tread lightly. These chariots will be dismantled and carried with our provisions. By law, no permanent roads may be made through the wild borders, although many trails pass through them. After all, do not the wild boars make paths of their own?"

If he could have dreamt of a world kept in balance, where nature was respected and upheld, he could not have done better.

"If Stonelake were a richer province, we would have a flying platform. As it is, we have to take the Road."

Liam looked at the forested hills in the distance. "This really is a paradise." The High Road was snaking its way through the plain. The air retained the cool freshness of morning, and he took a deep breath, invigorated. *The air is so clean.*

Morin chuckled. "We treat our worlds well, and have learnt some important lessons, but human nature remains the same. See the High Court first before you declare this a paradise. Besides, some would argue that we are too static . . ." Morin grew contemplative for a moment then sighed. "But that is a thought for another day."

They stopped for lunch at one of the small villages Liam had seen from the heights of the pass. There were animals everywhere. Big draft horses, and smaller rounceys. One paddock was filled with creatures that looked like a cross between a sheep and a goat. Morin was known to everyone. The image of bucolic medieval Europe was challenged by the high quality of the clothing, its modern lines, and the richness of the dyes. Unlike Stonelake, fires burned here. Logs glowed in the inn's hearth, sheathed by flickering flame, though far more heat and light came from the ubiquitous glowglobes and heatglobes, the latter which the locals insisted on called glowfires. Liam sat with Shane as they started in on their large savoury meat pies, but his attempts to get his friend into conversation hit a stone wall. Shane ignored him until they were halfway through their meal, when he said. "Having a nice conversation with your new buddy?" Liam realised Shane would be wondering how he spoke the Realm tongue.

"Yeah. The mind-bond—"

"Just shut the fuck up," said Shane, who went back to ignoring him.

As they set out from the town, they passed a tall mill, set not beside a stream for water power, but behind a pond that stank like a rendering plant.

"God. What's that?" asked Liam.

Moring signalled the charioteers to stop. "Come and have a look. Maybe your friend wants to see as well. Shane?" Morin called the last word across to Shane.

Shane had stepped down from the chariot to stretch. He shook his head and waved them off. There was something off about him that Liam could not quite put a finger on. A feral edge.

Morin led Liam into the building, where he was greeted by the miller, a thickset man wearing a sleeveless shirt. Inside he saw not a single mill wheel, but a whole series of them, fed grain by a complicated arrangement of pipes that carried the grain in an air stream. *Pneumatic conveyance.* The wheels were spun from a central shaft by a series of gears. The motive power was coming from a creature the size of a small elephant, but resembling nothing more than a vast grey slug. It sat in a stone tank, saturated by the stinking pond water. Every two or three seconds, its colossal body would flex and lengthen, driving a huge piston. That force was transmitted through a crankshaft and a network of gears to the drivetrain.

"It is a *musclesnake*," said Morin. "Non-sentient, of course."

Liam grinned at the thing, even as he continued to hold his breath against the stink. *More biotechnology.* It effectively brought the technological level — in terms of available power —up to something akin to the early days of steam power.

"Unaffected by a dampening field?" asked Liam. Morin had explained the basic ways in which the Realms defended themselves from Vault technology.

"Of course. It would be forbidden otherwise."

Morin's last comment had made Liam uneasy, although he was not sure why. There was so much about the Realms he did not know.

Shane had used the break to smoke a pipe of the noxious tobacco he had found in Stonelake. When they returned from the mill, Shane scowled at Liam, then tapped the pipe out on a chariot wheel.

By late afternoon, the plains had given way to forest as they entered the wilder border lands. Then later, with the sun setting at their backs, the High Road came to an abrupt end at the base of a forested mountain. The range dominated the eastern sky. It towered above them, rising to a high mist-shrouded plateau, and its distant, snow-capped peaks, caught the last rays of the setting sun in dazzling brilliance.

Bran eased the chariot to a stop. Liam looked into the forest ahead. It was gloomy under the trees, the shadows made deeper by dusk. There was no obvious path. Not even an animal track. It was daunting.

"The border forest," said Morin.

A cool, moist breeze drifted from the forest, bringing the smell of rotting vegetation. Liam could hear animal calls in the distance, haunting and mysterious. The trees species were unfamiliar, and with a jolt, the reality confronted him. This *was* an alien world, with rules, assumptions, and premises, he could only guess at.

There was a small clearing to their right. The ground sloped down to a narrow stream, running fast from the mountain. Liam and Morin stepped down from the chariot and walked stiffly through the clearing to the creek. Bran sprang down with all the agility and energy of a monkey. Liam and Morin sat on the bank. Liam took off his sandshoes and dangled his feet in the cool stream. "Ahhh. That's heaven!"

As the sun fell below the horizon, a loud chorus of crickets began. That much, at least, sounded like home.

Liam marvelled at the endurance of the charioteers. They went straight to work tending their horses and equipment, then started building a campfire. The Realm language was boiling over in his mind. Morin told him it would be so for a few weeks, and that the more he used the language in that time, the more he would retain permanently.

"We will camp here for the night and enter the forest in the morning," said Morin.

Shane walked over, his face white with exhaustion. "How long does this nature tour have to go on, Liam? Because it's no joke. I have spent the day in a bouncing box-cart with a South American or whatever-he-is who can't speak a word of English." Shane pulled the pipe and pouch of tobacco from his shirt with a violent motion and started to pack a pipe.

"I am sorry, mate. But there is nothing I can do. We are not in South America. We are not *anywhere* on Earth."

"Bullshit, Liam." Shane pulled a lighter from his pocket and flicked it on, igniting the bowl. "At least my lighter is working today."

Morin watched the exchange with interest. "Listen to your friend, Shane," he said in English. "This is the Fourth Realm of the Blessed. A world far distant from your own in space."

Shane glared at Morin.

"From what Liam has told me, your journey through the Gateway was an accident. If so, the High Court will do everything in its power to return you to Earth," added Morin.

"Don't worry. I intend to go home," said Liam. *After I have seen the High Court and more of the Realms, that is.*

Shane grunted and stalked away to the campfire.

"It is difficult for him," said Morin.

Liam watched Shane as he took a seat by the fire and exhaled a cloud of tobacco smoke. "*Shane* is difficult."

It was no surprise that Shane was in a crappy mood. He had hardly slept the night before. They had both been roused an hour before dawn for the trip. Shane had only got back to their room an hour before that. Liam, half asleep, had woken when Shane returned, roused by his muttering and cursing as he fumbled his way to bed. In the pre-dawn darkness, just for a moment, Liam could have sworn he saw a siithe. The vision was brief, but sleep had been impossible after that. He considered telling Morin, then decided against it. Even though Morin's intentions were good, the thurjun now controlled their lives. They could not afford any sort of misunderstanding.

The region around Stonelake was warm and temperate, in many ways similar to his native south-east Queensland. However, although it was summer beyond the Gateway, here it was late autumn, and a damp chill seeped down from the forest. Liam and Morin made their way back through the twilight to the warmth of the campfire, settling close to its edge. Liam nodded a greeting to Bran, who was busily preparing a stew. The horses shuffled as close to the fire as their tethers allowed.

The courier, Zanthis, took his sword from its scabbard and began to fuss over the blade, testing the edge and polishing the gleaming metal with a cloth. His movements were deliberate, fastidious. He was dressed in a brightly coloured shirt, light green silk breeches, and a dark cape. Liam had not met the courier before their journey, and was curious about him. "Zanthis, Morin tells me you are an officer of the High Court?"

The courier stared down his nose at Liam. "Yes, I am a senior member of staff for High King Torren's son, Sentas."

Morin poked the fire with a stick and looked at the stew appreciatively, seemingly unconcerned with anything Zanthis might have to say. Shane, unable to follow the conversation, blew a cloud of smoke over the stew, earning a black look from Bran, who had taken cooking duty.

"And what do you do on the staff?" asked Liam.

"Duties of the highest importance," said Zanthis, snapping his longsword back into its scabbard with a flourish.

"More like your master's chamber-boy," said Tres, the other charioteer.

"Aye, when Sentas calls, Zanthis yaps as loud as any lapdog," said Bran, laughing.

Zanthis glared at Tres and Bran, but said nothing.

"The truth is you are a minor servant of the High Court, and of equal standing as . . . for example . . . a humble charioteer," said Tres with a wicked grin.

"You should have heard him begging for passage after his mount went lame," said Bran.

The charioteers were obviously enjoying carving the pompous courtier down to size. Liam was puzzled by the antagonism, and was still curious about the First Realm.

"What is the High Court like, Zanthis?" asked Liam.

Zanthis sneered, brushing a small leaf from his cloak. "More grand than you could imagine, coming from the primitive worlds beyond the Realms."

"We have our own wonders," said Liam defensively. "We have cities as broad as this whole valley."

Zanthis' eyes narrowed. "Really. And what of technology? Weapons?"

"We have machines that fly through the air, and that travel on land. All sorts of advanced technology, and weapons . . ." Liam faltered, thinking of the horror of atomic warfare.

A quiet had descended on the fire. Even the charioteers grew tense.

"What sort of weapons?" asked Zanthis.

"Mainly firearms, I guess."

"Firearms?" asked Zanthis, his mouth struggling to form the strange word.

"Weapons that fire small pellets, propelled by explosives."

"Vault weapons!" snapped Zanthis, with a gleam in his eyes. "So you are from a Vault world!" The courier turned to Morin, his voice taking on an air of assumed authority. "Beware Morin. He could be a Vault spy."

"Still your tongue, Zanthis! Before you choke on it," snapped Morin.

Zanthis' shoulders sagged. He looked down at his feet. Despite his affability, there was no doubt of Morin's ultimate authority.

A gnawing fear began in Liam's stomach. He had been looking forward to his trip to the High Court as he would to a holiday, but how would they really view him? Would he be condemned because of his world? Despite his aid to Finn? He turned to Morin in a state of anxiety. The thurjun read the look.

"Do not fear the High Court, Liam," said Morin in English. "All will be well."

Bran ladled the thick stew into a bowl and passed it to Liam with a small loaf of bread. "Baked fresh in Stonelake this morning." Liam nodded his thanks. Starving and travel-weary, Liam tore into the food. It was delicious. The simple comfort helped to ease his fears.

Once the meal was done, Bran ordered Zanthis to clean the pots and dishes. Liam stifled a grin as the humiliated courier made his way down to the stream, balancing all the utensils between his arms. With Zanthis gone, Morin questioned Liam in detail about the weapons of Earth. To Liam's relief, Morin did not seem shocked or surprised at the mention of atomic weapons.

The fire was falling low when they heard hoofbeats.

A single rider galloped off the High Road to the campfire and drew rein. A young warrior dismounted, dressed in light armour.

"Guardsman, Keris!" said Morin in surprise, rising to greet him. "Take a seat by the fire. You look exhausted."

Keris shook his head. "Thank you, Lord Morin, but I prefer to stand. This is official business." He scanned the group. His eyes locked onto Shane, who was sitting back against a fallen log, smoking his pipe. He was watching Keris with dark, narrowed eyes. "I have disturbing news."

"Of what?" asked the thurjun, instantly alert.

Keris' eyes flicked to Shane then back to Morin. "Yesterday night, another siithe body was discovered beneath the fallen masonry at the wall."

Morin nodded. "Yes. I understand. Was it taken to the pyres?"

Keris shook his head. "No, Lord Morin. We could not touch it.

It had been buried too deep for the High God's Flame to reach. No blessing had been bestowed on the corpse before . . . it happened."

Morin's face creased in concern. "What happened, Keris?"

"One of the travellers from the Gateway," said Keris. "The one called Shane," he said pointing. "He was there. He. . . *touched* the corpse."

Morin nodded. "That alone establishes nothing."

Shane stood up and slowly backed away from the fire, his hand inching toward a bulge in his shirt, just above his waistband.

"Yes, but when the priestess from Jasper arrived to perform the ceremony, she said the Shade was gone!"

Liam did not know what a Shade was, but he could see that Morin and both charioteers were shaken by the news.

Keris' face, even his lips, grew pale. "And that is not all."

"What else happened?" asked Morin.

Keris took a breath. His hands trembled. "There was a . . . rape." His voice, strangled with emotion, dropped to a whisper. "It was my sister, Velis. 'It was one of the strangers,' she told us. 'The one with the pipe.' "

Keris drew his sword and advanced on Shane. "I demand justice!"

Morin threw himself between them. "Keris! *Stop!*"

Shane pulled the pistol. He pointed it at Keris.

"Enough of this bullshit!" yelled Shane. "Alien worlds, fucking jibber-jabber. *Enough!*" Shane swivelled the gun toward Morin. "You! You speak English. Get me out of here *now*, or so help me, I will blow every one of you away!"

Morin's face darkened. He turned toward Shane, his back now to Keris. "Give me the weapon," he said in English.

"No!"

Keris slipped around Morin and darted at Shane.

Shane turned and fired. The bullet took Keris high in the left shoulder. The young warrior was spun off his feet, but he did not lose his grip on his sword.

The intensity in Morin's eyes grew. Liam felt something sweep though him. The campfire went out like a doused candle flame.

With a howl of rage and pain, Keris surged to his feet and ran at Shane.

Shane fired point-blank at Keris. The gun now aimed at the young warrior's head. The hammer fell with a *click*

Nothing.

Keris' blade cut down, severing Shane's arm at the wrist.

Shane's mouth opened in mute agony. He fell to his knees in shock, staring at his severed hand on the grass in front of him, which still clutched the gun. Keris raised his sword, two-handed, up to the side. Liam recognised the move. It was a beheading strike.

"Don't!" shouted Liam.

Bran stepped in and grabbed Keris' sword arm from behind, staying the blow.

"*No! Let me end it here!*" yelled Keris.

Shane finally found his voice. He howled in agony, clutching at the stump. Blood gouted through his fingers in crimson rivulets. Dripped on the grass.

Morin walked to Keris and placed a hand on his shoulder. "Killing him will not end it, Keris. Only time and hope can heal the hurt you feel."

Keris let Bran take his sword. Liam watched as Morin skilfully crafted a healing magic to seal the young guardsman's wound and repair the tissue. "The bullet went right through the shoulder," said Morin.

Morin picked up the gun and Shane's severed hand. He carefully separated the two and gave the weapon to Liam. He took it numbly, hardly believing this was really happening. Morin took the severed hand and placed it against the bleeding stump. Shane hissed in pain, then gritted his teeth. Minutes passed, and sweat beaded on Morin's brow as he used the same healing magic to reattach the hand to Shane's wrist.

"That is the best I can do," he said to Shane in English. "You will have your hand, but I do not know how much function will remain. Perhaps the healers at the High Court can do better."

"Why?" yelled Keris. "Why do you heal him? He is a monster! He should be slain!"

Morin sighed. "Without mercy, Keris, we become our enemies. Besides you are not thinking. If a Shade has entered Shane, then slaying him only releases it once more. Would you care to take it in? No. I think not. He is better dealt with by the Temple in the First Realm."

Keris reluctantly agreed.

At a nod from Morin, Bran gave Keris back his sword.

"I must return to Stonelake," said Keris, mustering his control. "I beg you, Lord Morin. Make sure justice is done."

"I will, Keris. But should you travel now? Your horse is exhausted."

Keris' face was white from shock and blood loss. "I will be fine Morin. I would rather face the pain than spend a night here. With *him*."

Keris mounted stiffly, then galloped away.

"Point the weapon at the ground and hold it securely," said Morin.

Liam gripped the semi-automatic in two hands. Although his training with Aidan had focussed on ancient weapons, it had also included firearms. The pistol was a Sig Sauer P226, probably chambered for 9mm Parabellum rounds. He pointed it at the turf.

Liam felt something *release*. The campfire surged back to life in a rush of flame. The gun discharged in the same instant. The ejected shell springing away into the darkness.

"I have one more duty to perform," said Morin, taking the gun from Liam.

Morin gathered his power. The forms were subtle, and hard to catch. Liam caught only a glimpse before an intense heat engulfed the pistol. The bullets exploded, but the force was contained. Then the gun began to heat. The metal glowed red-hot, then white-hot, eventually melting like putty in Morin's grasp. How the thurjun's hand was not incinerated, Liam had no idea. The heat faded.

Casually, Morin tossed the useless weapon into the fire. "Bury it with the ashes, Bran."

Bran nodded, awed by the thurjun's display.

Liam walked over to Shane, who was struggling to pack his pipe with shaking hands. Memories of the vision Liam had experienced the night before returned. A chill ran down his spine. "You did it, didn't you? That's where you were last night."

Shane's glazed expression hardened. It was the same Shane, his calculating, narcissistic self, but there was a savagery behind his glare, a dark passion that Liam had never seen before. "Fuck off."

Liam stared at Shane, frightened by the darkness in him. He walked back to the fire.

"We should get some rest for tomorrow," said Morin. "Tres. I will leave Shane in your charge tonight. Chain his feet. I do not want him wondering around these hills at night. During the day, you and Zanthis can both keep your eyes on him. He cannot get up to much in the chariot with you."

Tres nodded and walked to his chariot, returning with a lightweight chain. He knelt at Shane's feet and began to secure the first shackle.

"You fuck off as well!" shouted Shane in English.

Tres slowly put down the chain. Then he hit Shane with a right cross that snapped his head back and left him stretched out and dazed on the grass. Tres casually picked up the chain and snapped the shackles shut on Shane's ankles. Then he seized the pipe and tobacco sack and stuffed them into his belt with a sigh of satisfaction. "That damned smoke's been getting up my nose all day."

Liam lay down to sleep, cold and unsure of the future. Something had happened to Shane. His own buoyant excitement at passing through the Gateway was gone, and for the first time Liam understood there were real dangers in this world. Dangers he did not understand. He could not shake the feeling that *this* Shane was not the one who had travelled to Fraser Island with him. The hard-case, but wisecracking friend who always seemed to win him over in the end, had been replaced by a stone-cold killer. A rapist.

The cool ground sucked the warmth right out of his back, and he wrapped his blanket tighter around him. His determination reasserted itself. He was a Keeper. The last thurjun of Earth. This was about more than him. Whatever the future held, he had to help shape it, not just for himself, but for Earth.

It took him a long, *long* time to get to sleep that night.

Chapter 34

Sydney, Australia – Earth
28th December, 1999

Finn sat cross-legged on the floor of his Sydney cell. He had just sent Genna a mental image of the prison building and its location. It had taken him hours to find the right spirit-wind, and he was exhausted. Without the mionanail set into the pommel of his sword, he was forced to use the power of his own mind for all magic, and spells that could be enlivened by such meagre resources. Many of those magics were ancient. Relics of a time before the Realms. This last spell had been more akin to shamanism. A feat only made possible by the training he had received from Morin in the thurjun's arts. It had required hours of constant concentration, and had been unutterably draining.

A bright fluorescent tube shed its empty light on the cell. The concrete floor painted dull grey, the block walls white. The tube's light reflected from the stark polished metal of the single bunk, toilet fixture, and small bench near the entrance that doubled as a table. There were also two white plastic chairs, lightweight and too flimsy to be used as weapons. One wall had a narrow, high window, set with bars, which nonetheless gave a tantalising glimpse of freedom. He closed his eyes, shutting out his view of the prison.

He had explained everything, a score of times. He had used the techniques Morin had taught him to bridge the language gap. They had interrogated him so often that his command of English soon equalled that of his own tongue, his mind even absorbing local expressions. But this facility with the local language had not helped him. In fact, it had made things worse. While using the bonding techniques, he had been able to convince them directly of his sincerity, but using English alone, his interviewers had put his statements through the filter of their own beliefs. His requests for a local thurjun – a *magician* or *sorcerer* in local parlance – had caused outright anger. To these *police* the concept of the Blessed Realms, of Gateways, and the perils of the Vaults of Sheol, were a fantasy. The cataclysmic wars of the past had been forgotten on

Earth. Those few with the thurjuns' blood lost to their own heritage. Escape, he now realised, was his only option.

Finn's eyes flicked open at the rattle of keys. The heavy metal door opened and a man dressed in dark trousers, white shirt, and blue tie, entered the room, escorted by a uniformed policemen. The civilian was slightly overweight, his wavy hair sparse and greasy. His eyes were deep blue, but dull like glass, the whites bloodshot and yellowed. His face was flushed, the skin blotchy and underlain with a sickly pallor. The man eyed Finn objectively, like a druid with a new specimen. Satisfied, he nodded to his escort. "Leave me with him, please."

The policemen's gaze moved to the small camera in the corner of the ceiling, then back to Finn. Then he backed out of the cell. *Remote video surveillance.* Some of the Vault worlds used a similar system. The door slammed shut. The key turned in the lock.

"Hello, ah . . . Finn is it?" asked the man, checking his folder.

"Yes. Finn Evenstone."

The man dragged one of the cell's two plastic chairs noisily across the concrete and sat uncomfortably close to Finn. He assumed a friendly posture and lowered his voice. "My name is Doctor Blundstone. I am a psychologist, and I work with the police on . . . special cases."

"Psychologist?" asked Finn, unaware of the meaning of the word, and too tired to establish a mental bond with the man.

"I help people. Part of that work requires me to establish their 'state of mind' as it were," the man smiled. Perhaps an attempt at reassurance? "I have read the initial transcripts of your interviews with the police. Very . . . interesting. They've asked me if at some stage we could go over a few of the things you've said there . . .?"

Finn was puzzled by the man's roundabout manner. He stood up and walked across the cell to take a seat on the bunk's thin mattress, turning to face the man squarely. "Why not now?"

The man nodded, neither pleased nor disappointed. "If you're happy with that?"

"Yes," said Finn, unsure what the man wanted from him.

"Great," said the man, clearly unhappy with his duties.

What followed was a litany of questions, some related to his journey and others more general. Blundstone apathetically scribbled the answers on his notepad. It was the nature of the questions, and the chilling emptiness of the man's eyes, that finally revealed the truth to Finn. *They think I am insane.*

Finn laughed bitterly.

Blundstone looked up from his notepad and studied Finn without blinking. With deliberate motions he made another entry into the margin of his notepad, then laid it aside.

"I would like to try something else," said Blundstone. "It's called hypnotic regression. It is a valuable technique, but I will only use it if you are willing."

Finn nodded slowly, realising how he could use the man. If he was studying him, as he thought, then Blundstone would have access to all his personal belongings. Amongst the clothing and other effects taken from him was the Ring of Evenstone. Within it was a tiny mionanail. Finn rarely used it, since it depleted rapidly, and the one set into the pommel of his sword contained much more power. But now it could mean the difference between defeat and freedom. And Blundstone could deliver it to him. Every hour that crept by took Procarrus and Sephany closer to the Vaults of Sheol. He may not have another chance.

Finn lay back on the bunk, as instructed by Blundstone, and let the psychologist attempt to lead him into a hypnotic state. But Finn had other plans. Although against the basic creed of the thurjuns, their range of spells included compulsions that could induce others to carry out their will. Use of these was strictly forbidden except in the direst circumstances. Against such a day as this, Morin had taught Finn a basic compulsion. He was low on energy, but Blundstone's bored mind seemed unfocussed, and Finn hoped, easily swayed.

As the psychologist was attempting to lead him into a deep state of hypnosis, Finn raised what little energy he could and wove the matrix of a spell. He would have only seconds after it was implanted to add his suggestion. Finn locked onto the gaze of his interrogator and sent the compulsion racing into the glassy depths.

"So Finn, tell me about the events leading up to—" Blundstone's eyes glazed over.

Finn seized his chance. *"Go to my personal effects and bring me the signet ring."*

The man's eyes resumed their focus. Blundstone was confused for a moment. He cleared his throat and resumed his questions. They all related to the activities of Procarrus, and centred around illegal substances. Finn repeated his earlier statements, and waited.

"Right. This is getting us nowhere," said Blundstone eventually. "It appears you have low hypnotisability." He looked at his watch. He wrote on his notepad. "Delusions remain," he muttered under his breath. He snapped his notebook shut. "That's enough for today. I will see you next week."

Blundstone walked to the door and waved to the camera in the corner of the cell.

Finn was elated, and grinned to himself as a policeman opened the door. It had worked! With the ring he would have a fighting chance.

The policeman looked at Finn. "You'll be having another visitor soon. Federal Agent Yolinda Paris. I think you remember her, don't you?"

At the mention of Yolinda, Finn's anger and frustration crested like a tidal wave. He turned away from the smirking guard and returned to his cot, trying to calm himself. Now more than ever he needed to keep a cool head. Yolinda symbolised so many of the things that were wrong with this world. Like Earth, she did not know her own heart. She had betrayed his trust, and that cut him deeply.

Finn did not have to wait long. Yolinda, dressed in a loose pair of dark blue trousers and a cream blouse, entered the cell escorted by the amused guard. Yolinda had one of the devices they called a "recorder" under her arm. She was stoic, and Finn noticed that the loose shirt she wore was buttoned right to her neck, as protective as armour.

She placed the voice recorder on the small bench, then took Blundstone's chair.

"That will be all," she said, without turning.

"Very well, Agent Paris."

The cell door slammed shut, leaving them alone.

The atmosphere in the room seemed to heat. The silence as

thick as an equatorial noon.

Yolinda reached across and touched a button on the recorder. A small green light came on, the only sign the device was active. Her gaze was fixed on the device, as if Finn were not even in the room.

"Tuesday, twenty-eighth of December. Ten forty-five AM. Federal Agent Yolinda Paris and subject identified as 'Finn Evenstone'."

She turned to him.

Yolinda's eyes, which Finn had not noticed in the darkness of the track, were a soft brown — not hard — yet closed to him just the same. Her blonde hair glowed in the bright lights, a far cry from the unwashed, lank locks, she had sported on Fraser Island. Her face was small and round, the skin still flushed with the health of youth, and set with determination. *How many smiles had graced that soft mouth?* Not many.

"Now," said Yolinda. "Tell me again what you were doing on Fraser Island."

Finn looked down at the recorder, then back at Yolinda. He had been so relieved to find a warrior of Kgari —Earth — to aid him in his quest. Under the moonlight, on that island track, he had put his faith in Yolinda. Over the years, and through the training he had received from Morin, he had learnt to trust his instincts. Had they failed him so utterly?

Although near the point of total exhaustion, Finn gathered his energy and sent a subtle tendril of spirit toward Yolinda, seeking the bridge of minds. Yolinda started in her chair as the bond was formed. There was a flash of vulnerability in the soft, yet impassable, gateway of her eyes. The hard determination returned.

"I ask again. What were you doing on Fraser Island, and what is your connection to the siithe drug ring?"

Finn gasped as a knife-thrust of pain stabbed through his right eye. Through the pain, he forced himself to concentrate. He breathed evenly to induce a state of relaxation.

"As I have told your other guardsman. I am a warrior of the Blessed Realms. A Captain of the High Court of Torren. I came into Kgari — the island you know as Fraser Island — through the

Stonelake Gateway in pursuit of the Archfiend, Procarrus," he said in Realm tongue.

Yolinda's eyes narrowed. She looked at her notes, seemed about to speak, then faltered.

Finn watched her steadily.

"Why do you maintain this story?" she asked, genuinely perplexed.

Finn smiled. Unconsciously, Yolinda had drifted into the Realm language. This bond, and the previous bond on Fraser Island, had been enough to give her a command of the language. That implied a natural talent.

"It is no story, Yolinda. It is the truth."

They looked at each other in silence. He felt her anger rising.

"Let me ask you a question," said Finn. "Have your physicians examined the siithe corpses?"

"That's none of your concern."

"I believe your physicians should be skilled enough to confirm that the siithe are not human. They are alien to this planet." The pain returned. Finn's concentration wavered. He would not be able to maintain the bond.

"The coroner's reports on the bodies are overdue," she said defensively, "but I'm sure—"

He looked up at her.

She blinked, then her mouth took a hard line. "You're here to answer *my* questions! What were you doing on Fraser Island? What is your connection to Procarrus?"

At Yolinda's outburst, Finn's own temper flared like a small sun. "Let me ask you a question. How often do you betray those who help you?"

Yolinda's eyes hardened.

"You want to know what my connection is to Procarrus?" asked Finn. "He was personally responsible for the deaths of my whole family. My father, my mother, my brothers. All dead. And they are only a handful amongst thousands!" Finn surged to his feet. "He must be found and stopped. Before it is too late. Too late for Sephany. Too late for Earth!"

Another shot of pain lanced through his eye, forcing him to gasp out loud. "It is the Vault that is your enemy," said Finn softly, gingerly touching his throbbing temple. "Not, Finn Evenstone."

Finn sat back on the bed and let the mind-bond drop.

The jailer appeared at the cell door. "Are you alright, Agent?"

As the bond dropped, Yolinda's eyes grew unfocussed. She looked across at Finn, suddenly unsure. She stopped the recorder. "Yes, Constable. I'm finished. For now."

Finn did not look up as the keys rattled against the painted steel of the door.

Yolinda followed the uniformed constable out of Finn's cell and down an adjacent corridor.

"Observation Room Two is right down there, on the right." The constable pointed. "We set up a feed from his cell, through the main monitoring room."

"Thanks."

He nodded in reply and returned to his duties.

She was angry with herself. She had spent hours prepping for that interview. Going over the police transcripts of his earlier interrogations, studying everything, poring over every last detail, each thread of cause and effect. She had been determined to grill Finn for hours, pushing him and pushing him until he finally gave up the truth. She had been ready for anything in that interview; anything except the appearance of her own feelings. When he had looked across at her, she had experienced that weird connection again. An overwhelming sense of *him*. Beneath the aristocratic lines of his face, and the bright green eyes, there was strength, integrity and determination. She had *felt* it. And liked what she felt. Then there was the sensation of hearing words beneath words. She had thought the dope was out of her system — that all these strange hallucinations were behind her — but apparently not.

There was so much that did not add up. The lack of any lighting system at the lake, the consistent failure of the firearms, the lack of evidence, the strangeness of the siithe. Shane and Liam, and the other man, Genna, had all vanished. The local police had been unable to locate them.

Inside the observation room, Superintendent Esco and two

local drug squad detectives had been watching the interview on a remote screen. A police constable sat at a desk in front of the video recorder. Esco led the Federal Drugs Task Force, and was technically the boss of her boss, but in reality he ran most undercovers directly. He was a big bluff man, with the hard edge of a former operational Agent.

Esco and the detectives watched Yolinda as she entered. She was unnerved by their united scrutiny. She gave her voice-recorder's memory stick to the police constable working the video. "Get this transcribed," she said. The constable took it with a look of bemusement.

"He might have a little trouble with it," said Esco.

"Why?" asked Yolinda.

"Replay the video," said Esco, without taking his eyes off her.

The constable rewound the video recording and started play.

Yolinda watched herself as she began the interview. A startled look came over her face momentarily, then she listened as Finn began to speak in a strange language, something akin to Gaelic.

"What language is that?" she snapped.

"You tell us," said Esco, pointing to the screen.

Yolinda gasped in amazement as she heard herself reply to Finn in the same language.

"But I conducted the interview in English!"

Esco looked at her with an unnerving gaze. "You have some explaining to do, Constable."

Yolinda's jaw clenched at the unspoken accusation.

"Just what is your connection to this man? And what language were you speaking?" asked Esco.

A hot denial sprang to Yolinda's lips, then she froze. The video track had continued to play. A cold feeling swept across her skin as she realised, that whatever language it was, she understood it. And she could speak it.

Oh, shit.

Chapter 35
Reil Range — Fourth Realm

The cool mountain breeze tussled Liam's hair, and numbed his face, but he hardly noticed. The view was stunning. They were now high in the Reil Range, which rose like a great basalt spine from the centre of the border forest. He had walked from their sheltered camp and up along the ridge to a natural vantage point to catch the dawn. The forest swept down the other side of the Range into a broad green valley, then on to the horizon. It was vast. Below him, mist shrouded the tips of the trees. A broad river flowed east from the flank of the mountains, glittering in the golden light of dawn. Everything was so fresh, so vital.

"I see you found the Old Road."

Liam turned to see Morin, dressed in his customary blue robes, walking through the grass toward him.

"One hell of a view," said Liam in the Realm tongue.

Morin puzzled over his words for a while, then smiled. "It is magnificent," said Morin. "Every time I look down on the vast, untamed wildness of a border reserve, my faith in the Realms is renewed."

This is how a world should be kept, thought Liam. In balance. Surely any sacrifice was worth this?

"You mentioned an old road? Where?" Liam looked around him, but could see only the long grass of the clearing, and the trees that bordered it.

"Do you notice how no trees grow here? And how this grassed area stretches back to our camp?"

Liam nodded.

"This is why," said Morin. The thurjun laid down his staff and knelt. With a grunt of effort, he pulled away clumps of grass, then clods of dirt. Beneath a thin layer of topsoil — no more than a handspan — was a solid base of black glass. He rose to his feet and struck the glass with the heel of his staff. The staff bounced off, leaving the dark material unmarked.

"This is the Old Road," said Morin. "In the dark years before the High King's law, a road stretched through here from

Stonelake. It rose from the western valley across the flank of the Reil Range, and onward. Only this small fragment of it — high on the range — remains. As you can see, it is quite durable."

"What happened to the rest?"

Morin smiled grimly. "Like the Vaults of Sheol, the Realms once possessed weapons of awesome destructive power." Morin walked toward the edge of the ridge and indicated the valley with a wave of his arm. "All of this was once a blasted wasteland. This section of road was spared because the bulk of the Reil Range sheltered it from the full force of the weaponry."

"But that must have been thousands of years ago," said Liam.

Morin smiled. "More, Liam. The Realms are old. Very old. Our laws bind us to the land, and protect us from the horrors of such destruction. That is why we oppose the Vault with such vigour. They would take and use the universe and leave nothing but a burnt wasteland in their wake."

They watched the view in silence for a while, then walked back to camp. The Old Road was obvious now. The tangled greenery of the forest ceased at its edge as though trimmed by a forester. The thin topsoil, and its unyielding base of glass, would support nothing more than hardy mountain grasses. They followed it back behind the flank of the range to their campsite, which also lay on the grassed corridor. Beside their camp, a mountain stream ran swiftly across a bed of dark mossy rocks.

The morning twilight had vanished, but the birds still sang a lively chorus in the thick canopy. Fragments of mist drifted through the trees, chased by the rising sun. Large forest birds, brightly coloured in blue and yellow, foraged on the camp borders. They had red throat crests, fierce yellow eyes, and wicked talons. They were much bigger than bush turkeys and strutted arrogantly across the forest litter in search of wriggling prizes . . . or unguarded food scraps.

Bran and Tres were busily stoking up the campfire, while their horses snorted and roamed about as freely as their tethers would allow. Zanthis was awake, and was inspecting the quality of his shaving in a small, hand-held mirror.

Shane was still in his blankets. Liam walked over and prodded his ribs with a shoe-tip, but Shane only groaned and pulled the blankets closer.

"Come on, rise and shine!" said Liam.

Tres walked from the stream with a bucket of icy water. He gave Liam a wicked grin, then threw the water over Shane's head.

Shane scrambled from his blankets. *"You f"ing bastards!"*

Liam and Tres burst out with peals of laughter.

They had been travelling for six days now, making good time up the forested slope. Without fail, Shane was the last to rise, and took delight in making them wait. *Not today.* Liam chuckled.

Shane stood and watched Tres as he returned to the stream for more water. After he had gone, he turned to Liam. "Laugh it up. When we get out of here you're going to pay for all this."

The pure venom in Shane's voice stunned Liam. Shane had always been self-centred and manipulative, but never vindictive. Liam looked into his eyes and saw a dark hatred there. Liam shivered. *The siithe Shade.* Shane was still in command, but underneath his posturing was a dark heart, longing for action.

Liam looked down at Shane's right hand, still clutching at the blanket. *It had turned black.* And the scar at the wrist, where Morin had joined the severed hand to the stump, was a red, raised welt, oozing thick green puss.

"Morin! Come quickly!"

As the thurjun hurried over, Liam saw the dark spirit vanish from Shane's eyes, leaving the calculating look he knew so well.

"Look." Liam pointed at Shane's hand.

"By the High God," said Morin. *"Bran!* Fetch the medical supplies."

Morin motioned Shane to the fire. "Sit down." He took the hand and inspected it carefully. Bran delivered a bulky leather satchel, and Morin went to work. He cleaned the wound, then prepared a compress of herbs to help fight infection. "Can you feel any sensation in your fingertips? Or your palm?" Morin traced a metal probe across Shane's skin.

Shane snorted. "As much as before."

"Move your fingers. Show me."

Shane moved his fingers, watching Liam coldly as he did so.

Morin sighed, carefully pressing the healing herbs around the wound and wrapping the hand in a bandage.

"This is very strange," said Morin, shaking his head. "The hand should be healing. Unless . . ." Morin met Bran's eyes.

"The siithe Shade," finished Bran.

Morin tied off the bandage and stood up, as though eager to be away from Shane. "We would have reached the First Realm in three days using the Peak Gateway, but we will have to take the Skyroad to Reil Tower. Perhaps they have a healer who can stop the infection."

Dead silence gripped the group.

Bran went pale. Tres shut his eyes and cursed under his breath.

"What does that mean? The Skyroad?" asked Liam.

"You will find out," said Bran. The charioteer looked across at Morin and grimaced.

*

Morin led them along the Old Road to the edge of the cliff.

"*That's* the Skyroad?" asked Liam.

A twisted remnant of the Old Road stuck out over the drop, glittering darkly in the morning sun. Turned into a spiral, its drawn edges looked razor sharp. At the edge of the cliff the glassy material blended seamlessly with the dark basalt of the range.

Morin drew out his mionanail pendant.

Through his thurjun's sight, Liam saw the air before Morin shimmer, then grow still. Some remnant lingered at the edge of his vision, but did not come fully into focus.

"Prepare the animals," commanded Morin.

Bran nodded. He and Tres set about blindfolding the four horses.

Liam walked to the edge of the cliff and stood beside Morin, who was looking out across the open expanse.

"Where do we go from here, Morin?" Liam's skin crawled as he met Morin's dark blue eyes, as though some latent power was communicating across the contact.

"Look at the pendant you wear," said Morin.

Liam nodded, lifting his green pendant from his chest.

"It is the twin of this," said Morin, lifting the brown mionanail

214

pendant that now hung freely outside his robe.

Liam studied Morin's pendant. It was etched with the same abstract design as his own — a representation of the Gateway interlace — and had the same teardrop shape. However, where Liam's pendant had a dull, dark gem set into the surface, Morin's was set with one of identical size that gleamed dull silver, like liquid mercury.

"Your pendant contains a mionanail, Liam, forged in the Thurjuns Tower in the First Realm. It is the soul of the thurjun, and is what grants him his power. It stands as a symbol of the High Court. It is only with the greatest of trust that one is granted.

"The power once stored in your pendant has gone, but can be restored."

Morin looked back over the cliff. "Look out over the valley, Liam. Tell me what you see."

"Trees. A great forest. A river . . ." He squinted into the distance. "More hills on the horizon."

"I have told you what the pendant means. What it can give you. Power. But what does the thurjun use, which is his own?"

Liam's head began to ache. Nausea squirmed to life in his gut.

Taking a moment to concentrate, Morin calmly stepped off the cliff. He seemed to climb, then turned to his right, supported by nothing but air.

Liam's jaw went slack. *What the . . .?*

Morin turned back to him. "Do you know the answer to the riddle, Liam?"

Liam numbly shook his head.

"From what you have told me, you have used your thurjun's powers many times now, perhaps hardly even realising what you had accomplished, or how.

"The power of a thurjun must be gathered, or given. Harvested and stored, such as within the mionanail. But the true skill of the thurjun is in the crafting of this power. The shaping of the tool that directs this power. The lens that focuses it."

"The interlace!" said Liam.

"Yes," agreed Morin. "But that is nothing more than a shape, crafted within the cradle of the mind. Tell me, Liam! What guides the hand?"

Liam looked down over the cliff, stomach lurching.

Morin had wandered further over the sheer drop, still suspended in mid-air.

Then he knew.

"*Sight*. It's sight. That's what the thurjun has, which is truly his own."

Morin nodded. "You have come to know your thurjun's sight. You have the grip upon it, the sense of it. Tell me, Liam. Can you command it? Or does fear still hold it from your grasp?"

Liam took a faltering step toward the cliff's edge. The headache had grown to a pounding intensity.

"*Let yourself see, Liam!*" commanded Morin.

Liam heard a loud popping sound. The headache and sickness vanished. Replaced by elation. The air was clearer, the forest more vibrant, the sun more intense.

And he could see it!

Ahead of them, stretching far into the distance, a narrow path of sun-bleached stone led out across the valley. Morin stood on the path. To either side of him were sheer cliffs, sparse vegetation clinging to the slopes. The mountain and ridge path were indistinct, as though drawn in watercolours.

"Where are you?" asked Liam, walking without fear over the cliff and onto the translucent path to join Morin.

"I am within both the Fourth and Second Realms of the Blessed. Only the nature of the Realms permits this. Within the Second Realm at this point is another of the border forests. Both have been unchanged for millennia. Both retain the essential essence that makes this possible. This is a Gateway. It is always open while the sun shines."

Morin clapped Liam on the shoulder. "To travel this road, you must have the thurjun's sight."

"Come on!" called Morin, waving the company forward.

Chapter 36
Reil Tower — Second Realm

Liam took another sip of the wine. It was a strong, well-crafted red. He was too tense to enjoy it. He sat at one of the huge dining tables in Reil Tower's main hall, where he had eaten with Lord Reil, members of the Reil family, and senior garrison officers. Its polished wooden surface was still scattered with the remains of their meals. Above them, large glowglobes and heatglobes hung in an alternating array, providing pleasant warmth and ambience.

On a raised dais, a travelling troupe from the First Realm played a lively jig, reminiscent of Irish traditional music. Liam's eyes drifted constantly to another table where Shane was deep in conversation with Fray, the youngest and most attractive daughter of Lord Reil. Liam turned to catch Morin's eye, but the elder thurjun, and the charioteers, had all gone. Lord Reil and most of the garrison officers remained. Liam had volunteered to keep an eye on Shane, and it seemed Morin and Bran had taken him at his word. It had been hours now, and he was beginning to feel uncomfortable with the responsibility. Lord Reil's eldest daughter Yunis, who sat opposite him, caught his eye and smiled. Like Fray, she had the trademark red hair and fair complexion of the Reils.

"We do not often get visitors from the Skyroad," said Yunis.

"It was certainly interesting," said Liam. That was an understatement. *Weird* would be a better word. It had been four anxious hours of travelling as the landscape of the Fourth Realm grew slowly more insubstantial and the Second Realm gradually solidified.

Shane stood up and walked out of the room, followed by Fray. Liam slammed his glass down so hard wine spilled over the rim.

"Is something the matter?" asked Yunis.

"No," stammered Liam. "I just want to get some fresh air."

"Shall I come with you?"

"No!" said Liam. "Oh. . . I mean that's very kind, but no. I won't be long," he said, manoeuvring along the low table before stepping over the bench seat. "I hope," he muttered under his breath.

Liam scanned the room to see if any of the other warriors, or Lord Reil, had noticed Shane leave with Fray. Liam ground his teeth in frustration. Even Reil's thurjun, Iress, who had listened gravely to Liam's account of the last few days, looked away.

Liam exited the hall and crossed a courtyard, searching for Shane. He heard laughter, and saw Shane and Fray pass through the gatehouse. *Now they are outside the walls.* His body tensed, as though with the threat of imminent danger. Liam trusted his instincts. There was no time to fetch Morin. He could alert the warriors at the feast, but what would he tell them? His friend had gone for a walk? They had all seemed so unconcerned. *"Damn it."* Liam set out after them.

That afternoon, the chief healer of the Tower had examined Shane's hand. He confirmed the presence of some infection, and praised Morin's work, but beyond that, he could not account for the skin discolouration, or the lack of healing. After that, Morin had left Liam to his own devices. Bran and Tres had gone to the stable yards to rebuild the chariots and care for their mounts, which were still anxious from their passage across the Skyroad. None of them seemed worried about Shane. Tres had even returned the pipe and tobacco.

Liam had to admit, since arriving at Reil Tower, Shane had been on his best behaviour. Polite and respectful, he had offered to help at every turn, thanked their healer graciously, and turned on the charm for Lord Reil and his family. It was like the old Shane, but Liam knew him too well to think it could last. Even the old Shane never did anything without a reason.

Ahead of Liam, Shane and Fray had stopped to sit on a low hillock beyond the Tower's influence. Liam squatted down, hidden in the darkness. The ground sloped sharply away from the Tower's walls, and he had a good view from the higher ground. Shane lit his pipe. The flame showed a brief picture of Shane's face. His eyes gleamed with malign concentration. The hairs rose on the back of Liam's neck. He almost went right then, but stopped. What the hell would he say? Minutes passed. He chewed his lip, cursing his own indecision. If something happened to Fray . . .

There was a high-pitched scream. A bellow of outrage from Shane.

"*No.*" Liam pelted down the slope.

Two figures resolved from the dark. Shane stood holding his groin. Fray had backed away from him. She looked at Shane, then quickly at the Tower, as though expecting something.

"You bitch," said Shane. His voice was savage. His face, so pleasantly schooled over the last few hours, twisted with fury and lust.

Reaching down to his ankle, Shane drew a knife and ran at Fray. She turned and fled. Shane pursued her, growling with animal fury. Liam realised Shane would overtake her and raced to intercept. Leaping from above him on the slope, Liam took Shane in a flying tackle just before he reached her. They both landed heavily on the grass.

Shane was the first to recover.

Fray screamed a warning. Too late.

Shane slashed out, aiming for Liam's neck. He blocked instinctively. The knife's razor-sharp edge sliced across his forearm. Liam gasped in pain, but was already moving, instinctively leaping back to get distance.

Shane followed him, lunging for the kill.

Liam launched a powerful inside kick that knocked the knife from Shane's hand. He followed with a jumping front-kick to Shane's chin. *Contact.* Shane few back across the grass. He hit the ground and lay stunned.

Bright light flared around him.

Liam shielded his eyes, and looked up to see a floating platform above him. Lord Reil and his thurjun Iress stood stoically on the hovering device, while Morin and a score of warriors from the garrison surrounded Liam and Shane. Then Liam understood. It had been a test. A test to see how Shane behaved in total freedom. And he had been duped as well.

Iress guided the flying platform to the grass and Lord Reil leapt down. Fray fled into her father's arms.

"Well done, Fray. Did you see the Shade rise in him?" asked Lord Reil.

"Yes, father. It is strong, and is bonded with his soul already. I do not think it can be banished."

Lord Reil nodded gravely.

Iress stepped off the platform and walked to Liam. He patted him on the shoulder. "My apologies, Liam, for the deception. But we had to know. Reil's daughter is a Seeker," said Iress, gesturing back at the platform where father and daughter stood side by side, "and a talented one. There would be none better in the High Court to conduct the test. But first we had to entice the Shade to rise."

"Thank the High God you followed as well," said Fray.

Reil stepped from the platform and walked to Liam. "Yes, we owe you a debt of thanks. We had no idea he would be armed," said Reil turning to Iress. "How did he get that knife?"

"I do not know, Lord," replied Iress.

Reil motioned for his troops to take the semiconscious Shane into custody. "Chain him. It is for the High King to deal with this matter now."

Morin picked up the knife, eyeing Shane warily. "I know where he got this. Zanthis! The fool probably does not even know it is missing." He grew grave. "It could have cost both you and Fray your lives. But you handled yourself well, Liam. You did not tell me you had been trained in unarmed combat."

"My uncle Aidan trained me. He knew a bit of everything. He taught me some sword work as well."

Liam gingerly touched the cut on his forearm, which bled heavily.

"Come, let my healer tend to that," said Lord Reil, taking Liam by the arm and guiding him to the platform. "For saving Fray I will make you a gift of a sword. Your choice of my own collection."

Liam stepped up onto the strange conveyance, which was rather like a flat-bottomed boat, with a low rail, and cushioned seats. A large mionanail was set into the prow. Through his thurjun's sight, Liam could see the flow of power that propelled and suspended the craft, shaped and guided by Iress.

The platform lifted and glided smoothly over the walls. Liam's heart was heavy. It was his fault that Shane had been drawn through into the Fourth Realm. Now he was in chains, and cursed with some sort of possession. The excitement of passing the Gateway, of coming to know his own talents, had gone, weighed down by guilt. But what else could he have done? Shane might have killed him tonight. He had *tried* to. Liam squeezed his eyes shut, but there was no denying anything.

This was all too real.

Chapter 37
Court of VoYannan — Vault of Seven Horns

Procarrus permitted himself a brief smile as he passed through the dank antechamber, but was sure to reassert his stern Roman visage before he entered VoYannan's smoke-filled court. The familiar, enticing smell of narcotics greeted him in the darkness. Procarrus adjusted his toga fractionally and continued on, secure in his triumph. Behind him, the priestess Sephany was displayed in a fine dress of white, her hair set with a silver circlet — as befitted VoYannan's bride. Procarrus could hear her muttering incantations to the so-called *High God* under her breath and suppressed a surge of irritation. She was nothing more than the booty of conquest. A prize to be delivered to his master.

Procarrus had reached the Dark City yesterday. There, he had eagerly taken a repast on the slaves of his estate, his siithe unable to keep up with the growing pile of corpses. Even they had grown fussy in the end, squabbling over the tastiest morsels in their feasting pits. Procarrus looked down at the exposed skin of his left arm and smiled in satisfaction. His powers had been restored, and with them his youth. Slaves could always be replaced. *He* could not.

VoYannan's bulk loomed through the darkness. Procarrus stilled his thoughts and checked the formation of his procession. Sephany was in light chains, set between his siithe captain Ossis and another of his most trusted siithe aides. Following at the rear was the ever-faithful Barsus. The huge man-beast snuffed at the air eagerly, scenting sex, but knew enough to keep his place.

Procarrus stepped carefully through the writhing bodies. He swallowed as he saw the veyr standing behind the throne, his grey wings folded about his body. The insectoid head turned at Procarrus' approach, the long proboscis quivering with hunger. The veyr's dark eyes glittered, the facets refracting the flames from the smoking censers into a thousand smaller lights.

"My Lord VoYannan!" proclaimed Procarrus, giving the Roman salute to his immortal Lord, right arm raised to the krell's throne.

Mucus oozed from the plates on the krell's wedge-shaped head, making the rows of yellowed horns there glisten. VoYannan's eyes opened. Huge green irises, framed in bloodshot white. The shock of that gaze was a physical blow.

"So, Procarrus," said the krell. "You have brought me my bride." His voice resonated with deep satisfaction. Sighs of pleasure rippled across the room as their master's delight communicated itself to his thralls. "Bring her closer."

Procarrus motioned to his siithe aides. Sephany was dragged to VoYannan's throne. She was pale with fear, and she kept her eyes shut. Her mouth moved feverishly in prayer.

"Forget your muttering. *Look at me!*" The krell's voice cracked across the room like a breaking storm.

Sephany's eyes flew open. Her hands trembled. Her prayer forgotten.

"Closer to me, my bride," crooned the krell.

Procarrus smiled as the arrogant Realm priestess tried to fight his master's will. She would soon learn that her defiance was futile. Step by halting step, Sephany was drawn to him, until she could have reached out and touched his slick, mucus-covered hide.

The krell's voice rumbled, deep in his chest. "I sense a powerful soul, my Archfiend. Such a prize. Such a feast!"

An erection grew at the krell's groin. The thick, twisted member, throbbed with his lust. In the puffy flesh at the base of the penis a shape struggled beneath the skin, as though seeking to tear its way free. "My spawn is eager to seek its place in your womb."

Sephany screamed. A sound of pure fear. She took one step back, then turned to run. The two siithe were waiting. They each took one of her wrists in their thick-fingered hands, halting her flight before it had begun. They grinned, faces full of pointed teeth.

"Take her to her chambers, and summon Balos to guard her. None may touch her."

The two siithe bowed and took Sephany away. She was only too eager to escape VoYannan's presence.

Procarrus straightened. Barsus sat at his right hand. He felt the man-beast's hot breath on the flesh of his exposed right arm.

"Well done, Procarrus," said the krell, his voice taut with lust. "Return to the world called, Earth. I have already commanded a siithe legion to proceed through the Gateway and establish an advance base there. Destroy the city of Sydney. Then gather slaves. Once I plant my spawn I will need fresh stock throughout the Vault of Seven Horns." The krell's voice grew hypnotic. "Take Earth and crush it. Then we can turn our sights on the Fourth Realm. *Go.*"

"Yes, my Lord!" Procarrus saluted and marched from the court.

*

When his Archfiend was gone, the krell motioned his veyr priest closer. "Tell me, Hoor. Are the omens still favourable?"

The veyr's dark head swivelled toward his master. His leathery wings unfolded, quivering with anticipation. "Yes, my Lord," he replied in his sibilant voice. "A spawn birthed from her broken spirit will be bound to you as surely as these." Hoor waved his thin, clawed arm at the krell's writhing thralls.

"Good. I have waited so long." VoYannan shut his eyes and sank back into his throne.

Across the floor, the thralls of the krell began to moan and writhe, copulating with renewed frenzy.

The veyr refolded his wings and slunk back behind VoYannan's throne.

*

Sephany sat on the narrow bed, staring at the wall's stained plascrete. There was no window. Instead there was darkness. Damp fetid air. Up until her confrontation with the krell, she had been able to still her mind, and put off thoughts of the future. Now reality sank in. She was trapped in VoYannan's fortress. The krell lord's plaything. Should she take her own life? *No. Life was sacred.* Was she doomed then? Doomed to become fodder for VoYannan's progeny?

224

With tears in her eyes, she knelt and began to pray, as she never had before. At first she felt only the icy cold of the floor through her knees. Then, slowly, a warm glow touched her heart, and she knew that even here the High God was with her.

The door opened.

The towering figure of Balos filled the doorway. Roughly humanoid, the angel's skin was a dark and featureless, nothing more than smooth armour stretched across a form of pure light. Like all seraphin, his facial features were unknowable, in a blur of constant motion. Red light leaked from the joins in his skin, and pulsed from the twin pits of his ruby eyes. Behind him, his six wings shimmered like tongues of red flame. He entered. The siithe guards shut the cell door, leaving them alone.

"You are the bride of VoYannan," said the seraphin. His voice was clear and powerful.. "I, Balos, will guard both you and the Spawn as it grows within you." His words rang like a proclamation

Sephany rose to her feet. Looked up. At the sight of this, this. . . *fallen angel*, her fear and bewilderment turned to anger. "How can you, of all beings, serve VoYannan?"

The flickering motion of the seraphin's wings quickened. "You are mistaken, priestess. I serve only Balos."

"So you deceive yourself," she said, unafraid of the seraphin, or its power. "How can you, of all the beings who once lived closest to the light of the High God, fall to the service of a krell?"

"Again, you are mistaken. Within the Realm of the High God, there is no freedom. His will is total, and must be obeyed. Here I have freedom. VoYannan has my allegiance because this aligns with my desires."

Sephany shook her head slightly. "You have fallen victim to his deceit. What of the purity of the Light? Here, even your power is coloured." His light bathed the room in lurid red.

The seraphin's wings slowed to soft blurs of red flame. "I have tasted the power of fury. The joy of freedom in action. If this colours me, then let it be so."

"But to hand out death, at the behest of VoYannan . . ."

"Do not the seraphin hand out death at the behest of the High God? In defence of the Realms?"

Sephany grew silent, amazed at the extent to which VoYannan had twisted Balos. It was typical of a seraphin, though. Their decisions were absolute. Their final judgements delivered without doubt. Fortunately for the Realms, they were an ancient race allied firmly with truth and peace.

"To me you are just another of the krell's minions."

Sephany turned away and knelt, raising her voice in a prayer to the High God. She closed her eyes, conscious of the seraphin's deadly heat, which bathed her in waves. But she did not fear. The terror she had experienced in the krell's court — at the prospect of rape by VoYannan — had pushed her beyond fear. She must trust her soul to the High God, and forget her mortal life, for she was convinced her sojourn here in the Vault could end only one way.

With her death.

Chapter 38
City of Tir — First Realm

Liam looked down on the vast city of Tir.

It was a city of towers. Thousands of them. They spread out from horizon to horizon, soaring above a pristine forest. The Dreaming Steed he and Morin rode flew so high that individual figures on tower balconies, or in elevated gardens and plazas, appeared as no more than dots of colour. This was nothing like the close-packed cities of Earth, where the natural landscape disappeared under a spreading shroud of concrete and bitumen. Here the forested landscape remained dominant at ground level, and the population itself lived far above the thriving habitat.

The towers themselves came in two classes. The shorter of the two —although none were less than a hundred storeys tall — resembled spires. They were slender in proportion and tapered to a sharp point. No two were the same, varying in decoration, colour, and construction material. More like works of art than buildings. The larger towers dwarfed the spires, and were of a more uniform design. These had hundreds of separate levels that were connected with those above and below by an impossibly thin central spine, like a vast stack of circular platters threaded by a spindle. The big towers were crowned with glass domes that glittered like jewels in the noonday sun. Each tower level was massive, multi-storeyed in its own right. The scale was mindboggling. Three hundred storeys tall, four hundred . . . it was impossible to judge. Higher than anything build on Earth, without a doubt.

"Tir," said Morin.

Dreaming Steeds, such as the one that now carried them from the Reil Gateway, swarmed through the air above the city. They were creatures of the First Realm. Some drifted sedately from tower to tower while others sped to and from the city at tremendous speeds. They had the bulk of a full-grown elephant, yet could fly in defiance of gravity due to their magical nature. Without any discernible head or limbs, it had been difficult for Liam to accept they were alive at all, let alone sentient . . . then their own Steed had touched his mind. Liam and the other passengers rode in a hollow in the back of the creature, surrounded by a chest-high wall of toughened skin.

Liam's head spun. He turned away from the view and took a step back from the edge. He focussed on Morin while the dizziness passed.

"Where to now?" asked Liam.

Morin pointed to the largest tower. It was so high its upper levels were lost in cloud.

"The High Court of the Realms," answered Morin, his voice hushed. It was comforting to see that even Morin was awed by this city. It made Liam feel just a bit less like a wide-eyed country boy.

Shane shuffled to the Steed's wall, shackle-chains clanking. His two grim-faced guards stayed within arm's reach.

Eager to take in all the sights, Morin walked across to the other side of the Steed, leaving Liam and Shane alone.

"It's amazing isn't it?" Liam smiled at Shane, energised by the incredible sight. "You still think you're on Earth?"

Shane studied Liam for a moment, then he gave him a sly smile. "Why do you think they've brought you here?"

"I am the last thurjun of Earth," said Liam with pride. "They need my knowledge of Earth to reopen their Gateway and help Finn Evenstone." He also thought that relaying his vision of Korbeth might be vital, but he stopped short of saying that. He knew how Shane reacted to that sort of thing.

Shane grunted. He watched Liam with a dark, hypnotic intensity.

"Look at all this, Liam," said Shane, nodding his head at Tir's endless cityscape. Its lofty towers spread out across the tangled blanket of forest. "Do you really think they need *you?*"

Liam's fears welled up, all at once. He trusted Morin, but what if the Realm thurjun had been telling him only part of the truth?

"How soon before you're wearing a set of these?" asked Shane, lifting his arms to show the manacles that bound his hands. "So you managed to get through one Gateway. Big deal! Look at that city, Liam. Can you imagine the power these people have? The wealth? They must have a thousand of these so-called *thurjuns* like Morin. Why should they need you?"

Liam felt Morin's hand on his shoulder. "Do not listen to him, Liam. The Shade inside him is devious."

"Get him back over there," ordered Morin, pointing to the far corner of the platform. "And do not let him talk to anyone. Do you understand?"

The two guards nodded their assent, and started to lead Shane away, but he shrugged out of their grip and surged at Liam. "They will use you, Liam! Then they will laugh at you. Who do you think you are, you fucking retard? Some sort of hero? All of your martial arts bullshit won't mean a thing here!" Shane was so close, drops of spit hit Liam in the eye. Shane's dark eyes gleamed. And the words . . . they burned like acid.

The guards took Shane to the other side of the Steed, where he sat meekly on the wrinkled floor. Shane stared out over Tir as though none of it had ever happened.

"Do not concern yourself, Liam. As a thurjun of Earth, you will be respected here, and no one will prevent you from returning to Earth should you wish it," said Morin. The elder thurjun looked over his shoulder at Shane and sighed. "As for that one. I am not sure what King Torren will decide."

Liam accepted Morin's assurances, but as they approached the High Court tower, his fears rose again. Each level of the tower was four storeys in height, each connected by that translucent, impossibly thin, central column. He lost count at seventy-eight levels.

The Dreaming Steed came to rest on the roof-top platform of one of the intermediate levels. Liam looked up nervously at the next level, no more than a stone's throw above his head. His heart twisted in panic as he thought of the immense weight above him. Up close, the tower seemed to be constructed of stone, with a smooth, featureless surface. *Stone?* The cumulative weight should have made the structure impossible.

Part of the Steed's wall unfolded into a debarkation ramp. Liam followed Morin down onto the landing platform. His head swam as he considered how far above the ground they were. Through the translucent walls of the central column, Liam saw people *flying* up and down between levels.

It was all so impossible.

Alien.

Despite everything he had seen, his Earth-bound horizons crashed in on him. The confidence he had gathered in the Realms, the discovery of the truth behind his visions, his newfound powers . . . these were eclipsed by Tir's sheer scale.

A brightly dressed courtier hurried across the roof. He was a small man, slightly balding, and dressed in a red jacket with an ornate white shirt and skin-tight pants of bright yellow. Out of breath, he bowed before Morin.

"Lord Morin. High King Torren . . . asks that you proceed . . . directly to the High Court."

"Yes, yes. Very well," said Morin, showing an annoyance with the man. "Tell Torren we are on our way."

"With your permission, Lord Morin." The courtier gasped a quick breath. "Torren commands that I conduct your party to the High Court immediately!"

Morin impatiently motioned for the man to lead the way.

"Do you see why I stay away from this place?" said Morin to Liam under his breath.

Liam stayed silent, lost in his own anxiety.

They made their way down a staircase. Inside, it looked much like the Stonelake tower. Incredibly, Liam realised it *was* built of stone. Interlocking blocks expertly joined without mortar. Not so much as a pin would have fit between the gaps. The walls were illuminated by the ubiquitous glowglobes, but rather than the plain bulbs he had grown used to, with a simple spout for refilling the glowbeast's nutrient solution, these were ornate orbs of coloured and etched glass, the spouts fluted works of art.

At the central column, Liam looked down into empty space with a sickening lurch. Far below, Liam glimpsed the blurred green of a grassed clearing, while far above, he saw open sky. His heart staggered into a sprint as he realised that the central column provided absolutely *no* structural support! That meant that each of the levels literally *hovered* in free space. His head swam, and he realised he was hyperventilating. He immediately slowed his breathing, concentrating on slow, deep breaths. Then he remembered the Skyroad. *OK.*

The courtier stepped out into the shaft. He floated in place.

"Come on, Liam!" said Morin, following.

The courtier and Morin waited impatiently in mid-air while Liam, Shane, and the two warriors, joined them in the middle of the shaft. Liam felt like he was standing on foam. Soft and yielding. Activating his thurjun's sight, Liam gasped in wonder as he saw the coloured lines of force that ran up and down the central column and surrounded the tower's whole structure. They were supported by a cushion of softly glowing force, which had formed the instant they entered the shaft.

"It is a sunsnake. A druidic device," said Morin, watching Liam with interest. "Non-sentient, but bred to act on simple mental commands."

They abruptly shot up the column, racing to the highest level. Liam gasped at the sudden motion.

Morin grinned with mischief. "The first time is always the most dramatic." His smile vanished when he met Shane's scowl.

Other groups or individuals sped past them going up and down. The green space below them faded to a distant blur. Their pace slowed as they reached the top. Here they stepped from the shaft into a corridor lined with guards wearing silver armour and equipped with halberds. These were no ceremonial weapons. Their sharp edges glinted in the light. Behind them, the walls were hung with delicately woven tapestries. They walked past the guards into a vast antechamber, filled with a noisy crowd. People talked in excited voices and waved their arms, trying to outdo each other in volume.

Morin smiled at Liam. "They are all waiting to see the High King. I do not envy Torren. Administering the law and defence of six worlds is a complex task."

The courtier pushed aggressively through the crowd, guiding them to two wide wooden doors. He motioned for them to wait, then disappeared through a small Judas gate set cunningly into the carved facade. Moments later the double doors opened and they were ushered inside.

Chapter 39
City of Tir — First Realm

The Court's hall was an immense open space. It occupied the full height of its tower level. At least five storeys. The walls and floor were white marble, chased with intricate curlicues of gleaming gold and silver. Light streamed in through tall windows, and the tapestries that hung between the balconies blazed with vivid colour. The hall floor, and the tiers of balconies that rose above them, were packed to overflowing. There was an audience of thousands here. The hall was quiet after the buzz of the antechamber, which was eerie, considering the size of the crowd. The men and women were either silent, or spoke in hushed whispers, like a theatre audience.

The room was dominated by the High King's dais — elevated from the hall floor by four wide marble steps — and by the presence of the man who sat there. High King Torren was a tall man. He sat rigid on his ornate throne, his dark eyes intent on the group of supplicants that now stood below him. Behind his golden throne rose a tapestry depicting a stylised dragon in red and white, writhing in fury on a bed of green, one wing extended toward a vibrant blue sky.

Morin followed Liam's gaze. "The dragon's colours, red and white, are the colours of the High King," he whispered.

Torren's gaze flicked to Morin's group. Noting their arrival, he dismissed the supplicants, and gave another signal. Now, even the low, whispered conversations of the upper balconies died away. Within the capsule of this silence, they advanced toward the throne, up a central aisle. There was packed seating on either side, crammed with haughty men and women dressed in finery that would not have been out of place at the court of Louis XVI in its lavish elegance, though of strange cut and design. Thousands of eyes followed them as they crossed the smooth marble floor. Liam and Morin led the group, with Shane walking behind, flanked by Reil's warriors. The metallic jingle of Shane's shackles was loud in the silence.

Torren drew Liam's gaze like a magnet. The High King's hair

was a reddish blonde, cut short with military severity. His face was long, but soft. Although of middle years, he had retained the vitality of his prime. He was flanked on his left and right by a series of low bench seats, conspicuously plain against the painted gold of his throne. On his left was a large contingent of men wearing multicoloured robes. From a strong and vibrant red at the collar, sleeves, and hem, their robes swept back through all the colours of the rainbow — orange, yellow, green, blue and indigo — to a vibrant violet diamond in the centre of the chest and back. The men were grim and silent, and watched Morin's small group advance with an almost palpable disapproval. On Torren's right, all but the front bench was occupied. Three groups sat there. The men and women of the largest group wore the light blue robes of a thurjun, like Morin. They sat with three women dressed in soft white robes. Each of the three women wore a thin circlet of gold set with a small purple gem. Also seated next to them, but slightly apart, were priests and priestesses of the High God in vestments of gold, orange, and white.

Below the dais, two groups were seated in comfort behind a low dividing rail that separated them from the main audience. On Torren's right, a group of richly dressed young men sat in various postures of arrogant confidence, most with gold or silver goblets in their hands. All wore ornate swords with jewelled hilts. One figure stood out in a loose shirt of vibrant red. The young man was lean, and watched everything through dark, narrowed eyes. His dark hair and oval face would have set him apart as handsome if not for his down-turned mouth. Across from the young men, below the dais on Torren's left, sat a tightly packed group of women attired in an array of bright, shimmering dresses with flared skirts, fitted bodice, and long loose sleeves. Liam had never seen so much lace. He felt awkward in jeans and T-shirt.

Morin halted their company at the base of the dais with a gesture, then stepped forward one more pace. "Greetings from Stonelake, High King Torren. Lord Thurjun Morin, servant of the Court, presents himself as requested."

Torren nodded. A smile played on his lips.

"Tirini and Kevrin have informed the Court of the abduction of Sephany, and of Finn's heroic — if not improbable — rescue attempt." Torren's voice was deep and clear.

Torren looked at Liam, then Shane. "And from my Lord Reil I learn that one of these Earth travellers has been taken by a siithe Shade — and stands accused of rape. A high crime."

Gasps of astonishment sounded through the room.

Liam was startled as the young red-shirted man surged to his feet. He was quite tall, and cut an impressive figure as he turned to address the Court.

"Is this not proof enough!" yelled the man, his hands raised in supplication to the crowded balconies. "Vault warriors within the Realms? Attacks on our Gateways? Attacks on our own people! Perhaps the betrayal of thurjuns?" He looked meaningfully at the seated thurjuns beside the throne. "We must take this in hand!" he declared. "We must secure this Gateway both in Stonelake *and* in this Vault world of Earth!"

Vault world?

A chorus of cheers and shouts rose from the balconies, along with subdued applause.

Morin leaned in close to Liam. "That is Torren's son."

Liam looked at Torren, trying to gauge his reaction. He seemed annoyed.

"If this is war, Sentas, then it is the time for cool heads and strategy. Not posturing," said Torren.

Laughter filled the Court. Sentas drew a breath to reply, but at a look from his father, he sat down instead. His cheeks flushed red. A momentary look passed between him and one of the rainbow-robed figures on Torren's left.

Torren's piercing gaze came to rest on Liam.

"How is it," asked Torren, "that after more than a thousand years, the Stonelake Gateway is opened by the Vault? And that — miraculously — an Earth thurjun is suddenly on hand to open the Gateway and enable Finn's premature pursuit?"

"For that we owe a debt to Korbeth, the High Priest of the Stonelake Temple. It was his sacrifice that enabled Liam to be found," said Morin.

Torren frowned, raising his voice. "I do not ask you, Lord Thurjun, I ask our newly found thurjun of Earth!"

Liam was drawn forward by Torren's powerful presence.

Thousands of people waited for his reply. *No pressure then.* He swallowed.

His mind went blank.

Shane's stinging words came back to him, eroding his confidence. Then, as if from nowhere, came the words of his uncle Aidan. *If ever in doubt, Liam, rely on honesty and courage. And I know you have a good grasp of both . . .*

Sentas surged to his feet. "Well! The Court is waiting!"

A chorus of laughter rang across the balconies.

What did lead him to Fraser Island? To the Gateway?

"I was led to the Gateway by a vision," declared Liam.

Silence settled on the room.

Then, the rainbow-robed figure, whose gaze Sentas had met briefly, rose to his feet. "When will this Court come to its senses? Visions? We talk of the defence and security of the Realms! Should we act at the behest of visions? We may as well act at the behest of a whim!"

Torren frowned at the man, his displeasure obvious.

The King waved to a grey-haired, dark-suited man seated nearby on the main floor. "Vikas. If you please?"

Vikas rose to his feet with stately poise and rapped his staff of office on the floor three times. "Order!" he commanded. "As Steward it is my duty to remind the Lord Druid Strannus that this Court is a place of discourse, not a racetrack!"

Subdued laughter echoed across the room.

"Any further outbursts will risk removal from the assembly!" continued Vikas. The Steward stared at Strannus until the druid reseated himself, then resumed his own seat.

"Now, shall we continue?" said Torren. "Liam. You call yourself a thurjun. Where then were you trained? From what I gather, our traditions have long faded on your world. By what right do you wear the mionanail pendant? Why should this Court lay its trust — the trust of the Blessed Realms — in you?"

"It has been others, not I, who named me thurjun," said Liam. His voice had strength and clarity, and he gained confidence. The acoustics were amazing. "As for this pendant, it was granted to my ancestors by the Blessed Realms, and I have been selected by my family to wear it." *Well, by the servants of my family, anyway.*

There are only two Durrows left.

"But what of your skills?" asked Torren.

"I will vouch for his skills," interjected Morin. "After all, who can doubt a thurjun who opens a Gateway, and learns our language in the span of a week?"

A thin thurjun rose from benches on the right side of the dais and waited to be recognised by Torren.

"Master Thurjun Kevrin," said the High King.

Kevrin's voice was thin, and edged with annoyance. "It is for the College of Thurjuns to assess Liam's skills." Kevrin studied Morin for a moment. "Be sure you bring him to the Tower at first light tomorrow." Morin nodded in answer. "We have enough to do without these distractions," Kevrin muttered under his breath.

Kevrin turned back to the High King and raised his voice. "The Court will gain a full report on Liam's capabilities by noon tomorrow. Then we can decide based on knowledge. Not emotion," he said, staring at Strannus with undisguised enmity.

Strannus stood abruptly. "I will not sit here and have a thurjun lecture me!"

Torren waved to his warriors, who promptly, but politely, escorted Strannus out of the chamber. The full company of druids filed out after him in silent protest.

The slightest of smiles played on Kevrin's lips as he watched them go. Around them, the room buzzed with excitement.

Once the huge double doors had shut behind the departing druids, Vikas rapped his staff for silence.

Sighing, Torren turned his attention back to Liam. "Your skills are one thing, what of your intentions?"

Despite the gathered scrutiny of the court, Liam was growing angry. But before he had a chance to respond, one of the white-robed women seated on the right side of the dais rose gracefully to her feet.

"His intentions are of the highest," she said, her high voice ringing musically across the room.

Liam was captured by her beauty. Her face was soft and rounded, her hair raven black, falling to her shoulders in gleaming lengths. Despite her slight frame, it seemed to Liam that half the audience shrank from her startling green eyes. Why though?

Torren nodded. "Thank you, Tirini. The judgement of a Seeker is always welcome."

Abruptly turning his attention from Liam to Shane, Torren waved the shackled man forward and studied him intently. "What are we to do with you? Possessed by a siithe Shade. Accused of dark crimes. What mischief will you cause, even in chains, if left unwatched?"

Not understanding the language, Shane remained silent. He had schooled his features into the picture of innocence.

"What say the Temple? High Priest Rolf?"

The High Priest rose to his feet. His face was lined and grave. Although well past middle age, his thick brown hair showed only a thread of grey. As he straightened, his belly pushed out against his voluminous robes. He turned his warm, dark eyes to the King. "He should be given over into our custody for now. Seeker Fray Reil suggests it is unlikely we will be able to cast the Shade out, but we will try our best. I believe in the end he must be returned to Earth. It is for the Temple there, if one should exist, to deal with his spiritual affliction. It may be that the Shade will fade beyond the Realms."

"Very well. Do what you can until the time comes for him to be returned to Earth. He will remain in your custody until then."

Torren rose. With a deafening rustle of fabric and scrape of chairs, the assembled Court rose with him. "As High King of the Blessed Realms, this is my judgement. Once the College of Thurjuns have determined the site of the Gateway that threatens the Realms, a company of warriors will be sent forth into the Vaults of Sheol to retake and seal that Gateway.

"The matters of the defence of Stonelake, control of the Gateways to Earth, and the suitability of Liam Durrow as thurjun, are yet to be decided."

Torren nodded to Vikas, who rapped his staff of office three times, declaring, "The assembly of the High Court is ended!"

The court dissolved in confusion.

Shane was marched away between two warriors, Liam overwhelmed with sudden guilt, while he and Morin were besieged by a mass of curious nobility. Liam caught a glimpse of

Tirini as she left the room. She turned and briefly met his gaze with a smile before slipping through the big doors. *What just happened there?*

Questions were being fired at Liam from all angles. Panic set in as he tried to focus on these strangers. Thankfully, Morin grabbed him by the arm and hauled him through the crowd. "I will take you to the Fourth Realm level, Liam. Rooms are being prepared for us. And some food, I hope!" It had been a long time since breakfast at the Reil tower.

"So what do you think of the First Realm?" asked Morin.

"Impressive. Overwhelming."

"Peace, Liam. You are a talented thurjun. Kevrin and the Council will ratify that. Besides, I have no small amount of influence here."

Liam's doubts exploded outward. "I'm no thurjun! Look at this," said Liam, indicating the huge and improbable structure of the High Court tower. "There are wonders here I couldn't begin to understand. Everything I've done so far has been more luck than skill. How can I pretend it was anything else?"

Morin smiled. "Have faith, Liam. From what you have told me of your uncle Aidan, I think you will find he has left you better prepared than you might imagine."

Liam thought with trepidation of tomorrow's journey to the Thurjuns Tower. "What if Shane is right? What if my knowledge of Earth is all the College of Thurjuns wants from me? Can they take this away?" asked Liam, clutching at the mionanail pendant.

"Listen to me, Liam. The skills you have already displayed are rare. This, and the fact that you are from Earth, makes you invaluable. You are needed." Morin paused at the threshold of the central transport column and faced him squarely. "Everything that has happened to date is no accident. In a time of dire need, you appeared to help us. No one will lose sight of that. Forget Shane. And put Strannus, and Sentas, out of your mind. The fact that a Seeker chose to support you speaks louder than those windbags."

As Liam stepped into the shaft, its glass roof caught the last rays of the setting sun, refracted them down the column. The effect was disorienting. "I hope you're right."

"I am," said Morin. "Although I do wish that Shane had stayed on Earth. I fear he will cause even more trouble for us before this is over. Torren's decision means that he will likely accompany us through the Vaults of Sheol to the Earth Gateway."

Liam had a bad feeling about that.

Chapter 40

City of Tir — First Realm

Uncomfortable in his new thurjun's robes, Liam followed Morin through the corridors of the Thurjuns Tower. His head was still dizzy from the rapid ascent up the central shaft on a flying platform. The thurjuns tolerated no druidic devices in their domain, and their tower had no sunsnake for personal transport. They passed blue-robed thurjuns of all ages, most walking with grey-robed assistants at their heels. Finally they came to a non-descript wooden door. Morin tapped lightly.

"What is it?" came the muffled reply.

Morin winked at Liam as he pushed open the door.

Inside, was a large study lined with bookshelves. A variety of mionanail devices littered the floor. Kevrin sat at the centre of a broad wooden table, besieged by a mass of papers.

"Thurjuns Morin and Liam reporting, as instructed by our beloved liege-lord, High King Torren," said Morin with a sly smile.

"Bah!" replied Kevrin. "Look at this," he said waving at the paperwork. "How am I supposed to keep up with these damned reports?"

"Get an assistant or three, like we have been telling you for about twenty years," said Morin.

Kevrin pushed aside a parchment and sat back in his chair, examining Liam with a critical eye. "Let me see that pendant."

Liam reluctantly removed the precious heirloom and handed it over to Kevrin. The Master Thurjun examined it thoroughly. Liam felt the play of subtle energies in the room as Kevrin turned it over in his hands.

"Interesting. This would have been one of the first ever crafted. But quite depleted." Kevrin handed the mionanail pendant back to Liam and stood up. "Shall we proceed?"

Morin nodded his assent. The filed into the corridor and soon arrived at another door. Kevrin knocked once and entered.

"Our Earth thurjun is here, Resulus," announced Kevrin.

The room was completely bare except for a large wooden desk

and two small, faded tapestries. Resulus was a solemn but portly figure with dark eyes set deep in a chubby face. His unkempt, straight black hair, was greying at the temples. Although he made notes in a tight, neat script on a parchment, there was not a single book in the room.

Resulus lay down his pen and stood, his vast blue robe unfurling around him. His eyes fixed onto Liam like a hunter seeking prey, and he nodded slightly. "Very well. Lead on." His deep voice rumbled in his chest.

Liam began to get anxious as the four of them walked to the central shaft. Here they boarded another flying platform. A young grey-robed pilot took them to the highest level of the Tower, which was a vast open space crowned with a stained-glass dome. In the middle of the floor was a huge sphere, around fifteen metres in diameter, supported by a grey metal structure. The sphere pulsed with a bright golden light.

"That is an ardanaith. The heart of all Realm defence," said Morin.

Power poured from the ardanaith in great shuddering waves. Around the room, a score of thurjuns busied about their tasks, scuttling between tables cluttered with all manner of strange looking devices; some constructed of a clear material like glass, others of crystalline or metalliferous materials.

Kevrin led them across the open floor to a small staircase, which circled up the inside of the dome to a small glass-enclosed room at the apex. As he entered the room, Liam struggled with a momentarily feeling of vertigo. It was as though he were standing unsupported and exposed at a vast height. If he looked through the transparent floor, he could see straight down the central shaft of the Thurjuns Tower, while above him, through the glass, was open sky.

Seated at a large oval table in the centre of the room was Tirini. The sun streamed in through the glass around her, making it seem as though her white Seeker's robes glowed with their own light.

"Morning, Seeker," said Kevrin in a businesslike manner. He looked away quickly.

She was so beautiful! Liam's heart clenched in terror and

ecstasy. "Hello," he managed. *It was the eyes. Definitely the eyes.*

"Hello, Liam," said Tirini. She gave him a brilliant smile. The effect was stunning.

"Sit here," said Resulus indicating a chair.

Liam sat, uncomfortably aware that everyone in the room was staring at him. It reminded him of a trip to the dentist, but with spectators.

"Now. Show me what you have been taught. Raise the matrices before your thurjun's sight, neatly and in good order."

Liam closed his eyes, and felt a mental bond with Resulus form with the rapidity of drying superglue. He opened his thurjun's sight, and concentrated. What matrices did he know? He dredged his memory, and swiftly constructed the interlace for the opening of a Gateway. He piled layer upon layer of delicate, twisting threads until it was perfect in its recreation, waiting only for the power of a mionanail for it to come to life. Letting the interlace fade, he drew the one he had first constructed in his flat. The interlace that had levitated his art equipment. He followed with the simple healing matrix he had rediscovered on the Fraser Island beach.

His mind went blank. He grew angry. He was never taught to be a thurjun. This was ridiculous! What was he doing here dressed in these blue robes? Everything had been an accident. He had stumbled through the Gateway —

Stop your rambling and concentrate!

With a shock, Liam realised Resulus could hear his every thought. Embarrassed, he grew even more determined to prove himself. Strengthened by his mental bond to Resulus, whose powers of concentration were nothing short of astounding, he began to examine his memories. The healing matrix he had taken from the pages of a childhood storybook.

Instantly, Liam was back on the Downs with Aidan, cradled in his uncle's arms. He watched the pages of the book turn and heard the kind voice of his uncle. The pages snapped into view. He remembered them all. Etched into his memory on all those long, fondly remembered afternoons, were each of the stories, and the carefully rendered drawings that he had endlessly marvelled at. A shock of realisation ran through Liam. Each drawing concealed an interlace, and each was as familiar to him as the scent of his childhood room.

Lost in wonder, Liam began to construct each of the interlaces. Here was the shape of the flower taken from the heart of the sun. *Ball of fire*, came the voice of Resulus in his mind. The shapes of the trees in the forest where the girl was lost. *Matrix of Finding*. The design on a piece of broken pottery, from the jar the boy smashed to get at the sweets sealed inside. *Blow of Force*. The heraldic design on the shield of the knight who fought the evil dragon. *Shield*.

On the next page, the weaving pattern of the basket that captured the dragon's flame became one of the most powerful matrices of all; the dampening field that quelled Vault weapons. With it, Liam could bring any city or army on Earth to a standstill. Liam went on, until he had reconstructed each of the matrices hidden in the pages of Aidan's storybook.

His head filled with knowledge. His thurjun's sight surged, his skill at constructing the matrices as sure as his hand on the easel.

Resulus withdrew. Blinking, Liam found himself back in the bright tower-top room. Above them, the sun shone down from high in the sky. They had been immersed in their bonding for hours.

Resulus stood and faced Kevrin. "The knowledge was embedded in his mind. I have helped to bring it forward. His skill with the matrices is good," said Resulus with a cynical smile. "I have never judged a student who started with the hardest, then worked backwards."

Resulus resumed his solemn manner and looked at Liam gravely. "I judge him well prepared in the skills of a thurjun. As for the rest — I leave that to you. Now if you will excuse me." He nodded to each in turn. "Morin. Kevrin. Tirini." He left the room.

Morin poured Liam a glass of water. "How are you feeling?"

Liam was exhilarated. He realised what a great debt he owed to Aidan. His uncle had been training him for this since he was a child, in ways he could have never imagined. "Fine."

"Well. Shall we continue then?" asked Kevrin. "We need to

discover where the Vault is entering Earth. To do that, Tirini will take you back there. To the place where Korbeth showed you the Gateway."

Liam blinked. *Back?* "But I don't know where it is."

"Your spirit knows, Liam," said Tirini. The slim Seeker circled the table and sat beside him. Her delicate perfume swirled around him.

He looked up. Met her eyes.

And was lost in green.

The mental bond was immediate. His thurjun's sight swelled and he was aware of her intimately. Her spirit felt like soft moonlight through the trees, delicately touching his skin. Her face was haloed by radiant white and violet. His chest tightened with longing. His body responded with physical desire.

Tirini giggled, her face suddenly girlish.

Embarrassed, Liam tried to banish his amorous thoughts.

Close your eyes, Liam. Think back to your vision of Korbeth.

Liam cast his mind back. It was after he had returned to the Downs. Images of Aidan's funeral passed through his mind, chased by the leaden grey of unshed grief. He remembered the chapel. The meeting with the Veniti thurjun. The journey across time and space with the spirit of the High Priest Korbeth.

Show me the Gateway, Liam.

Liam dredged his mind. *There.* He remembered the house. The party where black-clad women unwittingly opened a Vault Gateway, seduced by some dark watcher from another world. The collapse of the house. The ancient cave beneath . . . the opening Gateway.

Come, Liam.

Liam felt a rushing sensation, then looked about him to see he was floating above the city of Tir. Beside him, he could feel the luminous spirit of Tirini, and just discern her face within the burning flame of her soul. She held fast to his spirit.

This way! Her thoughts shot across the mind-bond.

Much as he had travelled with the spirit of Korbeth, they fled through space. The sky swept past in a blur of stars and clouded blue. The motion accelerated to the pace of a bullet train.

Then they were motionless.

It was a late, sultry afternoon.

Liam was back on Earth, hovering, insubstantial, above the mixed commercial and residential precinct where the Vault had entered Sydney. Tirini had led them straight to the Gateway, drawn like a bloodhound by the unmistakable resonance of the place. They hovered briefly above a grey industrial roof, then plunged through it, and through concrete and rock, to enter the cavern beneath.

The Gateway was closed. The cavern sunk in gloom. Six siithe warriors stood guard, standing motionless around the rough stone walls. The floor was scattered with debris and scurrying insects.

Tirini flew through the closed Gateway.

They emerged above a ruined city, and rose high into a clouded sky.

How did you pass through the Gateway?

Nothing is a barrier to the spirit, replied Tirini.

Below them, a ruined tower constructed of orange-brown stone blocks swarmed with siithe warriors. In the distance they saw a dark column of troops, marching in their direction. *Toward the Gateway.*

Tirini sped away. Everything blurred. Liam's stomach lurched.

They stopped an unknowable distance away. Through their bond, Liam could feel her anxiety. *What is it?*

I felt the twisted power of a Dark Thurjun at the Gateway. If we had stayed another moment, he would have sensed us.

Liam looked at Tirini. Within the formless golden flame, two eyes of green flared like emeralds. *We must discover the nature of this place. Torren and Kevrin were right. Earth is in danger.*

Remembering the warriors massing beyond the Sydney Gateway, Liam had to agree.

For hours they flew across a blackened landscape, burned in prehistory by colossal conflagrations. Huge craters had been blasted into the ground. At one point they hovered over a vast city, its skyscrapers nothing more than skeletal remnants of steel reinforcing. Other structures had been melted in place. *Vault weapons,* pulsed Tirini. Liam was shocked to silence. This had been a holocaust.

They continued on, until it seemed to Liam they had crossed the globe three times. Then in a rush, Tirini catapulted them back to the Thurjuns Tower.

Liam opened his eyes and sat back. His lower back ached, and his thighs were numb where they met the chair's edge. He shifted and tensed the muscles, trying to restore circulation.

Kevrin and Morin had been deep in conversation, but stopped to watch them revive. The sun was low in the sky. Tirini gently raised herself from the chair and stretched. She was lithe and lean, and the stretching tightened the fabric against her curves. Then she began pacing the room, deep in thought.

"What did you find?" asked Kevrin.

"A destroyed world," said Tirini.

"Show me," said Kevrin.

Tirini sat once more and, taking a moment to concentrate, formed a mental bond with Kevrin.

Liam watched as the eyes of the thin thurjun glazed over.

Morin came over and patted Liam on the shoulder. "You have done well, Liam. Very well."

"What are they doing?" asked Liam.

"Kevrin is our foremost expert on the Gateways. He has the knowledge. He can match what Tirini has seen against our historical records."

"Records? So he will search your library archives?" That could take days, thought Liam. Weeks. Months.

Morin was perplexed, then gave a short laugh of surprise. "You have picked up our language so well, Liam, I keep forgetting our ways are completely foreign to you. All our important records are kept in the mind. *The mind.* We are a living tradition."

Kevrin's eyes resumed their focus. His hands shook. "I have identified the world beyond the Sydney Gateway. It is the ruined Viri world." Kevrin sighed and rose from the table.

Morin paled. "The Dark City is on the Viri world."

"Exactly. VoYannan will be able to bring legions of siithe to Earth without having to pass more than one Gateway."

"Can we reach the Viri world?" asked Morin.

Kevrin nodded. "Yes. I know of a route through the Second Realm. We *must* reach this Gateway. We *must* seal it. Unless it is already too late."

Unless it is already too late.

Liam's heart went cold. Images of the siithe — destroying Earth —rampaged through his mind. Brisbane. Sydney. New York. London. All shattered and burned like those Viri cities.

He shivered.

Chapter 41
City of Tir — First Realm

Liam marvelled at the view.

Thousands of lights dotted the darkness, rising in scattered tiers, shining from the windows and rooftop platforms of Tir's towers. A soft breeze caressed his face, bringing the exotic scents of the city in through his open window. The smell of cooked food, tantalising with unknown spices. The earthy scent of the forest, rising up from the canopy below. The sweet bouquet of night-flowers.

It was a welcome moment of peace.

Tomorrow he would return to the High King's court as a fully-fledged thurjun. Morin assured him that none would question his powers. The responsibility weighed on him. He was not sure what that recognition meant, or where it would lead him.

There was a soft knock on the door. Two quick taps. Liam was puzzled. The servants entered without knocking, and Morin had retired for the night. He crossed the room and opened the door.

"Tirini."

The Seeker wore a shimmering dress of green and purple. Her golden circlet replaced by one of woven leather. Her delicate perfume washed over him. Once again, he was lost in her green eyes. His heart ached, as though suddenly caught in a capricious god's fist. He wanted to hold her. Touch her. He blinked, trying to shake the intensity of the attraction and get control of his brain. *I'm not usually this clueless, Goddamnit!*

"Are you going to invite me in?"

Liam had been standing in the doorway gawping at her. He stepped back, grinning like a loon. He could not remember the last time he smiled with such sheer delight. His face felt odd, underused muscles transforming it with a beaming smile.

"Please. Come in. Would you like something to eat or drink?" Thankfully, his brain had started working again.

Tirini smiled shyly. "That would be nice." She walked into the room. In her right hand she was carrying a small red bag made of woven fabric, which she set down by the door.

Liam pulled the chord beside his bed to summon a servant. A distant bell rang.

Tirini wandered across the room to the open window. She stood exactly where Liam had only moments before, looking out into the night. "It is beautiful, is it not?"

Liam looked at Tirini. In the soft light of the globes, she was as magical, and as perfect, as the night itself. "Yes, very beautiful." His throat was dry. Tirini turned and smiled. She wet her lips with her tongue. They shone, red and luscious. A pink glow rose in her cheeks, and she looked straight at Liam, her eyes wide.

The door opened, interrupting the moment.

A slight woman entered, dressed in the livery of the High King's servants, a black skirt and a white blouse trimmed with red. The woman looked in her middle twenties, with dark hair and brown eyes. Her gaze flickered to Tirini in the corner, then back to Liam. Tirini's entrance had not gone unnoticed.

"What can I do for you, my lord?"

"Ahh . . . could you fix up something light for us?" Liam turned to Tirini. "What do you feel like, Tirini?" Liam had no idea what sort of food they ate here for a late night snack. Send out for pizza? Not likely.

Tirini turned to the servant and smiled. The young woman jerked her gaze away, a guilty look coming over her face.

"Perhaps some chilled white wine, with fruit and cheese?" asked Tirini.

"Very good, my lady." The woman hastily backed out of the room.

Liam was puzzled by the servant's behaviour, but the thought quickly slipped out of his mind as he turned back to Tirini.

"So, do you live in the High Court tower?" asked Liam.

Tirini and Liam walked to the table under the open window. As she sat, Tirini flicked back her long hair, revealing the graceful curve of her neck. She tilted her head slightly and smiled. "No, I live in my own apartments, further into the city. Although, I could live in the Seeker's tower, should I choose it, which is not far distant."

They sat in silence for a time. Again, Tirini looked deep into

Liam's eyes. She seemed to be waiting for something. Expecting something. Perhaps even fearing some reaction from him. Instead, he found himself lost in her. It was like diving into a clear lake. Swimming in crystal. He was alive with joy. He knew he was staring again — but he could not help it. For a long moment they sat like this. Saying nothing. Tirini smiled and Liam saw she was crying. Her eyes were filled with joy, and inexplicably . . . relief. *Intense* relief.

"What's the matter?"

"Nothing," she said quickly, wiping away her tears. "Just something in my eye."

Just then, the tower servant entered with a large silver tray set with a silver jug, two slim silver goblets, and an array of chopped fruit and pieces of cheese, all cut into the shapes of trees and dancing figures. It was a work of art. Liam took the tray from the servant. He was still unused to being waited on. "Wow, that looks great. Thanks very much."

The servant smiled and bowed, turning first to Liam, then shooting a sideways glance at Tirini. She fled the room.

Liam put the tray down, then looked across at Tirini. She looked upset. "Are you OK?"

Tirini's face filled with determination. He waited, and did not look away. Her face lit with joy.

"Yes, Liam. I am well."

Liam poured goblets of chilled wine. He offered one to Tirini.

"Thank you. I cannot drink too much, the alcohol affects the Seekers' powers. Chilled wine is so nice though." Tirini giggled nervously and took a gulp of the wine. Then picked up a small piece of cheese, which she nibbled at appreciatively.

"So, Liam. Tell me of Earth."

They sat together talking for hours, long after the tray was empty. The same serving woman came to remove the tray, entering and leaving unnoticed. Despite what Tirini had said, she eagerly helped Liam empty the wine jug. They laughed and joked, Tirini listening in amazement to Liam's tales of Earth, while Tirini told Liam of her childhood in a distant province of the First Realm.

Liam felt alive. He just loved being with her. He felt as though he was *somebody*, instead of an orphan, pretending to be a thurjun.

They shared another joke, then lapsed into silence, enjoying the moment. Outside the window, a Dreaming Steed floated past, filled to the brim with lords and ladies in elaborate court finery. It was such a surreal sight, it pulled Liam back to reality. He looked around, and was struck anew by how alien everything was. Why had she really come? Surely not to just see him? Was she sent by Morin? By Kevrin? *By Torren?* Liam struggled for something to say, anything to ease the silence. He desperately wanted her to stay, but fear had sunk its claws in him.

"So. Why are you visiting a lowly thurjun?" asked Liam. He tried to make the comment seem offhand, but it came out flat.

"Why?" asked Tirini, taken aback.

"Business or pleasure?" asked Liam.

Tirini frowned, and Liam realised he was using Earth slang; phrases she would take out of context.

"No business, Liam. I just wanted to see you."

Looking out at Tir, Liam's fears peaked. Usually he would bury them, pretend that everything was alright, but with Tirini, he just had to let it out. "I thought I had passed the test this afternoon."

Tirini's brow creased in frustration. "This is no test! I am not here to test you!"

He could see he had really upset her, and cursed himself.

Suddenly Tirini was in tears. Liam instinctively rushed to her, taking her into his arms. She sobbed quietly. Against him, she felt small and vulnerable, like the young woman she was. "I just wanted to see you. You have no idea what it is like, Liam. People shun me. I have no friends outside my order. *Everyone* fears me. My own family . . ."

Tirini pulled away from him and wiped the tears away. She looked into him. *Through* him. To the depths of his soul.

"We have so little time. Tomorrow you will be leaving with Morin on a quest to close the Gateway to Earth," she said. "I know. I am part of Torren's War Council." She paused. "Then you will be gone. Perhaps to perish within the Vault. If you had died, and I had never had the chance to . . . touch you." She faltered.

Liam was amazed she would want him.

"People fear my power, Liam. They fear what I will see inside them."

Liam's heart swelled with compassion. She was so soft and gentle, like a fawn stepping lightly from the mists of a dawn forest. He felt his heart stir.

Tirini started crying, yet this time they were tears of joy. She reached up and placed the palms of her hands on his cheeks, on either side of his face, looking even deeper into his eyes.

"Do you know why I came, Liam?"

Liam shook his head. He had no idea.

Tirini smiled, and it was like the dawn of a brilliant day.

"It is this, Liam," she said looking into his eyes.

"This?"

"Oh, you idiot! You do not flinch! Not even a little. You open your heart without fear. I can look into your eyes and know you love what you see! Do you know what that means to me? In a world where every gaze is turned away? Where every thought is open to me?"

Liam felt a burst of love so intense it overwhelmed him. But whether it came from Tirini, or himself, he could not tell. This close to her, it was as though they were one being. Her lips were luscious and full. He longed to kiss her.

She pulled his head down to hers and kissed him passionately. "You cannot hide your desire from me, thurjun," she gasped between kisses. She backed Liam toward the bed, pushing him back onto the covers, then stepped onto the bed, straddling him. Her desire unleashed.

With one motion Tirini drew off her light shift and threw it to the floor. She was completely naked beneath, except for a slender silver chain around her waist, which glittered in the light. The chain held a single purple gem, which dangled below her navel.

Liam was dumbstruck. Her breasts were fuller than he might have guessed, and beautifully shaped, with dark red nipples. He felt himself harden beneath her.

Tirini giggled and lifted his hands to her breasts. He took a shuddering breath as he ran his hands across the silky softness of her skin and her nipples. She closed her eyes, feeling his touch. His eyes flicked down to her crotch as the heady scent of her own arousal flooded his senses.

"What about your vows?"

Tirini stepped back off him and laughed lightly. "I am no Priestess. I am a Seeker. We celebrate life. And love."

Tirini started undoing Liam's belt. Eagerly he reached to help her, but she pushed his hands away with a cheeky grin. "No, no, no. I will do this. I want to make this last."

As she undid the knots in his belt and slowly opened up his thurjun's gown, she talked to him softly. "I have waited a long time for this, Liam. For someone like you."

Liam was alarmed. *This was her first time!* Things were moving too fast.

Tirini giggled again as her voice appeared in his mind. She read his thoughts with ease.

Do not fear, Liam. Yes, it is my first time. And I could not have hoped for better. I have chosen.

Tirini finished undressing Liam, then lay beside him. She forced him to lie still as she traced gentle fingers across his body. His muscles were not built up like a weightlifter's, but were hard and defined from years of training. She ran her hands across his pectorals, palms hot, her fingers lingering on his nipples, then down across the sculptured muscles of his stomach. Then further down, across his legs, then up. Her small hand wrapped itself around his shaft.

Liam gasped in pleasure, then looked across at her. She was beautiful. Lithe and soft. His eyes drifted across the curves of her body, her slim waist and curvaceous hips, the taut nipples.

Liam tingled with adrenalin and excitement. He throbbed with urgent desire, and his heart raced. He wanted to push her down and take her. Then he was distracted by her eyes, the pupils now dilated with desire. He lost himself in their shared sense of wonder. She had come to him because she liked him, because she looked into him and saw goodness there. They kissed passionately.

Then Liam closed the distance, laying his body on hers. She was soft and alive beneath him, and he played his hands across her skin in a fever of desire, reaching down to the warm dampness of her crotch. The contact sent a shock of sensation through him, driving to a new pitch of desire. She groaned in pleasure and opened her legs wider, wrapping her thighs around his hips to draw him in.

"*Liam*." She pulled him down.

She cried out as he entered her. He stopped, fearing he had hurt her.

"*Do not stop!*" She raised her hips, and pulled him down with her thighs.

Then they were going furiously, building and building toward a crescendo. An energy grew within him, singing like a chorus of angels. It burst, racing toward his head as he orgasmed. Intense and beautiful.

Profound peace descended on him.

He was breathing hard, and looked down to see Tirini beneath him. Her face was flushed and she looked more beautiful than ever. She opened her eyes and smiled, then reached up to embrace him.

"Did you?" he asked.

Tirini giggled. "They told me men always asked. I did not believe them. They also told me to lie." She softly caressed his face. "I did not. But it was wonderful. Just hold me."

Liam melted into her embrace. Tears trickled down his cheeks, although he was not sure why. He felt whole, and wonderful. As though a part of him that had been dormant had come to life at last.

Tirini made a soft noise of sympathy and touched his cheek with a fingertip, gathering a tear. She put the fingertip on her tongue, and smiled. A wave of intense relaxation swept through him. Only now that it was shed, did he realise just how much fear and tension he had been carrying.

Although still driven by a high state of unsatisfied arousal, Tirini felt a supreme sense of contentment. She snuggled closer to Liam, and kissed his cheek lightly, tasting tears. When they had formed the mental bond earlier that day, she had known two things: that Liam was a good man, honest and courageous in a way few people were; and that he was deeply wounded. She loved the essence of him. It had stayed with her since the Thurjuns Tower.

She had sensed wounds, centres of pain where love had been torn, faith had been destroyed. Liam had the skills of the thurjun, but surviving the horrors of the Vault required inner strength that rested on solid foundations. She could not let him face the Vault without healing the inner wounds.

Liam wiped the tears from his cheeks. "I'm not sure why I'm crying. I feel awesome."

She giggled at his strange turn of phrase. "It is joy. At the healing." Tirini looked deep. Satisfied that the soul-wounds were now closing, the frozen pain eased, and shed, in the natural order.

"I shouldn't be crying," he said.

She felt the beginning of embarrassment, and shame, and headed it off.

"I love them. Because they are your tears." She plucked another from his cheek with a fingertip and used it to moisten her lips. Then ran her fingers across his hard pectoral muscles. "This is life. Sharing. A gift given freely."

He relaxed and kissed her softly.

"We do not defend the Realms to protect the stones of Tir. It is to defend life. The great wheel of love, and birth, and the passing of the spirit, which turns within the hearts of mother, father, son, and daughter."

Liam looked into her eyes and she felt that thrill again.

"You're right. *This* is worth fighting for," he said, cupping her breast.

Better, she thought.

Liam drew her into his arms, kissing her, at first tenderly, then with more passion. She pushed her hips against him, and he responded instantly, swelling to hardness. Tirini looked down and bit her lip. She rolled on her back and pulled Liam on top of her.

She felt him shudder with pleasure as he eased himself into her. She gasped and looked up at Liam in wonder, so young and innocent in the soft light. *No.* Not innocent. Pure of heart.

"This time it will be slower," he said. "Promise."

Later, as Liam slept, Tirini rested quietly by his side. The second time he had lifted her to a state of arousal she had not known possible, at last satisfying her. Now she was sated, but her mind was alive. She eased herself away from Liam and watched his face as he slept, tracing her fingers across his mouth and cheek. He was unique, and he could not see it. But she could.

"Come back to me, Liam Durrow."

She rested a delicate hand on her stomach.

Then smiled.

Chapter 42
City of Tir — First Realm

Sentas emerged from the forest into a decorative garden. All was dark and silent, as he had expected. There were no glowglobes here. It was a place of contemplation, of day use, well away from the main Temple entrances. The irritating clergy of the High God would all be abed, catching sleep so they could rise with the dawn and chant their prayers to the waking world. Beyond the garden, a neat lawn extended to the Temple wall. He walked on, weaving between flower beds and carefully manicured shrubs, then across the trimmed grass to the wall. Despite the pleasant surrounds, the Temple made his skin crawl, bringing up unpleasant memories of the endless tedium of Realm ceremony. His life had been filled with it. The night was humid, and he dabbed at the perspiration on his forehead with a scented silk handkerchief. Two dark figures followed from the tree-shadows to join him. Zanthis, recently returned from the Reil Gateway, and Fess, a young druid that Strannus had provided. Like Sentas, Zanthis sported a dark hoodless cape of fine material, which concealed his court finery and sword. Sycophants such as Zanthis were always aping his style. So tiresome. Fess wore a bulky cloak of coarse weave, its deep hood concealing his face. *You better not have led me out here in the middle of the night for nothing, Zanthis.*

A priest emerged from the wall's shadow. Sentas recognised the narrow, ferret-like face of the young priest Reld as he approached them across the grass. The priest had come alone, as agreed, and did not seem unduly nervous. Sentas nodded, satisfied there was no trap.

"Hurry up and pay him, Zanthis," snapped the King's son. "I want this over quickly." Sentas had no time for turncoats like this spineless priest, even though his various intrigues often relied on them.

Zanthis lifted a heavy coin sack from his vest and handed it over.

"And you are sure this world of *Earth* has forbidden weapons and technology?" asked Sentas.

Zanthis nodded, a satisfied gleam in his eye. "Yes, my prince. Even Morin grew defensive when the other one —Liam — let the truth slip out. I am sure they are conspiring together."

Sentas stewed with impatience while the priest counted his coin.

If what Zanthis claimed was true, the evidence they could gather from this man, Shane, would be crucial. If damning enough, it would prompt action. Mobilisation. With the right pressures applied to the right levers, Sentas could shift the mechanics of politics to put himself at the forefront of such a venture. It would be glorious . . . leading a Realm army into this primitive world of Earth to secure it and destroy the Vault contamination at its core. He would eclipse his timid father at last. These Earthlings were bound to be nothing more than ignorant savages. They needed to be saved from themselves. Ruled with a strong hand. After returning from such a triumph, there would be nothing the High Court would not grant him. They would surely vote that, of the eligible candidates, only he deserved to be confirmed as heir to his father's throne.

During the transaction, Fess remained motionless, his face hidden in the hood's shadow. The bulky shape of the translation device squirmed beneath the druid's heavy cloak, making him seem deformed.

Reld slipped the coins into his vestments. He walked to the Temple wall and pushed open a concealed door, turning back expectantly for them to follow. Sentas checked the gardens one last time. *Deserted.* He followed the priest through the Temple's western wall, up a tight spiral staircase, and then through a narrow tunnel between two walls. They emerged in a dark corridor lit by a single glowglobe.

"Most of the clergy are terrified of this man," said Reld, a gleam in his eye. Perhaps toying with the profane was a game he enjoyed. "They won't be anywhere near him until the morning."

"Good," snapped Sentas, barely containing his impatience. "Just open the cell and wait for us here."

Reld walked swiftly to a cell door, produced a key, then turned the ancient lock. As he swung the doorway open, Sentas pushed past him into the cell, looking for the hapless Earth man.

Reld caught Sentas' sleeve as he passed through the doorway. "Another purse as we leave? As agreed?"

Sentas snatched his arm away, watching the greed in the priest's eyes with a mixture of satisfaction and revulsion. "Yes, as agreed. Now wait here until we are finished."

Sentas pushed into the cell.

A single glowglobe illuminated bare stone walls and a single bed, on which the Earth man sat watching them through dark, narrowed eyes. At the sight of Zanthis, the man sneered and spoke. The words were unintelligible, but Sentas did not need a translator to recognise a curse.

Sentas snapped his fingers at the druid. "Set up your device."

Fess drew a large sack from inside his cloak and placed it on the floor. He took a long rubber glove from a cloak pocket and drew it fastidiously onto his right hand, fussing with the fit. Satisfied, he opened the sack's drawstring and plunged his hand inside, forehead creased with concentration. He gave a tight smile then drew out a writhing mass. Moist and grey, the thing was roughly spherical and surrounded by writhing tentacles. A ghastly medusa's head. The tentacles whipped out, some wrapping themselves around the glove, others reaching into space, seeking purchase. Holding the device at arm's length, the druid closed on Shane.

Shane backed away, cursing in his own tongue.

Zanthis threw back his cape and drew his sword in one fluid motion. He stepped forward and placed the point at Shane's throat, pressing forward with the blade until a thin trail of blood trickled from the wound. Shane grew still. He remained motionless as the druidic device's writhing mass was placed on his head.

Zanthis and Fess stepped back.

The tentacles wrapped around Shane's head and face, leaving the nose and mouth unobstructed, then tightened. The Earth man choked out a short scream, then grew silent as the symbiosis stabilised.

"Can you hear me?" asked Sentas.

The device achieved the same effect as a mind-bond, but with none of the benefits of language acquisition. Though Shane spoke in his native language, and the others in the Realm tongue, the device translated the thoughts directly, mind-to-mind, within its short radius of operation.

Shane looked around. He seemed surprised at the lack of pain, as though he had been expecting torture. "Yeah. I can hear you, dipstick."

Sentas' eyes narrowed. "I want you to tell me everything you know about this *Earth*."

"Why should I?"

"Because I intend to lead Realm forces there. I could take you back with me, and set you free . . . even reward you . . . if you cooperate."

Shane sneered. "I want out of this cell. And out of these." He held up his manacles.

Sentas nodded slowly. "Certainly possible. I could also get you moved to my own chambers in the High Court. There you would have your fill of wine and food, women . . . whatever you desire. Although we will have to keep you out of sight."

"And what you do want in return?"

"I have heard whispers that Earth uses Vault technology. I need you to tell me everything you know. Do the people of Earth possess weapons of mass destruction? Have you had any major wars of aggression? Genocide?"

A wide smile spread on Shane's lips.

"There's always an up side," said Shane.

Chapter 43
Sydney, Australia — Earth
30th December 1999

Finn gripped the bars of the high window, lifting himself up again and again. Each time he crested the painted concrete of the sill he had a brief view of the grey Sydney dawn through the dirty glass. His arm and back muscles burned, but he pushed himself on mercilessly, forcing strength into his body until fatigue made another lift impossible.

He dropped to the floor of the cell. Finn looked up at the camera's dark eye, burning with resentment. He had planned to elicit the aid of Earth warriors in his quest, and gain the support of an Earth thurjun. Instead, the *police* — the very men and women he had hoped would help him — had imprisoned him. And the only thurjun he had seen on this world, Liam Durrow, had vanished through the Stonelake Gateway.

Finn launched into an unarmed combat form. His hands and legs moved in a familiar sequence of sweeping arcs and elegant turns, then through a series of rapid, lethal strikes. He moved between patterns, each designed for a particular situation, or opponent. The Vault worlds had many different species of warrior, and the forms helped to polish his skills. He tried to clear his mind, but it was impossible. His thoughts circled around the same grim realities, like carrion birds above a corpse. There was little chance now to strike back at the Vault. He might be stuck here for years. Imprisoned. *No.* Genna *would* come. He had to believe that.

He broke off his training and looked up at the narrow slice of dawn sky visible through the high window. High King Torren would be alarmed by the Stonelake attack, and by Finn's disappearance. After years of ignoring his warnings, Realm forces would finally be mobilised. Too little. Too late. Without control of the Stonelake Gateway, any rescue was impossible. Prince Sentas, his foster-brother, would delight in his misfortune. The thought of Sentas, living at ease — and free — in the First Realm while he was trapped here, sent his heart pounding.

Sentas had hated Finn from the beginning.

Only days after the Archfiend's attack on Evenstone Tower, he and Tallandra found themselves in the First Realm. A sudden addition to the High King's household.

"Here Sentas. Here is a brother and sister for you at last," the High King had said.

The young Sentas had looked down his nose at them. "You are most welcome," he had said, but his eyes had communicated an entirely different sentiment. Finn had feared him then.

Sentas and Finn had shared tutors and weaponmasters. At first Sentas had delighted in embarrassing Finn in lessons, defeating him with ease and leaving him bewildered and humiliated. Finn had tried hard to win his foster-brother's respect, soon excelling in martial skills and scholarship. Yet if he had expected this to please Sentas, he had been terribly mistaken. As the butt of his jokes, Finn had been tolerable. As Sentas' equal — his better — he became the young prince's enemy.

Morin had shielded him and Tallandra from the worst of the manoeuvring, but there was little he could do to prevent the continual slights and torments Finn suffered from Sentas. Eventually Finn had given up trying to win over the prince, waiting for the day he would take his commission and earn his freedom.

But he could never have guessed how vindictive Sentas could be.

One day, a distraught and hysterical Tallandra had run to the training ground where Finn practised, her clothing in disarray, stammering out the name of Sentas. Finn had stormed through the Court in search of the High King's son, consumed by a flame of righteous anger, determined to challenge Sentas to a duel. He had found Sentas in the Temple of the High God, in the company of none other than his father the High King and his father's councillors. Thankfully, Morin had also been with the King that day.

Had Finn looked about him, he would have glimpsed the shadowed forms of Sentas' followers hiding at a safe distance within the huge building, yet close enough to watch their master's plot unfold. If Morin had not intercepted him, he would have struck Sentas to the ground and challenged him right there, breaking an ancient Realm law. It was forbidden to issue challenges within the Temple of the High God. An old law, and rarely invoked, but still enforced. The penalty would have been a period of exile, and a ban from holding any official Realm office. It would have meant the end of Finn's career, and the permanent loss of Evenstone.

Instead, Morin had apologised to the High King and led the outraged Finn outside. In the furious argument that ensued, Morin had confessed the truth of the attack on Evenstone Tower, revealing what the Archfiend had taken . . . and why. Finn had sobered instantly, understanding, in a flash of insight, why Morin had stayed with the last Evenstone scions, abandoning his own ambitions. Finn had left his childhood behind that day, and his destiny had taken tangible form.

Sentas need not have feared Finn's ambition after that. When Finn won his Captain's commission, Finn had been offered choice positions at large active Gateways throughout the Realms — one even close to his own home in the Third Realm — and field assignments warriors twenty years his senior could only dream of. Instead, he had astonished the High King by requesting Stonelake, an ancient, but now silent and ruined Gateway in the Fourth Realm. For his career within the High King's retinue, it meant a silent and slow death, far from any centre of power in the six Realms.

Keys rattled in the lock.

The constable assigned to his cell opened the door. He looked haggard, and there were dark circles under his eyes. When he saw Finn, the policeman tensed, his hand falling to the baton hanging from his belt. Finn smiled at the gesture. It was a compliment to think they feared him unarmed and unarmoured. Then he saw Blundstone. Finn's heart lurched into a gallop. The muscles of his shoulders and back tensed. *For the love of Lugh . . . please let it have worked.* The psychologist shuffled past the policeman and entered the cell, his face drawn from lack of sleep.

"There you go, Doctor Blundstone. I'll have to write this up though. An interview without prior clearance is highly irregular.

Why you want to come in here at eight-thirty in the morning in the middle of Christmas week is beyond me."

"Yes! I know what time it is!" Blundstone took a deep breath. "Thank you, Constable O'Neill. That will be all."

Blundstone stood just inside the cell, studying Finn. He looked angry . . . and bewildered.

"Finn Evenstone."

"Yes."

"I was . . . here looking in on some other clients . . . so I thought I would take the opportunity to look over your case again. Would you mind pulling up a chair?"

Finn drew up a chair and sat. He gripped its plastic sides with his hands to still their sudden tremor. He must appear calm. He had never used the compulsion before, and was not sure how it would manifest. He had to play along. If he did something overt that broke the spell, he was finished.

Blundstone sat directly opposite him and started leafing through his notes. The man tapped his folder thoughtfully, seemingly unsure how to proceed. Finn saw a flash of gold in Blundstone's hand. He froze as he saw the unmistakable shape of the Ring of Evenstone. *Should I take it now? By force?* Finn's eyes flicked to the camera. *No.* That would alert the watchers.

Blundstone stopped tapping the folder and looked at the ring in his hand, suddenly aware of it. "What the . . .? How on Earth did I manage to walk away from the evidence room with this?" Blundstone cleared his throat, clearly embarrassed he had spoken his thoughts out loud. The man looked weary, and his fatigue had broken down his usual reserve. "So, tell me more about these . . . " Blundstone checked his notes. "Blessed Realms." Blundstone seemed agitated, but launched himself into an interview regardless.

Finn forced himself to answer Blundstone's questions. He could still see the ring, clutched in the man's hand. Blundstone reached the end of the interview and sat blinking. The man clearly felt compelled to stay, but could find no logical reason to do so. Blundstone fidgeted. Shuffled in his chair. Finn's jaw clenched tight. His temples pounded in time with his heartbeat.

Blundstone flushed red. "Well that's about it then."

Blundstone rose awkwardly and waved to the camera. "I'll see you later in the week."

Blundstone turned toward the door, still tapping the ring idly against the folder. There was nothing Finn could do. His best chance to escape and fight the Vault was slipping through his fingers, yet he dare not alert his captors. Up until now they had assumed he was not dangerous. If he gave them a reason to bind him he would never get free. He needed stealth and surprise on his side to escape, even with the ring.

Finn watched Blundstone leave in silent fury.

As Blundstone stood waiting, he looked back at Finn. The psychologist's eyebrows rose and he opened his folder, taking a pen from his top pocket. "Initially elated . . . then sudden anger. Indicative of mood swings," he muttered as he wrote, unaware he was once more speaking out loud.

The door opened, then closed behind Blundstone. All Finn's hopes went with him. He cursed in frustration.

Then Finn's gaze fell on Blundstone's chair.

The Ring of Evenstone!

Finn leapt forward, driven by a surge of excitement, then made himself slow down. *Smooth and easy.* He turned his body to the camera to block his movements, and snatched up the ring, slipping it onto the first finger of his right hand. Of course! The compulsion worked through self-deception. All that fussing and shifting in place now made sense. Blundstone had wanted to go, but unconsciously knew he had to leave the ring. He had dropped the Ring and taken his own off as a substitute. *That* was the ring he had in his hand when he left. No doubt he would dutifully return it to the lockup and leave it with Finn's helm and personal effects, still convinced it was Finn's ring.

Finn made a triumphant fist, delighting in the familiar feel of the ring on his hand. All he had to do was escape, then wait. By now Genna would know where to find him.

Finn returned to his cot and sat.

He waited one agonising hour. Time enough for the guards to slip back into a bored routine. Then he launched into his plan.

The first part had been well rehearsed. He swiftly used his pillow and blanket to make the shape of a figure asleep in the cot with the sheet over its head. It just needed to fool whatever surveillance they had until he was out of the building. To slip out of the cell, he was relying on luck, and the natural laziness of guards everywhere. The men in the control room would not watch all of the prisoners, all of the time. Then he sat cross-legged on the cell floor near the door, his back to the camera. He took a few deep breaths and began. This was the hard part. He had to construct a Matrix of Confusion, which would enable him to project a lasting image into another mind. The minutes stretched out, and soon Finn was sweating with the effort. The spell had a confounding structure. At his first attempt he destroyed the subtle form with a misplaced curve, the second with a loop of the wrong shape. The task was at the very limit of his thurjun's skill. There was nothing wrong with his memory, at least. It had been years since Morin had shown it to him, but he remembered the shape well. The legacy of long years of training.

Around noon, Constable O'Neill returned to Finn's cell with lunch. The metal cover of the peephole in the door moved to the side, giving him a brief glimpse of O'Neill's pinched face. *Now.* Finn projected an image of the cell into the policeman's mind . . . with himself asleep in the bunk. Finn, cross-legged by the door, should remain invisible to O'Neill. *If* it worked.

The constable unlocked the cell door and swung it open.

"Goddamn nutter" O'Neill muttered. "Should be in the mental ward, not in the lock up."

Balancing the tray with one hand, O'Neill entered the cell and placed the meal on the small bench by the door. "Rise and shine, space-boy!"

Finn channelled more power from the ring's small mionanail into the matrix. The phantom Finn groaned and tossed in his sleep.

"Have it your way," said O'Neill.

As the constable turned, Finn slowly rose to his feet. O'Neill was looking straight at him, but saw only bare wall, totally immersed in the projected vision. Now came the tricky part. On top of the image he was projecting, Finn had to add a suggestion. Finn constructed the form and filled it with power from the ring. As the constable passed him he sent it into the policeman's mind.

You must get something outside the building. Immediately. Something important you have forgotten. O'Neill paused in his stride. His eyes glazed and he swayed, as though momentarily faint.

The man's vision cleared and a new determination took hold.

Before O'Neill could close the cell, Finn stepped out into the corridor. His heart surged with triumph. Soundlessly, he slipped behind the man and followed him as he made for the lifts in the centre of the building. Thankfully it was early, and there were not many people around. To a casual observer, it would look like O'Neill was escorting him.

They turned a corner. Two police were walking side by side toward them, dressed in a different uniform from O'Neill's. One was walking with a crutch, injured in the right leg, while the other had his arm in a sling. Finn recognised them instantly. They were two of the police he had fought on the beach at Kookaburra Bay.

Chapter 44
Sydney, Australia — Earth

Finn watched the two injured policemen walk toward him and O'Neil. He forced his exhausted brain to work, desperate for ideas as the two men drew inexorably closer. One on his crutch, the other with his arm in a sling.

"Esco is treating us like idiots. *He* wasn't there," said Sling-arm.

"Still. It *is* hard to believe. I was there and I can hardly believe it. Well maintained weapons just don't behave like that," said Crutches.

"He keeps us here all through Christmas week. Just to make us feel like a pair of incompetent hicks when he finally has time to interview us," snarled Sling-arm. "Arsehole."

Crutches sighed. "At least he could have let us fly home. Kathy is pissed I missed Christmas with the kids. But, at least we're getting paid."

"But no overtime," said Sling-arm. "That sucks for Christmas duty."

The two police looked at O'Neill and said nothing. Then they looked at Finn.

"Jesus, that's him!" said Crutches.

"What the hell is he doing outside his cell?" asked Sling-arm.

Finn had a single moment to act. He drew more power from the mionanail in the ring and used the matrix to project an image into the minds of the men. He fumbled, drawing too much power from the tiny device, and adjusted rapidly. Thankfully the matrix remained intact. The new image showed them a prisoner behind O'Neill, but one with Endar's face, not his. A face they would definitely *not* recognise. Both men were taken aback, then shook their heads, now embarrassed and eager to get past. Finn continued projecting the image. He could not risk discovery while he was still inside the building.

Then the trickle of power from the ring's mionanail died. Pain lanced into Finn's head as the matrix first drew power from his own mind, then collapsed, the tiny device exhausted to depletion.

The dual projections vanished like snuffed candle flames.

"What? What are you talking about?" asked O'Neill. " *'That's him.'* What do you mean?"

Finn held his breath. The two men were looking at him as though nothing was wrong. Enough of the enchantment had held. The implanted images would have a certain inertia in the recipient's mind. How much though? He had no idea.

"Forget it," snapped Sling-arm.

"We must be going crazy," muttered Crutches.

The two police shuffled past. They did not give Finn another glance.

O'Neill and Finn reached the lifts. O'Neill pressed the down button. They waited. Then waited. The lifts were slow. There was a bank of lavatories opposite the lifts, which the locals called *toilets.* O'Neill's eyes flicked between the lift lights and the male conveniences. The lift arrived, opening with painful slowness, but instead of going into the lift, O'Neill all but ran across the corridor to the toilet. Finn had no choice but to go with him. He could not stand alone in the corridor. Finn darted in through the toilet door, just before it closed.

O'Neill walked straight to the urinal and unzipped his fly.

"Ahh. What a relief," said O'Neill, looking down.

Outside the room, Finn could hear the lift chime. Should he make a break for it? *No.* He was still dressed as a prisoner. To make it out of the building he needed O'Neill. He watched the door to the washroom anxiously, wondering if he should duck into one of the cubicles behind him and hide until O'Neill was finished.

One of the cubical toilets flushed. Before he could do anything but turn around, a tall, overweight, and balding plain-clothes policeman emerged from the cubicle.

Superintendent Esco.

Esco swept the cubicle door back with a thud, and made for the washbasins. He looked tired and disgruntled. He swept his gaze across the room and stopped in his tracks as his eyes locked onto Finn.

"*Wha* . . . ?"

O'Neill zipped up his fly and turned around as though nothing was out of the ordinary. *He still cannot see me,* thought Finn.

"Morning, Superintendent Esco. Been in to take a statement from the Queensland boys? Bit strange aren't they?"

Esco went straight for his gun, reaching inside the left side of jacket for his shoulder holster. Finn darted forward, pinning the Agent's right arm against his body with both hands and trapping the Agent's left arm behind him, between his thick torso and the wall.

"What is the matter with you, O'Neill! *Get him!*" yelled Esco.

Esco pushed out from the wall, freeing his left arm and using it to help wrestle his right arm free. In a test of sheer strength, it was an uneven match. Esco was bigger and heavier than Finn. His face was screwed up in a murderous snarl as he forced Finn back.

The gun cleared the holster.

O'Neill rubbed his eyes and shook his head. "What . . . What's happening?"

Esco turned, swinging Finn against the wall. The Agent used the distraction to move his left hand, which he used to rack the slide on the top of his weapon. Esco hissed through his teeth as he forced the gun down. His finger whitened on the trigger. The barrel dropped inexorably lower. Soon he would bring it to bear, and he could fire point-blank into Finn's chest.

"*O'Neill!*" Esco's voice boomed in the confined space.

The constable looked around him as though coming out of a dream. His eyes lit on Finn and he yelped in surprise. He staggered back, tripped over the urinal's low wall, and landed heavily in the trough. He lay dazed.

Finn had to take Esco out of action. He had both hands on Esco's right wrist, while Esco now had both hands on his gun. Finn stepped in with a single sharp movement, while simultaneously pulling Esco's right arm forward. Finn's left forearm smashed into Esco's extended right arm just behind the elbow, while Finn simultaneously pulled Esco's right arm — and the gun — past him. Esco grunted in pain, but kept hold of the weapon. Keeping Esco's arm straight, Finn ducked under it, across Esco's body and behind him, using the Agent's straight arm to flip him in place. Esco thudded onto the tiles. His head bounced. He was momentarily stunned. Finn ripped the gun out of his opponent's hand and hit Esco in the temple. A precise strike. He did not want to kill the man. Finn waited, watching for signs of unconsciousness, but the Agent merely shook his head and levered himself up off the ground. *A hard head*. Esco lunged. Finn sidestepped Esco, then slammed the pistol butt into Esco's head again, in the same place, this time with more force. Blood flowed freely from the wound. Esco's eyes fluttered, his knees gave way, and he slumped to the ground. Unconscious.

O'Neill darted for the door.

"Stop!" shouted Finn in English. "Or I will use the weapon!"

O'Neill turned slowly, putting his arms in the air. "OK, just take it easy, fella. Why don't you give me that, hey? No one else needs to get hurt."

Finn advanced slowly. He turned O'Neill around and pushed him into the wall. He slipped the baton from its holder with his free hand and dropped it onto the floor, then checked the policeman for other concealed weapons. *Nothing*. Not even a communications device. He stepped back.

"I have another plan. You are going to get me out of here. I do not want to harm you, understand? Do not force me to." Finn pressed the weapon into O'Neill's back.

"OK! OK," said O'Neill.

Finn pushed O'Neill into a cubicle and told him to shut the door and stay there. Then he swiftly undressed Esco and put on the Agent's clothes. The trousers were big, but he tightened the belt and rolled up the legs. The shirt was loose, and stank of sour sweat. The shoes were a reasonable fit, if a little loose. He put the unconscious Esco into a cubicle with his discarded prison clothes and the baton and shut the door. Opening the other cubicle door, he waved the hapless constable out. He covered the gun with Esco's jacket, but kept the weapon trained on O'Neill. Together, Finn and O'Neill walked out of the washroom to the lifts. At Finn's prompting, O'Neill pressed the down button. The guard's eyes were fixed on Esco's jacket, and the gun beneath.

"Remember, policeman O'Neill. I want only my freedom," said Finn.

They descended the lift to the lower floor, and entered a wide, open lobby. Finn could see cars moving on the street outside through big glass doors.

They were halfway to the doors when the policeman at the front desk called out. "Hey, O'Neill. I thought you were on all day?" The policeman at the desk looked at Finn and his brow creased.

O'Neill turned back to the other policeman, his eyes flicking toward Finn, measuring the distance. Finn shook his head and lifted the jacket and hidden gun. "I believe the projectile will pass through the cloth without difficulty," whispered Finn.

O'Neill licked his lips. "Just out for a smoke, Williams!" he yelled.

"Yeah, right," replied Williams.

O'Neill and Finn continued on to the doors. They were only three paces away when Williams called out. "Wait a minute! You don't smoke!"

O'Neill turned back. A look passed between him and Williams.

Williams' hand stabbed for something below his desk. Finn understood immediately. *A lockout button.* Once he hit it, every entrance to the building — including the big glass doors — would be sealed tight. Finn pushed open a glass door with his free hand, then, swivelling his body, kicked the side of O'Neill's shin at full power, snapping the bone. The policeman howled in pain and went down.

A loud buzzing came from the glass doors. One by one, thick bolts dropped from the ceiling and shot up from the floor, closing them tight. But Finn was holding one open. He slipped through the door. As it shut behind him, he looked back to see at least ten armed police with thick black vests swarm from a concealed room. They reached the glass, but were trapped inside. Finn had a few precious seconds to make his break before the lockout was disabled.

He ran into the street, then around the first corner. As soon as he was out of sight he slowed to an even pace and merged with the crowd. He saw a large entrance up ahead, opening onto the street. People were emerging from it with bags in their hands, while others pushed metal-mesh carts full of food and produce. A crowded market. *Perfect.* He walked into the complex. Everything was bright and new, with many walls made of glass. Immediately in front of him were two sets of moving walkways with silver steps, one going up, another down. The steps folded flat as they reached the end of their circuit. *Ingenious.* In front of these moving steps was a plan of the complex. He nudged his mind into the thurjun's mnemonic state and absorbed the layout. Then he followed the crowd onto the silver steps and rode up into the complex. It had many levels, all around an open central atrium that rose to the height of the structure. He exited the moving stairway and moved around the first level, mentally comparing what he saw with the map. Shops, he realised. Most sold clothing. Others items of technology. He tensed as he passed a man dressed in a guard's uniform, but the man gave him no more than a cursory glance. At the far end of the floor, he found what he was searching for. The public conveniences. He did not recognise any English writing, but he listened avidly as he walked. "I'll just nick to the toilet," said one man, heading for an area that had been marked on the map with simple representations of men and women.

He followed the man into the toilet, entering an empty stall and locking the door. They seemed to be in constant use, and twice someone knocked on the door. He ignored the knock, and the curt questions. Finally, he found himself alone in the room. Using the toilet bowl and cistern as stepping stones, he reached up to the low ceiling. It was fitted with a light metal framework, with each rectangular space fitted with a white foam tile. He was beginning to see a pattern to Earth architecture. The very minimum amount of material was used for function, with little thought to longevity, or artistry. In this case, it suited his purpose. Finn lifted a white tile, finding a void between it and a bare concrete ceiling. Noting that there was plenty of space inside, Finn pulled himself up into the cavity and carefully replaced the tile. They would expect him to run, thought Finn, but he was not going anywhere. The police building was where Genna would come to find him.

Schooling himself to calmness, Finn began to wait.

Chapter 45
VoYannan's world — Vault of Seven Horns

VoYannan looked out across the Plain of Sorrow.

Stretching out across the Plain, all the way to the horizon, was a fleet of starships. Some of these raiders ranged far out into the cosmos, hauling back the plundered wealth of the Shadow Worlds through orbital Gateways, while others attacked star-systems he was yet to dominate. The Plain itself was red and bare, baked hard by launch thrusters. A grunt of satisfaction rumbled deep in his armoured chest. *All this I have wrought.*

VoYannan stood on a platform at the top of his Citadel, which was a vast pyramid of grey stone. Set nearby on the platform was a wide altar, its channels and stone collection bowls stained with ancient layers of dried blood. Ranks of siithe stood by impassively. The viewing platform was set into the sunward face of the pyramid and was large enough to land a starship on. Up here, away from the sulphurous clouds that hissed over the landscape, the stone was mostly unblemished, the writhing, twisted figures carved into every surface clearly recognisable. Near the base of the pyramid the stone was blackened, as though diseased. He sometimes saw this through the eyes of his thralls.

An orange sun dominated the sky, forever fixed in position. Its light was filtered through dense high-level cloud that plunged the planet's day-side into gloom. There was no night here, no dawn, no sunset. The shadows forever unmoving.

This was his world. The heart of the Vault of Seven Horns.

After countless millennia of occupation, not a shred of growth remained on the planet. Nothing but baked earth the colour of blood. Sand flew in biting, acid winds, abrading the bones of the world's vanished species to bitter dust. Nothing lived here that VoYannan did not give leave to breathe. Not a tree. Not a blade of grass. All food was flesh, plundered from the Shadow Worlds.

There were less than one thousand krell. Each of his brethren ruled another Vault, sitting like a spider inside a web of conquered worlds. Together they ruled the Vaults of Sheol. There had been more krell, but incessant war between the Vaults had removed the weaklings, leaving an uneasy balance of power. They were an ancient, powerful species, solitary by nature, evolved to reproduce without sexual union. Virtually immortal, the impulse to spawn was savagely repressed because a new krell spawn was a potential threat to its sire. Yet such progeny could also be a source of enormous power if subjugated . . . which was the lure. VoYannan had been leashed to his own sire for millennia, until he had managed to gain the upper hand. Then he had destroyed him utterly, draining him to a husk and feasting on his ancient flesh to absorb every last shred of strength.

The urge to expand their empires was strong in the krell. The destiny of the Cosmos was the extinction of all life that did not yield itself to their dominion. This they knew in their innermost core. It drove them outward. Some krell used the strength of a new spawn to extend their territories, then devoured their growing successor before it grew powerful enough to challenge them. It was a delicate balance. VoYannan himself had been cautious since his rise, conscious of his own destiny, which was to rule *all* the Vaults of Sheol. To leash all krell to his will, as he had once been leashed to his sire. To do that he needed to *fully* subjugate his spawn. Only Sephany could give him this complete control. With this enhanced strength, he could take control of each Vault, one after the other. Once he had harnessed the power of the combined krell worlds he could launch an assault on the Blessed Realms the likes of which they had never seen. Then there would be nothing, *nothing* that could stand in the way of total krell dominion.

VoYannan turned to Hoor, his veyr High Priest. The veyr's leathery wings were opened slightly, catching the orange light, his insectoid head and long proboscis raised in anticipation. His multifaceted eyes reflected a thousand Plain of Sorrows in miniature.

"The human-spawn. Do you have them ready, Hoor?"

"Yes, Lord," hissed the veyr.

"Bring me the Realm priestess. I am ready to plant my Seed."

"It shall be done, my Lord." Hoor waved to another veyr standing behind him. Without hesitation, the second veyr spread his wings and launched soundlessly from the platform, swooping down through the stinging air.

At the thought of planting his Seed — and the power this would bring him — VoYannan's lust grew. With a sucking sound, his member rose from its mucus-filled cavity, throbbing with the intensity of his need. Inside his penis, the Spawn struggled to tear its way free. He had waited so long . . .

Each krell implanted their parasitic seed into a host. The spawn destroyed the host as it grew, sucking power until it clawed its way free. Aeons ago, VoYannan had entered this world in a birth of blood, ripping his host asunder. His first memories were of a green wilderness, life thriving in the gentle, unchanging climate of the temperate zone of a tidally locked planet. He had found a score of brothers, already feasting, conquering, building their power through the enslavement of whatever sentience they could find. It had been a maelstrom of devouring lust. His sire had spawned them all, and watched them from orbit, waiting to leash the victor. They had fought bitterly, until the world was a ruin, and only a few of them remained. Like the others, he had at first sown his Seed throughout the world, siring a hundred krell, but these and their spawn became his enemies in turn — enemies who could find a way into his mind with ease — for a sire and his spawn were always linked. In the end VoYannan had triumphed. He had learned to hold his spawn while his brothers had let their lust go unbridled, sowing the seeds of their own downfall. He had learned patience, knowing that the right time would come.

Now was that time.

Through Sephany, he would dominate the mind of his spawn totally: doubling, *tripling* his power as it grew. The weakest of the krell lords would buckle beneath his growing power, making the next even easier prey.

A red light swelled across the platform, and VoYannan turned to see Balos arrive with Sephany.

Sephany's steps faltered.

In the dirty orange light, VoYannan looked even more fearsome, his enlarged member a horrific reminder of her fate. The bulky form of the krell was silhouetted against a stone altar. *So is it to be here? Spread on that bloody altar?* She wanted to scream, to throw herself from the platform and smash herself on the ruined ground below, but she did not. That was too much like defeat.

For hours she had prayed, through the unending darkness of her cell. She had opened herself to the Light and found peace and knowledge. Why had VoYannan not raped her immediately? The krell were notorious for their ruthlessness. She became convinced there must be a reason. The krell was seeking to break her will, to make her consent to carrying his parasitic seed. Well he would *not* break her.

VoYannan lumbered forward, his armoured bulk a sickly grey-green in the light.

"Come forward, my bride!"

Sephany felt the force of his command pulse into her mind. Half of her siithe escort stumbled forward dumbly, responding unconsciously. Sephany stood her ground. She drew the core of her consciousness beyond him, retreating into the Light.

The krell howled. The horns on his head extended like cat's claws.

Throughout the Citadel, screams rose onto the poisoned wind. The siithe fell to the stone, howling piteously as they writhed. Balos remained immobile, but the seraphin's wings blurred into lethal motion. Even the implacable veyr priests dropped to their knees.

Sephany trembled. She felt the cold kiss of tears on her cheeks. "I am no servant to be commanded, krell."

VoYannan loomed closer. The krell's eyes expanded, filling her vision. Pain ripped through her. She retreated into the Light, but a suffocating darkness drove her to her knees.

"Wake up, Sephany darling. Let me help you."

Sephany opened her eyes. She was kneeling in her bed, the covers tossed aside. Above her was the concerned face of Damast, her lover. They had been living together for years now. Damast put his arms around her. She felt an intense warmth in her stomach and groin, then a flowering of desire that made her gasp. His hands were all over her, pushing up her silky shift. They were rough on her naked skin. *Strange, his touch is usually so soft . . .*

Then he was laying her back onto the covers, spreading her legs with his knees.

"It was just a dream, darling. A bad dream," whispered Damast, his words hypnotic.

Something was wrong. His eyes were dark with lust. *Cruel*. He was pushing her down, *forcing* her down.

"Wait, Damast."

He was on top of her.

"No, Damast. Wait!"

Damast's face rippled, and his voice boomed. "DO MY WILL."

A rush of light filled her mind. The spell broke. She was on the rough stone altar, the huge bulk of VoYannan above her, his swollen member throbbing, dripping with mucus. Her stomach writhed in revulsion.

"No!" she screamed. "I do not consent!" Her heart fluttered at a frantic pace. A bird trapped in a cage. Its wings beating against the bars.

The krell threw his head back and roared. Every thrall in sight — siithe, veyr, and slave — bellowed his fury. The seraphin flared deep red. It seared her eyes.

She clambered off the altar and backed away.

The krell followed her, the hot force of his rage buffeting her. "Tell me, priestess. You, who are so pure. How many children would you see murdered?"

VoYannan waved and Hoor led forward a procession of child slaves, all in chains. There were hundreds of them, stretching in single file from the altar and across the platform, then down into the bowls of VoYannan's Citadel.

"Oh, no," said Sephany. "No."

The krell straightened. "Hoor. Bring forward the first."

The veyr priest came forward with a young boy of around five or six. He was beautiful. His clear blue eyes were stunned, broken. His blonde hair hung lank. Sephany swept her eyes along the line of children. Every one of them was perfectly formed. The flower of youth from a thousand worlds.

VoYannan nodded.

Hoor dragged the blonde boy to the altar. The boy screamed.

He turned toward her, crying out for help in his own tongue. Sephany took a faltering step toward the child. She trembled with dread as Hoor lifted him to the bloody stone. The priest drew a double-edged short sword from beneath his cloak. It was razor sharp, and tapered to a point. He looked to VoYannan, waiting for the krell's command.

"How many will you see die, priestess?" asked VoYannan.

The krell stood back and waved at the children. *There were hundreds of them!*

"How much blood do you want on your hands! Or is your life worth more than theirs?"

"These children have done nothing!" pleaded Sephany.

"In a second they will do no more," hissed Hoor with a buzzing chuckle.

"Yield to my will," demanded VoYannan.

Sephany looked away from the boy. She could not, *must* not, give in. Whatever the cost. There was more at stake here than her own life, or her fate. She was convinced of it. Sephany opened herself to the High God. Her mind filled with light. Peace descended on her. She opened her eyes and looked at the children. Silently, she raised her hands, calling down the blessing of the High God. *Banish their fear and guide them into the Light of the Tree.*

"Cease your prayers, *witch*, and answer me!" demanded VoYannan.

Sephany continued her prayers for the children. Along the line, their crying stopped, and their eyes, once dull, came to a bright focus on her. They stood unafraid.

The krell roared a command. Hoor lifted his blade.

The boy's screams died abruptly as the blade fell. Sephany turned away as the veyr priests gathered around, their proboscises eagerly dipping into the red, flowing channels. Muscles worked rhythmically in their throats, sucking up the boy's lifeblood before it even reached the collection bowls.

"There, priestess, now you are a murderer. How many more would you see dead? For every minute you delay, another dies." The krell spoke. His voice rumbled deep in his armoured chest.

Sephany remained motionless. A wave of power flowed

through her, surging in through the top of her head. When she spoke, her voice carried to the furthermost corners of the platform in perfect clarity. "It is you who are the murderer, VoYannan."

The krell stormed from the platform, calling back to his veyr priests as he went. "Kill them all! And make sure she sees every one of them die."

Sephany turned and made herself watch as the next innocent died, forcing herself to bear witness, using all her strength to lead the child's soul away from this place of darkness and toward the Light. Every time the blade struck it tore a cry from her throat. Her tears fell, to be lost on stone.

And beneath the orange sun, the blood flowed.

Chapter 46
City of Tir — First Realm

Liam and Tirini walked into the outer chambers of the High Court arm in arm. The buzz of excited conversation dipped and a wave of silence swept through the antechamber. Within moments, the whole crowd was focussed on them as they approached the High Court entry. Only the stoic guards in their silver armour ignored them. Liam looked around at the crowd, amazed and terrified by the reaction. He should have expected it — they were both celebrities — but there was something else. Something beyond the titillating nature of their liaison.

"What is it, Tirini?" whispered Liam, as they neared the doors.

"They fear my power," said Tirini.

"But you are no different to yesterday."

Tirini flashed Liam a smile. "Oh, Liam. They fear my *increase* in power. A Seeker does not take a lover casually. Should I bear a child, my powers will double."

A child! Liam's heart raced. Then he remembered the silver chain around her waist, and the purple gem that had hovered above her womb. A fertility charm? He had been so swept away in the moment, he had never even considered birth control.

As the huge doors opened for them, Liam struggled to frame a question. "But after one night — I mean, there isn't much chance of you being . . . pregnant . . . is there?"

Tirini studied Liam, then smiled. "Oh. I understand. I realise now that things are done differently on Earth. We do not hinder life, Liam. It is not the way of the Seekers. Have no fear, Liam. Should I conceive your child, I will love and cherish it."

Liam could not bear the thought of her carrying his child without him by her side. It made the thought of leaving her overwhelming. "I will tell Morin that I cannot come with him. I'll stay here with you."

Tirini's eyes misted. With a visible effort she stifled her tears. "Please, Liam. Do not. I also would give anything to be with you, but you must go with Morin. I know it. Then you must return to Earth. The Realms needs you there."

"But—"

Tirini silenced him with an embrace.

The people around them watched with shocked expressions, and Liam guessed that such displays of affection were rare in the High Court.

"I love you, Liam Durrow," said Tirini. She kissed him softly, then walked away. The crowd parted before her as she made her way to the Seeker's seats on the dais.

As he watched her go, Liam felt the joy drain out of him. The night they had, the unspoken promise of a life together, it was all slipping away. When Tirini reached the Seeker's seats, she sat alone, her eyes down. Even from that distance he saw tears in her eyes. *Not so simple then.* The crowd closed around him, and she was lost from sight.

Liam looked around, feeling bereft and ill at ease. He was angry at the world, angry at the High Court and the needs of the Blessed Realms that should draw them apart. But even so, he knew she was right. He had to fight the Vault, and Morin and the Realms needed him. He stood by himself for a few minutes, then noticed a stately woman making her way toward him. The last thing he felt like right now was talking with anyone, but he forced a smile and watched her as she approached. She was stunning. Dark-haired and elegant. She stopped three paces away and bowed slightly.

"I hear you aided my brother, thurjun." The lady had to raise her voice above the buzz of conversation.

Liam swallowed, uncomfortable in his new thurjun's gown. She must be Finn's sister. "Yes, although I didn't have time to meet him. I opened the Stonelake Gateway so he could follow the Vault forces."

A flash of fierce intelligence showed in the woman's eyes, then it was gone, replaced instead by a gentle amusement. "You have my thanks." She bowed again. "But I am forgetting my manners." She smiled and Liam's heart skipped a beat. She could have easily been a fashion model. "Tallandra Evenstone, sir, at your service." She raised an slim hand toward him.

Liam took Tallandra's fingers in his own, leant forward, and self-consciously kissed the back of her hand. Even though he knew the gesture was appropriate, he could not help feeling awkward. He glanced back toward Torren's throne, looking for Tirini.

"Delighted to meet you. I am Liam Durrow."

Tallandra smiled and their eyes met. For an awkward moment, which seemed to stretch forever, Liam could not think of a single thing to say. She seemed honest and sincere, and he felt as though he was being rude and vague, but his mind was still on Tirini.

Then prince Sentas entered the Court, High Druid Strannus walking at his right, Zanthis to his left. A whole entourage trailed behind them. First came a small army of druids, all dressed in their distinctive rainbow robes, followed by three priests of the High God, then came two Temple guards, alert and watchful, escorting a prisoner between them. Shane. A mass of confused emotions warred inside Liam at the sight of a man he had once called a friend. A man who tried to kill him.

The prince was tall and lean, and stood half-a-head taller than any of his companions. Straight dark hair, worn shoulder length, and dark, calculating eyes. He saw Tallandra and Liam standing together. His eyes lit up and a cruel smile curved his lips. He abruptly changed course, heading straight for them. The whole entourage followed. An intimidating wall of arrogant men assured of their own status, all clearly flaunting their allegiance to the powerful prince. Zanthis strutted like a peacock, chin tilted up with disdain.

Sentas' dark eyes flicked between them. Liam swallowed. He felt exposed under the prince's harsh glare. A fraud in the new thurjun's gown. *No,* he told himself. *I earned it.*

Shane smiled a Liam, but it was not a friendly smile. It was as though he was amused by a private joke told at Liam's expense. His eyes went flat and dead, just for a moment, as though something passed behind them. Then all was normal. He appeared relaxed and friendly. Liam had seen that mask before. The one that put people at ease before he ran a con. Sentas spoke, drawing his attention.

"Conspiring with Vault spies now Tallandra?" said Sentas, staring at Liam. Strannus eyed them both through a narrowed gaze.

Liam's heart burned hot with outrage. "I am no spy. Who the hell—"

He felt Tallandra's light touch on his arm. *A warning.* He looked sideways at her. She was relaxed and at ease. A ray of light fell across her face from the high windows, lighting up her blue-grey eyes. She laughed lightly, giving Sentas a radiant smile.

"Oh, Sentas, you have such a charming sense of humour." She swept on without giving him a chance to interrupt. "Have you met Liam Durrow? Do you not agree he looks fetching in his new, *thurjun's* gown?"

"We will see how good he looks in chains," snapped Sentas.

Tallandra took a small fan out of her sleeve, and looked up absently at the great windows above the throne.

"It is so pleasant here. Much more airy then the Judge's Court. Those proceedings are often so tedious," she looked straight at Sentas, "and so damaging to ambition." Behind Sentas, Strannus' eyes swept around to meet Tallandra's. It was a hot look, but carefully restrained.

Sentas went white with fury. He turned on his heel and stalked away toward the throne. Zanthis scurried after him, pulling at his sleeve. The druids, led by Strannus, followed.

"Get off me, you worm," said Sentas, shaking off Zanthis' hand.

"Bring the prisoner!" ordered Sentas.

The small group of priests moved forward, Shane shuffling between the guards.

"What did you say?" asked Liam, wondering at Sentas' reaction.

Tallandra kept her gaze fixed on Sentas and his departing group. She raised her fan to her mouth and whispered. "You have rank, Liam. As a thurjun, you have the right to meet any accuser in Court. And any accusation of treason is of the highest order. I merely . . . reminded Sentas of the fact." She laughed with delight. "He is more pompous and overwrought by the day."

Liam watched Shane as he passed. He was smiling and pleasant, nodding greetings to everyone who met his gaze. His natural charisma was blazing at full intensity. It made Liam uneasy. Once Shane had been a genuine friend, but Liam now realised that the friendship had died long before they passed the Stonelake Gateway. Only the memories of the good times had been keeping them together. Then had come the Shade. Who he was now . . . Liam could not even guess at. He felt enough responsibility for what had happened to make sure Shane got back to Earth. After that, he was on his own.

"You seem to have already made some enemies, Liam," said Tallandra. "I fear it is the help you gave Finn that has turned them against you."

"If they are your enemies, Tallandra, then I wouldn't want them as allies."

Tallandra, genuinely surprised, met Liam's eyes and smiled. He felt the thrill of contact as a physical force. She was very beautiful. "That was a most gallant thing to say," she said.

Vikas, the King's steward, strode to the front of the hall and hit the floor three times. At his signal, the mass of talking groups broke up and moved onto the hall floor.

"I fear I must away. Farewell, Liam." Tallandra leaned up to kiss him lightly on the cheek, then she was gone, moving gracefully through the crowd toward the ranks of nobility seated on the chamber floor. Above Liam, the noise from the upper balconies began to quieten as people seated themselves.

Morin entered through the huge doors with Kevrin at his side. Behind Morin and Kevrin, was the full College of Thurjuns, around thirty men and women in light blue robes. Morin and Kevrin split from the group and walked over to Liam, while the rest made straight for their seats on the dais in a loose-knit, but solemn procession.

"Ah, I see you have met Tallandra," said Morin.

"Yes. She—"

"The fate of the Realms is at stake and you arrive at court hand-in-hand with Tirini. Then start flirting with Tallandra Evenstone!" snapped Kevrin.

"Peace, Kevrin. I will take Liam in hand," said Morin.

Kevrin stalked across the room to rejoin the procession of thurjuns.

"Do not pay too much attention to Kevrin, Liam. He likes you.

If he did not, he would not stop to talk to you at all. He carries the weight of the Realms on his shoulders. It is Kevrin, with his knowledge of the Realm Gateways, who plots the strategies for our defence."

Morin led Liam through the hall and up the sweeping marble steps to the benches on the throne's right. As they walked, Liam told Morin of the confrontation with Sentas, and Tallandra's neat deflection of his spite. All the while Liam's gaze lingered on Tirini.

"Tallandra has become quite adept at Court," said Morin. "But she has taken no profession and remains a ward of the High King. Without any position, she must take care. Up until now, Sentas had hoped to wed her and take Finn's claim to Evenstone. If she makes her objections too plain, she could be in danger."

Liam took his seat with the other thurjuns. Tirini was sitting nearby, between two older Seekers. She would not meet his gaze. As the nobles and dignitaries took their seats, a silence descended on the room.

Vikas waited solemnly, his grey hair gleaming almost white in the morning light. His staff of office was held forward in his right hand at a slight angle, his head tilted back, his gaze fixed on the throne.

Torren entered, flanked by four warriors.

"By the grace of the High God, the Court of Torren, High King of the Blessed Realms, has gathered," declared Vikas.

Liam's stomach flipped. More nervous now than the first time he had attended the High Court.

Chapter 47
City of Tir — First Realm

Liam tensed as the High King approached the dais. Tall and severe, Torren towered over his subjects. A human embodiment of ultimate power. Earth had forgotten the terror and awe that a king could inspire. This man ruled six *planets*. He walked with energy and purpose. His short red hair free of any circlet or crown. He swept up to the top of the dais and turned his gaze on the room, pausing as though to subdue them all through sheer will. Finally, he took his throne.

Torren spoke forcefully. Precisely. "The principle matters to be decided today are the control of the Gateways to the world of Earth. The defence of Stonelake, and the suitability of Liam Durrow as thurjun." He turned and looked straight at Liam, seated with the assembled thurjuns. "I see the last matter is already decided."

Strannus surged to his feet. "I protest! How can this — *unknown* — be admitted to a position of high trust so quickly!"

"*Strannus!*" Torren's voice was a whip-crack. "If you interrupt me again, I will have you removed from your office. Do you understand me?"

Strannus nodded, a little shocked at Torren's threat.

"Take your seat. The time for comment will come. But be warned, I expect useful comments." Torren turned back to the Court.

"Also to be decided today, the fate of the Earth man, Shane." Torren turned to the Temple High Priest, who was seated with three attendants to the right of the throne.

"Rolf, have you made a judgement?"

Rolf rose to his feet, grave with duty. He was slow to straighten, and even then remained stooped. "Yes, my King. We have studied Shane at length. The original Shade, which was an ancient siithe, has gone, however its darkness found purchase in his soul before it faded. How large the new Shade will grow — that depends on how pure of heart Shane is. And who is to judge a man's soul but himself? There may be hope, if he has the will to fight it himself. But until that day, he will remain a danger to himself and others."

"Your judgement then?"

Rolf raised his voice to fill the room. "It is our judgement that he be taken back to Earth, to his own family, and given over into the care of a priest of Earth. There is nothing we can do for him, and to keep him here as a prisoner will not help him find the courage to fight his darkness."

Torren nodded. "So be it." He turned to the Seekers. "And what of the charge of rape? Have the Seekers made a judgement?"

An elderly Seeker rose to her feet. Her eyes were haunted, and when she spoke her voice cracked. "I looked into his soul, my King. Although he denied it, he is guilty of the rape in Stonelake." Beside her, Tirini reached up to gently touch the woman on the arm. The older woman's back straightened and her colour returned. The older Seeker retook her seat.

A quiet descended on the room.

"Then it is for the authorities of Earth to ensure he is punished for the crime. He will not be handed over until we have their assurances.

"Do you have anything further to add Rolf?"

"A priest from the Temple must travel with Shane, to protect and guide him on the journey . . . however . . . I would be loath to compel anyone to undertake such a hazardous task."

One of the young priests, who had entered with Shane, now seated just below the dais, solemnly rose to his feet. "With the help of the High God, I will undertake this task," said the priest.

Sentas smiled.

The muscles across Liam's shoulders tensed.

Torren looked across to the High Priest. "Rolf?"

"Do you feel you have been called to this duty, Reld?" asked the High Priest.

Reld nodded slowly. "Yes, Father. I will do the duty. I have carried it thus far."

Rolf nodded to Torren in confirmation.

"Very well," said the High King.

Rolf bowed his head and sat.

Torren turned back to the court. "In the matter of the defence of Stonelake, my council has decided that the garrison should be increased from three hundred to one thousand men, with a defence and containment tower to be built around the Stonelake Gateway. An additional thurjun will also be stationed there. Do any object?"

Silence.

"Very well."

"Kevrin has informed my council of the location of the Earth Gateway from which the Vault forces are gaining access to Earth. It is my judgement that a small company of warriors, thirty at most, be dispatched with two thurjuns to close the Gateway. Any greater force would alert the Vault and start a major conflict. But we must act quickly. They must leave at once.

"Thurjuns Morin and Liam will travel with the company. The man Shane will also join them, to be returned to Earth through the Gateway before it is closed. It is vital that the Earth thurjun operating the Gateway for the Vault is captured and brought back to the High Court for justice. Further strategies for defence will be decided once the Gateway is closed and Earth protected from imminent Vault attack."

There was silence across the room. Protecting Earth meant protecting the Realms.

"To lead the mission, I have selected a highly experienced warrior from the campaign in Minoras, Kyall Orin."

Strannus rose to his feet. He remained silent, but steadfastly matched Torren's gaze and waited for leave to speak.

"Yes, Strannus."

"Sire, all of us know of the importance of this mission. Perhaps a young noble should be selected to lead it, someone well aware of the strategic importance of closing the Gateway?"

"Kyall Orin *is* of a noble house. Make your point, Strannus."

"Is it not time for your son to show us his leadership?"

Torren's eyes widened. Before he had a chance to say anything, a noble from the floor surged to his feet.

"Yes! Send Sentas! The son of the High King should lead the mission!"

Then another rose. "The son of the King!"

"The son of the King!"

"THE SON OF THE KING!"

By the time the fifth noble had launched himself to his feet, the High Court was roused to a frenzy. The romance of the idea gripped the collective mind. What could be better? All knew the brash, outspoken son of the High King, what better way for him to prove himself than to lead this important mission?

Sentas stood and raised his hands to the crowd, smiling broadly. Without his habitual sneer, the prince looked handsome, even lordly. He shared his father's height and commanding presence. He nodded to each of the nobles who had shouted his name, and their deference to Sentas made Liam suspicious.

"It is my honour to serve the Realms!" shouted Sentas. "If this noble company sees fit to give me this duty, then I will embrace it as a warrior of the Blessed Realms should!"

Thunderous applause shook the room.

*

Torren looked critically at his son. He loved him. He knew his strengths . . . and his failings. He was highly intelligent, and yet harboured a knot of resentment that poisoned everything he touched. It was Torren's deepest wish that Sentas leave aside his antagonisms and petty manipulations and accept his duty with joy and humility, but to date this had not been the case. Perhaps . . . perhaps a taste of real responsibility would help him settle into his life.

No. As much as Torren's hopes led him to give Sentas the mission, his instincts sent warning signs. Sentas was not above manipulating events. Yet there was a compromise. He could send Kyall Orin to lead the troops. Sentas could be nominated as the official head of the mission, but in a diplomatic role, with Kyall and Morin retaining the final say on strategy. This would be a good way of testing Sentas' mettle — and his intentions.

The frenzied crowd continued to call out for Sentas.

Torren nodded to Vikas, who hit the floor three times with his staff. By the last blow, dead silence gripped the room, each of the nobles waiting to hear his judgement.

"Very well," said Torren, sweeping his gaze across the room.

"My son shall be my representative on the mission, however, Kyall and Morin will decide on all matters of strategy and warcraft."

Applause rang out.

Sentas smiled and waved to the crowd. Yet as he sat, he shot his father a look so full of anger and hatred that Torren's heart skipped a beat. *So, you had hoped to lead the mission outright.* If this has been staged, thought Torren, what benefit did Sentas see in leading a small, dangerous mission? A cloud moved across the sun, blocking the clear light from the high windows above the throne. A chill ran down Torren's spine.

"Sentas, you hold the safety of the Realms in your grasp. Remember your duty and lead well. You will take a lead role in any diplomacy, and will be responsible for organising logistics. I expect you to leave immediately. Kyall and his warriors are already waiting on the other side of our Gateway."

Sentas nodded, but remained silent. He turned to watch the Earth thurjun Liam with a predatory gaze, then shared a quick glance with the man Shane. Torren swallowed. His instincts sent a warning. The urge to turn toward the unseen blow. Shane was smiling, and watching Liam triumphantly. Sentas *was* up to something. The sky outside the High Court clouded further, plunging the room into darkness. Servants in the livery of the High King hurried about the room, turning up the glowglobes.

Torren put aside his worries and turned to the court. "Now, to other business . . ."

Chapter 48

Yolinda checked the magazine of her compact Glock for the third time. Just keeping her hands busy. *Yep. Fifteen rounds, just like last time.* She slammed it home. It was a brand new Glock 19. She had checked it out of the Federal Police armoury after returning to Sydney with Finn, determined never to be outgunned again. Lightweight and accurate. Laser sight. With a bullet in the chamber it held a total of sixteen 9mm Parabellum rounds. She was taking no chances. She knew the siithe were real, and that they were hard to kill. As for everything else? After the drugs — she was not sure which memories were real and which were imagined. They still had no idea of the siithe's nationality. East European? Some weird over-muscled racial subgroup with thick skulls and an enhanced pain tolerance? Procarrus, their leader, had a European look.

Yolinda sat in the front seat of an unmarked police four-wheel drive, the dull brown paint black in the night. Federal Agent Johnson, medium build with dark hair, was in the driver's seat. Johnson had been in her academy graduating class, yet somehow seemed too inexperienced for this.

Yolinda's hands began to shake. She slipped the Glock into her shoulder holster and clamped her hands between her knees. The tremors, the shakes and nausea, had started two hours ago. They came in waves. At the same time, images of her captivity with the siithe would flood through her mind. The deaths, the screams . . .

"Paris?" It was Johnson.

"What!" she snapped.

"You alright?"

Her whole body trembled. Behind her in the van, four police from the New South Wales Tactical Operations Unit watched her with knowing gazes.

Yolinda checked the time on her watch. "Just waiting for Y2K to hit."

"Y2K . . . what a crock of shit," said one of the TOU constables behind her, just like Yolinda knew he would. The argument had been going on for most of the night.

"The lights might go out . . . maybe," said the sergeant.

"What about all the nuclear arsenals? The computers will go nuts, sarge," said another constable, the one who had bought into all the conspiracy theories. "World War Three."

"They have safeguards up the yin-yang," replied the sergeant.

"I guess we'll find out at midnight. Not long now," said Constable Conspiracy.

"I'll find out what the delay is," said Yolinda, climbing out of the passenger seat. Outside, her stomach knotted with a sudden, intense nausea. She sprinted around the front of the building, into an alley, and threw up violently. Bile burned her throat. Her nasal cavity. *Gross.* She coughed and gagged. Then started crying. Her mind boiled over. Jay was dead. All those men and women, kept as slaves, were also dead, killed by the siithe in bloody violence. Those bastards had filled her veins with poison. Taken away her dignity. She remembered her escape from Procarrus' cruiser as though it was a dream. *A nightmare.* Three bullets. Three dead siithe. Indian Joe and Roberts. The swim for the shore.

"Agent Paris." *Esco.*

Yolinda wiped her mouth on her sleeve and flicked away the silent tears. She turned. Met Esco's gaze.

"Are you ready for this or not?" he asked.

"Are *you* ready for this, Esco? You should be in a hospital bed. We don't need to carry you." A warning voice, buried deep in her hindbrain, told her she shouldn't be speaking like this to a superintendent — especially one with her career in his hands. She suppressed it. Right now, an appearance of strength was more important than a demonstration of deference.

Esco's jaw clenched, then he took a deep breath and nodded. "We are rolling. This Siithe Gang will not know what hit them. I hope we find Finn Evenstone with those bastards." He touched the bandaged wound on his temple. "I have a score to settle with him."

"So do I," said Yolinda. "This time I will get answers, instead of a fairy tales."

Thinking of Finn, Yolinda's anger shot up like a geyser,

banishing her nausea. He had fooled all of them with his ridiculous stories of other worlds and evil warriors. In the end he had turned out to be some sort of conman. They had Research checking through all the international databases for records of any circus or theatre performers who specialised in hypnotism. Nothing else could explain her behaviour, or the bizarre actions of the psychologist Blundstone. It burned her to think Finn had fooled her so many times, earning her trust. Still . . . what about the language she had spoken? The language she could still understand when she watched the videos? What about the warmth of his green eyes . . . Yolinda growled deep in her throat. She screwed those thoughts down. *Tight.*

Esco walked back to the small convoy. Four vehicles, six Federal Agents, and thirty men from the local Tactical Operations Unit. Yolinda followed, climbing back into the front passenger seat of her assigned vehicle. Johnson looked sideways, but said nothing. Esco got in the lead van.

"OK. We're rolling." Esco's voice over the police radio.

One after the other, the convoy vehicles checked in. "Car four, ready," said Johnson into the mike, in turn.

They drove from the assembly point, all closing in on the disused industrial building the siithe used for their headquarters. They had been able to trace it from Yolinda's description and the name she had glimpsed on the doors.

It was time the siithe paid.

Across the street, in a red Landcruiser, Finn and Genna watched as the convoy rolled out.

"Follow," said Finn.

Genna pulled out from the curb, following the Feds further into Sydney's west. Genna had driven the "borrowed" vehicle all the way from Queensland to reach Finn, and had grown adept at handling it.

Finn watched Yolinda's car with mixed feelings. She had betrayed him, and yet, she was driven by a need to fight the siithe. In a way she was still his ally, even though she did not believe him.

Finn had passed the night in the shopping mall. When the

lights had gone out, he had crept from his hiding place in the ceiling space. He had swapped Esco's clothes for a white long-sleeved shirt, leather pants, vest and stout boots from a motorcycle shop. He had also taken a hunting knife and a motorcycle half-helmet. Finn curved his hand around the hilt of his sword, carried by Genna all the way from Fraser Island. He could feel the power in the pommel mionanail. If the Vault had to be fought on this world, he and Genna would make a good account of themselves.

The convoy travelled for around half an hour, then the four vehicles sped into a side street. They pulled their Landcruiser into an alley half a block away.

"Can you feel it, Genna?" asked Finn.

Genna nodded. "There is a wound in the Earth. This is the Gateway to the Vault worlds."

Finn cursed. "They are going to attack them head on."

They watched as police, with body armour, helmets, and automatic rifles, sped across the street in small groups toward a derelict building.

Finn grabbed his sword and opened the car door. "They have no idea what they are dealing with!"

Genna grabbed his arm. "Finn. You will be recaptured."

"Yolinda is there. They will be slaughtered, Genna."

Silence filled the cabin. Across the street, the police blew the glass doors that fronted the building with two small explosive charges, then swept inside. Finn stepped out into the street with a sword in one hand and the motorcycle half-helmet in the other.

"Come, Genna. It is time to fight." Finn strapped on the black helmet.

Genna grabbed his axe and shield and followed Finn. Rapid gunfire echoed inside the building. There were flashes of light from the police weapons. They heard the growl of a siithe warrior, then a humming discharge. The lobby flashed red.

"Pulse lasers," said Genna. "Use your sword, Finn."

"I dare not, Genna. It will make the police defenceless."

They stepped past the shattered doors and crept into the building. There was a rough staircase cut into the concrete and rock. At the top of the stairwell was a dead siithe armed with a pulse laser, a bulky weapon capable of destroying a small building. Surrounding the body of the siithe were three dead police, their bodies cut into cauterised sections by the blazing red beam of the weapon. From below came the crack of projectile weapons. In response came the low, thrumming discharge of pulse lasers.

Finn slipped his sword into his belt and picked up the siithe pulse laser. He was reluctant to use a Vault weapon, but until he could unleash the full power of his sword, he had no choice. They descended the stairs. Two more fallen police, cut into jagged sections, lay there. At the stairs' base, Finn stepped around the melted remnants of an assault rifle and entered a tunnel. They could see the bright disc of the Gateway ahead of them, surrounded by packed ranks of siithe. More siithe arrived through the Gateway, swelling the enemy numbers. The police had taken cover around the room behind piles of broken rock and debris. They had good positions, but they were hard-won. Finn could see another ten dead police, but it was hard to be sure of the count, since the bodies were dismembered. What was clear, was that the police were trapped. To escape they would have to cover at least twenty paces of open ground. Open ground on which they would be cut to pieces by siithe lasers.

There were almost a hundred siithe in the cavern, their ranks swelling as more arrived through the Gateway. They were in tight, disciplined lines, with heavy armour of black Vault steel instead of the usual studded leather, and were equipped with pulse lasers.

"I have seen these troops before," said Finn.

"Soulbreakers," said Genna.

Finn nodded. "VoYannan's advance force. He intends to take Earth."

They ducked behind a pile of broken, melted rock at the tunnel's end. They had not been spotted. *Yet.* Across the cavern Finn saw a squat man dressed in dark robes. He was operating the Gateway, opening it for the siithe forces. *A Dark Thurjun.*

A siithe broke from cover, swivelling his weapon toward Finn and Genna. Before Finn could react, Genna's hand snapped forward. His hand-axe whistled through the air in a tumbling blur. The blade thudded to a stop in the siithe's forehead. The beast barked in shock, then sank to the rubble-strewn floor. *Dead.* They dived for cover as another siithe targeted them. The beam swept past them and up across the roof. The smell of burned rock filled the air. Finn rolled out from behind the boulder, sighted his pulse laser, and burned a neat hole in the siithe's head. The siithe stiffened and fell.

Esco was pinned down with Yolinda behind a large boulder. The senior Agent had watched the siithe Finn shot advance across the cavern, and now saw Finn, holding the pulse laser. The Agent's eyes narrowed. Esco gave a terse command. Two armoured police turned their weapons on Finn. The Realm warriors dived for cover as high-velocity rounds pounded into the rock around them.

"Great," said Genna.

"They will soon have too much to concern them to bother shooting at us," said Finn.

Finn was right. A steady stream of laser blasts lanced into the police positions, illuminating the cavern in bursts of red light. The rifle fire directed at Finn and Genna stopped. Finn looked up over the rubble. The siithe were advancing in tight lines. One or two siithe were falling — the police demonstrated outstanding accuracy — but the rifle fire was having little overall effect. The siithe armour could slow a bullet enough to make it non-lethal. Only a well-placed head shot would drop them. The siithe were now only ten paces from the ragged police line. They stopped. At an order, the siithe front rank knelt. The second siithe rank detached bulky metal canisters from their belts and drew back their hands to throw.

"Fragmentation grenades!" said Genna.

Finn measured the distance with his eye. The mines would fall behind the police lines, bursting into fragments of razor-sharp metal that would shred the Earth forces into bloody meat. *Yolinda!*

Finn threw aside the pulse laser and drew his sword.

As the siithe mines sailed through the air, Finn shaped a matrix. The power of the mionanail flared. Above them, the line of incandescent bulbs went out like windswept candle-flames.

The laser bursts and the automatic weapon fire died. The mines landed with a series of dull metallic thuds. They bounced across the floor and lay inert. Useless.

The mercurial glow of the Gateway was the only light that remained, sketching the cavern in ghostly white.

Finn and Genna scrambled out from behind the rubble.

"For the Realms!" shouted Finn.

Finn sprinted at the siithe ranks. He hurdled the boulder that had shielded Yolinda and Esco. They looked at him, astonished, as he sailed over them. Genna was close behind, pausing only to recover his weapon from the forehead of the fallen siithe.

Finn screamed a battle cry and swept into the siithe ranks. The standing siithe threw aside their pulse lasers and drew heavy falcatas. But the front row — still kneeling — were too slow. Finn cut into them. Within a few seconds, twelve siithe were dead. The siithe, expecting an easy conquest on a primitive world, now lost momentum, unsure if they were going to be attacked by a full Realm force. Genna shielded Finn's back as he cut deep into their lines.

"We must reach the thurjun!" called Finn. If they could take down the Dark Thurjun, they could seal the Gateway.

The siithe commander yelled over the fray in the Vault tongue. "There are only two warriors! *Kill them.*" Finn, like most Realm warriors and thurjuns, had been trained in Vault languages.

"Send for the heavy crossbows!" bellowed the siithe commander. A siithe runner disappeared through the Gateway. Meanwhile, the siithe were recovering. Their lines reforming. Three packed ranks of siithe solidified between Finn and the Dark Thurjun. The forward momentum of the Realms warriors was countered. They saw it at the same time.

"We will never reach him!" yelled Genna.

Finn blocked a thrust. A second siithe surprised him, cutting down with a heavy blow that cleaved through the motorcycle helmet, grazing his head. Finn staggered. Two more siithe pressed him. He blocked one cut, but could only brace himself as another blade slashed toward his throat.

There was a sharp *crack*.

A whip curled around the sword arm of the second siithe,

halting the blade a finger's breadth from Finn's throat. It gave him the break he needed. He turned his sword over the blade of the first siithe in a flashing riposte that sliced the siithe's throat open. Then he turned and drove his blade into the second siithe's eye.

"Fall back, Genna!"

They disengaged. The break gave Finn enough time to see who was wielding the whip. *Yolinda.* She alone had followed them into the packed ranks of the enemy, armed only with a slave whip and a knife she had taken from a dead siithe. She lost the whip as the siithe fell, the Vault warrior's dead weight dragging the entangled weapon out of her hand. Instinctively, Genna and Finn fell back to either side of her, protecting her from the Vault falcatas. She hurled her knife at an advancing siithe, but the Vault warrior batted it aside with a dull clang.

They retreated to the police lines. The surviving police were now locked in hand-to-hand combat. Esco and some of the other police had armed themselves with falcatas from the siithe Finn had killed, and were fighting blade to blade. They were brave, but had little skill with the weapons. With the siithe lines advancing once more, the Vault warriors regained their ferocity. The surviving police would not hold.

The Gateway flared.

Scores of siithe warriors, armed with heavy crossbows, swarmed from the Gateway.

The siithe commander bellowed across the cavern. "Kill the warrior with the black helmet! He alone has a Realm weapon!"

With smooth precision, the siithe ranks parted. The front row of crossbow warriors knelt, the siithe behind them also raising their weapons, bringing about twenty crossbows to bear on Finn.

Finn, Genna, and Yolinda, dived for cover, skidding behind a wall of fallen rubble. A hail of crossbow bolts overtook them. One struck Finn in the helmet and speared the metal, another grazed his hip. Genna yelped in pain as one opened a bloody gash on his thigh, ripping through the trouser leather. They scrambled behind a large boulder, just as a second rain of iron-tipped bolts shot out. The deadly hail struck sparks from the stone.

"Esco! Get your men out of here!" yelled Finn in the English Earth-tongue.

Esco was fighting furiously with a siithe warrior. The siithe lunged. Esco sidestepped and swept his borrowed falcata into the side of the siithe's head in a vicious two-handed strike. The siithe dropped. Stone dead. Only six of the police fought on with Esco. The rest had fallen. Esco turned to Finn. The Agent's light strike-force helmet had been knocked off his head, and the bandage underneath was unravelling.

"Esco. Take your men and flee while you can!" yelled Finn. A rain of crossbow bolts thudded into the walls of the cavern, narrowly missing Esco and his police warriors. He nodded to Finn and gave a curt order. The police raced into the tunnel, and up the narrow stairs beyond.

Only the three of them remained.

"What's happening?" asked Finn.

Yolinda pushed herself into a kneeling position, crying out in pain. Carefully, she looked over the boulder. Finn looked down at her leg. A crossbow bolt had lodged itself deep in her thigh. Blood seeped from the wound. Finn tapped Genna on the shoulder and pointed down at Yolinda's leg. Genna nodded gravely.

"They are coming, Finn. The siithe with crossbows are leading," said Yolinda.

Finn calmed his mind. He had to find a way to contain them. Then his gaze fell on one of the siithe fragmentation grenades.

"Genna. *The grenades!*" Genna's eyes flashed with mischief as he understood Finn's plan.

"Got it," answered Genna.

"Yolinda, can you run?"

Yolinda's face gritted with determination. "I'll damn well run out of here!"

There were almost two hundred siithe in the cave now. The leading ranks of crossbow troops only paces away from their concealing boulder. More were arriving through the Gateway every minute. The Vault troops marched forward in packed ranks, silent and deadly. Soon the three of them would be flanked.

Finn closed his eyes and gathered his concentration. A matrix formed in his mind.

"Genna," said Finn. "Now!"

Finn stood. The double-rank of crossbows swivelled in his direction. Finn pointed his sword and let the power of the mionanail flow. A blinding flash of light exploded into the siithe's eyes. They cried out in rage and pain, their aim going wild. He dropped as crossbow bolts discharged around him. The siithe advance faltered.

Then Finn was in motion.

He supported Yolinda as they ran across the cavern floor to the tunnel mouth and the sheltering rubble there. Genna sprinted to the cavern wall where the police had held their cover, gathering all the siithe fragmentation mines in his arms, then looped back to Finn and Yolinda.

The siithe captain barked an order. Two hundred siithe drew their falcatas and charged. Behind them, their ranks continued to swell as more Vault warriors emerged from the Gateway.

Their retreat to the tunnel entrance had given them time. But not much.

Finn took most of the mines from Genna and packed them tightly into a crevice where the tunnel opened into the cavern. Genna hurled the rest into the ranks of the running siithe. With the mines in position, Finn, Genna, and Yolinda, retreated back through the tunnel and turned a sharp left up the stairs. They could hear the guttural curses and cries of the siithe echo in the tunnel. Finn could *smell* them. The rank odour of offal. Of rotten flesh. It was the stink of battlefields he would never forget. Bloody fields where Realm warriors he had know as friends and comrades-in-arms had fallen. His teeth ground together in repressed fury.

Finn released the dampening field.

All the mines, triggered when the siithe had thrown them earlier, now exploded with a deafening *thump.* There was a rumble of falling rock, followed by the screams of dying and trapped siithe. Dust and rock blasted through the tunnel and hit the rock wall at the stairs' base. Thankfully the narrow stairs were at a angle to the tunnel and they were shielded from the shock wave and its deadly cargo of debris. When the dust cleared, Finn crept back to the base of the stairs and looked down the tunnel.

As he had hoped, the mines had collapsed the roof, closing the tunnel, and burying the siithe advance force.

"It worked!" said Genna.

They had used the Vault's own technology against them. *Always satisfying.*

There was a muffled *crack* from overhead.

They looked up. In the blink of an eye, a long fissure raced across the tunnel roof, then up the rough-hewn ceiling of the stairway.

Finn's jaw dropped.

With a grinding roar, the ceiling of the stairway began to collapse. *No!* Finn knew there was no way to make it up the stairs before they were crushed. He pulled them back down the stairs and into the tunnel, where they flattened themselves against the tunnel wall. Their escape route vanished in a cloud of dust and rock. It swirled around them. The grit caught in Finn's throat, and he coughed. He blinked away the darkness, momentarily blinded. The tunnel to the Gateway cavern was sealed — so far so good — but now the stairway above was filled with a solid mass of rock. They were in a small tunnel section, sealed in both directions.

Trapped.

Yolinda took the radio from her belt. "CQ.CQ. This is Agent Paris." She switched the device to different frequencies and repeated the open call, but got no reply. "Nothing but static," she said eventually.

As Finn's eyes adjusted, he realised light was reaching them from the cavern. The explosion had not only buried the siithe, it had also blown a section out of the side of the tunnel. Through the narrow fissure Finn could see a flickering reflection of the Gateway's light. He could also hear the siithe, deeper inside the cavern, on the other side of the rock fall. He heard a low thrumming sound. The red glow of the pulse lasers blazed through the gap.

"The rock. It is heating up," said Genna.

The siithe were cutting their way through.

And they had nowhere to go.

Chapter 49
Kess planet — Vault Shadow World

Liam looked across the valley from the high ridge.

The planet's red sun clawed its way to the zenith, driving humidity up from the damp ground. The day was already hot. From the height, he could see the small village where they had spent the night, nestled at the base of the slope. It lay in a depression that hid it from the surrounding terrain. A delicate flower in the palm of a giant.

They had arrived at the village under cover of darkness, and Liam had seen little in the pitch black. Now, in the light of morning, he could not take his eyes from the view. The place had seemed larger in the night, but there were no more than ten houses and three ploughed fields clustered around a tiny lake. Here, a few families scratched a living from the earth. They had been overjoyed to see the Realm forces, knowing they would protect them. Now, three of the tall Kess, two men and a woman, all village elders, stood sombre vigil, watching them go. For the Kess village, the departure of Kyall's warriors meant a return to fear.

This was one of the Shadow Worlds. Lost between the Vault and the Realms, yet part of neither. His horse, a gentle mare, snorted and shook her head, plodding patiently up the trail. She was well used to moving with a mounted group and required little direction from him. Kyall Orin was already cresting the rise ahead with his men, leading them steadily higher into the hills.

Liam craned his neck as the trail turned, to keep the view in sight. Further down the valley, starting perhaps three kilometres from the small village and stretching to the horizon, was a shattered city. It was huge. Bigger than New York. Towers of concrete, glass and metal lay shattered, smashed by titanic forces, or melted to slag. Some buildings remained, but were ragged remnants, with huge chunks sliced out of them, as though with a gigantic blade. In the centre of the city there was a vast crater, the surface of the soil vitrified to dark glass.

A chill went down Liam's spine.

The Vault had discovered this world less than one hundred years ago. Now nothing remained of a starfaring culture more advanced than Earth's own. The Kess had been reduced to basic agriculture. Slavestock for the krell, who raided constantly from Gateways across the planet.

This was the third world the company had travelled through, stepping from Gateway to Gateway, gradually drawing closer to the Vault. So far they had travelled without incident. The route was familiar to the Realm warriors. There were staging posts along the way, manned by local allies — such as the Kess — who supplied and concealed Realm forces.

"Why don't the Realms fight for these people?" Liam had asked Morin the night before.

"Would that we could, Liam. The truth is we struggle to defend our own worlds. And the Vault continues to grow stronger."

Kyall was leading them to a secret tower in the hills, where the Realms controlled a Gateway to a world inside the Vault of Seven Horns. A world dominated by VoYannan's forces. Liam swallowed. Kyall rode as though supremely unconcerned with any impending danger. He was a squat, powerful warrior with an unruly mass of black, curling hair. He had a scar that started below his right eye and ran all the way down his right cheek, through both lips, and onto his chin. The disfigurement only added to the gravity of his demeanour. It had been obvious from the outset that the other Realm warriors respected and trusted the man, and even Sentas was guarded with him.

Liam and Morin rode together between Kyall's main force and Sentas' entourage at the rear. The prince had two family retainers and four other self-styled warriors — minor nobles who followed Sentas everywhere, seeking adventure and advancement. It was a strong enough force to act as an effective rearguard, yet Liam doubted their commitment. The prince and his men were dressed in court finery, sported fine mounts, and acted more like they were on a pleasure jaunt than a serious mission. They also had three female servants who seemed to do no menial work at all, and were all quite beautiful. As soon as they were out of the First Realm, Shane had been released from his chains. The priest, Reld, so contrite in the court of the High King, had swapped his austere robes for bright clothes and laughed and joked along with Sentas and his men. Shane rode at Sentas' left, seemingly as favoured as Zanthis, who rode to his right. The three of them had been inseparable.

Morin had taken both Sentas and the priest Reld to task about releasing Shane, but they had laughed in his face. "This is a serious business," Morin had replied to Sentas. "The last thing I need is you playing some political game." Sentas had merely smiled.

Sentas was the High King's representative, and although Morin and Kyall had the final say in most matters, Kyall was loath to take issue with Sentas over something that did not directly threaten the mission. Reld claimed the Shade in Shane was now bonded to his soul and had been brought under control by him. Only death could release it.

"Your friend seems to be enjoying the trip," said Morin, bring Liam back to the moment.

Liam frowned. "Yes." Every attempt by Liam to break the ice with Shane had earned him a cutting riposte. Much to Sentas' amusement. Shane had always excelled at putdowns. After the third unsuccessful attempt, Liam had left Shane alone. Liam was relieved, really. He could not forget the look in Shane's eyes when he tried to stab him at the Reil Gateway. The sheer *hate*. Other memories had surfaced too, little moments of spite that stretched back over years. Liam had dismissed them at the time. Now they revealed a vicious, petty nature that Shane had always concealed. He had always sought to strike back at imagined slights, or erode Liam's self esteem. As though Shane himself could not feel OK until someone else was taken down a peg. If he was honest with himself, he had been trying to reestablish rapport with Shane more through a sense of duty and obligation — and guilt — than a genuine desire to salvage the last remnants of their friendship.

For the twelve days they had been travelling, Shane had been having the time of his life. Each night he would drink and party with Sentas and his followers, sharing the camp women and any other local concubines that could be bought with the High King's gold. In contrast, he and Morin had been working late every night to sharpen his use of key offensive matrices, and to prepare him for combat. One of Kyall's men had been giving him a few basic lessons in swordcraft as well. Despite all his training, he was a novice to these experienced warriors. And he felt like it. Morin had promised to teach him quarterstaff, but as yet Liam had not seen him use the weapon.

By midday, they had reached the Gateway tower. A squat construction built deep inside a high, narrow valley, it was concealed from above by a massive overhang of dark granite. Here they stopped for a brief lunch before passing the portal.

Morin and Liam sat at a broad table in the Gateway's hall, with some warriors from Kyall's command. It was a relief to be out of the saddle . . . and out of the sun. Reld entered the hall. There was no room at the table with Sentas and his entourage, so the priest reluctantly joined Liam and Morin.

"You seem tense, thurjun," said Reld as he sat next to Morin.

"And you seem unduly relaxed, priest. Tell me, where have your vestments gone?" asked Morin.

Reld smiled. His reply was glib. "Being a poor priest, I only ever travel with one set of garments. Unfortunately they were ruined on the first day. Sentas was kind enough to lend me clothing."

"I see," said Morin, sweeping his gaze over Reld's brightly coloured tunic and breeches. "Strange that Sentas' clothes should fit you so well." Reld was a small man, far smaller than any other person in Sentas' entourage.

Reld flushed red. He ate in silence after that.

Liam watched Shane, noting that he was becoming reasonably fluent in the Realm tongue. He was on his best form, laughing and joking. Shane put his hand in the air and snapped his fingers, waving over a small, dark haired woman serving Sentas' table.

"I'm not a slave!" said the woman. "Don't snap your fingers at me."

Shane's face twisted with rage. Liam had never seen him like this before. In the face of this sort of thing he would usually play cool. Bide his time. Take his revenge slowly. This force of hate in him was something new.

Reld had noticed it to. He froze. A mouthful of food

suspended halfway to his mouth.

"Hey!" yelled Shane. He took the woman's arm in a painful grip. "I want another drink. *Now!*"

The woman shook off Shane's hand and swore at him in an unknown language. The men around the table burst into laughter. Shane's eyes swept around the group. Then Shane laughed too. But his eyes were as hard as stone, and never left the woman.

Reld dropped his fork to his plate and pushed the meal away.

"Lost your appetite, Reld?" asked Morin.

The small man met Morin's gaze. He looked quickly away.

"What is it, Reld? What did you see?" Morin leant forward. Intent.

Reld's eyes flicked to Sentas. "Nothing," he stammered. He fled the table. Food and drink abandoned.

Liam and Morin continued their meal, discussing some of the finer points of the thurjun's trade. They were contentedly sipping on ale when they heard the scream.

A woman's scream. Filled with pain and fear.

Liam's eyes instinctively swept to Sentas' table.

Shane was gone.

The conversation in the room dipped as people looked up, searching for the source of the disturbance. There was movement outside the hall. Tower warriors, alerted by the scream, hurried through the corridor beyond the hall doors. When there was nothing to be seen, the conversation in the room picked up, the incident forgotten. A few minutes later, a Tower warrior hurried into the hall and scanned the crowd, eyes narrowed.

Morin hurried over to the warrior. Liam followed.

"Is everything in order?" Morin asked the warrior.

"Yes, thurjun. We heard the scream, but so far have found nothing. Perhaps one of the cooks scalded herself on a cooking globe. We are investigating."

Kyall stood. "Finish your meals," he ordered his men. "It is time to make the transit." His men immediately began to rise.

Shane sauntered into the hall. He had a smug, satisfied look on his face. When he saw Liam he gave him a mocking smile.

Then there was another scream. This time from a serving woman in the hall. It was followed by the outraged shouts of warriors. The serving woman who had challenged Shane had staggered into the room, followed by a knot of Tower warriors. Her clothes were in shreds, and there was blood on her legs. A warrior stepped to her side to steady her, but she pushed him away. Something glinted in her hand. The woman pointed toward Shane and shouted in her native language.

Kyall pushed his way to the front of the group. "What is she saying?"

One of Kyall's men spoke her language and translated. "She says Shane raped her."

"Where is that priest!" demanded Kyall. Reld was nowhere to be seen.

Kyall waved to one of his men. "Find the priest. Bring him here."

Sentas pushed forward. "We do not have time for this! I have seen it a hundred times. False claims can be hard to disprove."

Kyall rounded on Sentas, his jaw clenched in anger. "This woman has clearly been assaulted. False or not we will get to the bottom of it. Bring Shane forward."

Shane was led to Kyall by two Realm warriors. The woman edged toward him. Her eyes hot with fury and pain.

Kyall turned to Shane. "What have you to say for yourself?"

Shane looked friendly. Innocent. "What can I say? I just went out for a piss. I never touched her." He stepped toward her and smiled. "I never did anything to her."

"There you have it," said Sentas, touching his brow with a handkerchief, clearly bored. "Just leave her for the locals to deal with Kyall, and let us be on our way. Or do you wish to challenge the King's representative over every small matter?"

Kyall cursed and called for the Tower Commander.

In the distraction, Shane looked down at the woman. His smiling face vanished, and just for an instant, it was replaced with a mask of rage and lust.

The woman gave an incoherent cry and lunged forward. A blade flashed. Blood spurted everywhere. It fountained across the floor in a wild pattern. Blossomed red on Shane's tunic.

Kyall's men took the woman's arms. One retrieved a razor-sharp skinning knife from her right fist. She was crying and shaking, howling in wordless pain.

Shane tried to speak but only a gurgling sound emerged. He sank to his knees as a thick curtain of blood ran onto his chest, soaking his tunic bright crimson. *So red. So impossibly red.*

"Damn you, woman!" said Sentas, furious. "I needed that man!"

Liam watched as Shane's face changed. It was innocent, shocked. The face of his friend. Instinctively, Liam reached out to help him.

"No, Liam!" Morin dragged him back.

The innocence was instantly replaced by a twisted mask of hate as Shane struggled across the floor toward Liam.

The circle around the body parted, admitting the priest, Reld.

"By the High God!" said Reld.

"Quickly, priest!" said Kyall. "Bless him, before the Shade takes one of us."

Shane's eyes glazed over and he fell forward onto his face. He hit the floor with a wet thud.

The woman cursed him in her own tongue, struggling in the grip of the two stunned warriors.

Reld looked at the corpse. His face whitened.

"No. *No!*" cried Reld.

Before they could stop him, the priest broke through the ring of onlookers and bolted out of the room.

"Get that priest back here!" roared Kyall. A warrior sprinted off in pursuit.

They backed away from the body, all except Sentas, who stepped forward and kicked the body savagely. "Get this corpse out of here, Kyall. I have not finished my meal." Sentas' looked over at Kyall, his eyes glittering as he waited for a reaction. His amused look fled, replaced with sudden pain. He gasped and staggered back, clutching at his temple. He straightened and shook his head. The crowd watched him silently. Sentas laughed lightly. "A moment of faintness, nothing more."

Reld reappeared, dragged by two of Kyall's warriors.

"Priest. Tell us. Is the body safe to handle?" demanded Kyall.

Reld calmed himself and examined the body carefully from a distance. He sighed with relief. "Yes. The Shade has gone. It fled with the man's death."

Kyall nodded. "Now. Look around this assembled group. Has the Shade touched anyone here?"

Reld turned and methodically scanned the group. When his gaze settled on Sentas his eyes widened and he shrank back into the warriors' grip.

"Be careful what you say, little man. If you utter one treasonous word my father will have you executed," said Sentas.

"Let him speak, Sentas! Or I will put you in chains," thundered Kyall. The Realm warriors tensed, ready to do just that.

Sentas' mocking smile became a thin line.

When the prince said nothing more, Kyall turned back to Reld. "Speak, priest. No harm will come to you."

Reld swallowed, then smiled. "I see no Shade, my Lord. It has fled." His voice was high and trembling.

"Send for a Seeker," demanded Morin. "We cannot risk the mission."

"Delaying even a single day endangers this mission, Morin. Finn is trapped on Earth. We must come to his aid before it is too late. And you know very well the nearest Seeker is at least a week away," said Kyall.

"Our orders are to seal the Vault Gateway to Earth," said Sentas, his pompous voice filling the room. "In all haste."

"And seal it we will. The matter is ended. We use the Kess Gateway as planned," said Kyall.

Around the room, warriors surged into action. Two took Shane's corpse by the arms. Liam watched as his body was dragged away, trailing blood across the floor. That was it. Shane was dead. He would never return to Earth, and any hope of redemption died with him. Shane should not have died here. He should have never even *been* here. Liam had no doubt of Shane's guilt, and knew it had been the choices Shane had made that had led him to this sudden end, but it had been the choices he *himself* had made that had put Shane in danger in the first place. To follow Korbeth's vision. To open the Fraser Gateway. To step through into a new world. Despite his faults, Shane had not deserved this. To be twisted by a darkness that only gained its power to corrupt in the Blessed Realms. A Shade, such as the one that possessed Shane, only manifested in the Realms. The weight of guilt that Liam carried grew heavier with regret.

Liam felt a hand on his back. *Morin.*

"Time to move on, Liam. It is Sentas we need to watch now." Morin's eyes lingered on the pool of blood, already growing sticky and attracting flies. "You can mourn your friend another time."

Chapter 50
Viri world — Vault of Seven Horns

They emerged from the Kess Gateway into a world of darkness.

Although it was day, there was barely enough light to see the ground ahead. The air was hot, and full of grit and smoke. Liam turned back to the Gateway, which stood like an archway of bright light on the hill behind them. The portal vanished, deepening the gloom. Gradually, Liam's eyes adjusted. The sky was a deep thundercloud grey, except where the heavy clouds blocked the sun, where it glowed dull orange red. Nearby was a circle of dead trees and a single standing stone. A Realm thurjun stood alone in the circle. Instead of a blue robe, he wore a leather tunic, leggings of dark brown, and heavy boots. He waved solemnly to Morin as they passed him by.

Morin waved back. "A lonely duty for a thurjun. And a dangerous one."

The lone thurjun walked back into the low hills, disappearing into the bleak landscape. Without him, waiting patiently for the call from the Kess world, the Gateway would have been closed to them.

Liam shivered involuntarily, despite the warmth. "What world is this?" he asked Morin.

"The world of the Viri," said Morin.

"Who are they?" asked Liam.

"They were a powerful and wise people, Liam. They were the first thurjuns, and taught us much. It is they who devised the mionanails and the ardanaiths. Without their knowledge, the Realms would have perished long ago."

"Will any meet us on the way?"

Morin shook his head sadly. "They are gone, Liam. For aeons they stood against the Vault. But they fell."

The company followed a narrow trail, which led down the hill and around the rusting hulk of a huge spacecraft. It lay broken on the hillside. A great titan born in a fallen world of technological wonders, now slumped across the slope like a metal blanket, bristling with turrets and antennae, struts and stubby wings. As silent as the grave. Riding past it was a truly surreal experience.

Two flat, wedge-shaped craft flitted by overhead and disappeared into the distance. Seconds later, two sonic booms crashed through the air.

"Vault fighter craft. Hopefully they did not see us," said Morin.

"How long to the Sydney Gateway?"

"If Kevrin's calculations are correct, the Gateway is in a ruined Viri city half a day's ride away."

A pack of lean dogs appeared nearby. One moment their mounted group had been alone in the empty landscape, and the next the beasts were there. Silent and intent. They had dark hides, and looked like greyhounds, built for speed, but with long jaws filled with sharp teeth. As they drew closer their size became apparent. *They're the size of small horses!* Their eyes were feral. Hungry. The pack paced them. The dogs' long snouts tilted up to taste their scent, eyes never leaving their prey. Kyall gave an order and the Realm warriors moved their mounts into a defensive formation. They drew their swords.

"Shadow Hounds," said Morin gravely.

The animals followed them for about an hour, periodically darting in to test their defences, always watching through their big, luminous eyes. Eventually they melted away into the hills.

"What do you think happened to Reld?" asked Liam. Reld had vanished before they passed through the Gateway.

Morin looked across at Sentas. "I think he ran for his life. Something he saw terrified him, and he did not dare go against Sentas." Reld was not the only one missing from the prince's entourage. Kyall had forbidden Sentas to take any of his female "servants" into the Viri world — much to the relief of the women. And when the time came to pass through the Gateway, two of Sentas' noble followers had been conspicuously absent. Either they had second thoughts about Sentas, or they had thought better of entering the dangerous Viri world, which, unlike the other Shadow Worlds through which they had travelled, was *inside* the Vault of Seven Horns.

Shane's death still had an unreal quality for Liam. What the hell was he going to tell Shane's parents?

"Do you think the Shade is inside Sentas?" asked Liam.

"It is difficult to say. One thing is for certain, we are in more danger than ever before."

Hours later, when the clouded sun stood high in the sky, they crested a rise and saw a vast, ruined city. From the height it looked majestic, and Liam could see the remnants of walls, towers, gardens and plazas between broad avenues. They paused in respectful silence, then descended along a cobbled road. Once they were inside the city, the illusion of order vanished. It became a wasteland of huge stone blocks, fallen masonry, rusted machinery, and smashed glass. They slowed to a crawl as they picked their way through it.

Hours passed. The sun dropped lower in the sky. A chorus of eerie howls echoed through the empty city. The sound clawed its way up Liam's spine. He thought of the Shadow Hounds, then remembered they had been completely silent. He tried to pin down a direction, but the sound came from everywhere. The howls stopped. Cut off as though by a signal. Or a command. The Realm warriors exchanged glances, but said nothing. Kyall raised his hand to signal a halt, then passed the word for Liam and Morin to join him in the van. The two thurjuns rode through the mounted warriors to the front. The ruined city around them was unnaturally silent.

Kyall leaned in the saddle until he was close enough to touch Morin, then whispered. "There. The ruined tower. Do you see it?"

Rising from the sea of shattered stone was a broad, square tower. It was mostly intact, and soared above the surrounding ruins. Their view of the tower's base was blocked by a collapsed row of three-storey terrace houses.

"Yes," whispered Morin.

"That is what Kevrin instructed me to look for," said Kyall.

Morin licked his lips. "Can we get closer?"

Kyall nodded and waved the group forward. Slowly they circled around the ruins.

To see a mass of Vault warriors.

They swarmed there. A black-clad cancer in the heart of the dead city.

Kyall signalled an immediate halt.

Liam's Sight swelled as Morin deployed a concealing matrix, channelling power from his pendant mionanail. Fortunately, only four of them had turned the corner, the very tip of their mounted force. The rest lay out of sight behind the collapsed houses. The matrix blended them into their gloomy surroundings, its radius of effect centred on Morin. It did not change what they could see.

"Sweet Mother," said Kyall. There were thousands of armoured siithe. Most were in an encampment to the north, but one contingent was drawn up in neat lines, right at the tower's base. "A full legion of Soulbreakers. Over ten thousand elite Vault troops."

"Probably a thousand at the tower itself," said Vale, Kyall's lieutenant, his eyes narrowed.

A huge section of rubble had been cleared to the north, to form a square of open ground. Inside it were rows of dark tents in regular lines, and dozens of bulky transport vehicles. A perimeter wall had been constructed with the gathered rubble, which enclosed the whole encampment. Perched on the wall's crest was a defensive ring of nine Vault tanks with laser cannon. Morin had educated Liam on the primary Vault weapons, showing him descriptions and illustrations. Seeing them was something else. He swallowed, trying to ease the sudden lump in his throat.

"I think we have found the Gateway," whispered Morin.

"Orders, Captain?" asked Vale.

Kyall took a breath. "We fall back. Plan. Find ourselves a good position and wait for our chance to break through their lines."

Kyall dispatched outriders to give them warning of siithe patrols and led the main force back into the city, always careful to keep the solid mass of ruined buildings between them and the Soulbreakers' encampment. They were still searching for a suitable building to use as a base when the setting sun dropped below the horizon. The gloom immediately deepened to black. It was a dark Liam had never known before. No stars. No moon. If not for the hot gritty wind, they might have been underground. Kyall ordered a halt until the scouts returned, then Morin shaped a light matrix, which blossomed into life just above their heads. The glowing sphere provided just enough light to ride ahead, Morin unwilling to risk any more illumination. The night beyond its radius remained impenetrable black.

Liam heard the leather of his reins creak as his hands tightened into fists. The mounts whinnied to each other, and snorted. Vale's horse shied suddenly, and it veered into another mount's shoulder, throwing the whole line into chaos.

"Liam—" started Morin.

Something dropped from above. A knot of black in the darkness, which plummeted down from the unseen sky. It landed on a warrior's back. The man screamed. Blood gouted. Liam had a brief vision of dark talons, sunk deep in the man's back. Broad leathery wings snapped with a surge of power, and the warrior was lifted from the saddle. Liam gagged at a pungent scent of stale urine and rank offal until it was snatched away on the hot wind. The man's screams continued as he was drawn up into the darkness, fading with height. Then, ominously, they ceased. The horses whinnied and fought their reins, terror driving them to run.

"Veyr!" hissed Morin. He raised his staff, shielding his head, then channelled a burst of power into the light matrix, which exploded into brilliance.

Liam touched his mionanail. "Shall I cover us with a Shield?" he asked, already sketching the interlace in his mind. He realised the problem immediately. A basic Shield that moved with him would be rudimentary at best, and leave the others exposed, while a larger Shield would need specific boundaries, and require him to remain stationary.

"No," said Morin. "We would be safe, but pinned down. Caught out in the open." Morin's brow creased in concentration. "I could destroy the veyr, but such powerful spells would alert the Dark Thurjun operating the Gateway to our presence. We cannot risk that. We must preserve the element of surprise at all costs. Kyall! Make for a building. Anything! Any kind of shelter."

Kyall let his horse have its head and galloped forward, dodging through the rubble-strewn street. They followed. Ahead of them, was a large, low building. The upper storeys were demolished, but the wide entrance was unblocked. Kyall turned his horse toward it.

A shape fell from the sky in front of them, smashing into a pile of masonry. It was the body of the warrior who had been taken from the saddle, now broken and twisted. Not a drop of blood remained. The warriors used their swords as more veyr swooped down, chittering with excitement. The winged predators slashed out with razor-sharp wing-tips and talons, seeking purchase on flesh and cloth. At least now they could see them coming, thanks to Morin's light, but they were *fast*. Another warrior disappeared, shrieking, into the sky. His horse followed, dragged aloft by five veyr. The horse's screams were awful. The warriors fought back, and two were killed.

Finally, they entered the sanctuary of the building.

"Set guards," ordered Kyall, dismounting. "Scout the building and seal the exits."

Some of Kyall's warriors took up positions around the large, low ground-floor room, while others took glowglobes from their saddlebags, activated them with a twist of the nutrient spigot, and carefully moved up the shadowed stairs to the upper storeys. For the moment, all seemed secure.

A hideous howling began outside. It echoed in the darkness. Tore at the fabric of their minds. Then, as before, it stopped abruptly. *Some form of communication?* Liam shuddered at the thought that whatever *thing* made that sound was intelligent. Somehow that would make it even more malign than a mindless beast driven by need.

Kyall sought out Liam and Morin. Sentas, whose small group had also dismounted, walked across to them. Sentas' face was pale, his eyes bright.

"We need to plan our assault on the Gateway," said Kyall.

"Surely you cannot mean to attack?" snapped Sentas, fastidiously pulling off his leather riding gloves.

"Your father did not send us here to fail, Sentas. We *must* attack."

"Out of the question," said Sentas, tilting his head back in a familiar gesture of arrogance. "We must retreat to the Kess Gateway . . . seek reinforcements."

"By then it will be too late. Two of my men are already dead, Sentas. I intend that their deaths mean something. Now — unless you have something constructive to add — be silent. Our strategy is not your business."

Sentas' jaw dropped. Just for a moment, he was at a loss, then his fury ignited. "You insolent bastard! You—" Sentas' threat died unspoken as he met Kyall's unyielding gaze. Sentas stalked away to his small entourage, only his stiff posture betraying his outrage. He had only five followers now. Two nobles, Lord Jonas and Lord Kar, two family retainers, and Zanthis.

"What did you have in mind?" Morin asked Kyall.

"Provided we have not already given ourselves away, we have one chance — and one chance only — to breach the Gateway."

"Which is?" asked Morin.

"The Soulbreakers are here to attack through the Gateway, but they will only be able to bring one small troop through at a time. Once they start to que for Gateway transit, their forces will be outside the perimeter defences of their encampment. They will be strung out, and vulnerable. As they move through the Gateway their forces will also be split. That is when we attack them. Drive a wedge through them and pass through the Gateway just behind their vanguard. We destroy the Dark Thurjuns and take control of the Gateway. Then the advance siithe contingent will be cut off — and unable to bring in reinforcements from the other side. You saw how narrow the entrance to that tower was. The other siithe forces will be unable to push through en masse. We will only have the siithe vanguard to deal with. A fraction of their forces.

"Once we have destroyed the siithe forces on the other side of the Gateway we can decide our next move." Vale sounded confident, but the red line of his scar showed livid against his pale skin, betraying his own tension.

Liam swallowed. He had only faced one siithe before, and that single Vault warrior had seemed fearsome enough. On Fraser Island, on the shore of the hidden lake, Liam had run. Now they planned to face thousands. He looked anxiously at Morin. The older thurjun was calm. *I can trust Morin. He knows what he's doing.* Liam buried his fear.

"We will need to find a position close to the Gateway. And be ready to strike as soon as they move."

"How long until sunrise?" asked Morin, thinking out loud.

His hand moved toward his pendant, then dropped again as he saw Kyall already moving.

Kyall touched the hilt of his sword and paused to concentrate. "Around ten hours." He dropped his hand. The mionanails could be set to track time on multiple worlds, as well as the movements of local astronomical bodies. It took only a brief mental connection to retrieve the information. Such precision was vital for Gateway operation.

"What can we do now?" asked Liam.

"Nothing more than wait, Liam. And try to sleep," said Morin.

There was shouting from above. A warrior appeared at the stop of the stairs, breathing heavily, his sword drawn. He sighted the commander and ran to him.

"What is it?" asked Kyall.

"More veyr. They tried to force a breach. Huris . . . is gone." Dark blood dripped from the point of the warrior's blade. Its scent acrid.

Kyall nodded in grim acceptance. He ordered more warriors to the roof.

"Is there *anything* you can do, Morin?" asked Kyall.

The old thurjun shook his head. "Not without alerting the Dark Thurjuns at the Gateway."

"Very well. Then we wait for morning." Kyall drew his sword and joined his men, leaving Liam and Morin alone.

The howls started again. Low and mournful. Filled with hungry desire. Liam's heart leapt wildly, driven by some deep, primal fear.

"Is that the veyr? Making that sound?" asked Liam, his nerves frayed.

Morin grimaced. "I am not sure, Liam. I hope we do not find out."

Chapter 51
Court of VoYannan — Vault of Seven Horns

VoYannan soared on a wave of power.

Thousands were dying. On many worlds. They fell in soul-deep agony, to feed his need. Their screams were delicious, and echoed across time and space as their core essence faded to oblivion.

His viewing platform was splashed with blood. A line of veyr priests stretched across its whole length, hundreds of them, each acting as executioner to the slain slave that now lay sprawled at their feet. The priests lifted the dead slaves easily, using their powerful shoulder muscles, and tossed them from the platform's edge. The bodies were swallowed by the sulphurous clouds that wreathed the Citadel. They tumbled down to the Plain of Sorrow in a rain of dead flesh.

Hoor, his High Priest, stood beside VoYannan at the main altar stone. Procarrus was also there, ready to bear witness, his slim and deceptively powerful hand gripping the bristled mane of his hound Barsus to restrain the man-beast, who was almost insane with bloodlust.

Hoor, observing his master's readiness, signalled to his priests. Hundreds of fresh slaves were brought forward, each in their prime. Each terrified. At a signal from VoYannan, the slaves were dispatched with a single thrust to the heart, the slim daggers of the veyr striking deep. The krell groaned with pleasure as the raw, red energies of their life force flowed into him. Then the bodies were cast down onto the Plain of Sorrow to join the rest. From these sacrifices he drew physical power and vitality, while from his leashed thralls across the Vault of Seven Horns, he drew the soul-essence that fuelled his mind.

His Archfiend, Procarrus, was trembling with suppressed fury. The human was suffering as the soul-essence drained out of him. For VoYannan, this was little more than a source of amusement. Like all of the krell's servants, Procarrus jealously hoarded his power. His chief servant would live to replenish himself, as he had many times before.

Deep in his groin, the Spawn burned with new strength. Normally he would starve it, weakening it, thus making it easier to control. This he had done for aeons, until it had grown dormant. Now, with Sephany under his power and its implantation imminent, he forced the Spawn to grow and swell, pushing its tiny mind outward with his will, giving it the skills it would need to prosper. For the stronger his spawn — the greater his own increase in power when he leashed it to him.

More slaves were brought forward and sacrificed.

As the released life force washed over him, VoYannan's internal reservoirs began to spill. Errant energies discharged across his armoured body in flashes of red light. His mind was already vast, stretched to the very limits of his massive empire.

"It is enough." VoYannan's voice was rich with the dark undertones of a thousand death-songs. The krell's timeless dirge.

After days of drawing power from throughout his Vault, and from many thousands of slave-sacrifices, he was ready. Now he could craft an illusion that would be irresistible to the Realm priestess. Not even the High God could stop him.

"Enough!" roared VoYannan, waving away his veyr priests. A chorus of chittering started. The veyr ran to the side of the platform. Their leathery wings snapped to full length and they sailed off into the mist — down to the smashed bodies below. He knew the priests would race each other for the freshest kills, eager to suck on the warmest corpse-blood. The other Vault dwellers who preyed on the sacrifices would scatter at their approach.

Hoor remained behind. He stepped slowly toward VoYannan and bowed.

"What now priest? What are the omens?" demanded VoYannan.

The veyr's wings flared slightly. "The omens remain favourable, my Lord."

"*Bring her.*" VoYannan's voice thundered with lust and impatience. Twin storms that flattened the air and made every thrall — from Procarrus to the merest dweller — tremble in sickening fear.

Hoor bowed, and dared to speak. "Her will must be broken, Lord. The Spawn must feed on a broken spirit. That is the key."

"Enough!" VoYannan thrust out his horns in fury, his body swelling with muscle. A pulse of crimson energy lifted him high above the priest. The krell hovered above the platform's bloodstained stone. "BRING HER!"

Hoor staggered back and fell. The veyr trembled beneath VoYannan's awesome presence. Awkwardly, for the veyr were clumsy beasts on land, he fluttered to his feet, then fled.

One by one, the other veyr returned, flying up from the Plain of Sorrow to stand before the ranks of siithe that lined the platform. The priests were sluggish, the dark chambers of their abdomens swollen to the limits of their chitinous exoskeletons.

"Do you wish us to leave, Lord?" asked Procarrus. Only he and Barsus remained beside VoYannan's altar.

"No. Stay my Archfiend. Stay and watch your lord plant the Seed of his power." VoYannan looked down at Barsus. The man-beast whimpered and backed away.

Hoor returned with Balos and Sephany. The priestess was dressed in a simple white slave-robe. Her dark hair was unbound. She betrayed no fear. VoYannan had ordered her food to be laced with narcotics, just enough to dull her wits. This time he was taking no chances. VoYannan drew on his vast well of power and reached delicately into Sephany's mind. She did not resist, did not even realise what was happening to her.

Sephany laughed with delight.

She had woken from a terrible dream to find herself in a verdant forest, on the bank of a clear mountain stream. Above her, the sky was a stunning blue, a counterpoint to the lush green grass. Her beautiful husband, Damast, was there, waiting for her.

"Come, darling. Lay beside me," said Damast.

He had spread out a picnic for them both, with bread, cheese, and good red wine. All on a thick red, woollen blanket. She lowered herself to the blanket and a delicious relaxation passed through her. She took a bite of the cheese. It was spicy and fresh. She met Damast's green eyes and a thrill went through her, along with a memory of the last time they were together in the sheets. A feeling of love overwhelmed her, coming with waves of desire so powerful she ached with arousal. Before she knew it, she was throwing off her clothes, spreading herself out on the luxurious blanket.

"I love you, Damast. Take me. Now."

Damast smiled his love and was suddenly naked. He lowered his hard, lean body over her.

Sephany swept her legs up, but somehow they got tangled, she could not get them around his slim hips. She felt pain in her leg, but ignored it. This was going to be perfect. *Perfect.* She fixed her eyes on the stream. It flowed crystal clear, trickling gently over rocks, pebbles and sand.

It is all so beautiful . . .

Then the water turned red. It became a torrent of blood that burned pain into her eyes. A foul stench assaulted her. She screamed and pushed back from Damast.

Damast waited for her patiently. "What is wrong, my love?"

Sephany looked around. Everything was perfect once more. The stream, the sky, the thick green grass. It was everything she would have dreamed for her first time. *First time . . .?* She looked at Damast. She knew she had been married for two years now. Happily married to Damast. Both longed for children. For a while she had felt drawn to the priesthood, but instead she had married.

"Come, darling," said Damast. "We can make a child for us to love."

She looked into Damast's eyes and her heart melted. She moved across the blanket and started to lie back. Then an image flashed through her head. *A Temple altar.* She was kneeling before it, giving her vows. The vows of the priesthood. She was to be a priestess.

Sephany cried out and clutched her head. She looked around, but the scene was as perfect as before. She thought she heard a growl of rage, as if from a rabid dog. Damast's face rippled. Then it was as before. She loved him so much!

"White lady."

"What was that? I heard a voice," said Sephany.

"I heard nothing, love," said Damast.

Before he could stop her, she slipped her simple dress back on and walked to the tree line. The woods immediately grew dark and forbidding.

"Come back to the stream, darling."

The stream sparkled with a thousand reflected lights. So beautiful.

"White lady."

Sephany turned back to the forest. "There it is again, Damast. There is a child in the forest. Perhaps the poor dear is lost? I should check they are alright."

"No!" commanded Damast.

Sephany was hurt that Damast would shout at her. He was never one to raise his voice. Despite his demand, she took a step toward the forest.

A young boy emerged from the forest's edge. He had the face of an angel, with blonde hair and blue eyes. There was a distant twinge of recognition in her mind.

"White lady!" said the little boy. His eyes swept across to Damast, but he was not afraid. He was beyond fear. A white light surrounded him.

"White lady." This time it was a young girl, also walking from the forest. Then they all came forward. And with each child, the light in the forest grew. There were hundreds. They ran to her, surrounding her. *White lady. White lady,* they chanted. She embraced them and knew they were not afraid. They had come from the High God. The light swelled, engulfing her.

Memories came like an avalanche.

VoYannan.

The illusion shattered.

Sephany screamed.

She was on VoYannan's platform, only metres from the edge. The red blanket was a blanket of blood, covering the krell's altar stone. On it, waited VoYannan, the skin of his erect member rippling as his spawn sought to rip its way free. Sephany looked down at her leg. There was a long gash where she had cut her inner thigh on the horns of VoYannan's hip.

Sephany's heart went cold.

VoYannan screamed in rage. The sheer weight of sound threw Sephany off her feet. The pools of blood in the carved altar-stone exploded into red mist. All along the platform, the minions of the krell were blasted from their feet. Siithe fell in heaps. Those who did not lay stunned, covered their ears. VoYannan flew at her.

Sephany began a prayer, but when the huge taloned hands closed on her arms, lifting her into the air, the words were torn away by terror.

"I have guessed your secret!" she screamed desperately. *"You cannot force me against my will."*

VoYannan slammed her body down onto the bloody altar.

"YOUR WILL? IT SHALL BE BROKEN!"

Sephany was plunged into darkness. She screamed in pain as taloned hands ripped her garments from her body. Then came a white-hot agony that left her breathless. Talons speared into her eyes, driving deep into the sockets, striking out her vision. She convulsed. A deep fear gripped her heart. *She would never see the sun again.*

"Submit!" thundered VoYannan.

Sephany heard herself whimper.

"My spawn does not need your arms and legs. Submit or I will take them all. One by one!"

"I would die!"

"My priests will keep you alive."

Fear swamped her. A heavy, suffocating blanket. Slowly, she distanced herself from it. Then she began to pray.

"No!" yelled VoYannan.

A taloned hand struck her face, ripping the skin.

"My, Lord. Beware you do not kill her." It was the hissing voice of Hoor, the veyr High Priest.

"You dare to dictate to me? I, VoYannan, who raised you from darkness to sentience?"

"I dictate nothing. But the omens, Lord. Her will cannot be forced!"

"Be silent, Hoor! It will be done my way!"

"But Lord, the Spawn—"

She heard the veyr's terrified death-scream.

Sephany felt a searing pain in her left leg. Razor sharp talons ripped through her flesh, severing the limb. Her body shook, her mouth gaped soundlessly. The pain was unbelievable. It snatched away her powers of speech.

"Submit!"

She steadfastly refused to answer. As soon as she could gather breath, she continued the prayer. A calm embraced her.

The talons pierced the flesh of her right leg, severing the flesh. Then her right leg was gone. She faltered. Tears of pain and blood ran down her cheek.

"Submit!"

Sephany gathered her breath. *"Never."*

She started the prayer once more. The agony had driven her above her body. Her mind hummed with light. She felt the beginnings of pain in her right arm, but this also faded, until it was nothing more than the ghost of sensation.

"SUBMIT!"

Sephany opened her eyes. She was whole. *It had been another illusion!* All except the blow to the face. Long slashes cut her cheek. Beside the altar was the smashed body of Hoor. VoYannan had killed his own High Priest.

"I reject you!" yelled Sephany. "I reject all your empty promises. Your illusions of joy, and your Vault of darkness!"

VoYannan bellowed. The sound shook the very stone of the Citadel. The horns on his head grew until they were almost a metre long. Razor sharp, they cut across her stomach, leaving a trail of intense pain. Within the krell's groin, the Spawn — bloated with power — began to tear its way free.

"I WILL NOT BE DENIED!"

The krell seized her in his taloned hands. He lifted her off the altar and forced her into his hideous embrace.

Sephany blacked out.

Distantly, she heard an animal howling in lust and triumph. Then a young woman, screaming in pain and despair. But she was calm. She turned away. In the distance she could see another altar. It was the altar at Stonelake. Beside it, in place of the Temple Flame, stood Korbeth. He was glowing — translucent — and yet real. She reached out to him and he swept her into his arms.

"Finn is coming," he said.

"He cannot fight the Vault alone, Korbeth."

"Have faith, Sephany." She snuggled into his broad chest and was overwhelmed with warmth and love.

She jolted to consciousness.

Finished with her, VoYannan had thrown her to the stone.

Blood flowed down her legs, and her whole abdomen flared hot with agony. She struggled to stand, but fell. A tall form, encased in ruby light, lifted her effortlessly into its arms. *Balos.*

"She must be prepared!" hissed one of the veyr priests.

"No one touches her," said Balos. "I alone will tend her."

A series of fragmented images followed. Dark tunnels. Nightmare faces. Then she was back in her chamber. At one point she remembered two veyr priests talking nearby.

"VoYannan planted the Spawn against her will," hissed one veyr.

"Be silent! Whoever speaks of it to VoYannan will die as swiftly as Hoor."

"But the omens! What will it mean?"

"All is reversed."

Then the powerful voice of the seraphin. "Be gone!"

Sephany opened her eyes to see Balos above her. They were alone. His red cloak of energy wavered, cycling from golden yellow to white and back to red. His power enfolded her, healing her wounds.

Inside her, something moved.

And began to feed.

Chapter 52
Viri world — Vault of Seven Horns

Kyall called a halt behind a ruined mansion.

They were north-east of the Gateway. Close to both the portal — and the siithe legion. The Realm warriors squatted down, reducing their profile, even though the pile of masonry, tile, brick and dusty glass that towered above them would easy shield them from sight. As soon as dawn had ended the veyr attacks, they had advanced on foot, leaving the horses behind. The men around Liam were exhausted. Faces drawn and streaked with dust. They had moved slowly, stealthily, through the eerily quite Viri city. Despite the slow pace, the strain had taken its toll on all of them, particularly the wounded. One warrior had a long gash on his face from a veyr's wingtip. The blood that traced the wound had dried to a dark reddish-brown, and looked almost black in the day's gloom. The warrior had slumped back against a block of marble, eyes shut to catch a moment of rest. One man had a bandage on his arm, another on his neck. All had been treated with salves to prevent infection from the veyrs' teeth and claws, which carried flesh-eating bacteria — and worse. It had been a sleepless night for them all. Liam and Morin had taken their turn on guard duty. Fighting the veyr in the darkness had been a nightmare. They were fast and vicious, and the bloody things *talked*. They would chitter amongst themselves, hidden in the night, the noise a distraction as the attack came from another quarter, then every now and then, they would taunt them from the darkness in Realm speech. Curses. Insults. Promises of death and torture. Lewd invitations that had sickened Liam. As underwhelming as dawn had been — merely a lightening in the east — Liam had never been so happy to greet a new day. The light revealed that the dead veyr on the roof had been cannibalised, everything eaten away by the other veyr except the tough leathery wings, steely talons, and the hardest parts of their exoskeleton. Even these latter parts had been gnawed. Then they had counted the cost. Three of the Realm warriors who had entered the Viri world were dead.

"We have to advance slowly," said Kyall, quietly. "Small groups. No more than three or four. Then we regroup behind that mound of fallen stone three hundred paces from the Gateway tower." Kyall pointed, then turned to each man to receive a nod or other unspoken acknowledgement that they understood the orders. Some warriors had stand to get a glimpse of the rally point. The mound was large, and would give good concealment. "The siithe forces are camped on the other side and will not see us — until we strike."

The warriors roused themselves, drawing from hidden wells of strength, and the company moved to the edge of the ruins. It was open ground from there to the tower, dotted with piles of rubble that might have once been anything. The Soulbreakers' compound was to the north-west. A shock of fear went through Liam as he saw the siithe. *Thousands of them. Everywhere.* The first of the small groups, led by Kyall himself, ran to the nearest rubble pile and ducked under cover. Other groups followed, leap-frogging from one spot to the next, gradually closing on the rally point. Finally, it was Liam and Morin's turn. They ran across to the first hiding spot accompanied by two of Kyall's warriors. Sentas and Zanthis were in the group behind them. Jonas and Kar had been left to guard the horses and supplies.

An hour crawled by as Liam and Morin wormed their way closer to the Gateway tower, sometimes crawling, other times running hunched over to decrease their profile. Finally, they reached the second-last hiding spot. Just one long stretch of open ground to a large stone block remained beyond that, then a short run from there to the rally point. From their new position, which was more elevated than the siithe compound, Liam could see beyond the rubble walls into the encampment. There were not only siithe warriors inside. There were slaves too. Hundreds of them. All with iron collars. A score of races, all humanoid, with mixed statures, weird faces, and a rainbow of skin colours. They cooked, and laboured, while their overlords dealt out casual cruelty with fist and lash. There were stacked cages near one of the larger tents, mostly empty now. Liam's eyes roamed across the dirty cubes of iron mesh, then snapped back. He saw a human woman, slumped in a cage, holding the ragged shreds of a black dress together with her hands. It was the Archfiend's Gate-opener. Her face was oddly stretched, and she was terribly emaciated, as though she had shrunken in on herself, but it was her. There was no doubt.

"Morin," he whispered.

"Yes," replied Morin.

"That woman in the black dress. In the slave cages." Liam pointed.

"Ah. I see her. Poor wretch."

"She is the Gate-opener. The one Procarrus used to open the Stonelake Gateway."

"The Earth thurjun?" Part of their mission had been to capture the thurjun who had opened the Gateway from Earth and return them to the High Court for justice. The underlying assumption was that they had been a willing participant in the Vault's schemes. This woman had not. She had been a slave to Procarrus. One look at her dejected form, and they both understood that. "There is no way we can get to her." Morin considered. "Both sides of the Gateway must now be manned by Dark Thurjuns. If we subdue them, we take the Gateway out of the Vault's hands."

"What if there are more Dark Thurjuns on Earth?" asked Liam.

"It is possible, but unlikely. Their talent is as rare as ours. There are not so many Dark Thurjuns that VoYannan can spend them carelessly. Our Seekers will keep watch. If the Sydney Gateway is reopened, Torren will act, I assure you."

"And—" Liam looked at the woman, slumped against the bars, her eyes glazed as she stared into nothing. He knew there was no way they could rescue her. Their whole plan relied on a surprise attack, then escape. They would be lucky to even make it to the Gateway. He forced himself to look away. She was another Vault victim, amongst millions.

"Stay strong, Liam. Protecting your world comes first," said Morin with a depth of sadness that spoke of witnessing many such tragedies and injustices. Morin understood such choices.

When the way was clear they crawled across the last piece of exposed ground, heading for the stone block, a huge thing that had tumbled from a fallen building to stand there alone. Liam heard Morin's harsh breathing behind him. They made it. Both sagged with relief behind the sheltering stone. Liam's hand stung where something sharp had slashed his skin. He had not even felt it. Morin's hand fell on his shoulder. Liam drew a slow breath, trying to ease his tension, and looked up. A squad of Soulbreakers came into sight, marching around the outside of their camp's perimeter wall. The Realm warriors froze. The regular crunch of boots grew louder. The siithe marched in tight, disciplined lines, and watched everything, pulse lasers — outlined with red power-lights — held ready. Soon they were only paces away. Liam tasted acid at the back of his throat.

Then they were past.

Liam let out a breath, aware of a sudden need to piss. *Now* for God's sake?

The Realm warriors began to creep forward again.

"I am not a worm," said Sentas indignantly — and loudly — behind them. Liam could hear the guards with him urging him to be silent. Liam turned. Sentas' group had reached the exposed open ground he and Morin had just crossed, and the prince was refusing to crawl on his elbows. No doubt worried about ruining his fine clothes.

"I am glad we left Jonas and Kar to mind the horses. Sentas is bad enough," muttered Morin.

"I am the son of the High King!" said Sentas, pushing away a helping hand.

The squad of siithe abruptly halted. The siithe commander turned back toward them. His dark eyes swept the open ground.

Two warriors grabbed Sentas. One pushed the prince to the ground, the other clamped a hand over his mouth.

"*That fool will kill us all,*" whispered Morin.

The siithe commander grunted and waved two of his men in their direction. The main troop continued their march. The two siithe warriors extended their bulky weapons, which were partially supported by slings, and advanced. The Realm warriors were spread out over more than a hundred metres. Exposed and vulnerable. The siithe were approaching on an angle, flanking them. In moments they would be in a position to see them all.

"The lasers. They could cut us down before we even have a

chance to move," Morin whispered to Liam. "The only way to counter them is to use the dampening field — but that will alert every Dark Thurjun for miles. We need to take them out, silently and swiftly. Steel and magic."

Although the two siithe warriors had started out in the direction of Sentas' voice, they were now heading for Liam and Morin.

"Liam," said Morin.

"Yes."

"Ball of Fire. Go for the head."

Morin turned to the two warriors with them. "As soon as they are down, drag the bodies back here." The two warriors nodded their understanding, and moved up into a crouch, ready to spring.

"Prepare the matrix, Liam. But wait for my signal. They need to be as close as possible."

Liam carefully constructed the matrix. Layer upon layer of twisting, turning loops. The siithe *were* close. Even as he thought it, one of the Vault warriors stopped dead. His black eyes fixed on Liam. Cold and dead. The siithe's mouth opened, showing rows of sharp teeth. The warrior grunted a single word in the Vault tongue. The other warrior turned. Both lasers swivelled toward Liam and Morin's group, the blunt barrel-ends gaping wide.

"Now!"

A small ball of fire shot from Morin's outstretched hands to the first siithe. It struck the Vault warrior's head, instantly transforming it into charred flesh. The siithe dropped without a sound. Liam's Ball of Fire blazed into being and raced to its target a fraction of a second later. It swelled as it flew, becoming a fireball more than five metres in diameter. An intense wave of heat washed back over him as it engulfed the second siithe. The flame burnt every strip of clothing, armour, and flesh, away from the siithe's bones in an instant. Then the power cell in the pulse laser exploded, shattering the siithe's charred skeleton to dust. Liam gaped in astonishment. He blinked dust from his eyes. He released the matrix in shock.

"Mother of God!" said one of the Realm warriors.

"Go!" said Morin. The men ran forward and grabbed the body of the first siithe and dragged it, and the laser, behind the block.

Goddamnit! That explosion was as loud as thunderclap!

They looked down at the siithe encampment, hardly daring to breathe. The Vault tanks sat huge and squat on the wall, laser turrets blunt and ugly, waiting to gout death. The gates were open, disgorging Vault warriors. They formed in long lines, while ahead of them, a siithe advance force marshalled at the base of the square tower. The patrolling squad was nowhere in sight.

"They are ignoring the explosion!" said one of the warriors.

"The power cells do explode sometimes. I have seen it before. Maybe they think it was an accident," said the other warrior.

"Or maybe they are too busy to care," said Morin. Columns of black-clad warriors steadily disappeared into the darkness of the Gateway tower.

"They are moving through the Gateway. We're too late!" said Liam.

"Come on," ordered Morin. They moved swiftly down the hillside to join the others at the rally point. Even though they were ridiculously outnumbered, Liam drew strength from the confidence of the warriors around him. The Soulbreakers' lines were less than a hundred metres away, between them and the tower. Close enough to hear them.

Sentas marched up to Kyall. "Kyall! I will not have your men—"

Kyall's hand swept up, knocking Sentas from his feet with a back-handed blow. The Realm captain stepped forward until he towered over the prince. "While we are performing a military operation, I am in charge here, Sentas. If you endanger my men one more time, I will have you bound and gagged. You understand me?"

Sentas' eyes flashed hatred. The prince's gloved hand came up to his mouth and came away bloody. He said nothing, but nodded to Kyall, who walked away and left him on the ground. Sentas' two retainers looked away. Zanthis reached down and helped his lord up.

Kyall joined Morin and Liam. They watched the siithe troop movements. At least two hundred siithe, armed with pulse lasers, had already moved through the Gateway. They had been followed by troops with heavy crossbows, running at speed.

"We are in luck, Morin. They have already brought their crossbows through," said Kyall. Then his eyes hardened as he considered the task at hand. "We must close that Gateway. Can you sense the Dark Thurjun?"

Morin closed his eyes. His brow creased in concentration. He shook his head and opened his eyes. "No. I am no Seeker, Kyall. I need to see him."

"Very well then. We must attack. Stand ready." Kyall turned to his men. "Form a fighting wedge! Forward on my command! Sentas and Zanthis, you stand in the centre with your men and act as reserve. Thurjuns at the top of the wedge with me."

The men smoothly took their positions. Those on the outside of the wedge swung round shields from their backs, forming a shield-wall. In total they had just over thirty warriors. Kyall drew his weapon, an ancient broadsword with a mionanail set into the pommel. His shield was dark and unadorned, painted black on both sides. Like all the Realm shields, it was made of a lightweight, tough alloy. The commander concentrated, forming a matrix. Liam felt the Realm dampening field sweep out through the city.

"Advance at the half run!" ordered Kyall.

The warriors drew their weapons and they all ran straight for the Gateway tower — and the packed ranks of the siithe guarding it. Ahead of them, at least eight hundred siithe stood in tight, disciplined lines. But the Vault warriors faced away from the approaching Realm force, their eyes on the tower entrance. Liam watched the broad armoured backs of the siithe draw closer with a sense of unreality, just waiting for the moment they would turn . . . and he would see his own death staring back at him. *Surely there is no way I can survive this?* Yet he felt no fear. Only exhilaration. After a night of terror, and a tense morning crawling toward the siithe lines, to finally act, to *move*, was an unbelievable relief. It was inaction itself that bred fear.

"Forward at the run!"

"Blow of Force, Liam. This time make it as big as you want!" said Morin.

Orders were barked out in the siithe lines. The nearest rank of troops turned, bringing their lasers to bear. They fired their weapons. Nothing happened. The siithe were close now. At least ten solid ranks of Vault warriors between the tip of the Realm wedge and the Gateway entrance. A second order rang out. The siithe dropped their lasers, which swung at their side on slings, and drew falcatas.

Blow of Force sprang into Liam's mind.

"Now, Liam!"

Liam opened himself to the raw, hot energy of the mionanail. He kept drawing power until sharp daggers lanced into his head, until his eyeballs felt they would burst with the pressure. Then he released it.

An invisible form exploded outward.

Morin's spell hit the siithe ranks a moment before his. Six siithe warriors were catapulted from their feet, slamming into the ranks behind them like missiles. Liam's Blow of Force missed the siithe ranks altogether, crashing into the wall of the ruined tower in a massive concussion that shook the whole ancient structure, and rained dust onto the Vault ranks. Liam felt wetness on his upper lip. He touched it, two fingers coming away bright crimson. It was blood. Streaming from his nose. He tasted copper on the back of his tongue.

"Straight through their ranks!" urged Kyall.

A sea of huge siithe warriors surged at them. Razor sharp falcatas rose and fell in the dull day. The Realm warriors turned every assault on blade, shield, and greave, then struck back with deadly skill. They left a low wall of siithe dead in their wake. Each one of Kyall's men was a master swordsman, handpicked from a score of garrisons. The wedge pushed steadily forward, and for the first few moments it seemed they would make it through the enemy ranks and into the Gateway tower. Then the sheer weight of numbers began to tell. One of the Realm warriors fell, then another. Sentas' retainers ran forward to plug the gap, snatching up fallen shields.

The wedge slowed.

Then stopped.

The fighting compressed. Too close now to use the long

swords to good effect, the combat dissolved into a shoving match, where the hulking siithe in their greater numbers had the advantage.

The siithe began to push them back.

There was a loud grating sound from above. Liam looked up sharply, expecting some new attack. Instead he saw that a whole section of the tower wall had fractured above the arched entrance. The great blocks ground together as they shifted. Blood splashed across Liam's face. He gasped as another Realm warrior fell, his face slashed open by a descending falcata. If they lost any more men, the wedge would break. Liam could feel it. That tenuous balance in the midst of battle. When the wedge failed, the warriors would be scattered and divided, and no longer protected by the line of battle, the shields of the warriors who now fought close by their side. They would all die, one by one. Gathering his energies, Liam fixed his eyes on his target — the apex of the arched entrance — and struck the tower wall with another Blow of Force. Three huge stone blocks were punched from the wall. *Direct hit.* With the keystones gone, the whole face of the tower collapsed, plummeting onto the packed siithe ranks, which were half inside, and half outside, the tower. The siithe bellowed, their harsh screams more animal than human. The Vault ranks broke as the surviving siithe scattered, and the pressure on the Realm wedge eased.

But the wall continued to collapse.

A vast rectangular block tumbled from the tower, some sort of support beam, easily ten times the size of all the others. At first Liam thought it would fall onto the siithe, but it crashed onto the ragged pile of fallen stones and bounced back *toward them*. Into the front of the Realm wedge. Liam gasped. His thoughts tangled as he tried to form a Shield. Morin was there ahead of him. Morin's Shield solidified in Liam's Sight. The monolithic beam struck the Shield without a sound and was flung aside, onto the backs of the retreating siithe. Dark blood flooded from beneath the stone.

Now there was open ground ahead, littered with dead siithe and fallen stone.

"Into the breach!" yelled Kyall.

Before the siithe could react, before the Vault forces could recover and drive back at them, the Realm wedge drove across the open ground and entered the ruined tower. Their warriors wove around the prone siithe and huge blocks of stone, swords sweeping down and rising wet with enemy blood as they efficiently finished them off. They passed through an outer bailey and entered a short tunnel. After a brief, but furious exchange, they broke through into a central chamber, which had a high vaulted ceiling of white marble.

The Gateway was in the centre. It was a sharply arched portal with elaborately carved side posts that stood tall on a circular dais. A dull, white light shone from the open Gateway, deepening the room's shadows. The Gateway was blocked by around seventy siithe warriors, who were slowly marching up the dais stairs and through the Gateway. Beside the arched portal was a tall, thin man in black robes. The man was almost bald, although a few wispy fragments of grey hair still clung to his pate. Around his neck hung the bulky, metallic shape of a Vault Accumulator, the device that fuelled the Dark Thurjun's talent.

"Kyall! Straight for the Gateway!" shouted Morin. "Liam! You and Kyall go through the Gateway. Take all the troops with you. I will deal with the Dark Thurjun and seal the Gateway from this side." Once established, the Gateway would remain open for as long as the interlace was fed sufficient power — or until it was forced closed.

"What about you?" asked Liam, concerned that Morin would not survive here alone. They had exploited a gap in the siithe lines, but virtually the full legion of Soulbreakers still remained.

"Do not fear for me, Liam. Provided they do not bring another Dark Thurjun against me, I will be able to hold them. When you are ready for me to open the Gateway, reach through with your mind. I will be waiting."

The plan had always been to leave one of their two thurjuns on the Viri world. Their remaining forces would fight through the Gateway, capture the Earth thurjun, destroy Procarrus' advance forces on Earth, deliver Shane to the "Earth Temple", then return. But now, with the Earth thurjun a slave stranded on the Viri side of the Gateway, and Shane dead, they needed only a quick thrust to take the Gateway out of Vault control. Liam was to be the one who would wait on the Viri world, with a handful of warriors, his only task to open the Gateway when Morin called through the portal. That was before they saw the Soulbreakers Legion. Now the roles were reversed, and Liam had to face a Dark Thurjun alone.

The fighting wedge hit the siithe rearguard at a run. They fell quickly, and the remaining Vault troops, which had been facing the Gateway, were thrown into confusion. Kyall fought like a demon, cleaving into their ranks in a blur of steel. Dark blood splashed in crazy arcs, drawing patterns across the ancient white stone as the siithe fell. The Dark Thurjun barked out orders. The siithe stopped their advance through the Gateway and all turned to face the Realm warriors. It had only been moments, but the Realm wedge had already split the enemy force. They were only twenty paces from the Gateway itself and gaining ground every second. *I'm going to make it!* thought Liam, in amazement.

The Dark Thurjun growled a harsh word in the Vault language and raised his hands. Razor sharp slithers of dark glass materialised in the gap between the fighting wedge and the Gateway and flitted through the air toward them. Dark blurs promising death. The projectiles shattered against Morin's swiftly drawn Shield in staccato *cracks*.

Then they were there. At the Gateway.

The Dark Thurjun stood alone, outlined by the Gateway's mercurial light. Two of Kyall's warriors stepped out from their shield wall to cut him down, but as their swords neared him, there was a sharp electric discharge. Both men yelped in pain and dropped their weapons. The Dark Thurjun laughed. His eyes glittered. Energy swelled and billowed around him, dark and foreign. Liam's stomach lurched, and the world tilted. His ears rang like a noonday chorus of cicadas in the bush. His mind slowed. He struggled to recapture the sense of urgency that had driven him here, but it slipped away. There was something he should be doing, he thought, but did not know what. The world steadied. He focussed on the Dark Thurjun, but his mind remained blank. Liam frowned, puzzled, disturbed, yet unable to gather a coherent thought. More warriors closed on the Dark

Thurjun, but they were driven back by bursts of lightning that arced across the gap, drawn by their shields, weapons, and armour.

"Let me through!" The ranks parted for Morin. The thurjun's wooden staff stabbed out, smashing the Accumulator to shards.

A red cloud hissed from the device, rapidly diffusing into the air. Liam felt the energy tingling across his skin, potent, yet tainted. It sent his heart racing with fury and strength. He blinked. The spell that held his mind shattered.

The Dark Thurjun inhaled, taking in as much of the escaping power as he could. The enemy thurjun's hand snaked out and grabbed the end of Morin's staff, pulling the thurjun toward him with supernatural strength. With his other hand the enemy thurjun unsheathed a long curved belt dagger. He drew back the blade, ready to stab it into Morin's throat. The Realm warriors nearby were still recovering from the shock of the Dark Thurjun's defensive field and did not see the danger.

"No!" Liam drew and cut in one movement. The blade sliced through the Dark Thurjun's hand at the wrist, releasing Morin's staff. The Dark Thurjun screamed and swivelled toward Liam, lunging with his dagger. In a practised reflex, Liam sidestepped the blade and sent a reverse cut to the Dark Thurjun's throat. The man staggered, then fell to his knees. The Vault mage gasped, horribly, and slumped to his side. A final exhalation gurgled through his slit throat, then he entered the total relaxation of death. Liam watched it all. *I've just killed a man.* The Realm ranks reformed, then he was pushed toward the Gateway. He turned back to see Morin beside the portal, forming an enclosing Shield that would protect him against any physical attacks. Morin nodded to Liam, then returned his concentration to his task, face grim. A dampening field pulsed outward from the thurjun.

Then Liam was through the Gateway.

The Realm warriors appeared in a large natural cavern. Roughly circular, and around forty metres across. There was no Gateway structure, merely a tall, pale flame that turned slowly in the cavern's centre. The light was weak, and much of the chamber lay in shadow. They advanced far enough for their own forces to exit the portal, then tightened their lines. Liam, Kyall, and Vale, remained together at the head of the wedge. On the far side of the cave, the siithe vanguard massed at the entrance to an exit tunnel, which was blocked with fallen rock.

"*Liam,*" hissed Vale, pointing behind them.

Liam's head jerked around. A man stood in the shadows beyond the Gateway. He was squat and swarthy, and his dark hair hung in long greasy strands. His stillness was ominous, like that of a spider, waiting in its web. He was dressed in black robes, like the Dark Thurjun on the Viri world, and a boxy Accumulator was strapped to his chest. His hood was thrown back. His yellow eyes fixed on Liam.

"He is yours, Liam," said Vale.

"Someone has activated a Realm dampening field here," said Kyall. "It has to be Finn! Look there," said Kyall, pointing at the bodies of the fallen siithe and their gaping red-mouthed wounds. "Swordwork. He has already been fighting them."

Those were not the only bodies. As his eyes adjusted to the light, Liam saw that some of the inert shapes on the cavern floor were police wearing body armour. Some had been sliced apart by energy weapons, others cut down by falcata. Seeing their familiar uniforms and weapons sent a spike of adrenaline through Liam, as though that very familiarity made their deaths more real. He swallowed and shut out thoughts of the dead. It was up to him to contain the Dark Thurjun.

Liam left the fighting wedge and circled around the Gateway. He wanted a clear field of effect for his magic. Liam sketched a Shield matrix, and began to draw power from his mionanail. Before he could bring his own spell to life, a dark blanket closed around him and drew tight. *Too slow!* His matrix shattered like spun sugar. Darkness soaked into his limbs. It numbed his arms, his legs. His mind. The Dark Thurjun's eyes flared in triumph. Liam tried to form another matrix, but the delicate strands fell into a tangled mess and dissolved. He had lost, and so easily. He would die here, in some unknown grotto, and Morin would be left to fight alone. They would lose command of the Gateway, and their mission would fail.

A series of curt orders rang out in the Vault tongue. The siithe turned in place so that they faced the Realm troops. Their heavy boots crashed on stone. Then the siithe charged, coming on with a chorus of guttural growls. With a battle cry, Kyall led the Realm warriors in a counter-charge, leaving Liam alone.

Liam watched it all, but could not move.

The Dark Thurjun stalked forward. He drew a long stiletto blade from his sleeve. The man's lips curled into in a vicious snarl. His eyes fixed on Liam's heart. *His target.* Protected only by the thin fabric of his blue thurjun's robe. Liam was paralysed. The weight of his sword, clutched uselessly in his fist, dragged his right arm down until the point rested on stone. He tried to call out to Kyall. His tongue was a dead thing. His eyes bulged as they fixed on the dark blade. A single thrust was all it would take. The story of Liam Durrow would end here. Under Sydney's concrete and steel. He saw Tirini's beautiful face. Wondered if she would cry for him.

Then the Gateway closed.

Chapter 53
Sydney, Australia — Earth

Pitch darkness fell around Liam.

Morin has closed the Gateway.

The Dark Thurjun's spell faltered, just for a heartbeat, and Liam's head cleared. He deployed a Shield. The Realm magic cut through the Dark Thurjun's spell. The paralysis vanished. His body came alive with unused adrenaline. The stiletto bit into his Shield and slid away. Liam turned to face the attack, guessing from the deflected blow where the enemy thurjun was standing. He dropped his Shield and stepped forward in a straight lunge. His sword arm shuddered as his blade met resistance. He twisted his wrist and pulled back, dragging the blade clear and stepping to the side at the same time. He heard a gasp of pain. Then the sound of a body slumping to the ground. A flutter of robes.

"Liam! Light!" yelled Kyall.

Liam formed Ball of Light. In his fear and anxiety, he made an error in the form, then channelled two much power from the mionanail. Instead of a single light ball, *hundreds* flared into existence above the fighting ranks. They shot around the cavern like super-balls, bouncing between siithe, Realm warrior and wall alike. They had no heat, but the effect was chaos. Adverse to bright lights, the siithe panicked, striking out at the balls in a frenzy, hitting any other Vault warriors who got in the way. Kyall's warriors exploited the confusion. They pushed into the siithe ranks, cutting them down.

The Dark Thurjun was not dead. He had crawled to the body of a siithe and retrieved one of the bulky Vault crossbows. It was drawn and loaded. He swivelled it toward Liam. Aimed low. Liam danced forward and stabbed his sword through the man's neck. The crossbow discharged with a deep thrum. The bolt sliced through the fabric of Liam's robe at his left hip. He tore out his blade with a vicious twist. As the man's yellow eyes widened in shock, Liam took a half-step closer and smashed the Vault Accumulator to shards with his heel. He stamped down. Once. Twice. Three times. Then he stood there. Breath harsh. Hands shaking. Staring at the dying man. A red cloud hissed from the shattered remnants of the Accumulator. Liam held his breath and shuffled back.

His balls of light slowed. They drifted up to the cavern's high roof to nest among a forest of stalactites.

The siithe retreated three paces and reformed lines. Around a hundred and fifty Vault warriors remained. Some were armed with crossbows, which they had not been able to use in the initial press. The siithe captain barked a series of orders. The Vault crossbow troops shouldered their way to the front rank. They cranked their discharged weapons, and drew iron-tipped bolts from belt-quivers. Kyall and his warriors had moments before the deadly barrage hit them. *Defence or attack?* Liam ran to the front of the Realm wedge, then loosed a Ball of Fire. The huge ball roared as it swept into the front siithe ranks. The crossbow men were engulfed, weapons reduced to char, bodies turned to writhing pillars of flame. The mionanail burned hot against his chest.

The siithe charged. There were still more than a hundred of them. Liam hit them with a Blow of Force, channelling every shred of energy he could muster from his mionanail. The Blow struck the centre of the Vault ranks like an immense battering ram, flinging dozens of siithe into the far wall. Liam hit them again, then again. The world spun. One of Kyall's warriors gripped Liam's arm to steady him. Then the siithe were on them. Liam was in the front rank. He parried a savage cut from a falcata, the jar of impact tearing something deep in his shoulder. The pain fled in a sea of fury. There were curses, warcries and blood. Howls of pain. The stink of the siithe. Eyes wild as his world contracted. He watched the blades around him, ready to block, always watching the black eyes of the siithe, alert for openings. Throats, groins and stomachs. One of Sentas' retainers appeared beside him, screaming in fury, his blade cutting left and right. Sentas himself hung well back behind the lead warriors, Zanthis at his side.

Then there was another battle cry. "FOR THE REALMS!"

Through the siithe battle-line Liam saw Finn and Genna attack. They carved their way into the siithe's rear ranks, a short blonde woman fighting beside them. *Yolinda!* The rear ranks of siithe tried to turn, but that left them exposed. Kyall's men cut forward without mercy, driving through the enemy formation. The siithe lines crumbled. The battle dissolved into individual combats. Finn killed the siithe captain in a furious exchange, then met Kyall in the middle of the melee.

"Nice to see you, Kyall!" said Finn.

"I was not going to let you have all the fun!" said Kyall.

The battle turned. The siithe, now without a leader, and sensing they were losing, broke and raced for the Gateway, even though it was closed. *A desperation manoeuvre.* The Realm warriors gave chase, cutting them down as they ran. The siithe formed a defensive wall at the Gateway, no doubt hoping a Dark Thurjun would reopen it, and that they could flee. One huge warrior surged at Liam. He hardly had time to raise his sword when a crossbow bolt took the huge warrior in the eye, knocking him back off his feet. Liam turned to see Yolinda standing behind the lines, busily cranking a Vault crossbow, a quiver of bolts hooked onto her waistband.

The siithe's last defensive wall buckled and broke. Swords and falcata met in a flashing, deadly dance. Siithe fell, then Realm warriors. Eventually only one siithe remained. The Vault warrior cried out then charged at them. Genna darted forward, side-stepping the siithe's attack. His axe swept in, underneath the siithe's helm, to take the Vault warrior in the side of the head. The siithe's warcry died. He staggered forward a single step, carried by his own momentum, then fell. Stone dead.

The Realm warriors stood drenched in blood and gore, their chests heaving. Twenty of Kyall's thirty warriors had survived. One of Sentas' two retainers had fallen on the Viri world, but the other, who had fought at Liam's side, had come through with only light wounds. Both Sentas and Zanthis lived . . . their swords unbloodied.

"We won," said Liam, astonished.

Kyall sheathed his sword and greeted Finn with a rough embrace. Morin had told Liam that they had trained together at the High Court, many years ago. Yolinda stood next to Finn holding a siithe long knife. She had discarded the bulky crossbow and shifted her weight, favouring one leg. Liam saw blood on her thigh. Genna ripped a strip of rough cloth from a fallen siithe and silently cleaned his axe-blade.

"It is good to see you, Finn. But what is that ridiculous contraption on your head?" asked Kyall.

Finn smiled and unfastened the motorcycle helmet. Two crossbow bolts protruded from it like antennae. Powerful blows from siithe falcata had sliced into the tough composite, opening it in three places. "This, my friend, was the best I could do at short notice." He tossed it over to Kyall, who caught it with a chuckle.

Finn's forearm stung where an enemy blade had sliced the skin. His left foot throbbed. A siithe had stamped down on his instep during the furious melee, trying to force an opening. He had been unaware of these minor aches and pains during the fight, but now they made their presence known. It was always the same. The post-battle exhaustion would follow. He scrutinised the ranks of Kyall's surviving men. They were excellent fighters, but so few remained. Finn had been surprised to see the Earth thurjun, Liam, with Kyall, and even more surprised to see him wearing the blue robes of a High King's thurjun. The young man approached him and extended his hand.

"I'm glad you are alive, Finn," said Liam, in the Realm tongue.

Finn took Liam's hand in a warrior's clasp, gripping his forearm. He grinned. "So am I."

"I'm sorry I could not hold the Fraser Gateway open for longer."

"Well — that hardly matters now," said Finn. He released the grip. "But please tell me there is another thurjun holding the other side of *this* Gateway."

Liam smiled. "Morin."

Morin!

Relief rushed through Finn. "Ha! Excellent." It meant more than he could say to have his old mentor with him.

"This is Yolinda," said Finn. "She is one of the local guardsmen, and helped me fight the siithe." He knew that she understood the Realm tongue well.

Yolinda responded with a tight smile. Pleased at the praise

perhaps, but also a little defensive.

"We've met," said Liam in English.

Finn looked between the two of them and raised his eyebrows.

"It was Liam and Shane who took me to the lake on Fraser Island," said Yolinda in English.

"I was led there by a vision from Korbeth," said Liam.

The hairs on Finn's arms stood up. Questions rushed through his mind, but he held his tongue. He knew he would not really understand the answers anyway. Some mysteries were too deep to plumb.

Kyall joined them. Finn introduced Yolinda, then Genna. "Genna is a warrior from the Fourth Realm," said Finn, reverting back to the common Realm language.

Genna nodded briefly to Kyall, gave him one of his enigmatic smiles, then left to help the wounded.

"Liam. What of the Earth thurjun?" asked Kyall. Their plan had assumed that the Earth thurjun would be on this side of the Gateway.

"They are on the Viri world. In the Soulbreakers encampment. In a slave cage," said Liam.

"You could recognise them?" Kyall frowned.

"Yes. From Korbeth's vision."

Kyall let out a long breath, his shoulders sagging, his face flushing red. He looked exhausted. "Good . . . good. That simplifies things."

Finn met Liam's deep blue eyes, trying to gauge the young man's character. There was more to him than he had first assumed. Liam nodded to Finn, a little uncertainly, then turned to watch Genna as he knelt to examine a wound. The young thurjun seemed anxious. Liam touched the mionanail pendant that hung free around his neck. The mionanail housing was an usual deep green colour.

"I should help with the wounded. Morin has shown me some healing matrices," said Liam.

"I'll help too," said Yolinda in halting Realm tongue, which drew a surprised look from Liam.

"Yes. By all means," said Kyall.

Liam joined Genna at the make-shift infirmary by the

Gateway. Yolinda found a police medical kit and began to bandage wounds.

Kyall shook his head and sighed, sweeping his gaze around the cavern. "Finn, you should be able to get some better armour from our fallen." He smiled. "But tell me. Do you want the good news or the bad news?"

"I always like the bad news first," said Finn.

"Well there are ten thousand siithe troops waiting for us on the other side of that Gateway." Kyall explained that the Gateway led to the Viri world, inside VoYannan's Vault of Seven Horns, and described the Soulbreakers' encampment.

"And the good news?"

"We are alive!" said Kyall.

The two warriors laughed, letting the tension of battle ease.

"What now?" asked Finn.

Kyall cleared his throat. "We organise things here, then move back through the Gateway. Morin is a capable thurjun, but we have no way of knowing what he is facing. The sooner we can break through the Soulbreakers' lines and put some distance between us and the Viri city, the better."

"And then?" asked Finn.

Kyall raised an eyebrow.

"I vowed to rescue Sephany, Kyall."

"Well . . . once the Sydney Gateway is closed, our orders are to return to the High Court."

"And?" Finn's heart beat fast. He would follow Sephany's trail on his own if he had to.

Kyall grinned, his teeth bloody around a lip that had been split in the melee. "I guess we can take the long way home."

Chapter 54
Sydney, Australia — Earth

Finn closed the Earth warrior's eyes. He laid the man's hands together on his chest, and covered the ragged stomach wound with a black cloak taken from a dead siithe. The elation of victory had completely gone now, replaced by lethargy. They all felt it. They had triumphed, against the odds, but the cost had been terrible. He and Kyall had worked with the surviving warriors to honour the Earth and Realm dead. They cleaned their faces, sponged away dried blood, and covered wounds.

Finished the solemn duty, Finn walked to stand beside Kyall. They said nothing. They did not need to. Each understood. They took in the carnage around the cavern. The surviving warriors sat back in exhaustion against piled rocks and debris. Finn pushed the dark morass of post-battle miasma down into his gullet. They had to get the men moving.

Kyall cleared his throat, then gave the command. "I want all of the Vault weapons collected and brought here for destruction." All the siithe were dead. Any that lingered had been given the mercy of the blade. A swift death.

Kyall's troops shuffled to their feet, moving like old men, feeling every torn muscle and stitched cut, but they obeyed. The men began to pile the fallen siithe weapons. Yolinda moved off to help. One of the badly wounded men started to rise. "Not you," said Kyall, more softly, speaking to the three men still being treated. Two warriors had suffered deep gashes from the heavy falcata, and their sewn wounds still leaked blood through their thick bandages. The third man was Vale, who had taken a deep thrust to the stomach — a wound that was normally fatal. Genna had stitched and dressed the wound, but could do little more. Liam hovered nearby.

Liam licked his lips nervously. "I'll try to close the stomach and heal the internal damage." Liam bent down. Vale's wound began to glow beneath his touch. Moments later, Liam took his hand away.

"How is it, Vale?" asked Kyall.

Vale looked up. His face registered surprise, then joy. He stood and touched his stomach. His face lit up in a smile. "It is healed!"

Liam was visibly relieved. Beside him, Genna nodded in silent approval.

"Excellent, I would not want my best warrior out of action," said Kyall thumping Vale on the shoulder.

Finn and Kyall walked over to the growing pile of weapons.

"Liam is a talented thurjun," said Kyall.

"Good," said Finn. "We will need him."

Sentas and Zanthis stood near the pile, watching Kyall and Finn with contempt as they approached. Finn ignored the fool, Zanthis, and studied his foster-brother. For so many years Sentas had made his and Tallandra's life a misery. Once he had even feared him. Looking at him now, he saw only a weak, mean-spirited, arrogant man.

"Nice to see you, Sentas," said Finn. "I must say you are the last person I expected to rescue me."

Sentas titled his chin up in the gesture of superiority that Finn remembered so well. "Surprised to see the representative of the High King on an important mission?"

"If you want to be useful, Sentas. You and your monkey can help collect weapons," snapped Kyall.

Sentas' eyes flared darkly. Kyall stared at him steadily until he and Zanthis turned away and began to help the other warriors. "Damn fool. I never liked that overblown court-boy," said Kyall as he and Finn also began collecting weapons.

A huge pile of pulse lasers, fragmentation grenades, portable missiles and mortars — even two small portable nuclear weapons — were gathered. Next to the pile was a stack of police firearms, most of which Finn recognised. With the last weapons gathered, the company stood together in a loose circle.

Finn walked over to Liam. "Tell me, how is Morin holding off the rest of the siithe legion?"

"He has raised a Shield and will maintain a dampening field as well. As long as no Dark Thurjuns are brought against him, he will be safe."

Finn was deeply concerned for Morin, but changed the

subject. "I fear we are too late to keep Sephany out of VoYannan's hands. She would have already passed through to VoYannan's world." Finn was silent for a moment. "But one step at a time. We have a siithe legion to contend with. I am sure between you and Morin we will be able to slip through their ranks."

Kyall waved at the pile of police weapons. "What are these?"

*

Liam looked down at the weapons. He recognised the assault rifles as Colt M4 carbines, although he had never seen one before. Dark, compact, and lethal. Capable of semi-automatic fire or three-round bursts. The handguns were Glock 17s. There were a few Heckler & Koch submachine guns, one tactical shotgun, and a dozen grenades.

"The larger ones are rifles. The smaller ones are called handguns. They fire projectiles. Bullets," said Liam. He ejected the magazine on a Glock and pulled back the slide to eject the bullet from the chamber, snatching it from the air. He handed it to Kyall.

"Yes. I see," said Kyall examining the bullet. "Simple, but effective. We have seen similar systems before." He handed the bullet to Finn who turned it this way and that in his fingers, then tossed it back onto the pile, where it clattered through the tangled metal.

Sentas smiled, his eyes measuring Liam. "They look like Vault weapons to me. One of each type should be taken back to the High Court for study. If Earth *is* a Vault world, we need to know everything we can about it."

Liam's stomach flipped. "Earth is no Vault world."

Yolinda watched the exchange with concern.

"Well. Not yet," said Kyall. "But Sentas is right. We should take some of these for study. They look basic, but you never know."

Sentas picked up a grenade, a handgun, and an M4 rifle. "As the High King's representative, it is my duty to convey these to the High Court."

Kyall nodded. "Very well."

350

"I also need half your men, Kyall," said Sentas.

"For what?"

"I intend to explore this . . . Shadow World . . . of Earth. The Court will need to know if it poses a threat. At least one Gateway from this world gives access directly to the Realms."

"True. But when and *if* Earth is studied, that will be a matter for the High Court. Our mission was to seal the Gateway," said Kyall.

"The Gateway is sealed," said Sentas smoothly.

"Morin is on the other side of that Gateway!" snapped Finn. "While we bicker he could be in danger."

"I am still in tactical command of this mission," said Kyall. "If you want to cart those lumps of metal all the way back to the High Court, Sentas, that is your affair. But once these other weapons are destroyed, we are returning back through the Gateway."

"And what of the Earth thurjun who opened the Sydney Gateway?" asked Sentas. "My father was quite specific. He must be located and brought to justice."

"The Earth thurjun who opened the Gateway is in the siithe encampment. In a slave cage," said Liam.

"So you say," said Sentas.

"You saw for yourself that the Gateway was being operated by Dark Thurjuns, Sentas. The krell keep their rarest treasures by their side. That man is on his way back to VoYannan's court — you can be sure of that."

"Woman," said Liam, his heart a lead weight. They all turned to him. "The Gate-opener was a woman."

Yolinda's eyes glistened with some inner conflict. She knew something, Liam was sure of it, but she kept silent. He had been surprised by her ability to follow the Realm speech, but had not had an opportunity to question her on it.

"Perhaps this woman has a thurjun's talent. But who is to say if she was the one who let Procarrus enter Earth? Perhaps someone else opened this Gateway for the Vault." Sentas' eyes flicked to Liam.

Liam drew in a sharp breath, hardly believing what he heard. A hot denial sprang to his lips, but Finn got in first.

"You are a snake, Sentas," said Finn, his eyes hot with fury.

"Liam at least fought the siithe. You and Zanthis did not even bloody your blades. Do not think I am the only one to notice your cowardice." A new tension gripped the warriors.

"Silent! Both of you!" ordered Kyall. "This is no time for accusations."

Sentas was unmoved. He gave Finn an insincere smile and handed the police weapons to Zanthis. Liam was uneasy. Sentas was up to something. And there was something way too familiar about his mocking smile.

"Liam, can you destroy these?" asked Kyall, his sweeping gesture including both siithe and Earth weapons.

"How is it usually done?"

"A thurjun will usually melt them in fire," said Finn.

"But won't they explode?" asked Liam. Then he remembered Morin's destruction of the handgun that Shane had taken from the siithe.

Kyall smiled. "Not with the dampening field in place." A Realm dampening field was still in place, powered by the mionanail in Finn's sword.

Of course.

"You better all stand back," said Liam, remembering the first time he had created Ball of Fire.

"Vale," said Kyall, indicating that the Earth weapons should be moved onto the pile of siithe armaments. The job was swiftly completed. Then Yolinda and the Realm warriors backed off.

Liam took his time constructing the matrix. He centred it on the weapon pile, tethering it in place. A small trickle of power still ran from his mionanail to the light-globes, drawn by the living matrices. He drew more power, steadily feeding the new matrix. A fireball erupted in place around the pile of weapons. Intense yellow, it had a diameter of around three metres. It was as bright as the sun — and as hard to look at. Heat radiated outward in waves, prickling sweat across his face. The lasers and firearms glowed red, then yellow, then finally melted, as though they had been dropped into a blast furnace. The grenades and missiles ruptured like rotten fruit and dissolved. The nuclear weapons liquefied and diffused into the molten mass, the fissile material dropping below critical mass as their remnants diluted. Liam released the spell and the Ball of Fire vanished, leaving nothing but white-hot slag.

Yolinda looked at Liam in awe. She walked over to him. "I don't believe I just saw that," she said in English.

The glowing mass groaned and cracked as it cooled, heat sucked away by the stone.

"What happened to the Liam I met on Fraser Island?" she asked, looking at his robes.

"I guess you could say I have discovered my talents," he said.

Liam saw her wounded leg. "Let me heal that."

Genna had drawn out the broken bolt and bandaged the wound. He gently unwound the bloody bandage to reveal a nasty puncture, made ragged by the bolt's broad head. He was quicker with the matrix this time. More focussed. The deep tissue knitted, then the lips of the wound drew closed, finally leaving a thin scar. She touched it, eyes wide. She blinked.

"So these Realms are real?" she asked.

Liam nodded. "As real as you and me."

"The last twelve hours have been . . . a whirlwind." She shook her head. "All this time, Finn has been telling me the truth." She bit her lip, then shook her head. A familiar look of determination returned. "What are you going to do now?" The question was almost a challenge.

"We have to return to the other side of the Gateway," said Liam.

She took a deep breath and let it out slowly. "I guess if I want to fight the siithe — and Procarrus — I'll have to come with you. I need to see these Blessed Realms, and these Vaults of Sheol, for myself."

Chapter 55
Court of VoYannan — Vault of Seven Horns

Xyth's gaze lingered on his master.

Since the passing of his Seed, VoYannan had sat unmoving, lost in the dreamscapes of his subjects. Sitting on his dark throne, he might have been a statue, carved from cold, unforgiving stone. The slight rise and fall of his slimy abdomen was the only sign of life.

Xyth was VoYannan's new High Priest. Supreme Loremaster of the Vault of Seven Horns. The ultimate position of power beneath VoYannan. Despite the untimely, and violent, demise of Hoor, Xyth still had to battle three of his fellow veyr Loremasters to take Hoor's place, two of whom he had reduced to mindless husks before dining on their power-saturated flesh. Now he waited with seven other veyr Loremasters for VoYannan to awaken. Each was a priest of the krell, a veyr male drone, preserved by VoYannan through the centuries, and gifted with extra life. Throughout his death-like rest, his Loremasters had stood vigil, waiting to answer their master's call. They could wait for days without moving, content to sup on the blood stored in their swollen abdomens. Around the room, the siithe warriors also waited, yet their hunger was growing.

Beneath the throne, the krell's court writhed in agony and pleasure. Xyth could sense VoYannan drawing power from them and others across the Vault of Seven Horns, trying to rebuild the reserves he had lost with his departed spawn. VoYannan had lost control, drawing too much power from the Vault. Now his hold on his remaining servants was weakened.

Xyth's mind wandered. His earliest memories were of the darkness and hunger of the hive. He would join the vast swarms that ranged through the Shadow Worlds, virtually alone amidst the mass of infertile female veyr, their minds focussed only on blood. Then came the day a Loremaster of VoYannan's court chose him from amongst the throng. A glorious day.

Xyth was troubled. The feasting had been good. The omens, however, had been bad.

A thick layer of grey mucus began to ooze from the joints in VoYannan's armoured hide, and the huge eyes opened. The green irises floated on a sea of bright, angry red.

VoYannan straightened on his dark throne.

Across the room, screams of horror rang out as the dreamers awoke. The siithe warriors waded into the packed mass of bodies, dragging away the dead. More than half of the court had perished. VoYannan had drawn deep.

The krell looked at Xyth.

"Where is Hoor!" demanded the krell.

Xyth trembled. "Destroyed by yourself, Lord, for his impertinence," hissed Xyth in his most placating tone.

VoYannan blinked. "Of course."

"I, Lord, am your new High Priest," said Xyth, spreading his wings and bowing low.

"Well then, Xyth, how grows the Spawn?"

"Magnificently, my Lord VoYannan. It should be fully grown and ready to rip its way free within a month. The energies you injected, and its repast on the priestess' soul, allow it to swell with bounteous life."

VoYannan made a harsh grating sound, which Xyth knew was laughter. He remained impassive. Like his brothers, Xyth was for the most part untroubled by emotion. He knew hunger, the exhilaration of victory, the satisfaction of the blood feast — and fear. It was fear that Xyth felt now. Fear that he would end up like his brother Hoor, smashed to the stone at VoYannan's feet. Still, the hunger kept him in place, and the prospect of a swift death outside the span of the Vault, without the energies that kept him alive.

"The Realm priestess could not resist VoYannan," said the krell. "And now my Spawn will grow to sit at my side. Not a single world will resist my power once I have harnessed and subjugated another krell to my will."

Xyth tried to still his thoughts, fearing they would betray him. VoYannan still had no conception of the vast energies he had wasted trying to break Sephany's will — only to force the Spawn on her anyway. VoYannan would need to grow strong indeed before its birth if he hoped to subdue the young krell.

VoYannan turned to Xyth. "Show me the omens!"

Xyth bowed. "We have recently cast the omens, my Lord. They are favourable! The Spawn will grow strong!"

"Show me the omens!" thundered the krell.

Xyth waved forward his human priests. They drew a hulking male slave between them, heavily drugged. Swiftly, they cut open the man's stomach. The slave screamed as they pushed the starved lizard into the cavity.

Blood sprayed in a huge fountain, striking the krell across his horned head.

Xyth hardly dared to move.

The slave fell to his knees, still screaming as the lizard fed. In a surge of manic strength, the man reached inside his own stomach and drew out the lizard. The lizard's tail whipped out across the slave's face, laying it open, and the razored claws tore at the flesh of the man's arms — but he did not feel a thing. The handlers rushed forward, but they were too late. The slave, summoning all his remaining strength, gripped the lizard in his huge hands and snapped its spine. With his last remaining strength, he forced himself to his feet. Blood sheeted down his legs. He hurled the lizard at VoYannan. The body of the animal fell short, but, inexplicably, it landed in a neat sprawl, the head pointing directly at VoYannan, the tail stretched out behind it. Before either the handler-priests, or the siithe, could reach him, the slave collapsed. Dead from blood loss.

Xyth waved a human priest of the First Tier forward.

Esseth was short and thick-bodied, his short greying hair unkempt. His skin glistened like hot wax. He walked around the dead slave, examining the stains of blood, drawing on the essence of the reading. A cape of human skin, stained deep red, billowed out stiffly around him. The Loremasters shared the power of VoYannan, but had no skill in divination. This was the domain of the priests of the Seven Tiers. The energies involved were delicate, and should the krell try to interfere, the reading would be destroyed. Xyth unobtrusively linked his mind with Esseth to share the reading.

Esseth's dark eyes fixed onto the pattern of blood and drew it in greedily. He saw a warrior of the Blessed Realms standing before VoYannan in chains, then the Angel of Destruction — it must be Balos — slain by a spoken word. Moving along the line of blood he saw the Spawn growing to strength in a distant place, the chains that bound him to VoYannan shattered. A wave of death and chaos spread outward from the Spawn. A great war was coming, and the future was balanced on a thread. In one future the Realms would fall . . . in another everything VoYannan hoped to build would be laid to waste.

It was as Xyth feared — no leash would hold the Spawn now. It would remain an uncertain weapon in their hands. Everything was in peril. They would need allies to turn the tide.

Esseth's eyes widened in fear.

"Speak!" demanded VoYannan.

Xyth stepped forward to take control as Esseth fled to the shadows. One wrong word, and Hoor's fate awaited him. He needed to find another target for VoYannan's fury.

"The handlers have failed to drug the slave properly. This has given us only a . . . partial omen. They have failed you, my Lord."

VoYannan's eyes widened. The krell raised his hand. The handlers fell to their knees, gasping like stranded fish. They shuddered as VoYannan drew every last shred of energy from their bodies. They collapsed. The krell drew in a breath of pure pleasure, feasting on their souls, then quivered as the energy flowed deeper into him. The horns on the krell's head slowly retracted, and he sank back into his throne.

"Now tell me, Xyth. What did Esseth see?"

"Good omens, my Lord! A warrior of the Blessed Realms will lie in chains before you. The Spawn will grow strong and its enemies will fall before it!"

"What of the death of the lizard?"

"It foretells the death of enemies, my Lord," replied Xyth smoothly. *The enemies of the Spawn.*

VoYannan waved Xyth back into his place behind the throne. Then he returned to his slumber.

Chapter 56
Viri world — Vault of Seven Horns

Liam took a sip of water from his canteen to clear his throat.

He shifted in the saddle, trying to ease his back, but the movement only sharpened the pain in his inner thighs, which had previously subsided to a dull ache. He sucked in a sharp breath, choking on dust, but could not afford to waste another sip of his carefully rationed water. *Damn it.* He screwed the canteen closed and fixed his gaze ahead. It was a stark landscape, devoid of vegetation, full of sharply eroded peaks and lakes of bubbling acid. At least it was cooler in the heights. A relief after riding in baking heat across dead plains of cracked, rock-hard clay the colour of blood. For two days their mounted troop had sawtoothed up an endless series of hills, steadily climbing, drawing closer to the Dark City. The Vault metropolis housed a Gateway to VoYannan's home world, and was their passage into the heart of the Vault of Seven Horns.

The deep rumble of distant thunder shook the air. Liam looked up to see dark storm clouds rolling in under the ever-present high cloud cover, staining the dirty orange sky. The planet's red sun was hidden by the high cloud, and it was impossible to discern its position in the sky.

"Here we go again," said Liam.

Morin, riding beside him, moved his horse closer.

The lowering clouds soon covered the whole sky, plunging them into gloom. They travelled on in silence, moving deeper into the Vault. Then the deluge began. Sheets of black rain pounded them, soaking their clothing. Clouds of crimson vapour rose from the ground, stinging their eyes. They pulled thick cloths up from around their necks to cover their mouths, allowing them to breathe in the suffocating mist. Liam's horse whinnied in fear. He drew a damp cloth from his saddlebag and tied it over his horse's head, covering the eyes. The mounted line slowed to a walk as they guided their horses blind through the mist. *Now we wait it out.*

They had emerged from the Sydney Gateway to find Morin

safe and well, alone with hundreds of dead siithe. In their absence, the Realm thurjun had pushed the Vault troops from the Gateway ruins with a series of magical assaults, sealing the whole tower with a powerful Shield. The siithe legion was still camped outside the tower, but with the Dark Thurjun dead and the Gateway in Realm control, they had attempted no further assaults.

They slipped through the siithe lines in the dead of night. There was no pursuit. Even the Vault troops feared the wild veyr. They sent a messenger through the Kess Gateway to the High Court, then made for the Dark City. Kyall and Finn were united in their determination to rescue Sephany, although Sentas had argued vehemently against it.

"Our mission is finished," Sentas had said, fuming at Kyall's decision to send Sentas' retainer as a messenger to the High Court, instead of one of his own elite warriors.

"True. So now we are free to help Finn," replied Kyall.

"My father said nothing about rescuing Sephany. If she is already inside the Vault, she is as good as dead."

"We don't know that, Sentas," said Finn.

Morin stepped forward. "What we have to ask is, 'Why is Sephany so important to VoYannan? Why go to all this trouble, just to capture one priestess?'"

Sentas had ground his teeth together in frustration.

"Because, somehow, she is vital to VoYannan's plans," continued Morin. "We *must* counter him. And . . . we cannot abandon her."

"I am the representative of the High King," said Sentas. "I order you to return to the Court!"

Kyall and Morin exchanged a glance.

"Kyall and myself have ultimate control of strategic decisions, Sentas. Or have you forgotten your father's own decree?" asked Morin.

Kyall stabbed a finger at Sentas. "We are in the Vault now. This is where the real fighting is done. If you have no stomach for danger, you and your lackey can return to the High Court."

Sentas' eyes bored into Kyall's with a murderous gleam. Kyall ignored the implied threat, clearly not intimidated by the prince.

But it had chilled Liam. He had recognised that gaze. The calculating look that promised things to come. It was Shane. The *dark* Shane. The one who had murdered his friend and taken his place. In that moment he knew it. The siithe Shade was inside Sentas, and it was growing in power.

A movement startled Liam, bringing him back to the present. He looked to his right and saw a horse approaching out of the mist. He squinted, trying to glimpse the rider, but could not see them. Their horse was coming fast though, and yet was making no sound on the rocky scree. He saw another horse. Then another. Too many to be from their own force. A shock of alarm gripped him.

"Morin! *Riders!*" called Liam, through the thick wadding. Morin turned. Even as Liam spoke, he realised he was wrong. They were not horses at all. They ran with a sinuous movement, and had dark hides, and huge, luminous eyes.

Shadow Hounds.

Before Liam could shout another warning, they attacked.

Chapter 57
Viri world — Vault of Seven Horns

Liam watched their mounted column dissolve into chaos. The horses had scented the Hounds. Warriors yelled warnings and warcries and tried to form a line, but the Hounds came from everywhere, shielded by the mist until the last moment. Horses screamed in pain as the beasts' razor sharp teeth tore into their flanks and throats.

A dark shape cannoned into Liam's mount, sending him flying. He landed hard on the sharp, unforgiving talus with a shock of pain. He lay winded, choking on fumes, eyes burning. The wadding around his mouth was gone. A Shadow Hound darted for him. Huge, elongated jaws ready to rip open his face. He reached for his sword, but it was pinned beneath him. He tried to clear his mind to form a matrix.

It was too late.

There was gunshot. The beast's head jerked back. It staggered, then collapsed. Then Yolinda was beside him, her left hand holding a cloth over her mouth while her right hand gripped her Glock. A second beast charged in. Yolinda swivelled. Sighted. Fired. The bullet ripped through the side of the creature's face. It yelped in pain and fled into the mist. *Not always silent, then.*

"Thanks," said Liam.

"Don't mention it," said Yolinda. "It's nice to be able to do something for a change. That damn field they generate disables my gun."

Yolinda helped Liam to his feet. The Hounds had gone. Warriors stumbled on the uneven ground as they searched for their scattered mounts. Many horses lay dead, others had been dragged into the mist by the Hounds, who had also taken their own dead.

Two shots rang out. Liam and Yolinda looked at each other in surprise.

"Who the hell is firing?" asked Yolinda.

Liam and Yolinda ran through the mist, along the line of

warriors. All around them, men were trying to find each other and remount. The clouds grew thick, then cleared.

Sentas stood over the body of Kyall. The Realm warrior had his sword in his hand, but was laying face down on the stoney ground. The prince was smiling, but his eyes were dark and dead. He was holding one of the police assault rifles he had taken from Sydney. Zanthis stood beside him. Sentas calmly handed the weapon to Zanthis, who hid it under his cloak.

Finn rushed out of the mist, three warriors behind him. Soon they were joined by more warriors, then Morin and Genna. Finn rushed to Kyall and felt for a pulse.

Zanthis slipped into the mist.

"No!" Finn looked up in disbelief. "He has no pulse! Morin! Genna! *Quickly!*"

Finn, Morin, and Genna began to strip away Kyall's armour. Two holes had been punched into the back of his breastplate, right at the heart. The clothes underneath were soaked with blood.

"By the High God," said Finn, his voice breaking.

"He was shot in the back," said Genna. The dark-skinned warrior shook his head. "He is gone, Finn. Kyall is dead."

"And there is the murderer!" said Sentas, pointing at Yolinda.

Yolinda's jaw went slack. She looked down to the pistol in her right hand.

"Did I not tell you these Earth people could not be trusted?" said Sentas.

Everyone looked at Yolinda and Liam. Then at the gun in Yolinda's hand.

"It's a lie!" said Yolinda, responding in Realm speech.

Liam turned quickly to Morin. "Yolinda is telling the truth! She shot two of the Shadow Hounds, but when we arrived it was Sentas who was standing over the body, with one of the rifles from Sydney in his hands."

Finn spun around. His eyes fixed on Sentas, and his face twisted with fury. He reached for his sword.

Morin seized Finn's hand, stepping between him and Sentas.

Sentas was unperturbed.

"If what this *spy* says is true, then where is the weapon?"

asked Sentas calmly. He turned to Finn. "As the High King's representative, I demand that Yolinda and Liam be arrested!"

Some of Kyall's warriors moved on Yolinda.

"Hold!" shouted Morin. "Torren put Kyall and myself in charge of this mission. No one will be arrested until I say so." Morin walked across to Yolinda and extended his hand. "Give me your weapon." Yolinda reluctantly handed over the pistol. Morin immediately turned to Sentas. "Where are the weapons you took from Sydney?"

"I have no idea. Perhaps Zanthis may know."

"Zanthis was here before," yelled a warrior.

"Sentas gave the rifle to Zanthis. He has it," said Yolinda. Her accent was thick, but her meaning clear.

"It's true!" said Liam. "He hid it under his cloak, then slipped away into the mist."

"All of you! Sweep the perimeter. Find Zanthis and the weapons from Sydney. Find what horses are still alive and gather them together," commanded Morin.

The warriors ran into the mists in groups of three to five. Minutes later, a warrior returned leading Zanthis. Then gradually the other warriors began to return with the horses.

"Where are the Earth weapons?" demanded Finn.

Zanthis' face was unreadable. "They were on one of our packhorses. It panicked and ran into the mist when the Hounds attacked."

"How convenient," growled Finn. His eyes never left Sentas.

"Finn, come over here with me," said Morin, leading Finn away from the group. "You too, Liam."

When they were out of earshot, Morin looked between Finn and Liam, then spoke in a low voice. "This is a tragedy, but we have to consider the situation carefully. We have only a handful of warriors left alive, and we are arriving at the most perilous part of our journey. We are planning to enter the Dark City and pass through a Gateway into the heart of the Vault. *VoYannan's own world*. For this we will need every warrior we have. Taking Sentas will mean taking Zanthis, Jonas, and Kar, as well. Then detailing at least two men to guard them. That would be six less swords. Six less warriors to fight our way to Sephany." Morin looked steadily at Finn, who nodded grimly. "On top of this, Kyall's men are seething with anger at his murder. Some of them would not even consider that the High King's son would be capable of such an act. Unfortunately, Yolinda is the natural one to hold accountable. Perhaps exactly as Sentas intended."

"We cannot let Sentas go free," said Finn. "That vile, arrogant bastard murdered Kyall out of spite. Because he stood in the way of his own ambitions. I cannot stand aside!"

Morin bowed his head. "Finn, if you care about Sephany. If you trust me. I ask you to wait."

The muscles in Finn's jaw worked. His eyes glistened with tears of rage.

Morin laid a hand on Finn's shoulder. "Come," he said softly.

Liam, Finn, and Morin, rejoined the main group.

"Here is my judgement," said Morin, looking around sternly at the assembly. "When we return to the High Court, it is the Seekers who will find the truth of this. Have no fear that whoever murdered Kyall will face the full wrath of Torren's Court," he said, looking right at Sentas. The prince returned the gaze with dark, triumphant eyes. "Liam is a thurjun of the High Court. I will vouch for him."

Morin turned to Yolinda. "I am sorry. But you will have to be bound."

Yolinda began to protest, then held her tongue.

The rigid tension in Realm warriors eased. The crisis had been averted.

"We should bury Kyall before the Shadow Hounds return," said Morin.

Vale and another Realm warrior reverently stripped Kyall's body of weapons and armour, then carried him into the mist.

"Wait!" called Morin, picking up Kyall's longsword, sheathed in its beautifully crafted scabbard, the ends of the sturdy sword belt and its heavy buckle dangling. It was a Realm weapon, and like Finn's, had a mionanail in the hilt. It was priceless. Morin held it out. "Bury this with him." It was the least they could do to honour Kyall. And here, in this desolate place, there was no risk the weapon would fall into the wrong hands.

Finn walked up to Sentas. "These men may be blinded by your

position, Sentas. But when we return to the High Court, I will see you hang for this. Not even Torren will be able to protect you."

Sentas laughed. "Small words from a small man. Who cares what some country commander thinks? Do not forget what you are, Finn. Nothing. You have no power at Court."

Sentas' words had no effect on Finn.

"I am not some trainee fresh from the provinces, Sentas. I know who I am, and what I do. I fight the Vault. I fight evil, Sentas. Wherever it finds a way to crawl into our worlds. Mark my words. You will pay for Kyall's death."

Sentas' smile faded, now genuinely irritated. He looked at Finn again, as though noticing him for the first time.

"Why should I pay for anything? I did not murder Kyall."

Finn took a deep breath and walked away.

Liam followed him. "Are you alright, Finn?"

The Realm warrior shook his head. "Walking away from Sentas, leaving him free after what he did to Kyall . . .?" He grimaced, as though swallowing something bitter. "That was the hardest thing I have ever done."

Liam was shaken. Kyall had been larger than life. His sword skills extraordinary. To have survived the impossible odds of their fight with the siithe, only to die at the hands of Sentas . . . it was impossible to accept.

All Liam's fears about Sentas had been borne out. He just hoped the prince's vendetta ended with the death of Kyall. He was unsure what lay ahead for them, but knew enough to realise that once they reached the Dark City, enough danger would be waiting for them already without adding the possibility of betrayal.

Chapter 58
Viri world — Vault of Seven Horns

Finn edged to the crest — and laid eyes on the Dark City for the first time. Infamous throughout the Realms, the city rose from the centre of a vast, lifeless plain. An endless expanse of eroded canyons and sinuous rivers that extended to the dirty horizon. The rivers that snaked through the plain were dead things. Open sewers that carried away the Dark City's filth. The Dark City itself was an ugly metropolis of concrete, glass, and steel, surrounded by vast dockyards. Thousands of spacecraft rested there, blunt sculptures of dark metal that bristled with turrets and antennae. Some of the craft were smaller than a house, others the size of a city block. Spaceships blazed up through the dirty sky in muffled roars of fusion power, while others manoeuvred down through the choking clouds to land in torrents of superheated gas and driven dust. An unending stream of pillage came to the Vault of Seven Horns from all corners of the krell's domain, and the Dark City was its greatest gateway.

Finn watched the roads leading to the Dark City and the ceaseless vehicle traffic they carried. Personal wheel-craft in every shape and colour raced along those blackened arteries, belching fumes as they wove between armoured troop carriers and Vault tanks. The military transports were all of the same design, bulky and cheap, cranked out in Vault factories, their front cabins and boxy rear compartments constructed of the same black metal sheeting. The squat, ugly Vault tanks that guarded them were dull grey, each designed with enough shielding to withstand the shockwave and radiation of a nuclear blast.

Finn slithered back from the crest and faced his waiting warriors. Yolinda, bound at the wrists, glared at him in silent challenge.

"Time to move," said Finn, avoiding Yolinda's gaze.

The Earth policewoman was still furious at being forced to stay behind with Jonas and Kar, who had been once more relegated to the care of the horses and equipment. Finn had originally given the duty to Sentas and Zanthis, but Sentas had pretended outrage and demanded to join Finn's expedition. Finn was surprised that Sentas would willingly endanger himself by entering the Dark City, and knew the prince must have some other reason for doing so, but try as he might, Finn could not guess at it. He had, reluctantly, agreed. It would give him a chance to keep an eye on Sentas . . . even if the sight of the prince's smug face made his heart burn with rage.

Finn led his force out of the steep, hidden valley. They scrambled over the rough ground until they neared one of the lesser-used roads to the Dark City, which passed through the hills here. Finn had identified a sharp bend ideal for an ambush. He carefully positioned his men and waited. Morin and Liam had swapped their thurjun's robes for plain clothing, while the warriors covered themselves with heavy hooded cloaks that concealed their armour and weapons.

Three troop carriers and a small armoured vehicle rolled by, their heavy rubberised treads grinding into the gravel surface of the road. A few minutes later a large transport came into view. It was moving fast and bouncing on the road. *Mostly empty. At last some luck!* Finn nodded to his men, then stepped out into the road. He raised his sword. The transport immediately lost power as the Realm field surrounded it. It shuddered to a halt. The driver ducked for cover, disappearing below the sill, as they ran for the vehicle. One of the Realm warriors tried to smash his sword pommel through driver's window, but it bounced off the bulletproof glass.

"Stand back," ordered Morin.

The old thurjun's face creased in concentration. An instant later, the glass exploded. Shattered by Morin's Blow of Force.

The door was wrenched open and the driver dragged out. The warriors dumped him on the verge of the road, two standing guard while a third swiftly bound and gagged him. The doors to the rear compartment were thrown open. Inside were six human slaves. They were in miserable condition, and cowered as the warriors approached. They began to cry out in a mix of incomprehensible languages. Morin and Liam used their thurjun's skills to calm them, reassuring them through direct mental contact that they would not be harmed.

Finn cut off the flow of power from the pommel mionanail. The dampening field faltered, then vanished. "Everyone into the back of the vehicle. Take the driver too. Liam and Morin, with me."

The Realm warriors, dragging the hapless driver, filed into the rear, shutting the doors behind them. Finn led Liam and Morin into the front cabin, then sat staring at the unfamiliar controls, trying to remember all he had been taught about Vault technology.

"Should I go back and get the driver?" asked Morin.

The sound of distant rumbling filled the canyon. On the vehicle's console, a video display showed an image of the road behind the transport. A long column of siithe troops were approaching. It looked to be a full Vault legion. There were hundreds of troop transports, nine Vault tanks equipped with laser cannon, and scores of support vehicles.

"By the High God," swore Finn.

"It is the legion from the Sydney Gateway," said Morin. "They are returning to the Dark City."

It was too late to get the driver. If they left the cabin, the siithe in the lead troop carriers would see them. Finn's hands worked over the console in a desperate fever as he tried to get the vehicle started.

The leading troop carrier reached the rear of the transport and skidded to a stop in a cloud of dust. Curt commands blared from a loudspeaker in the Vault tongue. The voice was distorted. The tone unmistakable. *Move or die.*

"Let me try," said Liam. The young thurjun swapped places with Finn and studied the controls.

"These Vault vehicles have internal combustion engines, right?" asked Liam.

Finn shrugged.

"There's no key slot . . . but the ignition . . . " Liam scanned the console.

A second warning boomed out. The laser turret of the leading tank jerked toward them, then adjusted its elevation. It locked into position. Finn swallowed. His fist tightened on his sword's pommel.

Liam tried a few buttons experimentally. Finally, as he hit an amber switch smeared with grease, Finn heard the high whine of a starter, followed by the cough of igniting fuel, and then the droning vibration of a big motor. A surge of relief swept him. *Now, Liam. Get us moving.*

"There's no steering wheel," said Liam, looking at a series of seven levers in front of him. "The largest two must be for steering. Then this one . . ." Liam lifted a small lever. The transport lurched forward. Using the two large levers, Liam steered the transport off the road, then eased off on the acceleration. The vehicle slowed to a stop, and the engine stalled. Behind them, the siithe column started moving.

"What are you doing!" snapped Finn.

"Letting them pass," said Liam. "I don't want them behind me all the way to the Dark City."

"Good thinking," said Morin. The older thurjun's breath was harsh, and sweat beaded his brow.

The Vault tank rumbled past, followed by a troop carrier. The rear doors of the transport were open, and filled with armoured siithe. They waved their weapons and shouted obscenities as they passed. More troop vehicles overtook them, then another Vault tank, the laser turret swivelling to keep them in its sights. The laser lingered on them, then, when its line-of-sight was blocked by the convoy, swung forward again. For twenty minutes they waited as the column roared past. Then, finally, the road was empty.

Restarting the engine, Liam manoeuvred the Vault transport onto the rough, gravel road, and followed the siithe troops down through the hills. Finn blinked sweat from his eyes.

Hours later, they merged onto a highway of dark, stained concrete, and picked up speed. Buildings appeared in the bleak landscape, and they were forced to slow on the outskirts of the Dark City as the traffic grew heavy. There were no road rules, and no lines of paint. If there was a gap, it was plugged by speeding vehicles, going in *either* direction. The noise and fumes filled the small cabin, swirling in through the shattered pane. Gradually, they were swallowed by the dark metropolis. The siithe troop column turned off the highway and disappeared.

"Keep going. Make for the centre of the city," said Finn.

Liam nodded and steered carefully through the dense traffic.

"Can you feel it, Liam?" asked Morin.

"Yes," said Liam. "It's like a beacon of power in the darkness."

Finn tried to sense it using his own thurjun's abilities, but could feel nothing. He smiled wryly.

"That's the Gateway to the Vault of Seven Horns. It has been open for millennia, like the ancient primary Gateways of the Realms," said Morin.

"Steer toward it," said Finn.

The crowds grew as they neared the city centre. A mix of races, many wearing slave-collars. Siithe patrolled everywhere. Lights and signs flashed in every colour of the rainbow, and aircraft darted overhead, flitting through the towering buildings like bats through a maze of stalactites. They rolled on. The crowds thickened, and they were forced to a crawl. Finally, they turned a corner and entered a wide plaza that swarmed with creatures, and was lined with tall, concrete and glass buildings, all housing heavy weapon emplacements. In the plaza's centre was a monolithic Gateway. It was rectangular, its two tall columns capped by a flat lintel stone. Through the Gateway, Finn saw a dark world, ruddy with light from an orange sun. Vehicles and people, even aircraft, passed in and out of the portal in an unending stream. They passed a gauntlet of siithe troops and Vault officials that controlled the traffic. Transports, flying craft . . . all crept forward under the ever-present threat of those big weapons.

"Turn into one of those alleyways, then stop the vehicle," said Finn.

Liam manoeuvred the transport to the curb, using its bulk to push aside a small mountain of trash. Men and women emerged from the pile and scrambled for cover as it mounted the curb, then shuddered to a stop. They hurled insults, but none of them dared approach. Liam let out a long breath then turned off the engine.

Finn patted Liam on the shoulder. "Well done."

Finn, Morin, and Liam clambered out of the cabin and opened the rear doors. Finn's warriors, and Sentas and Zanthis, all jumped down. They locked the six slaves and the driver inside, then crossed the busy street to the plaza, blending into the crowd. It hurt Finn to leave those poor men and women to their fate, but he made his heart stone. This was war. An ancient war for the Realms very survival.

They joined one of the lines inching toward the Gateway. Most of them were slaves, eyes downcast, carrying bundles, or chained together in large groups. They ignored the cloaked Realm travellers. Finn, Liam, and Morin, stayed at the head of the group, the other warriors following behind. Sentas and Zanthis were at the rear.

An hour later they were still waiting. They had reached the centre of the plaza and could smell the sulphurous air of the krell's home world billowing out of the colossal Gateway. Twice their whole line had been forced aside to make way for siithe convoys.

Finn looked back across his group, checking everything was in order. Sentas and Zanthis had been cut off, and were now separated from them by a group of slaves guarded by ten siithe warriors. "What in the name of the Vault is Sentas doing?" whispered Finn harshly.

Morin looked back. As he and Finn watched, Sentas and Zanthis fell even further behind. Others, eager to pass the portal, pushed ahead of them.

Finn met Sentas' eyes and waved him forward.

Sentas smiled.

"I am going back there," said Finn.

"*Do not*. We cannot draw attention," said Morin.

The line was moving faster now, and Finn's group were within a hundred paces of the Gateway. Three armoured troop carriers were positioned nearby, along with six laser cannon emplacements. Finn estimated there were around a hundred siithe warriors, as well as three veyr, whose dark insectoid eyes swept over each of the travellers as they approached the Gateway. There were *eight* Dark Thurjuns. A stab of fear sent Finn's heart racing.

The line surged, and suddenly they were at the Gateway. In seconds they would be on VoYannan's world. A siithe officer approached, studying the cloaked warriors. His dark face cruel.

Impassive.

"What is Sentas doing?" Finn snatched a glance behind him. *"We are going to pass through without him!"*

Sentas reached inside his cloak. Finn's heart clenched as he felt a Realm dampening field sweep the plaza.

No!

The building lights cut out instantly. Vehicles rolled to a stop, some slamming into others ahead of them through sheer momentum, their brakes inoperative. The drivers emerged and began to shout at each other. Two fights broke out. The siithe advanced. The commander barked orders. One of siithe held up a monitoring device, stabbing a finger at its dead display.

A dark shadow grew across them. Then another.

One by one, aircraft plunged into the packed crowd.

There were no explosions, just a series of crashing impacts, followed by terrified screams. The crowd panicked. Sentas and Zanthis ran with them, sprinting from the plaza. The Realm field faded, but not before another three flying craft plummeted down. Two slammed into buildings. Concrete and glass exploded outward.

One of the veyr Loremasters rose from his repose.

The veyr towered above the siithe. He swept his gaze across Finn and his group and raised a thin hand. "Open your cloaks," he hissed in the Vault tongue.

In an instant they were surrounded by siithe warriors wielding falcata. Finn measured the odds. They were heavily outnumbered, but if they were taken now, they would never leave the Vault alive. Sephany would be lost. They *had* to try and escape.

Finn threw off his cloak and drew his sword. "Make a break for the Gateway!"

Once more a Realm field swept across the plaza, but this time no craft fell from the sky, and the huge open space was empty except for Vault warriors. Finn could hear the sounds of a convoy in the distance. More siithe warriors approached. There was nowhere to turn.

They formed a fighting line and tried to break through the siithe ranks and into the open Gateway. Morin and Liam both sent a Balls of Fire racing toward the siithe, but the fireballs discharged against a solid, invisible wall. The Dark Thurjuns ahead of them bowed their heads and joined their power. A black cloud spread slowly toward them. Finn could see Morin and Liam struggling to combat it. For a moment they succeeded, then it passed through their combined defences and engulfed them all.

Finn's sword was torn from his grasp.

Savage blows rained down on him. Armoured fists. Heavy boots. His head slammed into concrete. A weight of stinking siithe pinned him down. Cold metal stung his skin. Shackles clicked shut on his wrists and ankles. He heard the rattle of heavy links.

Chains.

They had been taken by the Vault.

Chapter 59
Viri world — Vault of Seven Horns

Sentas pulled his hood down as the black rain fell.

He cursed this desolate world, and its dangers, and would be glad to pass the portal and begin his long journey back to the First Realm. Yet in a way, he would miss it. For it was here, in this barren wasteland, that he had been reborn.

Sentas led the mounted column, riding Kyall's tall gelding. Zanthis beside him. Jonas rode behind, one hand holding the reins of Yolinda's horse. The Earth guardsman had her hands tied. They had also blindfolded her, but somehow she had worked the broad cloth free over one eye, and it now crossed her face on a slant. She was watching him. Kar followed behind her, leading a long string of horses. No point in leaving such valuable horseflesh in the Vault. And Finn and his men certainly did not need them. Sentas chuckled. What a sad tale he would have to tell when he reached the High Court. The tragic loss of Kyall at the hands of the Vault spy Yolinda. The loss of Morin, Finn, and the remnants of Kyall's force to the Vault. His own heroic escape from the Dark City, thanks to his superior fighting skills, and tactical supremacy. Yes. Rousing material.

Zanthis looked pale and miserable.

"Cheer up, Zanthis. We will be at the Kess Gateway soon. Then we will have all the comforts of the Tower at our command."

Sentas felt stronger than ever. While travelling through the Viri world his thinking had become steadily clearer. Kyall had always been a problem, and yet for the whole journey from the High Court, he had been struggling for a way to subvert him and Morin, and take control of the mission. From the moment that pathetic Earth man, Shane, had died, everything had become so *obvious*. Why had he not thought of simply killing Kyall before? Getting the Earth weapons and laying the blame on Yolinda had been brilliant. Abandoning Morin, Liam, Finn, and his lowbred warriors to the Vault had been a masterstroke.

"Yes, my prince," said Zanthis, but without enthusiasm.

Sentas frowned in annoyance. Zanthis' behaviour was beginning to grate on him. The man had been out of sorts since Sentas had dispatched the transport driver and the six slaves. The fool had even had the nerve to protest at his action, and at Sentas' extended use of the knife, rather than providing a quick death by sword. He never thought Zanthis would become so squeamish. Who cares about Vault scum? Besides, Sentas had enjoyed their pleading . . . and their screams. He shivered in remembered pleasure. A vista of new experiences was opening up before him. He had been so blind!

Sentas refused to let Zanthis' weak spine ruin his ebullient mood. Everything was *finally* falling into place. Leading a Realm force to Earth would give him the support he needed to supplant his father. Based on all he had learned from Shane, Earth would provide him with an easy victory. Their weapons, equivalent to the most basic Vault technology, would be easily neutralised. Up until now, he had been prepared to bide his time. But now he knew the way. It was so simple! Yolinda, the spy from Earth, would once more kill for the Vault. This time it would be the High King.

Sentas could taste it. The sweetness of ultimate power. For too long he had lived in his father's shadow.

The rain intensified. Once more, the acid mists rose. *One thing I will not miss about this world.* Sentas pulled the kerchief around his neck up over his nose and mouth, then pulled a single layer of the thin material over his eyes. It restricted his view, but provided some protection. Zanthis copied him.

"Make sure the horses are secure!" Sentas ordered Kar, his voice muffled by the cloth. The horses already had their heads covered, but were unsettled by the sulphurous stink.

Jonas reached to cover his face. Still leading Yolinda's horse with his left hand, he had to drop his own reins and use his right hand for the action. It was awkward one-handed, and he fumbled the first attempt. Cursing at the acid sting on his skin, he raised his left hand — the one holding the reins to Yolinda's horse — to help adjust the rag. The reins slipped from his fingers. The Earth woman immediately yelled and urged her mount forward with her thighs and heels. Her horse, already unsettled by the stinking rain, lurched into a trot. In seconds, Yolinda, and her mount, were both swallowed by swirling mist.

Sentas reined in. "Fool! After her! You too, Kar." The long line of horses came to a halt "Incompetents! Why am I surrounded with them?" he said to Zanthis.

Zanthis did not reply.

They waited in silence, alone in the mist. Remembering the Shadow Hounds, Sentas drew his longsword and ordered Zanthis to do the same. Dark shapes emerged, and they both stiffened, ready for an attack, but it was only Jonas and Kar, leading Yolinda's horse. The saddle was empty.

"We found the horse, my Lord, but she was gone. Her hands were bound. If she fell, she would have landed heavily," said Jonas. "She is likely injured."

"Easy prey for the Hounds," added Kar.

A cold anger gripped Sentas. "With any luck she has broken her neck." He felt like killing Jonas, just to be rid of his pompous face, but Sentas needed him. For now. After they returned to the High Court . . . well that was another matter. So many things would change then.

"We will leave her behind," said Sentas.

A lone woman, bound and unarmed, would soon perish in the Vault.

*

Her room was dark, lit only by a dim orange lamp.

Hours passed, inside a shadow-world of dream. She saw visions of conquest, of darkness and murder. Sometimes she would sleep — the deep sleep of the exhausted — yet would wake to an overwhelming lethargy.

As she sat on the edge of her narrow pallet, swaying from side to side, her awareness of self dawned slowly.

"Who am I?"

There was no answer from the nightmare landscape of her mind. Fear rose then, but she gently held it to her, like a lost child, and let it fade away. Thoughts and images bit and tore, an angry flock of carrion birds, screeching and cawing in their frenzy. Loud and insistent. Demanding she attend their madness. She did not. Instead, she embraced silence. Her lips moved, forming the words to a prayer that came unbidden to her lips. Peace descended. Knowledge rose.

Sephany.

That is who I am.

A priestess of the High God.

But she was more than One. She was also Two. She looked down at her huge, swollen belly, watching as the Other moved beneath her skin. She knew him now. He was the dreamer of conquests. *A krell spawn.* Inheritor of an aeon of memory from his progenitors. She felt the tendrils of the Spawn reaching inside her, draining her blood, and health, even as his embryonic mind clawed at her soul, draining joy and will. A pulse of energy rose from the Spawn into her mind, and once more she felt herself descending into a dissociated state, a land of dreams where the Spawn would feed on her mind and soul.

Sephany forced herself to stand. Her legs quivered.

The Spawn twisted viciously, sending waves of agonising pain. The muscles around her womb cramped, doubling the agony. *Pain, I can deal with.* Sephany rose above it, her mind sharpening as she focussed her perception. It was the attack on her soul that made her truly afraid. When she was weak, her mind confused, the Spawn could reach into her soul, drawing away its bright substance. That joy was lost to her, leaving dead, empty space. This was the greatest rape of all. It frightened her as nothing in the Vault had before, not even VoYannan. Her very core was feeding an abomination.

She focussed on the prayer, losing herself in a timeless moment. VoYannan had taken her body, but he had never taken her faith. A white light flared in her mind, and with her second sight she could see it transforming the room around her, surrounding her, filling her. The Spawn grew quiescent. Its tendrils withdrew, and her heart soared as the reaching talons of its mind left hers.

She heard the door latch click.

Sephany opened her eyes. Balos stood in the doorway. He sensed the presence of the High God and did not enter.

"What is the matter, Balos? Afraid?"

A wave of red light rippled through Balos' frame. "I fear nothing."

The seraphin advanced. The guards outside her chamber closed the door behind him. The light of the High God surrounded Balos, and he trembled. The red light faded from his dark frame.

"If you fear nothing, Balos. Then why do you serve the krell?"

"I choose to. VoYannan is an ally."

"Yet when VoYannan commands, you obey. Is that not servitude?"

The seraphin remained silent. Motionless. Features dark and unknowable. He could have been a statue, carved from obsidian.

"Why did you leave the Realm of the High God, Balos? What does VoYannan offer you that the High God cannot?"

"The Realm of the High God is cold. His will is absolute. There is no passion. No fury. We destroy his enemies without emotion or judgement." The red nimbus grew around Balos once more, swelling to engulf his frame. His body rose up off the floor, and behind him six ghostly wings appeared. "VoYannan showed me the glory of combat. The joys of destruction. That is power. Warm and hot. That is life and colour."

"There are other passions, Balos. Other joys."

"What other passions?"

The light of the High God surrounded her, and she felt no fear. She stepped slowly toward Balos.

The glowing red sheath around Balos shrank as she approached, and the seraphin's body lowered to the floor.

He backed away. "What are you doing?"

"Are you afraid of a single touch, Balos?"

The seraphin immediately stood his ground.

As Sephany approached, the red light that had sheathed his form vanished entirely. Gently, Sephany laid a hand on the smooth, dark muscles of his arm. He felt cool, like marble. "There are passions and joys that create, rather than destroy. Love. Friendship. These can bring people together and strengthen the soul."

"Soul?"

"The heart of your feeling, Balos."

A golden light, hardly visible, even in the gloom, lit around him. "What other joys?"

"The joy of beauty. The joy of self-sacrifice. Giving yourself for others."

"But do you not hate VoYannan for what he has done? Would you not see him destroyed?"

"No, Balos. I forgive him. Hate will not heal me."

Balos swept forward. Sephany closed her eyes, expecting a death-blow. Part of her yearned for it. Yet no blow came. Instead, when she opened her eyes, Balos was kneeling at her feet.

"Teach me."

Chapter 60
Court of VoYannan — Vault of Seven Horns

Yolinda bit back a yelp of pain as she bent to pick up the food tray, the partly healed wounds on her back pulling tight.

She took a deep breath and straightened. The Overseer of Kitchens watched her every move with a leering gaze. Twice she had fought off his unwanted advances. The first time she had thrown a dish at him — which had narrowly missed his head — and he had ordered five lashes. The second time she had broken his nose with an elbow. Then he had given her twenty lashes himself, opening the flesh of her back. The next time she would have to kill him. Then she would be on the run.

She hurried through the labyrinthine corridors of the Citadel to VoYannan's court, carefully balancing the tray. So far she had managed to fool them, but time was running out. She had to find Finn. *Fast.* Evading Sentas and his pet lords had been easy, as had entering the Dark City and attaching herself to a slave gang in order to pass the portal. Following Finn had been a little more difficult, but she had always known where he was headed. VoYannan's Citadel. The Vault of Seven Horns' heart. A shudder ran through her as she remembered walking into the palace two days ago. One of the insectoid veyr, flanked by senior siithe captains, had stopped her as she slunk through the dark corridors looking for the dungeons.

"Who are you?" The veyr had demanded in the Vault tongue. Ever since her time in Procarrus' court, she had retained an understanding of the rough, guttural speech.

Yolinda had looked up at the veyr in silence. The Loremaster had leaned forward and placed a long forelimb on her head, the razored talons of his narrow hand draping over her crown to rest on the skin of her right cheek. She did not flinch as the points pierced her, even when blood trickled from the wounds, warm on her face and chin as it trickled down. As with Procarrus, Yolinda felt the invasion of a foreign mind. As before, she had hidden from the probe, retreating into her mind's depths, always one step ahead.

"She is a simpleton," pronounced the veyr, lifting his hand from her head. "Hardly sentient at all."

The veyr turned to a siithe captain. "Take her to the Slavemaster. She has obviously wandered away from her detail." The eyes of the siithe flickered over her, and he smiled, running a slimy tongue over his sharp, pointed teeth.

The siithe captain took her by the wrist and dragged her deeper into the palace. Out of sight of the veyr, the siithe pushed her into an alcove and started pulling at her garments. Yolinda acted dumb, letting him haul her to the ground. Her heart hammered inside her chest. She knew how hard siithe were to kill. In one swift movement, Yolinda drew a long stiletto and drove it all the way to the hilt, low in the siithe's abdomen. Finn had taught her a little about siithe anatomy, and she knew this was where their two hearts were. The siithe stiffened, and reached for his discarded falcata. Yolinda stabbed him again, through the other heart, then danced away. He slumped to the ground, then grew still. That was the first rape attempt.

Eventually, she was taken to the Slavemaster by a roaming siithe patrol. The Slavemaster, Axil, was a huge human, twisted by his long service to VoYannan. Over seven feet tall, he towered above her. The Slavemaster at first questioned her in the Vault tongue, then tried again in several other languages, one of which was the Realm tongue. Somehow, Axil detected a flicker of recognition.

"Oh? From the Realms? You are a long way from home. And so pretty too."

Axil ripped open her blouse and pawed at her breasts. Surrounded by siithe warriors and a score of other slaves, Yolinda endured it. Then Axil signalled for his attendants to strip her naked. She watched, terrified, as they took her stiletto. Axil turned her around, running his coarse, dirty hands over her skin.

"Too pretty to waste in the siithe pits. You can serve in VoYannan's court. Then I'll have you myself."

Yolinda steadied the tray. She paused for a moment to steel her mind, then entered VoYannan's court. She hunched forward, her eyes down as though she saw nothing more than the floor's dark stone, while she looked sideways from beneath her lowered eyelids. Her instructors in the Federal Police would never have dreamed their lessons in undercover surveillance would be applied on another planet, in the court of an immortal warlord. The muscles of her back bunched with tension as she saw that the krell was awake. The alien was huge. VoYannan projected a sense of menace that made the breath catch in her throat. Her legs trembled, until an answering fire ignited inside her, pushing strength outward from her core. A group of prisoners had been pushed to their knees before his throne. She could see no more than the tops of their heads through the crowd of naked bodies. She looked away. Yolinda had seen this before. First he would torment them, then he would drain the most defiant until they were lifeless husks. The rest would be thrown to the mercy of the siithe — ripped apart in the food pits.

Yolinda pushed her way through the bodies, adjusting her posture to remain unobtrusive. Unseen. As she worked her way closer to VoYannan's throne, she got her first view of the prisoners. She jolted to a stop.

Finn!

She forced herself into motion, but could not take her eyes off Finn. His face was bloody and bruised, but unmistakable. She tripped on a dreamer's twisted leg and lost her grip on the tray. She cried out as it fell. Immediately, a siithe backhanded her to the ground. Apart from that, she was ignored. Liam, Morin, Genna, and the rest of the Realm warriors, were there. Yolinda fought despair.

They would never leave the krell's court alive.

Chapter 61
Court of VoYannan — Vault of Seven Horns

Finn stared into VoYannan's green, mucus-filled eyes.

Heavy shackles bit Finn's wrists and ankles. Dark chain pooled around his knees. He tasted bile at the back of his throat and tried to swallow. The room's stench was overpowering. The fiend responsible for his family's destruction sat above him on a raised throne while he and his warriors were forced to kneel. For so many years he had dreamed of justice, of leading Realm armies against the Vault, freeing the enslaved millions crushed beneath the krells' cruelty. Instead, it had come to this.

VoYannan leant forward on his dark throne. "The son of Evenstone kneels before me. Captured with no less than two Realm thurjuns. What an unexpected gift." The krell's voice was deep and powerful. Charismatic. Almost hypnotic. Finn had not expected that. To look at, the krell was all the horror Finn had envisaged. The armoured grey bulk, glistening wetly in the dim light, the wedge-shaped head with its overlarge eyes and rows of yellowed horns. Those horns now slowly extended as the krell gloated over them. "My Dark Thurjuns will make good use of your devices . . . many Realm warriors will be consumed by their power."

Finn glared at the krell.

"Where is my Archfiend!" The krell's voice reverberated through the room.

"I am here, my Lord." Procarrus pushed through the ranks of siithe warriors and emerged from the dark smoke that swirled across the room. Finn pulled at his chains, unable to keep himself still any longer. His siithe captor gave him a warning growl and Finn dropped his arms. The dreamers of the court, naked and trembling, parted to let Procarrus through. The Archfiend advanced to VoYannan's throne, a hideous man-beast shambling along at his heels. The beast's gleaming yellow eyes bored into Finn's. It opened its jaws, showing rows of rending teeth. Finn's heart skipped a beat as it started toward him, its eyes fixed on his throat.

"No, Barsus," commanded Procarrus.

The hound froze, then returned to his master.

"Here, Procarrus. I give you the last son of Evenstone. A reward for my greatest servant," said VoYannan.

Finn looked up and met Procarrus' eyes without fear. His face and ribs throbbed where the fists and boots of the siithe had hit home. His knees were numb with the cold seeping up from the stone. All that was nothing compared to the pain of being forced to kneel *here* of all places. Finn's rage at Sentas' betrayal had passed now. Such things can happen in war. The important thing was that he had not flinched from the fight. For a time he had feared he would be trapped on Earth, but he had won his way free. Together with Morin, Liam, and Kyall's warriors, he had closed the Viri Gateway to Sydney. The Stonelake Gateway to Fraser Island was also secure. An unknowing Earth had been saved from the Soulbreakers and all the horrors of conquest. Millions of innocent men and women now lived because of their actions, and millions more kept from abject slavery. Together, they had thwarted the will of the krell and *that* was what mattered. The Realms would survive, strong and free. His heart tore at the thought of Sephany's fate, but perhaps there would be another warrior of the Realms to take his place and continue her rescue. He clung to that hope.

Procarrus smiled and drew his longsword. A swift, efficient movement. "I shall enjoy this, my Lord. A pity the sister is not with him."

Finn swallowed. This was it. The time of his death.

"Finn," said Morin.

He turned to his old mentor. Morin's face was also bruised from their beatings at the hands of the siithe. Beside Morin, Liam was white with fear, his own dark bruises livid against his pale skin, yet when Finn met the Earth thurjun's eyes, he saw only strength and determination there.

The Archfiend raised his sword, licking his dry, cracked lips in anticipation.

"Finn, I am proud of you," said Morin. "You have been my best pupil. My . . . son," Morin's voice broke. "I hope to know you in another life."

Finn returned the ancient death-greeting of the Realms. "I too Morin. I hope to know you in another life."

Procarrus' sword drew back. Finn looked up calmly, ready for death. *I'm sorry Sephany.*

"Wait," commanded the krell.

Procarrus reluctantly lowered his sword.

"I can sense in his thoughts that Finn led his warriors here to rescue the Realm priestess. I want Evenstone to see my bride before he dies. To know how he has failed." *Failed* . . . that last word boomed like a death knell. "Bring her."

His bride! Finn would never have dreamed that the krell would take Sephany for his own. *To . . . use her . . . to plant his spawn . . .* His mind recoiled in horror. Finn surged against the chains. He gained his feet. Ready for one last fight. A siithe casually elbowed him in the side of the head, driving him back to his knees. With a supreme effort of will, he reined in his fury.

Finn turned away from the krell, as though he could shut out this stark reality by looking elsewhere. He scanned the crowd of naked onlookers who cowered beneath the throne, searching for something, *anything* — and looked straight into Vespar's eyes. The thin, ascetic thurjun had changed beyond all recognition, yet Finn still knew him. The betrayer had been etched into Finn's memory since that night. His face had grown elongated, a roughly-drawn caricature of the one he remembered, with drawn eyes and open mouth. His back was bent over like an ancient's, while his genitals had grown enormously. Unlike many of the dreamers, his eyes were clear and free from insanity. They seemed to plead with Finn, perhaps asking for forgiveness. Vespar would receive none. Finn studied the pathetic group that cringed around the ruined thurjun, and his heart grew cold. Was this the fate of Morin and Liam? Would they cower here, naked and warped beyond recognition? Playthings and tools of the krell? He would not wish that on anyone, not even Vespar. Finn fixed his gaze on the stained floor and tried to focus.

He heard a surprised cry and the sound of plates crashing to the floor. He turned to see a siithe knock a slave-girl to the ground. Yet another senseless act of cruelty. His rage grew, once more swamping his calm. The Vault *had* to be stopped. Once he had thought he would be the one to destroy VoYannan, but it was not to be. His eyes lingered on the girl. *There is something familiar . . .* Finn was trying to puzzle it out when the room lit up with bright golden light.

Sephany entered.

Chapter 62
Court of VoYannan — Vault of Seven Horns

Sephany was flanked by siithe warriors, but they kept their distance, wary of the golden seraphin close beside her. Her face was drawn and white, her long dark hair lank and matted. Even so she walked with pride. He longed to fight his way to her. He felt a fierce satisfaction that VoYannan had not broken her spirit. Finn saw the swollen stomach, and with a sickening lurch, knew his worse fears were confirmed.

"You, bastard!" yelled Finn, levering up from his knees at VoYannan.

Procarrus rammed the heavy bronze pommel of his longsword into Finn's face, breaking his nose and sending him sprawling back into Morin and Liam. "Mind your tongue, Evenstone. You will die soon enough. Be thankful I grant you an honourable death, with your soul intact. VoYannan would not be so merciful."

"It is Balos. The Dark Seraphin," said Morin, voice raw and husky.

"My, God," said Liam, his jaw slack as the awesome creature approached.

Finn shivered. For years he had endured nightmares of the seraphin, visions of terror in which the dark form of Balos, sheathed in red, came for him, flying up the stairs of Evenstone Tower in a fury of destruction. He had never forgotten his mother's last cry of outrage . . . or the terrible screams of his brothers. Yet Balos had changed. The red nimbus replaced with gold.

The whole room was spellbound as Sephany approached the throne. The seraphin's golden light cut away the darkness, revealing the vaulted ceiling's ancient, carved stone.

Sephany smiled at Finn, her eyes full of compassion.

"By the High God, Sephany. What has he done?" asked Finn.

"Have no fear for me, Finn. I just wish you had not endangered yourself. It saddens me that more good people will have to die to feed the Vault."

Finn looked up at the krell, burning with hate.

"Yes," said the krell. "That is more like it. I think he understands now, Procarrus. It is time for him to die, and for the priestess to see what becomes of our enemies — and how any attempt to rescue her will end."

Procarrus raised his sword once more.

"No. Use the Axe of Evenstone. Let him die beneath the blade of his ancestor," rumbled the krell. "Close the circle. Use the instrument of our ancient defeat to seal our new victory. The first of a new era."

Two hulking siithe now pinned Finn's arms. He struggled in their grasp, to no avail.

"Balos," commanded the krell. "Fetch the Axe of Evenstone."

Golden light flared around the seraphin. "I am no servant to be sent on errands."

The krell was startled by Balos' reaction. He studied the seraphin for a long moment. "Your raiment has . . . changed, Balos."

Balos remained silent. Implacable.

"Very well," said the krell, waving at one of his siithe captains. "Fetch the Axe." The siithe lumbered into motion, leaving the room at a trot.

One of VoYannan's veyr Loremasters stepped close to the krell's throne and leant down to speak. His wings quivered in agitation.

"What is it, Xyth?" asked VoYannan.

"Master. You should not tolerate such insolence in your own throne room, even from your Champion." The veyr spoke in a furtive hiss, his sibilant voice only heard by those close to the throne.

"I can do as I please, Xyth. Be gone."

Xyth trembled, but held his ground. His jewelled, insectoid eyes fixed on Balos. "My, Lord. Your servants are bound to you by your strength. For most of your thralls your . . . shedding . . . was of no consequence. But Balos is mighty."

"Are you saying I cannot command him?" asked the krell.

"The change in his nimbus is a sign of his returning will."

"Impossible," snapped VoYannan.

"Remember how difficult it was to subdue him on the battlefield. Balos was beaten down by the power of no less than six Vault starships. Even then we could do little but imprison him in the Citadel. It took us years of careful manipulation to sway him to the Vault. You must test him. Immediately!"

The krell grew very still. His eyes glistened. For a moment they lost their focus. When they returned to acuity, his eyes burned with terrible intensity. "BALOS. COME. KNEEL BEFORE ME."

Each word boomed. Each hit Finn like a punch to the gut. He had been touched by the merest edge of their force, yet he still felt his own body begin respond against his will. Siithe and thralls alike shuffled closer to VoYannan. The dreamers came on their knees. Finn clenched his fists and fixed his feet to the stone.

Balos remained motionless. "I kneel to no one."

"You defy me?" More than a hundred pulse lasers turned on Balos. "I am the krell lord, VoYannan! I am your master."

"I am Balos! I have no master."

Balos moved in front of Sephany to protect her from the lasers.

Just then, the Vault warrior returned with the Axe of Evenstone, heading for the throne. The serving girl, forgotten amid the naked crowd, sprang up from the floor. She drew a long-bladed knife from a siithe's belt, danced through the reaching arms of the Vault warriors around her, and leapt onto the back of the siithe carrying the Axe. He grunted in surprise at the sudden weight. Before the Vault warrior could even turn, she rammed the long blade into his eye socket. Dark blood sprouted from the wound. The siithe howled and dropped the Axe, raising both hands to his ruined eye. The slave-girl's hair swung back from her face as she slipped off the siithe's back.

Yolinda!

She snatched up the Axe and ran at the two siithe holding Finn. Yolinda grunted as she cut up into the face of the nearest siithe. It was an awkward blow with a heavy weapon. Lean muscle corded through her whole frame. The siithe bellowed in surprise, and released Finn's arm as he flinched back from the great gleaming blade, which would have sliced through his face had he not moved. The other Vault warrior also let go, stepping back to draw his falcata. Yolinda hissed as she tried to control the Axe, its massive head dragging her off balance. Procarrus attacked, the elegant longsword snaking toward Finn's neck. Genna threw up his chains, trapping the weapon. Procarrus cursed and began a wrestling match with Genna to free his sword. All around Finn, Realm warriors surged to their feet, grappling with their siithe captors. They surrounded Finn with a shield of bodies.

"KILL THEM!" thundered the krell.

The siithe warriors in the room, who had been momentarily stunned by the turn of events, now jerked into action. They turned their pulse lasers on Finn and his group, but their aim was blocked by the Vault warriors who struggled with Finn's men, one of whom was Procarrus. Once they had a clear field of fire, Finn knew that he and his friends would die.

"Finn, hold out your arms!" yelled Yolinda.

Finn stretched the chain taut. Yolinda lifted the Axe and swept it down. The ancient blade sliced straight through the bulky locking mechanism of the shackle at Finn's left wrist. The dark metal bracelet opened and fell to the stone. Yolinda cut again at his right wrist. The Axe rang like a silver bell as the second shackle and its trailing chain fell away.

"Take it!" Yolinda threw him the Axe. It turned in the air, its huge cutting head making it spin. Finn's eyes widened. His hand shot out. He felt a flood of relief as its metal haft slapped into his palm. He gripped it two-handed and cut away his ankle chains with two precise blows.

A siithe clubbed a Realm warrior aside and ran at Finn. The huge siithe — who had been Finn's guard — lunged with his falcata. Finn locked blades with the warrior. The siithe tried to force him back and Finn found himself in a contest of strength. He heard a growl, and looked across to see Barsus shoulder through the struggling ranks and race at his undefended legs. *For the love of Lugh!*

Although weaponless, Yolinda darted in. She kicked the hound savagely in the side. Barsus skidded to a stop, then spun to face her, teeth bared in a fearsome snarl. The hound stalked toward Yolinda. There was nothing Finn could do to help. One false move and the siithe he fought would have him. Slowly he forced the siithe's falcata down as Yolinda desperately looked around for a weapon. Her eyes fell on the knife protruding from the eye of the dying siithe who had fetched the Axe. She dived for it, but Barsus was faster. He hit her in an avalanche of muscle and fur, bearing her to the ground. The hound snapped at her neck. Yolinda put up her arms to protect herself. The beast's teeth sank into her left forearm. She shrieked in pain.

One of the naked dreamers at the foot of the dais, a shrunken woman with an unnaturally lengthened face and shrivelled breasts, ran forward. She tugged the knife free from the siithe's eye socket and darted in. She rammed the blade into Barsus' groin, pulling it back to stab again and again. The beast stiffened, then howled. Barsus rolled off Yolinda, the siithe knife still embedded in his scrotum. Blood gouted from the wound. It spattered red across the stone. The hound stumbled.

"Vicki!" said Yolinda in surprise.

Barsus rallied his strength. His eyes lit on Vicki and he growled. The big muscles of his haunches bunched. He sprang. The huge jaws closed around Vicki's neck, and with a last surge of strength, he twisted sharply, snapping her spine just below the base of the neck.

"No!" yelled Yolinda, as the hound collapsed on top of Vicki's twisted corpse.

Yolinda ripped the knife from Barsus' groin and rammed it into the side of his head, burying it to the hilt. The hound quivered, then lay still, eyelids fluttering closed over his dimming yellow eyes. She tore the weapon free and turned, her face a mask of fury. Lean muscles rippled in her lithe frame, the slave dress baring her slim legs and midriff. Her eyes narrowed as she saw Finn wrestling with the siithe. She ran in. No hesitation. *None.* Finn's heart surged with admiration. She was fearless. The siithe grunted, and tried to turn away from her advance, but Finn held him in place. With both hands on his trapped falcata, the Vault warrior could do nothing, not even bring his weapon down to block as Yolinda thrust the long knife into his side. A perfectly placed strike that angled up underneath the base of his studded leather breastplate and skewered one of his two hearts. The siithe froze in pain, and his strength ebbed. Finn circled the Axe, breaking the hold, then batted away the falcata. He cut down through the gap. A savage strike that split the big siithe's skull in two. He twirled the Axe with a flourish. Dark blood flicked from the shining blade.

Finn went on the attack. He killed two siithe warriors with throat-opening slashes, then slew another with a quick lunge through the eye using the Axe blade's flared tip as a stabbing weapon. The rest of the Vault warriors fled, Procarrus with them. He felt one moment of triumph before he realised what that retreat meant. The shield of bodies was gone. They were exposed.

Bolts of red laser fire lanced through the chamber, shining lurid through the smoke. Two Realm warriors fell, their torsos cut through, their mouths open in silent screams. Procarrus ripped a laser rifle from the hands of a siithe and sighted it on a warrior shielding Finn, who tried to pull the Realm warrior out of danger, but was too slow. The energy burst cut up through the warrior's left side, opening up his torso and severing his arm. The Realm warrior fell screaming. Procarrus re-sighted the pulse laser. Aiming directly at Finn. In the split second before the Archfiend fired, Vale leapt in front of him, taking the full force of the blast. Vale fell without a sound.

All around the room, thralls began to wail. It was a hopeless sound. A terrible sound.

"The krell is drawing power!" yelled Morin.

VoYannan rose from his throne. "BALOS! I COMMAND YOU TO DESTROY THEM!"

Chapter 63
Court of VoYannan — Vault of Seven Horns

Balos trembled.

The seraphin's aura shifted from bright gold to orange, then flickered, before returning to a dull gold, his power diminished, but not broken.

Finn reached for the Axe's mionanail. For one terrible moment he feared it was empty, that it had been drained by the Vault, but then he was rewarded with a surge of power that lit up his mind like summer sunshine.

A Realm dampening field swept out.

The siithe weapons went silent. Procarrus screamed in rage and threw the laser to the chamber floor with enough force to shatter its metal frame on the stone. The power cell bounced clear.

"Falcatas!" commanded Procarrus.

The siithe hastily drew their heavy, cleaver-like weapons.

Finn used the pause to cut Liam, Morin, and the surviving Realm warriors free. The Axe, an ancient Realm weapon, sliced through the Vault steel with ease. Each time it sang with that same silver chime. A beautiful clear note.

"Follow me!" Finn launched himself at the siithe guarding Sephany. The first Vault warrior barely had time to raise his blade before the Axe sheared through his abdomen, cutting up on a diagonal to exit from his right shoulder. He batted away the blade of the second siithe at the end of the same rising arc, then cut back, taking off the second Vault warrior's head. He darted in, stabbing the rising point of the blade straight through the throat of another siithe. Fury boiled in Finn's guts. A whirlwind of vengeance rose up through the Realm steel of the Evenstone Axe as though the ancient weapon had merely been waiting for this moment. He would not leave Sephany to face this horror alone. They would die together. Free and unbound. Realm warcries rent the air. He did not need to look behind him to know that his warriors had taken up fallen siithe weapons and formed a fighting line at his back.

The siithe before him retreated, while Procarrus rushed in

from the flank with reinforcements. Sephany was close now, only three steps away, but Procarrus would reach her first. Finn's warriors were falling. His own final stand was coming, he knew.

Procarrus shouted an order at the two siithe warriors guarding Sephany. "Take her back to her cell!"

The siithe started to drag Sephany away. Finn's heart sank . . . then something astounding happened. Balos' dark limbs swept out, smashing the two siithe guards from their feet. Their twisted bodies spun to the floor. Spines shattered. Procarrus, eyes wide, slammed to a stop. The Vault warriors behind him also halted. In a single moment, the battle had turned.

Finn surged in. He cut at the last two siithe between him and Sephany, the Axe shearing through them both at the waist. Their severed torsos jerked and slid to the floor in flood of dark blood. He stopped in front of Sephany. He looked up at the tall seraphin warily, not daring to touch the Priestess, lest he share the same fate as the last two Vault warriors who tried.

"Sephany. Come quickly," said Finn.

She came to his side. He tensed, expecting at any moment to face the seraphin's terrible onslaught, but, incredibly, the creature let him lead her away.

"Balos has given them Sephany!" yelled Procarrus.

The air around the krell shimmered.

"Xyth, stop them!" roared VoYannan.

Xyth and his Loremasters joined their power. An ink-dark cloud gathered, roiling above their heads. It thickened, then swelled out toward the embattled Realm force, expanding like a living creature, its tentacles racing ahead of its swirling core.

Finn stopped dead. His breath came in great gasps, his muscles only now registering the monumental effort of wielding the heavy Axe. His warriors formed a fighting circle around him and Sephany. There was open space around them. The dreamers of the krell's court had fled the fighting. The twisted creatures watched, alert to the horror, as far away from the sharp blades as they could get.

Think!

Only a Realm thurjun could contain that dark, numbing cloud. *"Morin!"*

Morin had seen it. "The Axe!" he called back.

Finn extended the Axe toward Morin, who put his hand on the haft.

"Liam. Join me!" yelled Morin.

Liam came to Morin's side. He put his hand atop Morin's.

Finn saw movement. He tensed, expecting another attack, but it was not Procarrus, or the siithe. It was a group of naked thralls that had been cowering at the base of the krell's throne. They rose as a group, and slunk toward them, crouching beneath the rising cloud. *Vespar.* With six others. *What is this? Some strategy of the krell's?* But when Finn looked back at VoYannan, he saw that the krell lord was locked in a silent battle of wills with the Dark Seraphin.

Finn felt Liam and Morin join their power. Matrices bloomed in Finn's inner vision as Morin took control, but his Sight was too narrow to follow the loops and turns, which formed and coalesced at frightening speed. He felt the Shield as it came into being, dropping like a dome over their fighting circle. The dark cloud hit the unseen barrier. Its tentacles swam around the circular Shield until they reached its far side, where they wove together, then *tightened.* The Shield trembled, then contracted. Liam hissed in effort. The young thurjun's eyes bulged as he tried to balance the flow of essence from the mionanail, the white sclera around his deep blue iris' threading with red as capillaries burst from the effort. The Shield buckled, but Morin — somehow — reformed it. Through the Axe, Finn could sense the titanic struggle. *The Loremasters are too strong.* The Shield would not hold. Morin staggered, and Finn steadied him, taking his arm.

"Press them!" ordered Procarrus.

Siithe warriors flooded in from all sides. Procarrus stalked in behind his advancing troops. His cold blues eyes fixed on Finn. Devoid of mercy. The seven thralls reached the edge of their fighting circle ahead of the siithe. In moments they would be caught between the Shield and Vault blades.

"Let us help," said Vespar from outside the circle.

Finn's guts churned as he looked at Vespar. He fought disgust at the sight of the naked, twisted beings gathered with the Realm traitor.

Vespar's eyes pleaded. "You cannot match the Loremasters with two thurjuns. For the sake of what I once was. Let us help. We are . . . we were . . . thurjuns who fought the Vault and lost."

Finn's heart burned with frustration. If not for Vespar's weakness, and his betrayal of Evenstone Tower, Finn's family would be alive today. His father, his mother, his brothers. He would have grown to manhood surrounded by hearth and family. Finn bit his lip, tasting blood.

"Quickly! While VoYannan battles Balos we can stay out of his control," pleaded Vespar.

"Finn. We have no other choice," said Morin.

"Let them in!" ordered Finn.

The circle parted, the Shield opening to admit them before slamming back into place.

The stinking, crooked things crowded around Finn, reaching. Nine thurjuns gripped the Axe of Evenstone, all drawing on the power of the ancient mionanail. The Shield strengthened, pushing back the Loremasters' dark spell.

VoYannan bellowed in rage. The krell abandoned his struggle with Balos and leapt down from his dais. He waded through the ranks of the siithe, throwing them aside like sacks of wet paper. The power in VoYannan's squat armoured frame was terrifying.

The siithe closed on them. The Vault warriors hammered at the Shield, knowing that every blow drained the mionanail's power. Behind their ranks, Procarrus watched. Waited. The Realm warriors, exhausted and bruised, readied themselves to fight, although if the Shield fell, they were all finished.

VoYannan roared. Finn was momentarily stunned by the blast of sound. The huge krell flew at them, driving through his own warriors like a battering ram.

"*Mother of God!*" Liam gasped.

"Make for the exit," gasped Vespar. "Blow of Force. Then Arrow in Flight!"

The Shield vanished.

The Loremasters' black cloud swarmed them, driving into their minds like acid, obscuring sight.

Finn heard the boots of the siithe. Tensed for the first blow.

Morin drew a Matrix. All nine thurjuns channelled power into it from the Axe's mionanail. The air shimmered as something vast, yet barely glimpsed, exploded outward. *Blow of Force.* The wall of siithe in front of them became a mass of tumbling limbs, armour and steel. Thralls were thrown aside. They crashed into each other, into stone, into the siithe. Then the veyr Loremasters, safe until now behind the krell's throne, were smashed from their feet. Their black cloud vanished. Another running column of siithe were pulverised as they tried to enter the chamber. The huge chamber doors behind them, already open, were slammed back against the wall on either side.

For an instant, a wide path lay open.

Finn was lifted into the air, drawn up into an invisible cocoon of force. Then they *all* lurched into flight, Realm warriors, thurjuns, Vespar's twisted escapees, all accelerating *fast*. Thralls shrieked. Siithe bellowed. VoYannan's voice thundered as he flew toward them, horns extended. A colossus of armoured hide, his eyes expanding as his mind reached out ahead of him in a psychic shockwave. The Loremasters were one thing, thought Finn, but none of them would survive against the focussed might of a krell. Amid the chaos, Balos stood rigid and immobile. An implacable golden statue. The full force of the krell's mind crashed down on Finn. His vision flattened, as though pressed down by an immense weight. The room became a blur of colour. They sped along the channel that the Blow of Force had carved out of the crowd, and through the open doors. They raced through the Citadel corridors. Finn sensed Morin and Vespar in mental communication, and he guessed that the twisted thurjun was showing Morin the fastest way out of VoYannan's dark pyramid. Vault slaves and warriors were knocked aside as they hurtled past.

They shot out of an opening high in the side of the pyramid. Sulphurous clouds swirled around them, and for a moment Finn had a clear view down to the cracked plain below. His stomach lurched as he realised how high they were. He saw a dark highway below, crammed with traffic, and glimpsed a ragged stream of aircraft approaching the Citadel. Far behind them, on the Plain of Sorrow, what looked like a endless city of towers was in fact a fleet of grounded starships. The dirty clouds closed around them, cutting off vision. Through his connection with the Axe, he knew the dampening field continued to surround them, moving with them. As fast as they had gone before, they picked up even more speed, flying faster than a Dreaming Steed. They hurtled through the sulphurous clouds toward the city of Seven Horns. It was a sprawling metropolis of concrete and rotted steel that languished on the surface of VoYannan's poisoned world, a vast cancer that would have died long ago, but for the Gateway at its heart. VoYannan's ancient capital, and the portal to the Dark City. The barren plain gave way to a dead cityscape of blackened concrete and abandoned towers of rusted steel and shattered glass. They were dead things, like rotted teeth. Aeons past, these areas were inhabited, until the dying ecosystem of YoYannan's world finally collapsed. As they neared the centre of Seven Horns, huge domes of acid-resistant glass rose in clusters like boils on the planet's skin. Here the krell's servants lived in artificial atmospheres. Huge laser cannon emplacements dotted the surface of the domes. Already alerted, they swivelled into action. Long-range targeting picked up their tiny flying group in the clouded skyscape and the barrage began.

"Hold on!" yelled Morin over the rushing wind.

Bursts of laser fire, orange and red, seared past them. Morin wove through them, and — incredibly — increased their speed again. Finn squeezed his eyes shut against the stinging air, then forced them open again. *By the High God, I am not going to my death with my eyes shut!*

Finn drew deep on the mionanail. He pushed the Realm dampening field to its limits, elongating it so it reached ahead of them like the tip of a spear. Morin cut sharply to the right, and dropped closer to the ground. Warriors and thralls alike yelped in surprise as their stomachs lurched. A bolt of shimmering orange roared past, just above them. *Too close.* One of the rescued thurjuns shrieked in pain and patted out his burning hair in a frenzy. The smell of ozone hit the back of Finn's throat. A big geodesic dome swelled in his vision, the individual panels vast transparent polygons. They were closing fast. He could see the lights of the buildings inside the dome through the dirty glass. Then, at last, the Realm's technology met the Vault's. Lights winked out inside the dome, darkening in huge segments. The siithe laser emplacements went silent, their blunt, ugly turrets drooping down to rest position as they lost power. Finn saw tiny figures in the cannon command capsules, working their controls in manic desperation, yet to no avail. The Realm had touched this place.

Magic and steel.

"I see it!" yelled Finn, his words snatched by the wind.

He pointed. Finn was not the only one. The Viri Gateway was the twin of the Dark City Gateway. Two huge columns, topped by a single lintel stone. It meant escape. *Salvation.* The scene below was chaos. At the base of the Gateway, traffic was jammed, the vehicles transformed from living things to lumps of useless metal as the dampening field killed their engines. Skycraft dropped like lead weights, smashing into the Vault troops, into the crush of traffic, and through the glass of the enclosing domes. They were moving so fast Finn only had a moment to take in the scene. The Viri Gateway swiftly grew from something on the horizon to a towering structure that struck awe into their hearts. The glowing membrane between the pillars, which separated one world from the next, expanded to fill their vision.

Then they were through.

Chapter 64
Viri world — Vault of Seven Horns

Finn forced his stinging eyes open.

They emerged above the Dark City's huge central plaza. Morin took them straight up. They dodged towers, darkening buildings, and tumbling air cars, then broke free into empty space. They flew on, high above the Dark City. An empty plain spread out around them. He recognised the range of hills to their right. That, and the city behind them, were the only features to mar the plain's flat immensity. Finn's heart lifted in relief at their escape, then he grimaced as he remembered Sentas' betrayal. There would be no horses and supplies waiting from them in those distant hills. They were alone . . . and still inside the Vault of Seven Horns.

"Finn! The mionanail is almost exhausted!" called Morin.

Finn cursed. They were more than twenty kilometres from the hills. "Set us down."

Their headlong flight slowed, and they lost height. The hills vanished below the horizon as their perspective changed. It felt like it was the promise of sanctuary that was disappearing, not just a geological feature. The plain grew closer and closer until Morin touched down gently on cracked blood-red clay. The thurjuns released the Axe and Finn stood alone. His eyes and throat burned. His whole body sang, an aftereffect of the wind's torrent. He released the dampening field.

One of the naked court thurjuns — a thin, emaciated being like a kangaroo with legs as thin as sticks — collapsed. Vespar knelt at her side and felt for her pulse. The twisted thurjun hung his head, overwhelmed. His hands gripped her matted fur, as though he could keep her spirit in place through sheer desperation.

"She is dead."

*

A gust of wind blasted gritty dust into Finn's eyes.

The plain was endless. Empty. Its bone dry surface was

shrunken clay, cut into a ragged patchwork by endless cracks that ranged in size from the width of a thumb to the size of a fist. It was completely devoid of vegetation. The soil itself felt dead. There was a sense of menace too, as though death lurked here, invisible, in the stinking air, sucking away hope as it slowly drew near. They were far from the poisoned rivers, and an atmospheric haze hid the horizon. He could see the tops of the Dark City's largest towers to the north, shimmering above the haze as though floating there with no support. *Still dark.* After the roar of rushing wind, the quiet was stunning. Finn had seen this plain from the hills above the Dark City. To actually stand here made him aware of its bleakness in a way he had never understood before.

The naked thurjuns groaned in torment as the abrasive dust stung their naked skin. They huddled together. Sephany sank to her knees and said a Prayer of thanks for her deliverance.

Deliverance?

Finn blinked. Shook himself.

He walked over to Morin and held out the Axe. "How much power is left in the mionanail, Morin?" He did not have enough of the thurjun's skill to sense that.

Morin waved away the Axe. He did not need to touch it to answer. "It is almost exhausted. We could reactivate the dampening field for a time, but if we use any more than that, we will not have enough power to pass the Kess Gateway."

Finn's heart twisted. The brief flare of hope — that impossible hope that they would live and escape with Sephany — drained away. After everything they had suffered, all they could achieve here was a good death. The Axe, which had come alive in his hands in VoYannan's court, grew heavy. His arm trembled, and he let the Axe drag it down. He was exhausted. They all were. They had been given no food or water since their capture. He looked to his men. Kyall had chosen well. All of them were living on their last reserves, yet they were drawing on deep wells of strength. *Pure heart.*

Morin's eyes showed concern. He patted Finn on the shoulder. "The Arrow saved us all . . . but it uses a tremendous amount of power. It . . . it was only possible with the combined focus of so many thurjuns. But that joint focus drains a mionanail fast."

"I know, Morin." There was nothing more to say.

The distant towers lit up, one by one. The Vault was regaining its strength. The dark metropolis coming back to life. Finn's heart hardened as he saw shapes in the sky above the Dark City. They were too far away to identify, yet he knew what they were all the same. Fighter craft. Armoured starships.

"Here they come," said Liam. His voice trembled.

"Should we run?" asked one of the warriors.

Finn shook his head. "We cannot outrun them."

The leading aerial shapes resolved into a wing of Vault fighter craft, flying in a tight vee formation. A second squadron appeared to the west, another to the east. Behind them came vast lumbering spacecraft, bristling with weapons. Then, emerging from the haze, came the first of the troop transports, speeding across the flat plain. A long column followed, dotted with the squat shapes of Vault tanks. It snaked toward them, growing in length.

The men and women around Finn went silent. Stunned.

Finn crushed his fear and desperation. He became what he was trained to be. A Realm commander. He watched it all with a dispassionate, discerning eye. Seeking patterns. Considering strategies, assessing them, discarding them. The fighter craft, troop carriers, and lumbering spacecraft resolved into a familiar pattern. The standard Vault deployment against Realm forces. There would be no rapid attack. No attempt to overwhelm them. The Vault would come at them slowly and carefully, approaching at first to a point just outside the range of a Realm dampening field, then advancing with heavy crossbows, spears, and falcata.

"Damn them!" said Finn. *They had come so close to escaping*. He looked west to the hills, hoping to see Sentas galloping toward them with their mounts, but knew he would not. The traitor had abandoned them to their deaths. He and his lackeys would be long gone.

Finn felt a gentle touch on his arm. It was Sephany. The thought of what she had endured at the hands of the Vault made his heart boil. He longed to take her in his arms and comfort her, but something held him back. A new strength in her.

"Do not lose faith, Finn."

Procarrus crouched above the controls of his fighter craft. Through the armoured glass of the cockpit, he could see Finn's small group cowering on the plain below. He shook with fury. Barsus was dead. The priestess stolen. The Fragment gone. The Earth thurjun Vicki dead. Both Earth Gateways closed.

The siithe general Boreth sat in the copilot's chair, beside Procarrus. The ancient Vault warrior had been rewarded many times with extended life, growing in wisdom with each additional lifetime. Boreth was now senior Vault general below Procarrus.

"Nuclear strike?" asked Boreth.

"No." *Fool*. Procarrus bit back the rebuke. "VoYannan needs the Spawn unharmed."

"Yes, my lord. Continue with the standard deployment?"

"Yes, but no crossbows. We can risk no harm to Sephany."

Procarrus focussed his hatred on Finn's small group, using it to clear his mind. Evenstone. *How he hated that name!* After hundreds of glorious victories for VoYannan, the first Evenstone had defeated him decisively at Stonelake. It had been a terrible setback for his ambitions. VoYannan had punished him cruelly for the defeat, removing him from his inner circle. It had taken him centuries to reestablish himself as VoYannan's most powerful and trusted servant. Was he to have this taken away by the last warrior of the Evenstone line? No. This *disaster* has gone on long enough.

"Send in the probes," ordered Procarrus.

Boreth issued a curt command across the link. Hundreds of small Vault probes hurtled from the airborne fleet, deploying at regular intervals between the Vault forces and the small group of Realm warriors. Boreth examined the returning datastream. "None have ceased to function, lord. As yet they have not activated the dampening field."

"Send in the ground troops," said Procarrus.

"Why not send in fighters?" asked Boreth. "They would make short work of them."

Procarrus struggled to hold his temper. "I will take no more chances. Finn Evenstone is too well trained. At the first hint of fighter craft he will engage the Realm weapon. No. We approach on foot."

Huge starships, each carrying thousands of siithe, descended to the cracked surface of the plain and settled under their enormous weight. Hatches opened, disgorging streams of black-clad warriors. These joined forces from the Dark City that had arrived in troop transports. Soon there were more than thirty thousand siithe on the plain. They surrounded Finn's small group, cutting off any line of retreat.

"Take me to the ground, Boreth. I will lead them in myself."

"What of the seraphin? VoYannan ordered him cast into the sun."

Procarrus looked behind him at the inert, dead form of the seraphin. The limbs and body had melted into a dark, formless shape, like black glass. The surface was featureless, except for the eyes in the misshapen head, which had become dull oval mirrors, like twin lozenges of polished metal. Lifeless, but eerie. "He can do us no harm now, Boreth."

"VoYannan has commanded —"

"Here I command!" snapped Procarrus.

When the small group of Realm warriors had sped from the room with Sephany, VoYannan's rage had exploded across the court. Procarrus, the veyr, and the siithe, had been knocked to the ground, senseless. Balos had tried to follow Sephany, but VoYannan had unleashed his full power.

"So you will not kneel before me! *You will kneel now!*" The krell had raised his hands, a thick cloud of bloody red billowing out across the room, enveloping Balos. The golden sheath around the seraphin had flickered, then vanished. Balos had surged at VoYannan, dark limbs extended to tear and rend. He had moved no more than a pace when, with a high-pitched cry of agony, he was driven to his knees.

"Siithe!" called the krell.

Like marionettes, the siithe warriors around the room jumped to their feet and sighted on the seraphin. More than a hundred lasers discharged, encasing Balos in a blazing corona. Procarrus had shielded his eyes, and backed away from the heat, and the screams of dreamers caught in the inferno.

Inside the lurid conflagration, Balos struggled in pain and agony.

With a supreme effort, Balos had pushed himself to his feet, then staggered toward VoYannan. His long, dark fingers hooked like claws. He took one step, then fell forward, full length on the stone, unable to rise. Balos roared. Once. An almost musical sound that made Procarrus lose vision for a moment. When his eyes refocussed, Balos lay unmoving. The siithe continued to fire, reducing the dead seraphin's unknowable form to a dark, twisted, molten mess.

The fighter craft touched down, bringing Procarrus back to the present. He looked out through the armoured glass at the mass of siithe troops gathering on the plain. *Yes.* Finn Evenstone will pay dearly. Boreth commanded two siithe warriors to drag the grotesque remnants of the seraphin from the small craft and stand guard over it.

Procarrus left the craft and walked rapidly to the front lines. He looked down expecting to see Barsus at his heels — then remembered Yolinda delivering the death blow. In that moment he had recognised her as the woman from his Sydney court. She *had* proved to be more than she seemed. Not killing her had been a mistake. It was not one he would repeat. She would die — but not quickly. First he would strip away every shred of memory and will she possessed. Boreth joined Procarrus just behind the front rank. The siithe general drew his falcata.

"Short swords and heavy shields!" commanded Procarrus.

The siithe drew their weapons and smoothly moved into formation. The shields crashed together into a solid wall. The small group of Realm warriors were surrounded in a ring of Vault steel.

"Use your little Axe now, Evenstone. It will avail you nothing. *"FORWARD. SLOW MARCH."*

This was fighting that Procarrus could understand. The fighting he had been trained for, all those years ago in Rome. Siithe boots drew dust from the plain as they stamped down in perfect time. He wanted Finn Evenstone and his pitiful warriors to live every moment left in their lives in terror — watching as their death approached. As they closed on their prey.

"No one is to kill the Axe-wielder!" shouted Procarrus.
"He is mine."

Chapter 65

Plain before the Dark City, Viri world — Vault of Seven Horns

Finn watched the Vault forces approach.

His small group of warriors formed a circle around the thurjuns and Sephany. Genna was standing on his left, armed with a siithe short sword. His surviving twelve Realm warriors were the best of the best. Swordmasters with honed talent, almost supernaturally gifted with speed. Yet the odds . . . were unfathomable.

Finn had eight thurjuns and not a mionanail pendant between them. If they were equipped with a fully charged mionanail each, then the siithe would know fear. He struggled to control his frustration.

"What should we do, Captain?" asked one of the warriors.

Finn watched the approaching Vault ranks. Knuckles white on the haft of the Axe. There was not enough power left in its mionanail to fly even one of them to safety.

The siithe were advancing in low-tech formation. Swords and metal. If Finn had a thousand men, or two thousand, perhaps they would have a chance for a fighting retreat. If only he had the means to strike at them! Give him a full Realm legion and a company of thurjuns and he would drive them all the way back to VoYannan's Citadel. Then it would be VoYannan kneeling before *him*.

"What do we do!"

Finn could hear the panic in his warrior's voice. He turned to meet Morin's eyes, then Liam's. The young thurjun was stoic, and Finn noted the absence of fear. Earlier, Liam had offered to fight in the circle, but Finn had refused him. Liam was competent with a sword, but nothing more. It was vital the circle held and for that he needed warriors of equal skill. Sephany smiled at him and, incredibly, hope kindled in his chest.

She sank to her knees, closed her eyes, and began to pray.

"What should we do, sir?" asked the warrior again.

Finn fought nausea as Sephany's abdomen rippled and

bulged. The Spawn fought against her words, her thoughts. She gasped in pain, but continued to pray. If he needed a lesson in courage, he had found it. The Spawn's motions grew even more violent, and blood began to appear on her white gown, flooding from her groin. Even so she did not falter. One by one, the thurjuns from the court of the krell, dressed now in an odd assortment of borrowed cloaks and tunics, fell to their knees beside her.

"You want darkness, dreams and death — but I shall not yield," whispered Sephany.

Finn's grip on the Axe relaxed. He felt the peace of the High God descend on the plain. A quiet majesty he had never experienced before, not even in the Temple. His frustration eased, to be replaced by resignation. Around him he watched the fear leave the men and gave his own private words of thanks.

"We all die," he said finally, pitching his voice so they all could hear him. The warrior who had questioned him listened intently, eyes shining. He, like Finn himself, was unmarried, and had left no children behind to keep his memory alive. "But only a few of us get to die well. Together we have spit in VoYannan's eye. If we are to fall here, then so be it. But we will not let them cow us! We will die like warriors of the Blessed Realms, doing what we have devoted our life to. Fighting the Vault!"

His warriors' resolve strengthened. The man who had questioned him nodded in acceptance and turned to face the advancing siithe. Finn took his place in the circle. The men readied their weapons.

Sephany's prayers continued.

The siithe lines were less than a hundred paces away. They would have perhaps minutes of combat before the enemy's sheer weight overwhelmed them.

There was an explosion of bright golden flame behind the siithe lines. A siithe warrior was thrown through the air, as though from a Vault landmine. *Accidental detonation?*

"Balos rises up from the shell of his last life. The Dark Seraphin is no more!" cried Sephany.

Balos soared into the sky on six wings of golden flame. He rose, then turned into a dive, speeding low across the plain.

Closer and closer, until he stopped above them, wings flaring in a flash of gold.

"Sephany," called the seraphin. His voice thudded into Finn's chest, ringing with Light's hidden symphonies.

Sephany's face shone in the seraphin's golden glow. Her eyelids fluttered and Finn knew she was struggling to maintain consciousness.

The seraphin remained passive. He hovered on his six golden wings, attention fixed on Sephany. Waiting.

"Are you here to fight with us?" demanded Finn.

The seraphin ignored him. Finn's heart sank. The minions of the High God were always remote, acting at the behest of imperatives and commands that were never understood by mortals. Enigmatic at best. More typically pitiless in pursuit of their goals. Balos' focus was Sephany. The rest of them might as well not exist.

We meet the Vault alone.

"Turn and face the enemy!" yelled Finn.

*

When Procarrus saw the golden form shoot through the air, he knew a moment of true fear. Balos. *Reborn.* VoYannan had ordered him to send the inert seraphin into his world's sun. Procarrus had chosen to postpone that duty. If he should fail now

. . .

Procarrus looked around him at rank upon rank of siithe, all approaching the Realm warriors without a single item of high-tech hardware. Procarrus had ordered it, determined to beat the Realm warriors without the complication of the Realm dampening field. Yet now they were defenceless against the seraphin. Without lasers, without cannons or missiles, Balos would be unstoppable.

"Boreth, order the fighter craft forward! Destroy the seraphin. Use lasers. Missiles. *Anything.*"

"But, my lord, VoYannan's bride!"

"*Do it!*"

Procarrus fixed his gaze on Finn's small group, driven by

urgency. He had to slay Finn and neutralise his Realm weapon before the Vault fighter craft arrived.

"FORWARD AT THE RUN!"

The siithe troops smoothly increased their pace.

Procarrus pushed into the lead, sprinting directly for Finn Evenstone.

*

Finn flinched as a wall of harsh sound crashed around them. The battlecries of thousands of siithe. An answering defiance rose inside him that steeled his spine. The leather binding on the Axe's half creaked in his tightening fist. He could only imagine how the violent chorus would tear at his warriors' resolve as they watched death approach.

"Steady!" called Finn.

The siithe were coming fast. The Vault shield-walls were already collapsing as the four approaching fronts raced to close on the tiny Realm force.

"There are so many," said one warrior.

"There will be less when they get here," said Genna, grinning.

"Keep steady!" Finn's warriors were armed with siithe weapons taken in VoYannan's court. Most with heavy falcatas, unwieldy for a Realm warrior, some with short swords, others with siithe long-knives. They wore thin tunics, trousers and boots. In contrast, the siithe were heavily armoured, and equipped with shields. Everything would depend on whether Finn and his men could withstand the initial charge.

Someone forced their way into the circle to his right. Yolinda, armed with a siithe long-knife, all but naked in her slave outfit, every line of her body set with determination. He wanted to order her back, but did not. Twice she had saved him in combat. What right had he to deny her this? Instead they shared a quick smile and turned to face the Vault line, ready to fight and die. The krell's army roared toward them. A tidal wave of steel, muscle, and hate.

"HOLD THE CIRCLE!" shouted Finn.

Procarrus! Right there in the front line. *Running straight at me.*

"Help us, Balos!" called Sephany.

The seraphin rose into the air. A high-pitched whine sounded as the seraphin's wings quivered, then expanded in a flash of golden light. The approaching Vault warriors were momentarily blinded, and their advance grew ragged. Procarrus shielded his eyes and stumbled. Vault warriors ran past him.

Balos began to spin, faster and faster, until he became a dark blur inside a golden whirlwind. He streaked into the siithe ranks. First in front of Finn, then circling back around to hit the Vault forces on all approaching fronts. He smashed the front lines. Armoured bodies tumbled through the air in his wake. The Vault forces slowed, struggling to restore their formations. Balos blazed back to Sephany, hovering above her. The angel's golden light swelled around them.

"Let me take you to safety," said Balos.

Finn grew weightless as Balos lifted them all slowly above the plain.

A sonic boom sounded from overhead, then another.

"Vault fighter craft!" said Morin.

Two missiles struck Balos, exploding with hot fury just above their heads. The golden light vanished. They crashed back to the ground. Finn landed hard, the cracked clay as unyielding as concrete under his boots. He tensed, waiting for the explosion's heat to sear his flesh, but it did not reach him.

"He shielded us!" Morin's eyes followed the seraphin.

Balos had been thrown high into the sky. Twelve Vault fighter craft now converged on him. A barrage of missiles struck home, bursting against his dark form in single colossal impact. The shockwave battered them, almost taking Finn and his warriors off their feet.

Finn studied the siithe lines. They had reformed and were coming at them again, Procarrus once more in the lead.

"Finn!" called Morin. "Activate the dampening field! Balos will be overcome!"

The lines met with the dull clatter of metal on metal. They braced, and their boots slid on the clay until they had absorbed the initial impact. Then the Realm warriors pushed back, their ragged warcries swamped by the roars of the thousands of siithe behind the enemy's front line. They were toe-to-toe with them. Their unwashed stink, ripe under a clouded sky heated by the unseen Viri sun, made Finn gag. Procarrus came at Finn. The Archfiend shouldered aside a siithe and lunged. The Axe deflected the blade. Procarrus cruel face filled Finn's vision, his blue eyes filled with a cold rage, his cruel mouth twisted in fury. The longsword slashed down again, this time in savage overhand cut, right at Finn's unprotected head. Finn tried to form a matrix. He desperately blocked the cut from Procarrus' longsword only to find the light, razor sharp weapon darting back at his heart. *There is no time to think!* Finn twisted and the longsword slithered past him, slicing the fabric of his tunic. He stepped to the side, gripped the Axe with both hands, and launched a vicious cut at Procarrus' head. The Archfiend deflected the blow with contemptuous ease. The shock of impact jarred Finn to his shoulders. The ancient Vault warrior appeared thin, even emaciated, but that was a lie. Procarrus was unnaturally strong. He pressed Finn, coming in with a swift, controlled strike. Finn brought up the heavy Axe. He blocked — just in time — only to find the sword cutting in from the right. At his throat! Even as he lifted the heavy Axe to intercept the strike, he knew it would be too late. Procarrus' blue eyes shone with glee.

And Finn watched his death come.

Chapter 66

Plain before the Dark City, Viri world — Vault of Seven Horns

Procarrus' weapon met steel.

Finn hissed through his clenched teeth. He looked back along the dark blade that had stopped Procarrus' longsword to its hilt. Saw the slim hand that held the weapon, and knew its wielder.

Yolinda.

She had turned Procarrus' longsword aside with her siithe long-knife, deflecting it, rather than meeting the Archfiend's massive strength head on. The siithe pushed in, wild with blood lust, driven by the massed ranks that continued to arrive behind them. Procarrus was shoved aside by his own incensed warriors.

"My thanks!" gasped Finn.

Finn fought with desperate fury, Yolinda at his back. Her eyes missed nothing and her hands were fast and sure. Two Realm warriors fell, both stabbed through the stomach by the heavily armoured siithe. The Realm line buckled. The survivors had seen the danger, and their circle contracted, but not before one of the siithe broke through. The Vault warrior sprinted at Sephany and the court thurjuns. Finn felt the terrible dynamic of the press around them, and knew that not a single one of the Realm warriors could leave the defensive circle without the whole thing collapsing. His men were achieving the impossible, holding back a furious tide of Vault warriors, but it could not last. Still, he fought on. When Finn fell, he would die knowing he had never faltered, never backed down, even here, inside Vault's steel-toothed maw.

Vespar and three of the court thurjuns joined their meagre powers, sending a narrow beam of hot light at the siithe, searing into his left eye. There were few matrices that could be powered by the native energy in a thurjun's body, but generating heat was one of them. Even so, it required expert focus. The Vault warrior fell, howling in agony. Liam seized a knife from the siithe's belt and rammed it into his throat. The siithe flailed, throwing Liam across the circle. The young thurjun landed heavily, flipped back onto his feet with surprising agility, then darted back at the siithe.

Finn was caught in a furious exchange. The next time he looked back, he saw that Liam and Vespar's group had swarmed the siithe, pinning him down. They had also wrestled away his short sword. Liam took the blade and drove it deep into the siithe's abdomen, killing him instantly. As Vespar and the other escaped thurjuns stripped the siithe, Liam ran toward Finn, passing the short sword to Yolinda. Then there was no time for thought. Finn and his warriors fought for their lives, for each precious second. He saw other thurjuns pass a steady stream of scavenged weapons to the Realm warriors in the front rank. *Including shields!*

Two siithe ran at Finn simultaneously, swinging in with falcatas. Genna blocked one of the blows and killed the siithe with a precise lunge that passed through a gap in the Vault warrior's armour. The siithe fell, but Genna's sword was trapped. Before he could turn away, a huge siithe clubbed Genna off his feet, the blow sending the slight warrior back inside the circle, unconscious. Liam, Morin, and Vespar, dragged him to safety. His head was bleeding heavily.

The circle contracted. The backs of the warriors were now only paces away from the unarmed thurjuns.

"The skull is not cracked!" called Morin.

Finn risked a glance. Balos spun through the sky, dazed. For years Finn had puzzled over how to defeat such an awesome adversary, yet now, as an unlikely ally, he wished the seraphin was as invulnerable as he had always feared.

"What is wrong with Balos?" shouted Finn, blocking a low thrust and countering.

"The powers of his new form have not fully manifested," said Sephany, pausing for a breath. "And the missiles have drained him."

Balos righted himself. The Vault fighter craft turned in formation and powered back. The seraphin's wings flared as the gap closed. Missiles raced ahead of the fighter craft in a streaking cloud. Balos twisted majestically, sailing through the entire barrage. The seraphin's arm swept out, a dark adamantine blur that ripped right through a fuselage. The stricken fighter craft was consumed in a blazing fireball. The stunning *crack* of the explosion came a moment later. A second fighter tried to avoid the flames, but was caught in the conflagration. It detonated. The other ten craft banked sharply away. As the flames vanished, Finn saw the seraphin tumble through the sky, limbs flaccid.

Finn had a ferocious exchange with a huge siithe, finally delivering a powerful lateral strike that cut through the Vault warrior's helm. The Axe sheared through the Vault steel, and then the siithe's skull, exiting in a bloody spray.

The remaining ten fighter craft turned in formation and raced back to Balos. Their laser turrets flared. The beams converged on Balos. Flared red. His dark form vanished in a furious blaze. The seraphin's wail of agony resounded across the plain, tearing at Finn's ears. Balos broke free and hurtled skyward, trying to escape, but the fighters followed. The lasers glowed a more intense red as the fighters diverted all available power to the attack. Balos' flight slowed, halted, then he was falling again. The fighters turned smoothly, keeping him in the centre of their converging fire.

"Finn!" called Morin. "*The dampening field!*"

"I know!" Finn's heart tore in frustration.

The siithe collapsed, but there was no respite.

Procarrus stepped into the gap.

The Archfiend's mouth twisted into a snarl. He attacked in a whirlwind of controlled fury and supernatural strength. Finn blocked cut after cut, his eyes searching furiously for the next strike. Procarrus was tireless, while Finn's arms burned with fatigue. The Axe was a heavy weapon. A slow weapon. Accustomed to his Realm longsword, he struggled to match Procarrus. The Archfiend cut from left, right, high and low . . . all in the passing of a breath. How could he win? How could any of them survive? Balos was lost, and they were surrounded by thousands of Vault troops. He could feel himself weakening.

"Stop using the Axe like a sword, Finn!" called Morin from behind him. "Think of Sephany!"

At the thought of the Spawn clawing at Sephany's womb, he was filled with a hot flame. New strength flooded his limbs. He had battled through half the worlds of the Vault trying to rescue her. Was he going to let her be taken again, after what the krell had done to her? *No!* The Axe suddenly felt light in his hands. He swept it around him and Yolinda dived for cover. Two siithe fell, the flared axe-blades slicing through their Vault armour. The Archfiend ducked, then fell back.

Procarrus looked for an opening, but the Axe made a whirlwind of blurred Realm steel that promised only death. He retreated. Finn followed him into the siithe ranks, cutting down siithe warriors left and right. The Realm circle moved with Finn. All around them, the siithe picked up the change in the battle and hesitated. Finn's warriors, now equipped with captured short swords and siithe shields, fought with new confidence. So many siithe dead surrounded the small circle that the Realm warriors had to take care with their footing as they moved deeper into the siithe lines. Procarrus tried to fall back again, to give himself distance to manoeuvre around Finn, and to work his longsword past the Axe's deadly sweep, but the weight of the siithe ranks pushed him forward. Finn smiled. The Archfiend could retreat no longer. The Axe of Evenstone flashed toward Procarrus' head in a silver blur. Finn drove all his weight, his physical power, all this fury, into the strike. Procarrus' sword swept up, but a siithe's shoulder slammed into him just as he struck. His longsword turned, its angle awkward, the Archfiend's unnatural strength misdirected. The blades met with a ringing chime. The heavy Axe slammed into the flat of the longsword's blade, just above the hilt. The longsword's blade flexed — then cartwheeled right out of Procarrus' mailed fist. Unhindered, the Axe drove on, crashing into the Archfiend's helm. The high-tech alloy, gifted only to senior Vault generals, folded around the axe-blade, and held, but Procarrus was driven to his knees by the massive force of the blow.

"Mercy!" called Procarrus. "I swear I will let you all live!"

Procarrus' eyes measured the distance to his sword. *A distraction.* Finn knew the Archfiend would never let them escape. Never let them surrender.

"It is too late for mercy," said Finn.

"No! *I was going to forge a new Roman Empire —* "

The Axe whistled softly as Finn drew it back, and cut forward, slicing the Archfiend's head from his shoulders. His severed head struck the ground with a heavy thud, and the dented helm bounced free. Procarrus' eyes widened. They followed Liam as he darted forward to retrieve the longsword. The Archfiend's mouth worked soundlessly. Finn braced himself for a last blast of Vault magic, but nothing came. The light faded from Procarrus' eyes and the mouth grew still.

Finn stepped back. The fighting circle closed around him. He paused to concentrate, shifting his mental state. He formed the dampening field matrix, carefully adjusting its shape. He lifted the Axe, drawing every residue of power from the mionanail and sending it up through the construct. The field blossomed, swelled, and extended above them, to where Balos fell through the sky, still bathed in hot laser-light. The flames of the fighters' tail thrusters extinguished. The lasers vanished. The fighter craft fell. The air screamed around their sleek bodies as they smashed into the siithe ranks. Hundreds of siithe were crushed, and hundreds more maimed by flying debris. The wounded Vault warriors bellowed in agony . . . and fear. For above them, the seraphin had halted his fall. He floated in place, his six golden wings beating slowly as his dark, implacable gaze searched out his enemies.

"Retreat and reform!" The orders were issued in the Vault tongue by a squat siithe general who had been fighting behind Procarrus. The orders were relayed down the line and the siithe began to draw back. But not fast enough.

The seraphin swooped down. A golden inferno.

Finn gave a whoop of triumph.

This time there was nothing to stop him. Balos hit the siithe ranks. His dark limbs flashed. Crushed. Destroyed. The siithe, who had been retreating in orderly ranks, panicked and fled.

Finn and the tiny circle of Realm warriors were left alone on the plain, inside a ragged circle of siithe dead. Men sank to their knees, gasping for breath. Others laughed and slapped each other on the back.

Finn blinked. A sense of unreality overwhelmed him.

We . . . are to live?

Realm warriors gathered around Finn, excited, congratulating their Captain. Finn responded automatically, struggling to gather thoughts from a fractured, exhausted mind.

Balos returned.

The seraphin's wings expanded, then gently curled around them, embracing them all. They lifted from the plain, held aloft by the angel's power. Pale golden light flickered across Sephany's white tunic, the ethereal flames dancing and crackling. She smiled up at Balos. "Your colour has changed, Balos."

"It changes still," said the seraphin. "I have been lost for so long. Rest."

Balos placed a gentle hand on the priestess, encasing her in golden flame. The struggling form of the Spawn was instantly inert. Sephany fell into a deep, healing sleep.

Genna jerked awake. He started as he saw they were airborne, held aloft on six huge golden wings. "Where are the siithe?"

"We beat them," said Finn.

"This is a nice dream," said Genna, looking around him in wonder.

Chapter 67
Viri world — Vault Of Seven Horns

Liam's abdominal muscles tensed as Balos approached, as though he was bracing for a blow.

The seraphin's pale golden nimbus lit the scattered debris around the old Gateway tower, cutting through the Viri world's daytime gloom and making sharp-edged shadows that swung and danced around them. Liam, Finn, Morin, Yolinda, and the surviving Realm warriors from the battle on the plain, were all gathered in a loose circle around Sephany. They watched in tense silence as the seraphin closed on the priestess. There were so few of them now, even less since Vespar's group had left them, electing to stay behind on the ruined Viri world.

Liam was wary of Balos, but the powerful, enigmatic creature had no thought for him. In fact, apart from the priestess, the seraphin had ignored them all since the rescue. Balos glided toward Sephany until he was close enough to touch her. The seraphin dwarfed the priestess. His six wings were insubstantial, feathered out behind his dark body in streams of ethereal light. Huge stone blocks lay tumbled around them. The entrance to the Sydney Gateway, which they had fought so hard to win, gaped open beyond the collapsed Tower wall. The siithe and Realm dead, seared into Liam's memory of the battle, were long gone. All that remained were shredded remnants of armour, torn apart by veyr talons.

Balos' featureless ebony-dark face tilted down toward Sephany. "I cannot thank you enough, Priestess. After an aeon of darkness, you have brought me back into the Light of the High God. So much destruction. So many dead at the order of the Vault." His voice, coiled and potent, vibrated in Liam's chest.

Sephany laid her slim hand on Balos' dark arm.

Balos shivered.

White light ignited around the priestess and the angel. Liam gasped and shielded his eyes. Liam squinted through the intense glare, heart thudding. Sephany's eyes remained wide and alert, wild with wonder. She looked up at Balos, and *through* him, at something Liam could not see, her eyes lit with knowledge, and alive with life. "Leave aside your fear, Balos. Now is the time. Return to your own realm."

Balos lifted skyward, yet not through his own effort. His body remained in the same posture, wings motionless. It was as though the earthbound grip of the planet below them had simply been released, and now ceased to rule his physical form. There was a final flash of brilliant white. Then he was gone.

"Vanished!" said one of the warriors.

Liam let out a long breath. His neck ached with tension, the pain flaring in concert with his heartbeat.

"I, for one, am glad to see him gone," said Finn. Liam could only nod in agreement. Balos was a powerful ally, but he had also been one of YoYannan's most fearsome weapons.

"He has returned to the High God," said Sephany. Her eyelids fluttered, and her face creased with sudden pain. Her knees buckled.

Finn ran forward to catch her. Liam close behind. They each took an arm. She strengthened and smiled, recovering enough to stand unaided. Her face remained deathly pale. Her swollen belly, taut against the fabric of her white gown, rippled as a formless lump thrust up from beneath. Liam and Finn exchanged a worried glance. The Spawn *had* been inactive. Now it moved with new urgency.

"I am well," said Sephany. She pulled her borrowed cloak around her, concealing her body. The black cloak had been taken from a huge siithe, and was voluminous enough to wrap around her twice.

Morin took Liam's arm and guided him away. "We must pass through the Gateway. Quickly."

Liam's heart lurched in his chest, galloping on a new wave of worry. They had never intended to return here. Their flight from the Kess Gateway, carried by the seraphin through the gloom of the Viri world, above its ruined landscape and decaying cities, had felt like defeat. Their mission had been to *seal* the Sydney Gateway, not open it up for use. There was no thurjun on the other side to establish the mind-bond and reach back across the vast gulf of space. The Kess Gateway had always been their planned escape route out of the Vault of Seven Horns and back to the Realms. What they were going to attempt now had not been achieved in living history . . . and Liam was the only one who could do it.

They had arrived at the Kess Gateway exhausted, yet buoyed by their impossible victory on the plain, high on the sheer joy of survival, thrilled by the swift airborne journey, and bonded by their travails. They had recovered Kyall's broadsword from his grave on the way, giving them one precious mionanail between them, guaranteeing their passage even if the Realm thurjun stationed there had been sent on another mission, which had at first seemed the case. They had found the hidden cave of the Realm thurjun deserted. That had not overly discouraged them. They returned to the Gateway and Morin established a mind-bond with a thurjun at the Tower on the other side of the closed portal. Then they learned the truth. Sentas' betrayal had been thorough. The Kess Gateway had been sealed on Sentas' orders. The Realm thurjun stationed there was not absent on Realm business, but was gone from the Viri world entirely, ordered back to court. It was an act of astounding vindictiveness . . . and an inexplicable one. Closing the Gateway hurt the Realms, removing a great strategic advantage. The Realms now had no access to the Viri world. No way to strike at VoYannan's massive war machine here, or erode the foundations of his slave empire. The news was worse even than that. Despite command of a mionanail, and any number of capable thurjuns on this side of the gate to open it, the thurjuns at the Kess Gateway on the other side of the portal had been ordered to block all access. This had seemed like some mistake. Morin had appealed directly to the commander of Kess Tower using a mind-bond, but the Realm commander had merely confirmed the order. It seemed inconceivable. The Tower commander had refused to budge, no doubt wary of Sentas' political power . . . and sensitive to his own advancement. What Sentas had promised the man, they could only guess at. Finn had been too furious to speak. After their impossible victory, after coming so close to safety — to have it all snatched away — was a crushing blow.

Vespar had left them at the Kess Gateway. He and the other

five surviving thurjuns from the krell's court had elected to stay on the Viri world. The group filled the Realm thurjun's snug cave to overflowing, but it was still a paradise compared to VoYannan's court. There were stocks of food, spare clothing, and a spring at the rear of the cave yielding clear water. Together, they would be able to gather enough power from the ruined world around them to open the Gateway should the call ever come from the Realms. Finn, sickened by everything he had seen in VoYannan's court, had grudgingly allowed Vespar to escape from Realm justice, but made it clear that even his help in their escape did not square the debt between them.

Liam had gone from uncertainty and fear of his own unruly mind to discovery of a family history that spanned millennia. He had found a purpose that brought his own being into alignment with his abilities and native temperament in a way that he could never have imagined. That had been a revelation. His doubts had been banished by Tirini, his confidence boosted by his public recognition as High Court thurjun. He had faced the numbing fear of battle, and experienced the overwhelming relief of survival. Known the pride of facing death without flinching. Then capture. The horrible inevitability of his fate as a dreamer beneath VoYannan's dais, the corruption of his soul, and the morphing of his body into a twisted *thing*. Then escape. The impossible surge of hope, coming on the heels of despair. The sharp feeling of fate's cruelty as they realised that despite everything, the Vault would retake them on the plain. Then Balos' astounding rebirth, and the courage and skill of the Realm warriors, which saw them snatch victory from the jaws of that defeat. *Now this . . .*

Liam was quiet as they entered the ruined Tower. Finn and his warriors checked everything carefully, alert for Vault booby-traps. There was little power left in Kyall's hilt mionanail, and they needed what remained for the Gateway matrix. Without a Realm dampening field, the Vault tech remained deadly. Despite the slow pace, they arrived in the vaulted Gateway hall way too quickly for Liam's liking. He felt the stares of the Realm warriors on him, the weight of their expectation, and flinched. He was about to attempt something not even a master thurjun like Morin had ever achieved. *In theory* a thurjun could return to his own world by reaching through the portal and drawing the energies of his world toward him. Those energies were deep in his being, implanted since birth. It was the same principle as using a Gateway artefact that had been imbued with the energies of an open portal for centuries. Procarrus had used such a relic to open the Stonelake Gateway from Fraser Island, yet the energies in such an artefact were thousands of times stronger than those embedded in Liam's physical body. Even sensing such faint resonance required a rare talent, more akin to a Seeker's skill, than a thurjun's.

He reached the Gateway dais and began the climb up its ancient steps to the arched portal at the top of the raised platform, Morin beside him. His body was drained of all strength, his leg muscles sapped, each step a weary contest. He clung to the memory of Tirini, and their time in the High Court, a bright vision of another life, one that could keep him afloat in this sea of uncertainty. He reached the top and walked across to the nexus, dreading the moment.

Then he touched one of the Gateway posts.

He drew in a sharp breath. The hairs on his arms and the back of his neck stood up.

Morin squinted at him. "You feel it?"

"Yes," said Liam in wonder. Relief flooded him. He had never expected another miracle, and yet here it was. The first step. There was a chance now, that he could do it. That he could save them all. That he would hold Tirini in his arms again.

"Good. Good. Let us begin." Morin squeezed his shoulder in encouragement. The older thurjun lifted Kyall's broadsword until it was between them, point down. Liam automatically put his hands on the hilt, preparing to draw on the mionanail's power.

Liam's mind expanded as the mental bond formed. He and Morin drew the Gateway matrix together. It came to life as the hilt mionanail flowered.

Liam took a deep breath and reached into the Gateway. Initially he found only darkness. Endless, empty space. *Reach within yourself, Liam, find your home,* sent Morin through the mind-bond. Liam tuned into the unique essence that he sensed through the Gateway . . . and felt an answer within him. He lost himself in it. It expanded to fill his senses. Through the lens of his own being, he looked once more into that empty darkness. A point of light appeared there. He focused on it, and it slowly grew. After an eternity, it swelled to fill his vision. *I see it!* A yellow sun and a blue planet.

Earth.

Liam let the energy build until he felt he would burst apart. Then, all at once, it rushed through him.

"You have done it, Liam!" Still linked mentally with Morin, he could feel the older thurjun's relief and awe. "I have always known this was possible, yet in all my years as thurjun, I have never seen it."

Liam opened his eyes.

The Sydney Gateway was alive.

A shimmering silver curtain hung inside the arch.

"Quickly! Go! Take the sword," urged Morin.

Liam stepped through, cradling Kyall's longsword. From one step to the next, he passed from a ruined Viri Gateway into a dark cavern on Earth. Just like that, he was home. He felt it so keenly now. The unique energy of Earth soared through him, saturating every cell. A pale silver glow lit the cave. The bodies were gone, replaced by painted outlines, and the whole area was roped off with yellow plastic tape bearing the words "CRIME SCENE". Liam moved forward, and the remaining Realm warriors filed through behind, two of them supporting Sephany, who was thickly bundled in her cloak. Then came Yolinda, Finn and Genna.

"So good to be back home," said Yolinda with a mocking smile. She drew her own borrowed cloak closer around her skimpy outfit, as though suddenly conscious of her modesty.

Last of all, came Morin. Once the portly thurjun had stepped through, he released the matrix. Liam did the same, and the light vanished. Then he used the longsword's mionanail to create a small ball of warm yellow light that hovered above his head. *No errors this time.* Liam smiled to himself.

"Now what?" asked Yolinda.

"Now we make for the Stonelake Gateway," said Finn. He turned to Liam. "Can you get us there?"

Liam nodded. This was precisely what the Durrow fortune was for. All it would take was one phone call.

Finn led the group through the darkened cavern, up through the tunnel and carved stairway, which had been cleared of debris, across the empty concrete floor, and through the gutted offices to the old industrial building's deserted foyer. Sephany was barely conscious, her face drawn in pain. They carried her up the stairs. As they crowded together, Liam heard her praying to herself in a low voice.

Two swift kicks from a boot heel were enough to dislodge the unpainted sheeting that had been bolted to the brickwork outside to block access to the shattered entry doors. Then they were outside, in the Sydney night. The surrounding area, a mix of dowdy residential homes and old commercial buildings, was quiet. The street itself, deserted. The house where Vicki had unwittingly opened the Gateway for the Vault was gone. The collapsed structure had been removed, leaving bare ground, and the lot barricaded off with tall chain-link fencing supported by unpainted concrete bases. The only illumination came from a row of sodium vapour streetlamps that dotted the far side of the narrow bitumen thoroughfare with pools of wan yellow light. Liam took note of the building's number, and the street name. He would make sure this property, and the one next to it, were purchased by the Darrow Trust . . . and well secured.

Finn shifted his grip on the Axe and turned to Liam. "Lead the way, Liam. This is your world."

"Right then." Liam looked right. Darkened industrial buildings showed there, with a scattering of window-lit residences. To the left he saw much the same . . . but there was a faint glow in the sky beyond that hinted at neon and nightlife.

He walked down a short flight of brick steps, turned left, then led the rescued priestess, Morin, Finn, Yolinda, and the ten surviving Realm warriors through the Sydney suburbs in search of a phone box. All of them were dressed in ragged, bloodstained clothes. All of them bruised, unwashed, and streaked with grime. The Realm warriors carried heavy shields, Vault short swords, knives, and falcatas, and were ready to meet any threat, but the night was silent. The air clear and sweet. The sky above filled with familiar stars.

And around them, the Earth slumbered on in innocent bliss.

Chapter 68

Hervey Bay, Queensland, Australia — Earth
February 28th 2000

Yolinda tossed her keys onto the laminated bench under the mirror. She put the siithe short sword on the table by the bed, shrugged off her borrowed cloak and started stripping off her clothes. They stank, and were stiff from sweat and blood. Her shoes were the only thing left from Earth, the rest of her clothes had been replaced by the crudely stitched slave outfit supplied by the Slavemaster, a cross between a rustic bikini and a stripper's outfit, designed to show as much flesh as possible. She shuddered as she peeled it off, then threw the dirty rags straight into the trash. Her shoes and socks followed. Even stuffed into the bottom of the rubbish bin, their stale, rank odour pervaded the small motel room. Naked now, she cracked the curtain, checked that no one was visible in the motor court's parking area, then put the bin outside the door. She piled the stolen siithe cloak on top.

Yolinda darted back inside. She walked into the bathroom, snatched the little bottles of shampoo and conditioner from the white sink-top, and slipped through the glass doors into the shower recess, pulling them closed behind her. Turning on the shower, she unwrapped a packet of soap and eagerly stepped under the hot spray. Her back stung, particularly over her left shoulder where the lash had broken the skin. It was healing well and unlikely to scar badly.

"Ohhh. This is heaven." She put her head under the flow and soaped her hair liberally with shampoo. She washed it again, then again by rising out the empty bottles to get the dregs of the shampoo and conditioner. She closed her eyes and leant against the tiled wall, under the nozzle, letting the hot water sear her skin. Her hand relaxed, and the empty shampoo bottle dropped from her fingers to clatter on the white plastic recess floor.

They had travelled through the night and into the next day to reach the Gateway at Fraser Island. On the way she had read a selection of old Sydney newspapers dated from the New Year, which she had scrounged from a service station's newsprint recycling bin. The monumental conflict in the cavern beneath the old Teros Graphics building had gone unremarked by the press . . . no doubt suppressed by the Australian Federal Police on advice from the government. The whole incident had merited only one small article on page twelve of the Sydney Morning Herald, which speculated about the link between a power outage in western Sydney and the much feared — and hyped — Y2K bug. *Finn's dampening field at work.* They had hit Urangan, a mainland town on Hervey Bay, opposite the great sand island of Fraser, only hours ago, to find that the last ferry had already left for the night. Finn was frustrated at the check, but Yolinda was relieved. By that stage she was desperate for a shower. They had rented rooms in a old motel and hit the nearby tourist shops for new clothes.

Yolinda used a flannel and soap to scrub away the accumulated dirt and blood from her skin. Grime gathered through the Shadow Worlds, and at VoYannan's court, swirled away and circled down the drain. She kept at it until the water at her feet ran clear. Then she shut off the flow, stepped out of the shower, and dried herself with a thick, white towel. She put on the complementary cotton robe that hung in the bathroom and wrapped a towel around her head. Then she walked out into the hotel room. It was a generic motel unit, decorated in shades of beige. The old curtain was dusty, the carpet worn thin. There was a single queen-size bed, and a long bench across the far wall with a wall-length mirror above it. A tiny bar fridge. A rack of mini-bar snacks with a price list below it. A paper breakfast menu with check boxes and a hole so that it could be hung on the door knob for room delivery the next morning. A worn plastic folder with delivery menus and tourist information pamphlets in plastic sleeves.

A laminate table with two plastic chairs.

A siithe short sword.

Black ugly metal, with a keen cutting edge that was stained brown with old blood.

Reality swirled around her. Memories of the battlefield flooded her mind. Fighting beside Finn as the siithe closed in. The furious exchange between the Archfiend and Finn. The Citadel of the krell. The veyr Loremasters. The endless slaves surviving in misery, and those she had seen die savage unmourned deaths in the siithe feeding pits. The sound Vicki's neck made as it snapped, inside Barsus' jaws. The Archfiend's severed head flying through the air trailing a fountain of blood.

Yolinda trembled, conscious of her shaking knees.

She turned her back on the blade. Hid her face in her hands.

Yolinda swore under her breath and stalked across the room to the bed. She emptied the shopping bags onto the bedspread. She had bought new shirts and underwear, loose blue jeans, and a stout pair of hiking boots, as well as sunglasses and a hat for the drive tomorrow.

It was over.

It was over.

She sat on the bed and started crying. She was not sure why. She just knew she could not stop. Finally she forced herself to stand up. She threw off the towel and robe and dressed swiftly. She had planned to get a meal in her room, but suddenly she could not be alone. She had to be close to someone who had been there, who had shared the fight, seen the blood, seen the death.

She grabbed her keys and walked to her door. She paused. "Do you know what you are doing, Paris?"

She shook her head and pushed through the door, slamming it behind her. The soft summer evening was a balm to her soul. Urangan was an old fishing area, right on the bay. The air was fresh and clear, with a tang of salt. She walked along the portico's undressed concrete to Finn's door. She remembered being lifted up by the seraphin's wings, surrounded by a golden nimbus as they flew through the clouds.

Crickets sounded from the motor court's garden.

She hesitated. Then knocked.

Finn opened up. He had showered and changed into black jeans and a Hervey Bay T-shirt, with black boots. Kyall's sword was strapped to his waist. "Guardsman Yolinda. Come in."

Inside, Genna was sitting in one of the room's chairs, sipping a drink. The bench below the mirror was lined with cans, spirit bottles, and potato chip packets from the mini-bar.

"Would you like some refreshments, my lady?" asked Finn.

"I'd be surprised if there is anything left," she said, conscious of how harsh she sounded. She took a deep breath and smiled. "Yes, thank you. That would be nice."

The rooms only came with two chairs, so Yolinda sat on the bed, while Finn got her a can of bourbon and cola from the fridge.

"There you are. Not sure what it is, but they have been pleasant enough so far."

Yolinda laughed and opened the can, wincing at the sweetness as she took a sip. She usually drank beer, but at the moment she did not care what it was. She just wanted to be with someone else.

The three sat in silence. Yolinda looked at Finn. There was so much she wanted to say, she did not know where to start.

Genna took one look at the pair of them, finished his drink, then stood up. "I think the sky is calling me."

"Calling you?" asked Finn, eyes narrowing suspiciously.

Genna winked at Finn and moved to the door. "I feel like sleeping on the beach tonight. I will return at first light."

The door shut behind Genna. Yolinda and Finn looked at each other in silence, then spoke at once.

"Thank—"

"I'm sorry—"

They burst into laughter.

"Thank you for saving my life, Yolinda," said Finn.

He was about to say more, but Yolinda held up her hand. "Please, let me go first. Before I lose my nerve and become a bitch again."

Finn raised his eyebrows, but said nothing. He took another sip of the neat scotch in his glass.

"I'm sorry for the way I treated you when you first arrived through the Stonelake Gateway," she said. "What I did on the beach. It was unforgivable. I should have tried to believe you. But what I've seen. . . I never *could* have believed it."

Finn shook his head. "I was angry with you. Furious. But I was angrier with myself. From the first mind-bond, I was sure I could trust you. It was what I took to be my error in judgement that really frustrated me."

Finn put down his glass and knelt before Yolinda. He took her drink and set it down on the table. He took each of her hands in one his, the grip gentle. "But Yolinda, I was not wrong about you. You have been the most steadfast ally. You have saved my life on the battlefield. You saved Liam's life when the Shadow Hounds attacked, and have stood firm with us in the darkest of moments.

"Without you, we would have never left the Vault of Seven Horns alive. Never would have been able to save Sephany. Now we can return to the First Realm in triumph."

Finn stared at Yolinda, his clear green eyes filled with conviction, and the integrity that was so central to his character. "Thank you, Yolinda."

Yolinda remembered all the things she had first felt about him when they were bonded on the forest track — and how she had liked what she felt. She had never met anyone like him.

Memories came again. The fury of battle. Blood and death. What she had suffered at the hands of the Archfiend. The fact that Procarrus was dead, that his evil was ended, meant nothing. She started to shake. Felt nausea rise.

"Hold me, Finn."

He took her into his arms. Warmth surrounded her.

Yolinda hugged Finn as hard as she could, as though the more intense the embrace, the more she could escape the images in her mind. She began to cry, releasing all the fear, all the terror. He stayed with her, until she was empty of tears, and her heart grew quiet. Until the grief was replaced with lightness.

"Do you want me to walk you back to your room?" asked Finn, standing up.

"No, Finn," said Yolinda, stepping into his arms. She drew him down into a kiss. His stubble was rough on her soft lips. Something ignited inside her.

She pulled him down onto the bed. He loosened the sword belt. The weapon thudded to the floor. Clothes followed in a chaotic heap. They kissed hungrily. Then slowly, gently, they made love. Finn was an accomplished lover, but it would not have mattered. It was his compassion, and the softness of his touch, that Yolinda needed.

They held each other through the night, and slept inside the warmth of love, safe from the terrors of the Vault.

Chapter 69

Liam slowed the Landcruiser and manoeuvred it off the track, swinging the bulky four-wheel-drive in beside a fallen tree. He cut the ignition, slid out of the driver's seat, and stepped down from the high-slung cabin to the sandy soil. The grass was high, the ground littered with gum leaves from the surrounding trees, which had been dried dark brown by the summer heat. The sun was high in the sky, climbing toward noon, and the bush was quiet.

The living vitality of Fraser Island swelled around him, and beneath him, rising from the land's heart. After experiencing the desolation of the Shadow Worlds, and seeing the power of the Vault first-hand, he realised just what a miracle of precious life his home planet was. He no longer feared his own mind. He welcomed his occasional visions, knowing now that they hinted at a latent talent, something akin to the skill he had used to open the Sydney Gateway from the Viri world. His thurjun's sight was sharp. What he had once merely sensed was as clearly visible as summer sunshine. The pulsing flow of the living world circulated around him in a continuous energetic movement. It was a flow he could tap, if he chose, to fuel minor matrices. Magic. *Real magic.* This was the sort of power his uncle Aidan would have had, remarkable enough in a world of scientific rationalism, but with a mionanail he could bring any Earth city — any modern army — to a standstill.

A crow cawed in the distance. Another answered it.

A second Landcruiser, driven by Yolinda, pulled in beside him. She wore a red cap and dark sunglasses, her blonde hair tied back in a single ponytail. Her soft, elfin face made her look young, but her expression was intent, and expectant. *Constable Yolinda Paris, on the job.* She wound her window down.

Liam blinked and looked around the clearing, eyes narrowed. It was different in daylight, but he was sure this was the place. It was not something he was likely to forget.

"Well?" asked Yolinda through her open window.

"This is it," said Liam.

Liam waved to Finn and Genna in confirmation, and they filed out of Liam's Landcruiser. All three of them walked to the rear door to help Morin and two Realm warriors lift the unconscious Sephany out of the vehicle. She was wrapped in heavy blankets, and shivered uncontrollably. Her face dripped with fever-sweat.

"We have her now," said one of the warriors. Finn, Genna, and Liam stepped back, anxious, while the two men settled Sephany onto a portable stretcher and gently turned her onto her side.

More Realm warriors piled out of Yolinda's Landcruiser and formed into loose ranks. All of them felt the same urgency. Sephany had grown increasingly ill since they passed the Sydney Gateway. She had lapsed into unconsciousness just after arriving on Earth. Liam gritted his teeth in impotent fury at the idea of that *thing* inside her. They had to get her to Realm physicians and Seekers before the Spawn killed her.

They locked up the Landcruisers, rented courtesy of the Durrow Trust, and set off. The whole area had been closed to visitors for some time. From the start they had to fight their way along an overgrown path. The lead warriors cut a trail through the heavy wallum heath with captured siithe falcatas, which were perfect for the task. Liam walked behind Morin and the warriors carrying Sephany. Yolinda was at the rear, lost in thought. Every now and then she would look at Finn and smile. There was something going on there, but Liam's worry soon banished any speculation.

Liam could not look away from Sephany. From her limp form. Her sweat-soaked black hair. Bile rose in his throat as he thought about the horror she had endured. Still he could not look away. "Are we going to make it?" As soon as he said it, Liam cursed himself for voicing his worry.

Morin replied anyway, his voice grim. "I am not sure."

"Let's just get her through the Gateway," said Liam. He ground his teeth together.

Morin nodded, smiling at Liam.

Liam caught the look. "What is it?"

"You have changed. Grown in self-assurance. As well you should. The young man who started his journey through the Blessed Realms and the Vault worlds has been well tested. You have come through it all, Liam. Without you, we would never have been able to rescue Sephany."

Liam felt a glow of pride at the acknowledgement. It was true that they had all achieved the impossible. Yet with Sephany still in the grip of the krell spawn, none of them felt inclined to celebrate.

Morin looked down the trail at Finn. "You are not the only one who has changed."

They broke through the last of the thick growth and hurried through a stand of open scrub to the lake. The warriors carrying Sephany gently laid the stretcher down on the lakeshore. A hot wind blew across the lake's surface, shivering ripples from its deep blue.

Finn turned to Morin. "Well?"

Morin gestured to Liam. "Do not ask me, Finn. Ask the thurjun of Earth. This is an Earth Gateway."

Finn bowed formally to Liam. Liam tensed, yet relaxed when he saw Finn's ironic smile. "Thurjun of Earth. If you judge us worthy, allow us to pass your Gateway and return to the Blessed Realms." He drew Kyall's broadsword and presented it to Liam. "Just do it quickly."

Liam took the weapon, immediately sensing the power in the mionanail. They all watched him in quiet expectation, and with respect. He paused to take in the moment, measuring the men, and the determined woman standing with them. Warriors of the Blessed Realms. Together they had battled the Vault and survived. *To hell and back.* Liam's throat choked with emotion, and he felt joyful tears spring to his eyes. He knew he would not be able to say anything without letting those tears flow, so instead he just nodded and walked into the lake. He waded thigh-deep. The cold water was a shock on his hot skin. He drew the Gateway matrix with a swift series of mental strokes . . . and reached through time and space.

An image of the Stonelake Gateway grew in his mind. It was swarming with workers, and manned by a single young thurjun.

Liam touched the Realm thurjun's mind. The startled man jerked upright, almost losing his balance and falling into the lake. The thurjun took a firm hold of one of the two ancient obelisks that framed the Stonelake Gateway and paused to concentrate. Lines furrowed his forehead. Their two open minds met. The mind-bond formed. His name was Uren. Through the bond, Uren swiftly confirmed Liam's identity.

"Everyone off the Gateway!" commanded Uren. His words echoed through the mind-bond. The construction workers looked up from their work, then fled down the wide Gateway steps like startled insects.

On Fraser Island, light blazed above the lake, outshining the noonday sun. A whirling maelstrom formed as the magical portal swirled into existence. Liam immediately started directing people into the lake.

Balancing on the ancient Gateway lintel in the Fourth Realm, Uren helped the travellers onto the new Gateway structure as they emerged from the Stonelake portal. In his mind's eye, Liam saw them hurry across the new Gateway platform, then down the ancient steps to the lake shore. Morin was last.

Finally, it was Liam's turn.

He hesitated, feeling a moment's panic, but Morin had assured him he would be able to open the Fraser Gateway, as he had the Sydney Gateway. Then he thought of Tirini, and his last reservations vanished. He stepped through. The Gateway closed behind him.

Liam looked up at the green mountains and the familiar turrets of Stonelake, drawing in the fresh, wild air of the Fourth Realm. He helped Morin and the two warriors carrying Sephany manoeuvre the stretcher across the new, partially completed platform, and down the steps.

Sephany's eyes fluttered open. She looked up in wonder at the clear blue sky. "I had a dark dream."

"You are home now." Morin took her hand.

"My heart feels free, Morin. Free." Tears streamed down Sephany's cheeks. "Finn," she muttered weakly.

Morin called to Finn and he rushed to her side. His eyes lit up as he saw she was awake. They feared she would die without regaining consciousness, the Spawn tearing its way free from her cooling corpse.

Sephany saw Finn and smiled. She was terribly pale, lips red against white skin. Her eyelids fluttered. "I can sleep soon. Without dreams." A shadow crossed her eyes. "*Gone.*"

"What is she saying, Morin?" asked Finn.

Morin shook his head. "I am not sure."

The old thurjun leant closer. "You can rest now, Sephany. We will take you to the High Court as soon as we can."

Priests and priestesses from the Temple of the High God rushed across the grassy strand toward them, calling out in excited voices. Sephany closed her eyes. Her head lolled to the side.

"Unconscious?" asked Liam, uneasy.

"No. Just sleeping," said Morin.

Chapter 70
City of Tir — First Realm

Tallandra pushed her way through the crowd, all niceties forgotten.

Every balcony and patch of marble in the High Court swarmed with onlookers, all in their best Court finery. Buckles, cane-tops, diamonds and jewellery sparkled. Dresses dazzled, shimmering through every colour in the rainbow. The wealth of the First Realm was on display. For hours now, new arrivals, including red-faced nobility, had been turned away at the doors, despite the increasingly opulent bribes on offer. *Finn had returned!* The news had flashed through the First Realm. The golden silk of her floor-length gown swished across the floor in time with her hurrying feet. She wore the gold-set emerald earrings and necklace she had set aside for the day when she and Finn returned to Evenstone, their full rights restored. *Hang that.* Nothing could overtop this moment.

Her brother was alive!

It was less than a week ago that Sentas had arrived back with only three companions. He had been acclaimed a hero, the tale of Kyall's death, and the loss of Finn, Morin, and Liam a terrible, tragic end to a brave mission. The news of Finn's death had driven Tallandra to despair. A lifetime of work, lobbying for their return to the ancestral Evenstone lands, had burned to ashes in a moment. It meant nothing to her without Finn. Now that desperation had been turned on its head. Sentas, that black-hearted, manipulative bastard, had been arrested on charges of treason, and even now lay imprisoned in the Temple of the High God. Today, Torren would have to pass judgement on his own son.

Tallandra caught sight of Finn at the far end of the hall, near the steps that led up to the High King's dais. He was in conference with Torren himself. Morin was there, and the Earth-thurjun, Liam Durrow. They were surrounded by a thick mob of gawkers, which only gave them a respectful distance because of the High King's presence. There was also a small blonde woman in an ill-fitting dress, who Tallandra did not recognise. The woman stood slightly apart from the others, warily scanning the crowd.

"Finn!" she called.

Her brother's sombre weariness transformed to delight at the sight of her. Her heart leapt into flame. Tallandra ducked past Torren and ran into Finn's arms. They collided in a rustle of silk. She melted against his muscular solidity, overwhelmed with relief. He was leaner than she had ever known him, just muscle and bone. Her mind settled, and she became aware of her gross breach in etiquette.

She broke away from Finn, smoothed down her gown, and bowed her head to Torren. "Apologies, my King."

Torren's lips twitched into a smile. "No need for such formality. I think Finn is entitled to some congratulations from his own sister." At these words, the blonde woman beside Finn suddenly relaxed. *Interesting,* she thought.

Tallandra took Finn's arm and leant against him, feeling his warmth through the thin material. Her shock had been profound, and some part of her needed this direct contact, this tangible proof of his survival. Torren accepted her presence, and her brother and the King continued their conversation.

"You are certain then?" asked Torren.

"Yes. Sentas triggered a dampening field to get us captured. And I am convinced he killed Kyall," said Finn.

Torren absorbed the news. "I had hoped . . ." The High King's mouth made a grim line. He straightened his shoulders. "Your testimony only confirms the Seekers' verdict." His voice was flat. Emotionless. "Zanthis broke under questioning. He helped Sentas conceal Kyall's murder. Sentas had hoped to implicate Guardian Yolinda." The High King waved a hand at the blonde woman. *Yolinda.* Hearing her name, the short blonde looked across to the High King.

"Perhaps the Shade. . . ," began Finn. They could all see how hard this was for Torren.

"I need no excuses for my son. Or myself. I could see what Sentas was becoming, yet I looked away. He . . . he is the image of his dead mother. He has the same smooth olive skin. The same dark eyes." He shook his head. "Now I now realise there was never anything of his mother *in* him. She was soft and kind, whereas Sentas always harboured a deep antagonism. Only now do I see how this well of spite poisoned him, and everything he touched."

"Perhaps if the Shade is cast out . . .?" said Morin.

Torren shook his head. "No. Enough of this. It is time to get it over with."

The High King turned on his heel and climbed the dais to his golden throne, shoulders broad and powerful. He nodded formally to the ranks of druids on the long bench seats set behind and to the left of his throne, each dressed in their distinctive multicoloured robes. The greeting was returned by a rather subdued Lord Druid Strannus. The rumours were that Torren had given the senior druid a private rebuke for the part one of his druids had played in Sentas' plots, although no one knew the exact nature of that assistance. Strannus, of course, had been careful to insulate himself behind the flunky. Then Torren gave the same acknowledgement to the Seekers, thurjuns, and clergy of the High God, in identical seats to the throne's right. They each responded with individual gestures or nods of respect. The purple gems set in the Seekers' golden circlets flashed with the movement.

Torren then turned to face the room, his noble visage grey against his reddish-blond hair. *He is under tremendous strain.* Torren gave a curt signal to his steward, Vikas, who immediately rapped his silver-tipped staff on the marble floor. Once. Twice. Three times. The sound rang across the huge hall. Thousands of murmured conversations swiftly hushed, like a raging fire deprived of air, until only a quiet expectation remained.

Torren took his throne. For a long moment he just stared at the ranks of nobles and onlookers. "Bring in the prisoners." His voice fell hard on the Court. Devoid of mercy. A hammer slammed to an anvil. The High King spoke. Not the father.

The whispers died as Sentas was brought in. He was flanked by two Realm warriors dressed in the High King's white and red livery. Behind him came Zanthis, Jonas, and Kar. All were in chains. Sentas was defiant. Zanthis resigned. Jonas and Kar looked down, eyes to the marble, tense and silent.

"The prisoners have been questioned at length, and the Seekers have confirmed the truth." Torren's voice resonated through the chamber.

"Jonas and Kar," continued Torren.

The two lords looked up, faces pale and grim.

"You are guilty only of following my son. For this you will have to examine your own hearts, but apart from this, I find you innocent of the death of Kyall, or the betrayal of Finn and his Realm force.

"You were part of Sentas' schemes, however, and that cannot go unpunished. You are hereby stripped of all titles. You have the choice of ten years prison, or three years in the High King's garrison. Which do you chose?"

"The garrison," they said in unison, their relief obvious.

"Take them away," ordered Torren.

Their chains clanked into the silence as the former nobles departed, flanked by their guards. The chamber doors opened to let them pass, then boomed shut. All eyes returned to the throne.

"Zanthis. You have confessed to the crimes of murder and treason."

Torren turned to his son. "Sentas . . ." He faltered. "As the representative of the High King, your acts of murder and treason are the most reprehensible. It is true that the Shade from the Earth man Shane coloured your actions, perhaps pushing you over the edge, but the priests of the High God, and the Seekers, assure me the motivations were yours."

Torren straightened. Although his face was impassive, Tallandra could sense his pain. "It gives me no pleasure, but there can only be one sentence for both of you. Death." The last word hung in the air, hovering above them all like a spectre. A buzz of talk rippled through the crowd, quickly swelling to a cacophony.

"Mercy!"

The conversations ceased. The crowd before the throne parted to reveal a short priestess with long dark hair, outfitted in the gold, orange and white vestments of the High God. She moved gracefully, her face set with purpose.

Tallandra gasped. Her hand tightened on Finn's arm. *"Sephany."*

The priestess stood before the throne and looked up at Torren. So slim, lithe and vital, it was hard to believe she had ever been host to a krell spawn.

"There has been enough killing, my King. Let them live. The Temple can take them. They need not be a threat to the Realms again. Perhaps, in time, Sentas may throw off the Shade and repent his darkness."

"They must pay for their crimes," said Torren, his voice almost breaking.

"Only the High God can truly judge men," she replied evenly.

Rolf, High Priest of the Temple, stood in his place to the throne's right. Middle-aged, and grey haired, he waited in solemn silence for Torren to acknowledge him. Torren met the priest's dark eyes and nodded. Rolf lifted his head, straightening as far as his stooped posture would allow. "There is wisdom in what Sephany says, my King. Let them live out the span of their lives in the Temple. Confinement, and living with the knowledge of their actions, is punishment enough."

Torren sank back into his throne. He closed eyes for a second to recover his composure, then stared straight at Sentas, his gaze inscrutable. "So be it. Take them away."

Sephany smiled and bowed. She walked up the dais to sit with Rolf. The priestess was still pale from her ordeal, but her eyes were clear and free.

Torren straightened. "Now to more pleasant duties. Finn. Bring forward your party."

Chapter 71
City of Tir — First Realm

A surge of excitement shot through Liam as he walked forward beside Finn, Yolinda, and Morin. Finn waved, and Kyall's surviving warriors broke away from the crowd and joined them below the dais. Tallandra, glittering, refined and beautiful, her dark hair coifed into a neat tiers, watched from the Court's main floor. Liam grinned as she bounced up and down like an excited child, her hands clasped together in expectation. Her stunning looks and effortless sophistication made her a little intimidating, but now her sheer joy had stripped away that veneer, revealing her native warmth. Talking to her was usually like trying to have a conversation with a supermodel that had the IQ of a NASA scientist . . . who was — incidentally — from another planet.

The High King watched them with a benevolent gaze, visage pleasant, knowing, and kindly. No trace of grief or heartbreak in his dark eyes. "Where is Genna?"

"He stayed in Stonelake, my King," said Finn. "He said something about getting back to his wives."

Laughter broke out around the court, and Torren nodded to himself. "Well, let him know he has the gratitude of the High Court, and if there is any service we can do for him, he has but to ask."

Torren's dark eyes rested on Finn. Narrowed. "Lord Evenstone. Come forward."

A woman squealed in the audience. Liam looked back. *Tallandra.* Her hands were over her mouth like the "speak no evil" monkey. Her eyes glistened with tears.

"Henceforth, you will resign your commission at Stonelake and remove yourself to your ancestral home, to take command of the defence of the Evenstone Gateway. You have proven yourself more than worthy of that trust." Then softer. "It is time for you to go home, son."

The applause built and built, and Torren let it continue. It died away as Torren finally lifted his hand.

"Liam Durrow."

Liam came forward. He swallowed, his throat dry, conscious of the power of the Realms that was personified in this one man. This High King.

"You have proven yourself a loyal and true thurjun of the High Court. I have great pleasure in presenting you with another mionanail to replace the one lost to the Vault, and appointing you as our liaison to the world of Earth." Whip-thin Kevrin, head of the College of Thurjuns, rose from his place and handed something to Torren. Liam ascended the dais and took the new mionanail pendant, which was set on a silver chain. It was teardrop shaped, and much like his old one, but brown like Morin's. The central gem glowed silver. An unblinking eye that promised power. *Fully charged.* Kevrin nodded to Liam and retook his seat.

Torren gave Liam a wry grin. "I expect you to check in a little more regularly than your predecessors."

Laughter filled the room.

"Yolinda Paris."

Yolinda walked to the throne.

"I understand you have refused an offer to be trained as one of our warriors."

"Yes . . . I have my own duties on Earth, King Torren. I must return as soon as I can." Her Realm speech had become quite fluid.

Torren was thoughtful. "Very well. But we have a gift for you." Torren beaconed her to him. Yolinda ascended the steps warily. One of the warriors on the dais produced a metal bracer, which he handed to the King. Torren clamped it around Yolinda's left forearm.

"I understand from Morin you have some latent talent as a thurjun," said Torren. "This bracer is a Realm weapon. It contains a small mionanail, which Morin will show you how to use. With it, you will be able to fight with our warriors against the Vault should the need arise. I advise that you learn to use a sword, however."

"Have no fear for her, your majesty. Yolinda is a steadfast companion," said Finn.

Yolinda smiled at Finn, relaxed for the first time since arriving at Court. Liam had not forgotten how strange Tir had seemed when he first arrived here, with its colossal floating towers, sunsnakes, and Dreaming Steeds.

"For the rest of you warriors, you have the thanks of the Realms, and more — I have a commission for each of you, and the gift of weapons, armour, and titles.

"Once more the Realms thanks you," said Torren. That was their cue to retire, and they all stepped back into the crowd.

Torren rose. "That concludes the court."

The High King swept down from his dais and out of the High Court, flanked by his guards.

Vikas' staff hammered out its three-part rhythm. "The assembly of the High Court is ended!"

The hum of conversation from the huge crowd quickly filled the room, and many began to leave the Court. Liam remained with Finn, Yolinda and Morin, in a small group near throne. They had come through so much together. Tallandra was in conversation with a gaudily dressed lord, but she kept looking across at Finn as though worried he might disappear.

"Torren gave you nothing, Morin?" asked Liam.

"Ha! I have what I wanted," said Morin.

Liam let the cryptic comment pass. "Have they found the Spawn?" he asked instead.

Morin shook his head. "No. It was gone from Sephany by the time she reached Stonelake. That was what she was trying to tell us. It must have left her during a Gateway transit . . . used its own power to move itself out of her body at the very moment she passed between worlds. It is the only explanation. If it tore its way free, Sephany would not have survived."

Liam remembered the Spawn moving inside Sephany, just before they passed the Sydney Gateway. It had been suddenly active then, as though it had sensed the departure of the seraphin and was ready to seize its chance. The ruined Viri city was vast, and filled with the Vault's minions. The perfect place for a newborn krell. He knew from Morin that a krell spawn was born with innate power, and the memories and knowledge of its sire. It would be able to subdue and dominate the wild veyr with ease. To have another krell so close to Earth, on the other side of a single Gateway . . . It was frightening.

"The Viri city," said Liam.

Morin grimaced. "Yes. Most likely. But with her swathed in blankets, and unconscious—"

"Will there be a mission to find the Spawn and destroy it?" asked Liam.

"Yes. But let us not dwell on it now. It is the time for celebration."

Liam let out a long breath. "It must have been hard for Torren to sentence his own son."

Finn sighed. "It was the assassination attempt that broke his heart."

"Assassination?" asked Liam.

"Yes, some poor hapless fool duped by Sentas into an attempt on the King's life. They discovered him sneaking into Torren's apartments. He broke quickly. Told them everything," said Finn. "So what will you do now, Liam?"

"I need to get back to Earth. But I think I'll stay in Tir for a while." Liam looked past Finn into the crowd, searching for Tirini. He had sent her word as soon as he arrived, but she had been on duty in the Seeker's tower. He was dying to see her. To get his arms around her.

"What about you, Yolinda? Would you like to stay in the Realms for a while?" asked Finn, eyes sparkling with mischief.

Yolinda went red, but tried to sound nonchalant. "Oh, I need to get back to Earth as well, but perhaps not right away."

Finn smiled. "I was hoping you might all return with me to Evenstone for a little holiday feast."

Tallandra hurried over to rejoin their group. She hugged Finn, wrapping him up in a flurry of gold skirts. Her perfume teased at Liam. She broke away and touched Finn's face, as though marvelling. "Home, brother. At last. We will rebuild our family."

Finn told Tallandra of his invitation for Yolinda to come and visit with them. Tallandra caught a look between Finn and Yolinda and touched her brother lightly on the arm. "Brother, you have *not* been telling me everything." She leant toward the Federal Police Agent, and spoke in a low, confidential tone. "You have to come, Yolinda. Finn will be heartbroken if you leave him now."

"Well . . . a short stay wouldn't do any harm," said Yolinda, beaming with delight.

Morin took Finn and Tallandra into his arms, embracing them both. "Finally, the return to Evenstone. You have no idea how long I have dreamed of this day. Longed to see you both safe and back on your ancestral lands." Morin sighed, his eyes misting with tears. "And I am looking forward to a *long* rest."

Ah. Liam knew what Morin had meant now. *This* was what he had wanted.

"What about you, Liam? Are you sure you do not want to visit the Evenstone Gateway?" asked Finn.

Tallandra opened her fan and looked at Liam speculatively. "Perhaps, brother, Liam may be more inclined to visit if he knew a certain Seeker would be visiting as well?"

"What?" asked Liam, amazed.

"It is all arranged. I have petitioned Torren, and he has granted Tirini a month's leave of absence," said Tallandra.

Just then, Liam saw Tirini enter the Court. The young Seeker's eyes lit up as she saw him. The crowd parted as she ran into his arms. They kissed passionately. Hungrily.

"Is it true?" asked Liam, eagerly.

"Yes. A whole month!" said Tirini.

They looked into each other's eyes, lost in timeless bliss. Then, gradually, they became aware of those around them. Tirini melted into Liam's side. "I was so dreadfully afraid you would never return," she whispered.

"Well, it is all settled then," said Tallandra. "Tonight you shall all stay in the Third Realm apartments. Then tomorrow, we travel on to our home." Tallandra stepped into Finn's embrace. "Oh, Finn," she said, wiping away silent tears of joy. "*Home.*"

They walked out of the High Court together.

Tallandra took Yolinda's arm and she, Yolinda, and Finn led the way. Liam and Tirini followed with Morin. Tallandra was already chatting with Yolinda, drawing the quiet policewoman out of her habitual reserve with consummate skill. As they left the Court, and walked through the long antechamber to the shaft, people bowed, cheered, and applauded.

Liam felt the warmth of Tirini against him and his smile broadened.

It was going to be a good month.

Epilogue
Fraser Island, Australia — Earth
April 1st 2000

"Stupid turkeys," said Pavlo, under his breath. He took another drag on his joint.

His eyes narrowed as he looked back at the two women in the car. He flashed them a smile. "You don't know what you're missing! Come on!" They waved in reply, but did not move.

Pavlo turned his back on them and scowled. He sucked the joint down to the end, then flicked it away with a low curse. He stripped off his jeans, jocks, and T-shirt, and slipped into the lake. He gasped as the water hit his skin. He swam on until he was out of his depth, then turned on his back. He waited. Still they didn't join him. The sun dipped below the surrounding hills, dropping the little valley into twilight. It was cold, just floating there, so he struck out across the lake to warm himself up. He used a powerful breaststroke, but soon grew out of breath. *My lungs are fucked. Too many bloody fags.*

Pavlo was angry. He had managed to convince Jean and Patti to come out to the lake, but do you think those stupid bitches would join him for a skinny-dip? Not a chance! They had turned up their noses at his joint and stayed in their car listening to Enya. *Fucking Enya* for chrissake!

When he had met the chicks at Kookaburra Bay they had seemed cool enough. They were easy going, and getting them to drive him out here had been a snap, but then everything had started to go wrong. How was he ever going to get into their pants if they would not even get high with him? Where were they from? Some happy-clappy Christian commune? Still, it wasn't a total loss. He knew both girls drank. All he needed to do was get them down to the resort bar, then he could slip them something. They would not even remember it in the morning. He would. *And* he had a nice little video set up to catch every precious moment. There was always an upside, he told himself. You just have to think things through.

Pavlo made for the shore.

Something swept past below him. A vague shape in the water. A shadow on the edge of his vision. He stopped swimming, and looked into the depths. Without the sun, it was hard to see. The crystal clear water was dark now, but there *was* something down there. An eel maybe? It would have to be a big one.

A razor sharp talon bit into his leg.

Pavlo gasped. Then he screamed.

He fought, but in his drug-addled state, the world soon contracted to a confusion of dreadful pain and thrashing water. Claws pulled him down. His head slipped beneath the surface. He kicked out, trying to swim up. A new wave of pain shot through him and he instinctively gasped for air. Instead he choked on water. He sank, losing strength. He could feel the talons on his leg, and the reaching tendrils of *something* all over his body . . . looking for a way in.

He saw two green, glowing eyes, surrounded by red. Then the tendrils found their entrance. Pavlo's mouth opened in a last, silent scream, as the talons ripped into his anus, pulling him apart. The Spawn clawed its way into Pavlo's body. Inexorable. Merciless. Blood filled the water. His abdomen swelled enormously as the krell spawn squeezed its way in. Tendrils slithered up his spinal column, tracing nerves, and slid into his dying brain. A young, powerful mind reached into Pavlo's, ripping aside any resistance.

Pavlo surfaced. Face slack. He took long lungfuls of air, reviving his brain tissue and organs. His body resumed a normal shape as the thing inside him rearranged itself.

Once more Pavlo struck out for the shore. His movements were mechanical, his eyes dull as they scanned the shoreline, noting the trail of footprints. He walked up onto the sand, exactly where he had entered, body dripping.

*

The Spawn feasted on Pavlo's soul. Unlike his previous host, the Spawn encountered little strength of will, and none of the dreadful white light that had seared and confined him. He gobbled down the little bundle of emotion, pulling it apart in moments, eagerly boosting his powers. The krell took a moment to establish a bond with the host's brain and nervous system, examining the memories. *Good,* thought the krell. *There are more humans nearby.* His hunger was overwhelming. Staying dormant for so long had been taxing. He needed to feed. To build up his strength before he burst out of his host as a fully formed krell. Carefully, he cleaned the body's wounds. Then he healed them with a delicate trickle of power. He dressed his host body from Pavlo's discarded pile of clothes and considered his next move. He must hide for now. Conceal himself in the guise of a human as he fed his body through his host. But first he must get closer to these two others, bind them, and fuel his nascent talent with their minds and souls.

He retraced the host body's steps, careful not to damage the flesh as he negotiated the tangled scrub. Experimentally, he tried a few words from the host's language. Bonding was soon complete. The last vestige of Pavlo consumed.

He walked to the car. Slow and easy. Two human females looked up. The Spawn could tell they were nervous. He reached into his host's brain for information, then made his plans. He knew the thrill of the hunt. The anticipation of domination and feast. He had thousands of years of memories, yet this was the first time he had experienced these emotions himself. He was pleased.

It was the work of a moment to enhance his host's hearing.

"Here he comes," said the one called Patti, smoothing her long brown hair with a quick movement. Plump and good natured, with a rounded face, she was the shy one.

"Why couldn't you have just said yes?" asked Jean, shifting impatiently in her seat. She had a solid build, with dark brown eyes, and a light complexion. Her arousal state was high.

"There is no way I am going to skinny-dip with a stranger," said Patti.

"He just seemed so nice," said Jean, biting her lip.

The Spawn approached the car. He smiled. It was a smooth, disarming smile, which had been used frequently by his host to good effect. He saw Jean's eyes dilate as her arousal increased.

"Hey, is that Enya?" he asked.

"Yes," said Patti.

"I love Enya," said the krell.